W9-BDG-931

OCT 1 0 2000

TAPS AND SIGHS

edited by

Peter Crowther

Subterranean Press ✤ 2000

FIRST EDITION
July 2000

ISBN
1-892284-37-5 (limited)
1-892284-74-x (trade)

Subterranean Press
P.O. Box 190106
Burton, MI 48519

Website:
www.subterraneanpress.com

Table of Contents

Douglas E. Winter
OF TAPS AND SIGHS

What lips my lips have kissed, and where, and why,
I have forgotten, and what arms have lain
Under my head till morning; but the rain
Is full of ghosts tonight, that tap and sigh
Upon the glass and listen for reply.

— *Edna St. Vincent Millay*

Ghosts? I've never met one. And to tell the truth, I've never been eager for a supernatural encounter. Perhaps it was my conservative religious upbringing, which urged that faith was far more crucial than any experience of the miraculous. Perhaps I'm just a cynic. Perhaps it is why I choose, on occasion, to write about the ghostly.

Others whose fiction ventures into the murky realm of the uncanny seem, more often than not, to share my disbelief—and dread. H.P. Lovecraft, despite his epic imaginings of elder races and gods forever threatening to intrude upon our reality, was insistent in his mechanistic materialism; I suspect that his fear of the unknown, expressed so capably in his fiction, was best managed in life by denial. For every Russell Kirk or William Peter Blatty, writing from a confident metaphysical stance, there are many uneasy explorers whose stories peer into the shadows of the cellar or the grave with a mingling of hope and horror.

My own view is one of indulgent skepticism. I was born in the "Show Me" state, Missouri, and when it comes to the extraordinary, that philosophy is mine: Show me.

I'm working my way toward a half-century in the world, and I'm still waiting for that glimpse, that moment when my eyes and my brain agree that what they've seen (or what I've heard or touched) is something more than the imaginary. So, yes, I believe that Elvis is dead; that Oswald was the only gunman; that night flights, atmospheric anomalies, and even swamp gas are the closest we've come to visitations from other planets; and that the thing over there in the corner, yes, the one that's misty and white and curling up through the floorboards, well . . . it does look a bit like Aunt Edith, but really, truly, it's mist, that's it, yeah . . . mist.

7

Since I've never seen a ghost, despite a few conscious tries, I'm much like the screenwriter who narrates Richard Christian Matheson's eerie "City of Dreams," the lead story of this auspicious anthology. "I don't believe in ghosts," he says, "unless they are of the emotional variety; aroused by seances of personal misfortune, you might say." He learns to think differently, of course—that is often the fate of characters in ghost stories—and it is his moving epiphany, his comprehension of the symbiosis between life on earth and that on the silver screen, that is crucial to the power of the ghost and the ghostly—and to understanding their enduring sway over our imaginations, and our beliefs about life and death.

In the best fiction, you see, the importance of a ghost is rarely its objective reality. Whether spawned by a trick of the light, faulty vision, confusion, prank, trauma, madness—or even supernatural visitation— these spectres are compelling because of their penchant for metaphor and meaning. In a time when surface, particularly the visual, is exalted in popular entertainment—compare, if you will, Robert Wise's G-rated minimalist masterpiece, *The Haunting* (1963), with its overwrought and forgettable remake—the imagery of horror is insistently defined (and confined); but the ghost remains vague and subjective. It is a boundless source of discomfort, its manifestations ranging from a single, ill-heard footstep in a quiet house to a scream transmitted around the world. Little wonder that the ghost is a constant of world literature—and likely to endure as a central motif of great horror fiction.

The indefatigable Peter Crowther has assembled, in *Taps & Sighs*, a worthy new look at ghosts, real and imagined, through the eyes of some of the best writers now working in the realm of the horrific. These stories challenge the ordinary and the expected while acknowledging the legacies of Charles Dickens and M.R. James; in these pages you will find styles and structures that are traditional and those that are unique, but mostly you will find stories that are not simply about ghosts but that seem unerringly to confront the reader with the issue of their meaning.

Ghosts, like Biblical angels, invoke that curious mingling of terror and awe that defines the emotion of horror; the very sight of them might drive one man insane while touching another as wondrous—as Ed Gorman confirms here in the noirish "Ghosts." A lingering spirit reminds us of the imminence of death, but suggests something else, something profound yet fearful: the possibility that death is not final—that life, of a kind, persists after death. And it is not always the afterlife promised by religion.

Although some of these spectres haunt old dark houses and are seen only at night or in shadow, some brave the sunlight and grace curious places: telephone booths, railroad boxcars, airplanes. The sight of a ghost is a common theme; but, as our title suggests, seeing is not the only means of believing. Sound is an insistent motif: taps and sighs that may find expression in more modern and sophisticated ways—through the telephone and, in Ian McDonald's bleak and brilliant "White Noise," even the blower of a toilet hand-drier.

Whether by sight or sound or other means, the dead offer messages as complex as the unknown realm they inhabit: hope, fear, forgiveness, threat, and above all, caution.

If there is a singular theme to this collection—and, indeed, to the vast literature of the ghostly—it is that the dead have certain lessons they wish to teach us, and that we should be wary students. That most archetypal of ghost stories, the campfire tale, indulges the spirit (and often the very text) of urban legends, providing a way of mediating very real anxieties about ourselves and our world into entertainments, cautionary tales that amuse or excite—yet instruct—us.

"I've come to warn you," says the ghost of Brian Stableford's "All You Inherit": "That's what apparitions of the dead are supposed to be for, after all. The first time's just to let you know that we're around, to keep you on your toes. The second time's to tell you that you're going to need to be strong if you intend to see it through." And the third time?

For Michael Marshall Smith, the third time is the aptly titled "Charms," in which the darkness yields to the light, offering redemptive wisdom; but more often the voice of the beyond heralds destruction, if not damnation. In "The Homeless Couple," Ray Garton's tale of loss and obsession, the sound of the otherworldly proves poignant yet perilous . . . and why not?

The dead, after all, are dead; their appearance among the living, however welcome, upsets the order of things. Perhaps they are weighted to this plane by emotional baggage, as one of Charles De Lint's characters proposes in "The Words That Remain" : "What else can they be but unhappy? If they weren't unhappy, they wouldn't still be hanging around, would they?" Perhaps they serve some higher purpose, as Peter Crowther and Tracy Knight suggest in the arch "Circling the Drain," whose ghost—a self-styled "janitor of the unseen universe"—helps the living "decide to go back when they're trying to die out of order." Or perhaps they heal, or at least soothe, the wound of time.

Graham Joyce's melancholy "Candia" depicts a reunion of two former co-workers in a strange and increasingly surreal locale—a city of lost bars and missing streets and "ruined temples dedicated to gods glimpsed only once in a lifetime." Candia offers no escape. The narrator feels only "the hollow ache, the hunger, the yearning to make one moment snap together with another to form a chain of some consequence, some meaning." It is a place not unlike our own present, a place where past and future intersect; and the ghost story, which is insistently temporal, strives to help us find that "chain of some consequence, some meaning" that binds the difficult, enigmatic future to the unrecoverable past.

Writers of ghostly fiction have never needed Santayana's famous maxim about the lessons of history—for them, it is a given. And we have writers of our own to quote: Dario Argento, whose *Inferno* insisted that "the only true mystery is that our very lives are governed by dead people"; or Jack Cady, who noted with convincing simplicity, "We are formed and directed by forgotten words, spoken by forgotten ancestors."

The antiquarian stance of the ghost story, immortalized by M.R. James, remains strong in this anthology. In "The Prisoner's Tale," Thomas F. Monteleone returns us to the nineteenth century and Solferino, site of the fiercest battle of the Franco-Austrian War, where a prisoner of war's only hope of escape is the ghost said to haunt his cell. Graham Masterton's sardonic but touching "Spirits of the Age" imagines a millennial reunion of Prince Albert and Queen Victoria, and reminds us that there are rifts of the heart that neither science nor the supernatural can heal.

Poppy Z. Brite's "Nailed" is postmodern antiquarianism (or as close as one might come to such a thing) and indulges another ghostly tradition by proving the perils of neglecting—or, worse, poaching—the past. It is a vengeful place, the past, lingering to remind us of things we'd prefer to forget; but its imprint, however dire, is only inescapable if we permit it. Thus, in Brian Stableford's "All You Inherit," his protagonist, Amelia, must live in the shadow of an empirical "family curse"—the risk of cancer from the blood of her mother, which Amelia passes on to her own child. Yet as her mother's ghost reminds her—and us: "All you inherit is the risk."

As beings whose essence is the intangible, ghosts have a fondness, and occasional fervor, for possessing the material—and using objects in symbolic, if not malefic, ways. From the sublime (Shirley Jackson's Hill House) to the ridiculous (the television series "My Mother, the Car")—and in several stories of *Taps & Sighs*—hauntings find power through the investment of the ordinary, transforming the utilitarian into the mythic.

In Ken Wisman's "The Glove," an old baseball mitt fields an entire life of conflict between father and son. In Gene Wolfe's "The Walking Sticks," a curious legacy brings a bloody past into collision with an equally bloody present. Ramsey Campbell's wryly titled "Return Journey" offers an apparition that is surreal and somber. A child's train ride, and its descent into a dark tunnel, marks her as part of a generation that has grown up in the inescapable shadow of world war:

"She remembered little of the blackout. The war had been over before she started school. The few memories she could recall just now seemed close to flickering out—her parents leading her past the extinguished houses and deadened lamps of streets that had no longer been at all familiar, the bones of her father's fingers silhouetted by the flashlight he was muffling, the insect humming of a distant swarm of bombers, the steps leading down to the bomb shelter, to the neighbours' voices as muted as their lights. She'd been safe there—she had always been safe with her parents—so why did the idea of seeking refuge make her yearn to be in the open?"

Why, indeed? Because the past cannot easily be consigned to the blank realm of faded memory. An object from that near but distant conflict—a gas mask—takes on some semblance of life, shattering all childhood illusions of safety. Elegant in style and stunning in emotional truth, "Return Journey" is one of the more profound antiwar fictions I have read in recent years.

Inevitably, ghosts haunt even our art. In Charles de Lint's "The Words That Remain," a writer (himself a kind of ghost, whose "favorite haunts" are used book stores and libraries) finds epiphany in the ultimate ghost story—one told by a ghost. In Terry Lamsley's "His Very Own Spatchen," a dilettante covets the final painting of an arcane artist only to learn the delicate balance between reality and its depiction on canvas. The past, Lamsley reminds us, cannot be restored, just as it cannot be escaped; and efforts to reclaim its territory are traps that bind us even tighter to its sway. In each story, haunter and haunted circle in a mating dance, each yearning to supplant the other.

As Ian McDonald notes in "White Noise," however: "Ghosts do not need to be from the past." Even our best-remembered ghost story,

Dickens's "A Christmas Carol," makes clear that the past is not the only dominion of the dead. Its ghosts of Christmas present and future find horrifying echoes here in Mark Morris's holiday fable "Coming Home"— and in "White Noise."

"Ghosts of the future, speaking from the past. Warnings? Prophecies?" Neither, McDonald's protagonist soon understands. "Ghosts are merely the blind replaying of some tremendous trauma, an outrage so far beyond normality that it has imprinted itself on the white noise that is the hiss of reality continuously recreating itself." Proof of the existence of the paranormal brings him a startling revelation—that ghosts offer us nothing, save to remind us that life is life, nothing less but certainly nothing more, and that reality, however we may imagine or believe it is interpenetrated with the spiritual, is ultimately material and dictatorial: "He does not have to do anything. There is nothing he can do. There is nothing that can be done."

If there is sadness in that thought, there is also a strange hope, the kind of hope that sears through the anguish of Chaz Brenchley's "The Insolence of Candles Against the Light's Dying." In this fitting conclusion to this fine anthology, the narrator confronts the death of his uncle— and the inevitable death of his lover (and thus, obliquely, of himself). "I believe in being haunted," he says. "By the living or the dead, or some dream that was never properly either one of those." His lover responds, so very acutely: "What, you mean we make our own ghosts?"

This, then, is the final truth of *Taps & Sighs*: Whatever we may believe, or disbelieve, about the existence of the supernatural, we make our own ghosts. If not, then the ghosts—our past, our parents, our failed potential—make us.

In the pages of this anthology you will find many well-made ghosts, summoned from the shadows of time—and places beyond time—for your entertainment and, perhaps, edification. Tonight the rain is made of words, not water, but it is full of ghosts, that tap and sigh . . . and listen for reply.

Douglas E. Winter
Oakton, Virginia
August 1999

Richard Christian Matheson
CITY OF DREAMS

It was June when the Royal moved in.

I knew because high, metal fences started going up, perimeter shrubbery doubled and two sullen Dobermans began patrolling. Then, overnight, an intercom, numerical keypad and security camera were mysteriously installed at the bottom of the Royal's driveway, which ran alongside mine. Whenever I drove by, the lens would zoom to inspect me, staring with curt inquisition.

The Royal was obviously concerned who visited.

Had the Royal been hurt? Was future hurt likely? Were death threats being phoned in hourly? It seemed anything, however dire, was possible. I was already feeling badly for the Royal.

I didn't know if the Royal was a him or her. Rock diva? Zillionaire cyber tot? Mob boss? Pro-leaguer? My mind wandered in lush possibility.

But all I ever saw was a moody limo that purred through the gate and crunched up the long driveway. By the time it got to the big house, the forest landscaping hid it; a leafy moat. I found it all rather troubling. In my experience, concealment is meaningful; trees can be trimmed, the fears which lurk behind them are a different story. Ultimately one cannot hide, only camouflage. Orson Welles certainly understood it; in *Citizen Kane* tragic privilege never seemed so rapturous nor incarcerated.

As days passed, I tried not to listen to what went on next door. I'd play jazz CDs, sip morning espresso, scan the entertainment section, for reviews, to distract my attentions. But the community is exclusive and quiet, and birds' wings, as they groom, are noticeable. It made it hard to miss the Royal's limo as it sighed up the driveway, obscured by the half million dollars of premeditated forest.

Once parked, doors would open and close, and I'd hear footsteps, sometimes cheerless murmurs; the limo driver speaking to the Royal, I assumed. Russian? Indo-Chinese? Impossible to tell. Then, the front door to the house would slam with imperial finality.

It went on like that for two weeks.

I began to think, perhaps, I should be a better neighbor, make the Royal feel more welcome; a part of the local family. Which is somewhat misleading considering the neighborhood is an aloof haven and I barely know anyone. I'm like that; keep to myself, make friends slowly. I'm what they call an observer. Some dive, I float with mask and snorkel. But the instinct seemed warm; welcoming.

I was also getting very curious.

❖

I was up late writing, one night, and decided to mix-up a batch of chocolate chip cookies. My new screenplay was coming along well, if slowly, and I thought about love scenes and action scenes as I peered into the oven, watching the huge cookies rise like primitive islands forming. They were plump, engorged with cubes of chocolate the size of small dice; worthy of a Royal, I decided.

I let them cool, ate three, wrapped the remaining dozen in tin-foil. Crumpled the foil to make it resemble something snappy and Audubon, the way they make crinkly swans in nice places to shroud left-overs. I wrapped a bow around the neck, placed the tin foil bird into a pretty box I'd saved from Christmas, ribboned it, found a greeting card with no message. The photo on the front was a natural cloud formation that looked a bit like George Lucas.

I used my silver-ink pen that flows upside down, like something a doomed astronaut might use to scrawl a final entry, and wrote "Some supplies to keep you happy and safe. Researchers say chocolate brings on the exact sensation of love; an effect of phenoalimine. (Just showing off). Welcome to this part of the world."

My P.S. was a phone number, at the house, in case the Royal ever "needed anything." I also included a VHS of Francois Truffaut's *Day For Night*, a film I especially love for its tipsy discernment.

I debated whether to include exclamation marks, thought them excess, opted for periods. Clean, emotionally stable. Friendly but not cloying. Being in the film business, I know first impressions counted.

It's one reason I'm sought after to do scripts, albeit for lesser films with sinking talents. But I'm well paid and it allows me to live in this secured community near L.A., complete with gate-guard, acre parcels and compulsory privacy. I'm an anonymous somebody; primarily rumor. I wish I could've been Faulkner, but there you are. Instead, I'm a faceless credit on a screen, my scant reply to a world's indifference.

I left the cookies and card in the Royal's mail-box, at the bottom of the driveway, and spoke tense baby-talk to the Dobermans, as I made the deposit, like one of those pocked thugs in *The French Connection*. A beautifully directed film, by the way. The package fit nicely, looked cheerful in there. Too much so? I considered it. Every detail determines outcome; it's the essence of subtext, as Preston Sturges once observed. And certainly if the Royal were an international sort, I wanted there to be room for some kind of friendship. I could learn things. Get gossip that mattered; the chic lowdown.

I waited two days.

Nothing.

I'd sit by my pool, every morning, read the paper, scan box-office numbers, sip espresso. But I wasn't paying full attention. I was watching my Submariner tick.

At ten-thirty, sharp, the heavy tires would crunch up the driveway and the door ritual would begin. I couldn't make out a word and tried to remember if I'd left my phone number in the P.S. Even if not, there was always my mailbox. Concern was devouring me by ounces and I disliked seeing it happen.

In self protection, I began to lose interest in the Royal; the inky sleigh, the seeming apathy, the whole damn thing.

At least that's what I tried to tell myself.

❖

Two weeks quickly passed and I'd heard nothing. I felt deflated, yet oddly exhilarated to be snubbed by someone so important; it bordered on eerie intoxicant, even hinted at voodoo. Despite efforts otherwise, the truth was I continued to wonder what the Royal thought about me, though it hardly constituted preoccupation.

I'm a bit sensitive on the topic because my ex-wife often said I paid unnatural attention to those I considered remarkable, though I found nothing strange in it. The way I see it, we all need heroes; dreams of something better; perhaps even transcendent. A key piece of miscellany: she ran off with a famous hockey player from Ketchikan, Alaska; a slab of idiocy named Stu. *Time* and *Newsweek* covered their nuptials. Color photos, confetti, the whole bit. A featured quote from her gushed:

"I've never been happier!"

Real pain. Like I'd been shot.

I feel it places things, as regards to my outlook, in perspective. She certainly never could. Strangely enough, I've been thinking about her lately; how she drove me into psychotherapy after she left and took our African Grey, Norman, with her and never contacted me again, saying I'd made them both miserable. Over time, I heard from mutual friends that she was claiming, among other toxic side-effects of our marriage, that I'd caused Norman to stop talking, and that once they'd set-up house elsewhere, he became a chatterbox. I took it personally; couldn't sleep for weeks.

More haunting facts of my teetering world.

❖

The fate of the cookies preyed on my mind for days, affecting work and sleep, a predicament rife with what my ex-shrink, Larry, used to term "emotional viscosity," a condition I suspect he made up, hoping it would catch on and bring him, and his unnerving beard, acclaim. Still, I wrote half-heartedly and my stomach churned the kind of butter that really clogs you up.

Another few days went by and I made no move. Any choice seemed wrong; quietude the only wisdom. I was feeling foolish; mocked. My heartfelt efforts had been more irrelevant than I'd feared. I continued to work on my screenplay, and joked emptily with my agent, who seemed an especially drab series of noises compared to the person I knew the Royal must be.

It's true, I had no real evidence. The Royal might be an overwhelming bore. Some rich cadaver in an iron lung, staring bitterly into a tiny mirror.

But I didn't think so.

In fact, I was beginning to think anyone who went to such trouble to avoid a friendly overture had something precious to protect. On a purely personal level, if cookies, a card and a badly executed foil-swan could scare a person, their levels of sensitivity had to be finely calibrated. Perhaps the Royal had been wounded; given up on humanity. I've been there. I wish somebody like me tried to crack the safe; get me the hell out.

But when's the last time life had a heart? Let's face it, unsoothed by human kindness, souls recede. It's in all the great movies; pain, sacrifice, hopes abandoned.

It's how people like me and the Royal got the way we are. We flee emotionally, too riddled by personal travail to venture human connection. Sort of like Norman. We're just recovering believers, choking on the soot of an uncaring world.

I understood the Royal. Yet I had to move on; get over it.

But it was hard. Maybe I was simply in some futile trance, succumbed to loneliness and curiosity. I admit I'm easily infected by my enthusiasms. You read about people like me; the ones who do something crazy in the name of human decency only to find themselves stuffed, hung on a wall; poached by life.

So, despite rejection, I found myself listening each morning, over breakfast, to the Royal's property, gripped by speculation. Awaiting the door ritual, sensing the Royal over there, alone, needing a friend. It was sad and nearly called out for a melodramatic soundtrack; something with strings; that haunted Bernard Herrmann ambivalence.

It made me recall a line I once heard in a bleak Fassbinder movie; this Munich prostitute whispered to her lover that a person's fate "always escorts the bitter truth." She blew Gitane smoke, pouting with succulent blankness and, to my embarrassment, it just spoke to me. I don't know why. It got me thinking, I suppose, the ways movies can; even the sorry, transparent ones.

It was the first time I began to consciously wish I could do a second draft of me; start things over; find my life a more worthy plot, tweak the main character. Maybe even find a theme. A man without one has nowhere to hide.

Ingmar Bergman based a career on it.

⹁

Two days later, the note came.

In my mailbox, dozing in an expensive, ragcloth envelope. It was handwritten, the letters a sensual perfection.

> *"We must meet. How about drinks tonight over here. Around sunset?."*

I must have read it a hundred times, weighing each word, the phrasing and inclusion of the word "must." It seemed not without meaning.

I debated outfits. Formal? Casual? I was able to make a case for either, chose slacks, a sweater. I looked nice; thought it important.

Before heading over, I considered a gift. Cheese? An unopened compact disc? Mahler? Coltraine? But it all strained of effort and I wanted to seem offhand; worth knowing. The way Jimmy Stewart always was; presuming nothing, evincing worlds.

I used the forgotten path between the two driveways, dodging the dobermans who seemed to expect me, tilting heads with professional interest, eyes ashimmer.

I walked to the front door. Knocked. Waited two minutes, listened for footsteps, and was about to knock, again, when the door opened.

She was *exquisite*.

Maybe twenty. Eyes and dress mystic blue, dark hair, medium length. Skin, countess pale. She wore a platinum locket, and gauged me for a moment.

"Hello," she said in the best voice I've ever heard, up till then, or since.

We spent an hour talking about everything, though I learned little about her. At some point, she said her name was Aubrey and I'm sure I responded, though I was lost in her smile, her attentions colorizing my world.

It seemed she told me less about herself with each passing minute, which I liked; genuine modesty looks best on the genuinely important.

She asked me about my work and listened carefully as I spoke about why I loved the music of words and the fantasy of movies; of creating perfect impossibilities. Her rare features silhouetted on mimosa sunset, and she said she's always loved films, especially romantic ones, and when her smile took my heart at gunpoint, I felt swept into a special effect, a trick of celluloid and moment, as if part of a movie in which I'd been terribly miscast; my presence too common to properly elevate the material.

She took my hand and when we walked outside and watched stars daisy the big pool, I thought I must be falling in love. I still think I was, despite everything that was soon to befall me.

After a slow walk around her fountained garden, she said she was tired and needed her rest, that she'd come a very long way. I wish I'd thought to ask for details of that journey; an oversight which torments me to this second.

Aubrey slowly slipped her delicate hands around my waist and it almost seemed a recognition of some dire subtext between us, a moment nearly cinematic in composition.

She said she had a secret gift for me and led me to a wrapped package that rest, on a chaise, near the pool.

"For you," she said.

"A painting?" I guessed, reaching to open it, until she gently stopped me.

"Tomorrow," she suggested. "When you're alone."

It seemed she was being dramatic. I wish it had been anywhere near that simple.

"Goodnight," she said.

I protested, wanting to know more about her, but she placed her mouth to my ear.

"I've always looked for you out there," she said, voice a despairing melody. "In the dark. I've wondered what you were like."

"What do you mean?" I finally replied, lost.

She never answered and I watched her disappear into the mansion, with a final wave, and what I'd describe, in a script, if I had to tell the actress what to convey, as veiled desperation.

❖

The next morning, I slept so deeply I didn't even hear the car that sped up my driveway. It wasn't until the knocking that I finally awakened.

When the detective spoke, I felt the earth die.

"A break-in?" I repeated in a voice that had to sound in need of medical attention.

He explained the missing piece was valuable, purchased in London, at auction. The chauffeur had told the police the owner of the house was a collector, but provided no further details.

"It was a gift. She gave it to me," I explained.

"She?"

"Aubrey." I could still see her plaintive eyes, desperate for connection. "The woman who lives there."

He said nothing, then asked if he could see it. I nodded and took him to my living room, where it leaned against the big sofa. He slowly, silently unwrapped it and my world began to vanish.

The poster was full color, gold-framed. It was from the thirties and the star was a stunning brute, named Dan Drake; unshaven, clefted. His beautiful co-star was Isabella Ryan, and she was held in his embrace as the two stood atop Mulholland Drive, windblown; somehow doomed. Behind them, a stoic L.A. glittered, morose precincts starved of meaning. Though striking, no splendor could be found in its image, merely loss. The movie was titled *City of Dreams*, but I'd never heard of it.

Isabella's eyes and dress were mystic blue, her flowing dark hair and pale skin more regal than the platinum locket adorning her slender neck. From any angle, no matter how inaccurately observed, she not only re-sembled Aubrey, she was her. It was shocking to me in a way I'd never experienced and I nearly felt some cruel director zooming onto my pained expression for the telling close-up.

Both stars had signed at the bottom.

"To everyone who ever loved. Yours, Dan Drake"

Beside his, in delicate script was:

"I've always seen you out there. You're in my dreams. Love, Isabella Ryan"

She seemed to be looking right at me.

❖

Charges were never brought against me, and the sunken-faced detec-tive said I'd gotten off easy, that my neighbor, still unnamed, didn't want trouble and was giving me a second chance. The Royal only wanted the poster back, nothing more. For me, this generosity stirred further mys-tique; intolerable distress.

❖

It's futile to determine who I'd actually spend the evening with; I don't believe in ghosts unless they are of the emotional variety; aroused by seances of personal misfortune, you might say.

But this thought brings no peace, no clarity.

I looked up *City of Dreams* in one of my movie books and found it; **1942, MGM. Black and white. Suspense. 123 minutes.** There was a related article about Isabella, an air-brushed studio photo beside her hus-band, the obscure composer Malcolm Zinner. Zinner was bespeckled, intense. It appeared their marriage had been loveless.

Despite promising reviews, the article said that she'd never done an-other movie and suffered several nervous breakdowns . . . but then, don't they all? She'd died in a plane crash, in 1953, near Madrid. The book said her real name was Aubrey Baker.

Truffaut said that film is truth, twenty-four frames per second. Mine seems to be moving rather slower these days, my heart circling itself. I feel drugged by confusion; a lost narrative. I'm drawn to unhealthy theory and wonder if perhaps I am dying.

Maybe I've just seen too many movies.

My ex-wife used to say the thing about irony is you never see it coming; that's how you know it's there. She used to talk like that, in puzzles. I'm not sure what she was getting at, but there you are. All I know is a movie poster with a long dead beauty is the most genuine thing I can remember in a lifetime of misappropriated and badly written fictions; it seems a bad trend. Not even a particularly worthwhile plot, but I was never much good at that part.

❖

It's been two months now, since that evening by the pool, and still no sign of the Royal who remains at large in elite silence. I suppose I've given up thinking we'll ever actually meet, barring the extreme twist.

Sometimes I find myself staring at the handwritten invitation, which I saved, though I have no idea who really wrote it. I stare until my focus and faith untie, and the words slowly lift from the paper and fly away, scattering grammar into sky; an image Vittorio De Sica might have sparked to.

❖

After much search, I finally found a copy of *City of Dreams* at a specialty video store which had to track it down for me.

When I watch Aubrey, despite her astonishing beauty, I keep thinking she looks trapped; not by bad dialogue or plot, but an apprehension of her life to be. Its imminent ruin.

Today, I tried to tell my agent why the dumb script I've been working on is late and when he heard all of what had happened, he sighed and said writers were always getting themselves in crazy messes. He said he thought I'd probably seen Isabella's movie when I was a kid and forgotten about it. He nearly accused me of drinking, again, and wondered if maybe I'd had too much one night, wandered around the Royal's house and seen the poster; decided I had to have it, succumbing to stupid nostalgia. To bring back my only good childhood memory; going to the movies. The rest had been awful, loveless; an ordeal that lasted for endless seasons of pain.

I'm sure he's right. I do drink when I get lonely. I could take many evenings out of your life failing to convey the dread and hurt I often feel. I've had nights where I stared pointlessly, out at the world, and thought no one could ever love me, just as, it seems, Isabella watches it from her lurid, heartbreaking poster, searching for the one face, out there in a heartless city, who will truly care.

❖

Bunuel said every life is a film. Some good, some bad. We are, each of us, paradoxes in an unstated script; pawns who wish to know kings, souls divided, hearts in exile. We're all tragic characters, one way or the other; the vivid Technicolor glories, the noir hurts, the dissolve to final credits.

Fellini believed movies were magic, itself, awakened by light. That theaters were like churches, dim and velvet; filled with incantation.

All I know is that when you feel lost and wounded, movies always welcome you, like a friend, inviting you to forget the painful truth. To dream of better things.

Life pales.

Michael Marshall Smith
CHARMS

Once she reached the high street Carol's walk slowed. She took a few deep breaths and shrugged her shoulders to dislodge some of the tenseness, making slow fists of her hands and releasing them quickly, as if trying to flick off insects. The street was crowded in the sunshine, and she threaded her way down the wide pavement, wondering where to go. She had no reason to be in town, and before her parents had started arguing had been looking forward to a desultory afternoon at their house.

Then something had happened.

Nothing unusual; the same old thing. Whatever it was.

She always missed it, somehow, the actual moment when things turned sour. Most of the time being at home was like wading in a stream of warm flowing water, comforting and secure. She knew the history of everything in every room, and the spaces were secure, dependable. So too her parents: Mother would potter about in the kitchen, asking her how she was, what she was doing; Father would read the paper and listen to her answers while Mother pounced in with another question.

Then the warmth would be gone, as if Carol had carelessly stepped into a deep cavity filled with icy water. Suddenly the air was taut with the unspoken, and the objects in the room seemed to stand isolated with an unpleasant starkness, cut adrift from each other, as what her parents said to each other started to take on cutting subtexts. Until she'd left home Carol had subconsciously blamed her father, probably because it was always him who ended up storming out of the room. Distance had helped her see that her mother was at least as much to blame.

She'd left the house fifteen minutes after stepping into the cold. By that time Mother was furiously cooking unnecessary brownies, and father was in his study. As she walked down the drive Carol winced at the music coming loudly from the window. The arguments always ended in the same way—with her mother burying herself in trivia, and her father in his study, sitting bolt upright in his chair and listening to his old 45's. Early Beatles, Stones. Other bands whose names fate hadn't blessed with memorability. Carol had never been able to hear those songs with pleasure, and always flinched when they came on at parties. They were irretrievably associated with suddenly finding herself in a wasteland, lost between two warring factions whose feelings and grievances she had never understood.

Everyone in the high street seemed to have somewhere to go, urgent tasks to perform. A glance at their faces showed they weren't even seeing the high street, just running breathlessly on rails. Carol felt strangely dislocated, in a town that was no longer hers, wandering aimlessly among projectile people as they ricocheted from car to shop to shop to car. At last a task occurred to her, and she crossed the street and headed for Tony's Records. It was her mother's birthday in a couple of weeks, and she might not get a chance for a leisurely shop again before then. She could probably find something in the record store her mother would like, though she'd have to be diplomatic about giving it to her.

Her mother had a CD player, and classical tastes. Her father had his 45's. And never, it appeared, did the twain meet. She'd always been a little perplexed by that, as it had been her father who had encouraged her to have piano lessons when she was young. Every now and then she caught a glimpse of something irrational between her parents, something made so rigid and obscure by time that even they probably didn't understand it any more. The still water between them ran very deep, and the smallest coin created huge ripples. She'd give her mother the CD on the quiet.

Saturday afternoon in Loughton was a time for the big guns of shopping, the DIY mercenaries and the Sainsburys SWAT teams. The record shop was almost deserted, and as she headed for the classical CDs she cast a glance at the only other customer. He was in his late forties, and she was a little surprised to notice herself finding him rather attractive. Older men weren't her thing at all, but there was something about him that kept the eye.

The classical section of Tony's was laughably small, market forces evidently having declared proper music played by actual musicians to be a cultural dead end. The single rack of CDs hung like an appendix on the end of the Soul section, and in five years it probably wouldn't be there at all. But by then Tony's would have probably have folded anyway, and you'd have to go twenty miles to buy music from a hyperstore the size of Denmark. For just a moment, Carol suddenly felt terribly old.

She spent five minutes flicking irritably through the CDs, trying to find something that wasn't either music from a TV advert or Nigel bloody Kennedy playing the Four sodding Seasons. She was about to give up when a hand reached from beside her and plucked a double CD case from the "B" section.

"What about this?"

Startled, Carol turned to see the other customer standing beside her. Now that she could see his face properly she couldn't imagine how she could have thought him middle-aged. He was no more than early thirties, and had a smile that was younger still.

"Are you buying for yourself," he asked, "Or someone else?" His grin was infectious, and Carol found herself returning it.

"For my mother."

He nodded, and looked at her for a moment. "I think these, then."

He handed her the CD, and she turned it over to read the cover. It showed a relatively youthful Paul Tortelier, sternly poised behind a cello.

"Bach Solo Cello Suites," she said, looking up at him, "I don't think I know them. Are they nice?"

He frowned at her. "They're not 'nice,' no. To the best of my knowledge they have not helped sell a single brand of car, bank or nationalised industry."

She laughed. "Good. They sound perfect."

"Would you like an ice cream?"

Carol double-took at the question, but the offer was evidently serious. She shrugged. "Why not?"

As she waited for the teenaged assistant behind the counter to remember that she had a role to play in helping customers make purchases, Carol glanced at the man. He was waiting near the door, and raised his eyebrows at her. She smiled at him, then turned back. For some reason she felt quite excited. From the minute he'd first spoken to her she'd known that he wasn't trying to pick her up. She'd fielded more than enough charming lechers and drink-buying madmen to be able to tell immediately. He had talked to her because he wanted to, nothing more. And when he'd spoken, he'd spoken to her, to Carol, not just to a pretty girl who might be worth a try.

It was so unusual it was a bit weird. But nice.

On the first warm day suburban England goes into Summer mode as if a giant switch has been thrown somewhere. Men walk around with no shirts on while still wearing trousers, every moron with a white car cruises the high street pumping out anonymous dance music, and sure enough, there was an ice cream van only ten yards down the street. The man's courteousness in ordering their ice creams so blew the frazzled kiosk attendant's mind that he even got a smile from her. Then he led Carol to the bench that sat beneath the one tree in the high street.

As she sat and lapped her cone, Carol felt curiously cool and calm, and she turned to look at the man.

"So why that CD?"

"What brought you out to this mayhem this afternoon?"

"I asked first," Carol said. As she did so she felt a faint brush of embarrassment, then realized she didn't really feel embarrassed at all. It was like being with someone back in the days when things were simple, when you didn't have jealous ex-boyfriends on your back and weren't talking to someone with a closet full of hang-ups and probably a wife somewhere in the background; when the game had been fun, instead of just a tortuous and repetitive way of ending up with a record collection you didn't even recognize any more.

"And I shall answer," he smiled. "Eventually."

"Well, I came out," Carol paused, then decided to go on anyway. "I came out because my parents were having a row."

"Over what?"

"Over nothing. Over everything. I don't know."

He nodded at her, and she noticed that his eyes were very green, with a ring of brown round the irises. They reminded her of leaves, some fallen, some still on the trees, down by a stream in the autumn.

"I've never known. They're both . . . they're both so *nice*. I mean, individually, they're the two nicest people I know. They must have loved each other once, otherwise they wouldn't have married each other, but somewhere down the line . . ."

She trailed off. Somewhere down the line two people who had loved each other very much had simply drifted off course.

"Maybe something happened, maybe nothing," the man said.

Carol looked up at him, startled but grateful to realize that he'd picked up the train of her thoughts. Then she looked down at her lap again.

Something had simply gone wrong somewhere, and now her father sat in his study listening to old records that had lost their magic, and her mother grew old in the living room. She found her eyes filling with tears. Although she'd thought about her parents many times, she'd never had the realization before. This was all they had, it wasn't working, and they were just waiting for everything to be over.

Maybe something, maybe nothing. That's all it had taken.

It wasn't fair, wasn't right that people who had loved each other should end up bound together by their feelings for two people who weren't there any more, and she suddenly felt very miserable.

The man turned from looking out across the road, and smiled gently at her. "Shall I tell you what I like about that CD?"

She nodded. She was happy to listen to him talk about anything.

"Bach is very different from any other composer," he said. "When you listen to Vivaldi, or Handel, you can tell that the music was composed for an audience. It's like a blockbuster film: it's good, but it's good because it's *supposed* to be good. It's been designed that way. When you listen to Bach, it's different. You're not being performed to. You're being allowed to overhear."

An open-topped white Golf cruised by, spilling trance jungle garage at a volume that would have had Led Zeppelin shaking their heads in grim disapproval.

The man smiled. "Ten years from now, no one will be listening to that crap any more, thank Christ. It's moment music, no more. But it's the same with the better stuff too. All the old 45's stashed in people's rooms, they're like a butterfly collection. They look as if they're still alive, as if they could fly away, but they've been dead for decades. Old feelings and memories pinned to pieces of vinyl. In a hundred years no-one will have associations for those songs any more, and most of them will be dead. But in five-hundred years, a thousand years, when people sit in houses on planets we don't even know exist yet, they'll still listen to Bach, and they'll still hear the same things. It's like listening to a charm. It doesn't fade."

His smile broadened, ridiculing the flamboyance of what he was saying. She smiled back, properly this time. He nodded approvingly.

"Better. And there's something else about that record, too." He reached across and took the CD from her. "Look. Recorded in 1961. When you listen to it, remember that."

Slightly puzzled, she grinned. "I will. But you still haven't answered my question. And I'm intrigued now, I want to go listen to this and it's not even for me."

"Well maybe you should."

"But," Carol fought hard, but then said it as simply as she could. "It's nice being with you." Great, she thought. You sound, what—about fourteen years old?

"That's alright," the man said. "I'll come with you, if I may."

Carol leapt at the chance. Quite apart from anything else, her turning up with a guest might diffuse the atmosphere back at the house. Her parents always liked meeting people she knew.

"Of course, I mean, yes. I'll say I bumped into a friend by accident."

Which wouldn't, she thought as they headed for his car, feel as if she was straying very far from the truth.

❖

Carol knew nothing about cars, but there was something undeniably classic about his, a diffident and unassuming open-topped sports car in darkest green. It looked like something from another era that had lasted very well, like the deepest pockets of Epping forest where the trees had never been pollarded, and still looked like trees.

There was a comprehensive-looking CD player built into the front console, but she couldn't see any CDs anywhere, and she didn't want to break the wrapping on the Cello Suites. It was still going to be a present for her mother, though not for her birthday, and it would only take a few minutes to get home.

When they pulled up in the drive all was quiet, and Carol knew from experience that her father would now be out in the garden, pottering quietly, thinking his own thoughts.

Her mother looked a little quiet when she opened the door, but brightened considerably on seeing Carol had a guest.

"Hi Ma," Carol said, "I ran into a friend in town, thought I'd bring him home to meet you."

"How nice," her mother said warmly, reached out her hand.

Realizing too late she didn't know the man's name, Carol scrabbled and came up with one that would have to do.

"So, er . . . Mother—*Mark*, Mark—Mother."

The man accepted this without batting an eyelid, and took her mother's hand.

"How do you do. I've heard a lot about you."

"Oh, I hope not," her mother laughed.

"Are you bored with people saying how alike you and Carol look?" he asked as she led them into the sitting room. Carol blinked: how did he know her name? Had she told him, and forgotten? She must have.

"No, not at all," her mother giggled, and Carol stared at her curiously. She didn't think she'd ever heard her mother giggle before. Certainly not like that.

Carol felt the house relax about them as mother set about making tea, chatting with the man. She'd never been like this with any of the boyfriends she'd brought home. Polite, yes, friendly in a reserved and parental way, but not like this. "Vivacious" was something she hadn't realized her mother had in her armory.

"And that," said the man, nodding out at the garden, "is presumably your husband, Mrs. Peters?"

Carol steeled herself. It was generally a few hours after an argument before either of them would acknowledge the other's existence.

"Yes," said her mother, "that's John. And call me Gillian."

"Okay," he said, "Is that your name?"

Giggling again, her mother punched him lightly on the shoulder and turned to hand Carol her tea.

"Your friend is a twit, Carol," she said.

"Perhaps I should go introduce myself to your father," the man said. His eyes drifted over the small package Carol held in her lap, and she realized that he was giving her a chance to present it to her mother undisturbed.

"Do you want me to . . ."

"No, I'll be fine."

They watched him go, and then mother and daughter turned to each other.

"Well," her mother said after a pause, "if you're not going out with him yet you want to bloody well get a move on."

They looked at each other soberly for a moment and then started laughing. When they tailed off, still hiccuping every now and then, Carol felt an enormous wave of relief. Not only had the tension in the house disappeared as if it had never existed, but her mother looked so relaxed, so vital.

"I bought you a present," she said.

Her mother hadn't heard the Suites either, and they decided to give the first one a quick listen. Carol settled back in her chair as her mother set up the CD, realizing that was something that she liked about her mother that she'd never noticed before. Most people past a certain age seemed to make a decision to refuse to come to terms with new technology. To give up, and become old. But not her mother: as she wielded the CD remote she looked just like Carol's flatmate Suz. Or like a capable older sister, the kind who goes off traveling round the world and doesn't come back with dysentery.

There was a faint hiss before the music started, and Carol remembered what the man had said.

"Recorded in 1961," she observed to her mother, who nodded.

Then there was the sound of the cello.

It had something of the austere beauty of an equation, an irreducible expression, but it touched you very deeply: it was like seeing truth with your ears. It *was* like a charm, she realized, like looking at the inside of a perfect crystal and observing an expression of natural forces which you could appreciate but not understand. That was why, she realized, you could often tell what was coming next when you listen to Bach. Not because it was predictable, but because it was right. When clouds darkened, it was going to rain: when they broke, the sun would shine. Some things happened after something else. That was all there was to it.

All her favorite songs, the albums in her flat and the battered singles archived in her old bedroom upstairs, they captured moments. This music captured time.

As they listened she focused on every note as it passed, listening to sounds recorded in 1961: before the Beatles, before the Stones, before the Sixties themselves got into their stride. On the day those notes were recorded the world was a completely different place, yet however you listened to it, in those grooves, in that tape, in those digits, was 1961. Outside the room Tortelier was playing in was another room, where men with Brylcreamed hair ran an old-fashioned recording desk which was state-of-the-art to them. Behind them was a window, and outside the birds were singing. And somewhere out there would be a newspaper seller, and he'd be hawking papers with the date 1961 on them, maybe a Thursday. Perhaps if you listened hard enough you could hear him, and the moment had never really died.

Charms

As the Prélude finished, reducing itself to a broken chord which hung on the air, Carol turned and looked at her mother. She was crying gently, and pressed the Stop button on the handset. Then she looked up at her daughter, and Carol saw that her mother had heard the same things.

In a different house, on a different planet, it would always be there to be heard.

Her mother wiped her eyes and smiled with genuine warmth. "They've been out there a long time."

They walked into the kitchen, to look out of the window into the back garden. The man was standing talking to her father, and though you couldn't hear what they were saying, her father's laugh when it came drifted through the window to them. Carol glanced at her mother, and held her breath when she saw the expression on her face. There was a faint smile on her lips, and small tears still in her eyes. It was the face of someone who was looking at a photo of a friend who'd died long ago, and finding that the mourning was not over yet.

When she spoke, her voice was fractured, and hesitant. "It's funny. Standing out there, he looks just like he used to look."

As they watched, the two men laughed again, and her father ran his hand carelessly back through his hair. Carol heard the intake of her mother's breath.

"He always . . ." Her mother reached her own hand up, and ran it gently through her own hair, at the side. "I loved him for that."

The two men burst into a fresh gale of laughter, her father almost doubling up. They looked like two young friends out there, planning old-fashioned devilry, and it would be very easy to love either one of them. Tears ran down her mother's face.

"Mum—what happened?"

Her mother looked at her, her face clouded. "Nothing," she said, shaking her head with puzzled misery. "Nothing that I can remember."

As they watched the two men looked back towards the house, and then headed towards the back door, still talking.

"They're coming back," her mother said, wiping her face with a tea towel. "Is the tea still warm?"

As Carol poured two cups the back door opened and her father came in, followed by the man. Her father made it halfway across the kitchen, and then stopped, faltering, rubbing his hands nervously on his hips. He looked about sixteen.

Carol watched her mother. She was looking at her husband, eyes bright and wide, also nervous. They seemed awkward, unsure of themselves, as if meeting for the first time, or after a long time apart.

Then her father ran his hand unconsciously through his hair, and Carol noticed his grace as he smiled tentatively, a lopsided grin that could break anyone's heart. Her mother handed him a cup of tea, not taking her eyes off his, head tilted to one side.

"Never mind tea," said the man from behind her father. "It's a lovely day. Let's drive."

He led Carol out to his car, and she stood to one side to let her parents climb into the back seat, which they did with an agility Carol doubted she could have mustered. They settled back, and as Carol noticed her father's hand brush her mother's, and saw her grab hold of it, her father drawled in a surprisingly good American accent.

"So what are we waiting for?"

The man pulled the car quickly out into the road and turned away from town, out to where the houses shaded away to fields. "In the glove compartment," he said quietly.

Carol opened it, found the CD, and slotted it in the machine. The sound of the cello whipped up into the wind as they flashed towards the country, but she believed that if you strained your ears hard enough, you could hear those sounds, you could hear that year: you could slip through that channel and step out into the fresh sunlight of that day. As the fields spread out beside them and the car shot out into the afternoon, her mother whooped deliriously, and Carol turned 'round to see them, faces bright and hair dancing in the wind, clasping each other tight and waving at the trees, the wheat, the birds.

Ken Wisman
THE GLOVE

It was as though the thing was waiting for him—for how many years?—twenty-five, thirty. Paul stared in disbelief at the fielder's mitt lying at the bottom of the crumbling cardboard box. He had uncovered it moments before in his search for old books.

It looked malevolent in the dim attic light, like a swollen, severed hand. Paul reached in and plucked the glove between his thumb and forefinger, handling it as though it were a dead animal.

The moment he touched the leather, a stream of images flashed through his mind.

Ghosts.

Of him.

His father.

He heard voices. Angry. Strident.

Frightened, Paul dropped the glove.

He took a deep breath, recovered. He chuckled and whispered to himself: "If I didn't know better, I'd swear the damned thing was haunted." He decided to throw it out with the other accumulated trash.

"What's that, Dad?"

Startled, Paul turned to see his son's head and shoulders poking up through the trapdoor.

"Junk," Paul called. He knelt by another stack of boxes and rummaged through them. Absorbed in his search, Paul didn't see his son come all the way up and kneel behind him.

"It's a fielder's glove," Jackie said.

Paul turned to see his son putting the mitt on his left hand.

"Where'd you get it, Dad?"

"My father bought it," Paul said. "A long time ago."

"Grandpa? What was he like?"

More ghosts beckoned; Paul beat them back.

"We didn't talk much. I really don't know."

"Hey, Dad, this old mitt is neat." Jackie pounded his fist into the pocket. Then he fished inside the box. "What's this?" Jackie held up a small bottle.

"Castor oil," Paul said. "They used that to soften the leather."

"It needs it. It's stiff." Jackie unscrewed the top. "This stuff's still good." He smeared the discolored oil onto the pocket, across the webbing and fingers.

Aside from the dim bulb over the trapdoor, the only light in the attic was a shaft of sun streaming through a vent. Paul watched the disturbed dust drift through the sunbeam—a thousand dried hours and dead days, thirty years of dust and old, bad memories.

Damn you, father, Paul thought. Damn you to hell for sending that thing back into my life.

"Take it off!" Paul shouted.

Suddenly the attic space seemed smaller and more stifling. Jackie let the glove drop into the box.

"I came up to find some more of my old books," Paul said in a soft voice, trying to smooth things over. "I'm sorry I yelled."

Jackie shuffled closer, nodded. "It's okay, Dad."

Paul pulled a copy of *Kidnapped* and *Robinson Crusoe* from a carton. "I loved these books. I wanted you to have them."

Jackie held out his hand. "Hey, these are first editions, Dad. Thanks. I read the other ones you gave me. The Hoffmann and Dunsany. I guess I liked the Lord Dunsany best."

"Then you should like the Bradbury I have around somewhere." Paul handed him an illustrated *Gulliver's Travels*.

Jackie leafed through the Swift, looking at the pictures. "Dad?"

"Yeah, Jackie?"

"The mitt—"

"I was going to throw it out."

"I don't have one of my own," Jackie said. "Maybe I could work the stiffness out."

Paul felt a welter of emotions—guilt for having yelled at his son, embarrassment for cursing his father, downright stupid for accusing his father's ghost of reaching from the grave.

"Okay," Paul said. "Take the books and the glove, too. But, Jackie?"

"Yeah, Dad?"

"When you're through with the glove, throw it out?"

"Okay."

❖

The following day, Paul drove Jackie to the first Little League game of the season. Jackie was intently pounding a ball into the pocket of the glove, when he looked over at his father.

"Dad? Some of the guys on the team can really get on you. I mean rag you, if you pop up with a guy on base or miss an easy grounder."

Paul remembered saying something similar to his own father twenty-five years ago. Paul recalled his father sneering at him, ridiculing him because he let the other guys get to him.

Paul knew he couldn't shield his own boy from all the hurts in his life, but he did want to soften some of them.

"It's only a game, Jackie. Some people take it more seriously than others. They're the ones who take the fun out of it."

"Yeah. The coach says things like that. But you know he hates when we lose, too, and he doesn't want to play the guys who aren't so good. Except now they've got rules that say he's got to."

"Sports aren't the only thing in the world," Paul said.

"I know, Dad."

"Keep that perspective. How'd you like the books?"

"Neat," the boy said. "I was going to start on the one about the guy stranded on the island."

Paul parked the car in the grammar school parking lot and walked with his son to the field in back of the building. Jackie left to help with the unloading of the equipment.

Paul sat in the bottom row of the bleachers. A dozen parents, talking animatedly, sat scattered in the benches above. Jackie's coach, Tony Cangelosi, came to where Paul sat.

"Hey, Carter," he said to Paul, "didn't see you much the end of last season."

Paul didn't like the burly, balding man, and he'd be damned if he'd apologize to him.

"Busy," Paul said, frowning, not wishing to invite more conversation.

It had taken Paul awhile to admit it, but he started avoiding the games because Jackie wasn't a very good player. Paul couldn't endure reliving his own pain when his son missed a ball or struck out. But this year he had made a commitment to be there for Jackie, no matter what.

A boy in uniform approached. "We're ready, Mr. Cangelosi."

"Gotcha, Scott," he said and turned back to Paul. "Maybe we can put together a winner this year, huh, Carter?"

Paul shrugged.

Cangelosi left to prepare his team.

A winner.

The phrase kept repeating in Paul's mind. Another ghost. One of his father's favorite terms.

Be a winner.

Competition was good.

Sports built men.

For Paul, undersized and skinny, sports had been a continuous source of pain and humiliation. His father never saw it, or if he did, never accepted it. The man had been a huge, threatening figure, one who constantly exhorted Paul to do better.

It was true that Paul's father was patient and supportive at first. But as Paul's peers developed beyond him and Paul got worse, his father openly displayed his disappointment. Finally, he erupted in anger shouting at the boy when he didn't keep his eyes on the ball, didn't drop his glove fast enough for grounders, didn't stand correctly in the batter's box.

It was the pain and humiliation that Paul wanted to keep from Jackie.

Lost in thought, Paul didn't notice that the game had started. By the time he looked up, the opposing side had three men on with two outs.

Paul searched the field for his son. Jackie was out in right. He was playing far back near the fence so that when the batter hit a soft pop up, Paul didn't think the boy could get to it.

But Jackie made the effort, running in as the first baseman backpedaled. The ball was going to fall between them. Then Paul saw Jackie dive. He skidded across the grass, and the ball landed impossibly in his mitt.

The parents stood and cheered.

Paul sat frozen on his seat, stared at the glove. "A fluke," he whispered to himself.

The next three innings were uneventful.

In the top of the fifth the first two opposing batters went down in order. The third batter hit a vicious line drive to right, and the ball went straight into Jackie's glove without him moving a muscle.

"Hey, Carter," Cangelosi called, "that mitt have eyes in it or what?"

Nothing unusual happened the next few innings. In the top of the ninth, Jackie's team was ahead by one. The pitcher struck out the first two batters, then gave up a single.

The opposing team's clean-up hitter got up, and with the first pitch, hit a towering fly to right.

Paul watched as Jackie went back. Paul's eyes were on the glove, which seemed to have a life of its own—taking the boy along to the edge of the field, arcing up and around and reaching back to pull a sure home run from over the fence.

"You put a magnet in that mitt, Carter?" Cangelosi called. He turned away to celebrate the victory with his team.

In the car, Jackie talked nonstop. Paul hardly listened. Every time he looked out the side windows he thought he saw a hulking, threatening figure standing in the misty rain that had begun to fall. And every time he glanced down at the glove he swore he could hear his father whispering.

Be a winner, Pauly.

Ghosts.

. . . and a winner . . .

❖

Midweek Paul sat late at night in his study working on his novel. The glove, which he had secreted from his son's room, lay on the desk. When Paul was done writing, he'd decide what to do with it.

Paul tried to concentrate on the chapter he was outlining, but his attention kept wandering to the glove.

He put down his pen, picked up the mitt and placed it on the legal pad. Touching it made the ghosts stir up again.

❖

Paul remembered the day his father took him to the special sports shop in New York where the pros bought their equipment. His father was excited, kept repeating that money was no object—as though the amount spent could somehow make Paul a better player.

Paul acted excited over the glove his father picked out. It cost $49.95—a lot of money at the time. The following day Paul's team had an important game. It was for the regional semis, and Paul's father wanted him to be prepared.

It was not likely that the coach would play Paul in the game. They didn't have the "everyone plays" rule in those days. But the day of the game, three players turned up sick with the flu. The coach sent them home. Paul had to play.

He was put into right and batted last. Everything went fine through nine innings. Paul managed to walk twice, and anything hit out his way was handled by the center fielder.

In the ninth, Paul's team lead by one. A fresh pitcher was put in, and he struck out the first two batters. The next one hit a triple.

Then the fifth kid up hit an easy pop up along the line in right. All Paul had to do was take three strides sideways and snag it. But he tripped, and the ball bounced over him and clear to the fence.

By the time the center fielder got to the ball, the hitter was rounding third. The center fielder threw, but the runner was safe at home.

Paul had to pick himself up and walk past his teammates, the parents, the coach. Worse, he had to face his father.

But as Paul approached him all the years he had been placating his father, pretending interest, lying about practice rushed through his mind. Something snapped.

He couldn't keep up the façade any longer.

Paul shouted. "I hate you, Pop! I hate sports. I've never been interested in your damned baseball!"

Paul threw the glove in the dust at his father's feet. His father swung, and hit the boy across the mouth. Paul ran home, tears and blood streaming down his face.

Paul never played baseball again; his father never asked. Paul brought books into the house—reading was something his father sneered at.

"Sports'll teach you how to compete in a man's world," his father had told him over and over. But at twelve, Paul knew that there were other ways to make it. He developed his mind, got a reputation for being a "bookworm" in high school. It paid off later.

Paul studied literature and writing in college. He finished near the top of his class. He went away to Europe to try his hand at writing. His father died before Paul sold his first novel—not that it mattered, his father wouldn't have cared.

Paul was now a successful novelist with two National Book Awards to his credit.

✣

Paul picked up the glove, turned it over and over in his hands. He knew he was being ridiculous, bordering on superstitious—but he couldn't help but feel that his father was interfering through the agency of the glove.

Cursed objects? Spirit possessions?

The glove's appearance in Jackie's life at the same age as it had been introduced into Paul's life was too much of a coincidence. And there was the uncanny way that the boy caught as though something were guiding his hand.

Superstition or not, Paul would throw the glove out while the boy slept.

✣

On the weekend, Paul waited in the car to drive Jackie to his second game.

The boy climbed into the seat and put the glove between them. "Look what I found in the garbage, Dad. Mom must've thrown it out by mistake."

Paul looked down at the glove, heard the ghosts stirring again, felt a prickling at the back of his neck.

"We're late," he said, pulling out of the driveway.

The boy prattled on about the glove being his good luck piece. Paul found himself vacillating between guilt and anger.

When Paul and Jackie arrived, the teams were ready to play. Jackie's team got up first, and the batters made three quick outs. Nine players drifted out on the field. Jackie took his position at shortstop.

Paul stood behind the metal link fence of the backstop. He wanted to be as close as possible to Jackie. Paul squinted into the bright June sunlight as the team threw practice balls back and forth in the infield. He couldn't be sure, but he thought he saw a dim outline around the boy.

"Play ball!" the umpire shouted.

Paul didn't take his eyes from his son. The outline grew thicker, sprouted arms that shifted the boy to the left—one foot, two—pressed on his hand lowering the glove a few inches.

The first batter hit a grounder that bounced into the glove like a dart into a bull's eye. Jackie swung around and threw the runner out. Two outs later, and Jackie's team left the field.

Jackie led off the next inning.

Paul saw the hulking outline.

Ghosts.

Of his father.

Kneeling behind Jackie.

Putting Jackie's feet into the right stance.

Positioning the bat.

Jackie swung and hit the ball cleanly into left. He rounded first, went for second. The shadowy presence ran with him, slid with him under the second baseman's tag.

"You can't have him, Pop," Paul whispered under his breath. "I'll fight you to the end."

❖

After the game, Paul came into his son's bedroom to have a talk. The boy sat on the edge of the bed carefully oiling the glove, his back to his father.

Paul fought the urge to grab the glove from Jackie's hands and send it sailing through the window. He was afraid of it, there was no denying it now.

"Jackie?"

Startled, the boy turned.

Before Paul said anything else he noticed the stack of books on the boy's bureau. He went to them. They were placed exactly where he and Jackie had put them two weeks before.

Paul ran a finger through the dust on the cover of Swift's *Gulliver's Travels*.

"You haven't read them, have you?"

"I—no, dad. Not yet. There wasn't time. With practice and all."

In three strides, Paul was at the bed. "It's started already." He yanked the glove out of Jackie's hands. "Because of this! Get rid of it now! No more damned baseball!"

The boy looked cowed and apologetic. Then his own face twisted in anger. He ran to the bureau, swept the books to the floor.

"I'm tired of having to lie to you, Dad!"

Ghosts.

"I hate your books!"

They swirled and swooped and sneered and yelled.

Paul saw them everywhere.

"I've never been interested in your damn books!" Jackie said.

Paul raised his hand in anger.

I wanted him to be a professor, a doctor, a novelist like me, he argued with the ghosts.

But he knelt . . .

"I'm sorry, Jackie. I've been blind."

. . . pressed the glove between his son's hands . . .

"I love you."

. . . and put the ghosts to rest.

Thomas F. Monteleone
THE PRISONER'S TALE

Like all prisoners, Fritz was innocent of any crime, and dreamed of escaping his cell.

Especially *this* cell, in a military keep on the highest cliff overlooking the hill-town of Solferino. But tonight, he lay in his bunk with a fragile smile on his angular face—he had discovered a way out.

❖

Corporal Fritz Essrig had been the gunner of an Austrian battery in the Army of the Emperor Franz Joseph. He'd never considered himself a very good soldier, but had no way to escape the conscription by the young and headstrong Emperor. Besides, Fritz had been a butcher in the village of Berndorf—and no one expected him to understand the subtleties of European geo-political strategies.

It was enough for him to know that Franz Joseph believed Napoleon III possessed too much land . . . and that Napoleon III believed the same crime of Austria's Emperor.

One such possession was none other than the entire country of Italy, and so both Emperors sent their armies into the rolling hills of Tuscany in hopes they might stumble upon one another.

Which meant the time was coming when many young men would surely die.

On the battleground, the field infirmaries, and in the sewers that served for prisons.

And Corporal Essrig had seen them die—of the 320,000 men who created the Battle of Solferino on the night of June 24, 1859, more than 40,000 of them were dead before the next sunset. Another 70,000 left crippled, maimed, and mutilated by the savage clash of new technologies and old avidities.

As French grapeshot riddled Fritz's position, he'd dropped down behind his cannon. Looking through the spokes of its wheel, he watched a squad of Austrian grenadiers wither under the fire of Algerian sharpshooters. The air became fetid with the stench of blood seeping into the soil, tanged by the sharp edge of spent gunpowder. In the valley below, he'd watched battalions of opposing infantry melt together in sparkling flashes of bayonettes. The poor young boy who'd been Fritz's flagbearer had been suddenly shredded by a cannonblast of nails, chain, miniball; Fritz puked violently as he tried to tear his gaze away from what was left of the 16-year-old youth.

He'd seen bigger chunks in the trough below his butcher's block.

Another soldier picked up the fallen colors, the black and yellow flag emblazoned by the Austrian eagle, and had not charged forward 10 paces before a cannonball had taken his legs at the hips.

Enough. Corporal Fritz Essrig, of the 34th Artillery, had seen quite enough. After whispering a brief prayer to a God he'd long ago stopped worshipping, he ducked his head and lay as still as the dead about him. Sooner or later, the chaos rampaging around him would pass . . . or it would take him with it.

❖

Fritz had no idea how long he lay in the blood-soaked earth, but he was yanked to awareness by a hideous silence. An utter *stillness* that blanketed the battlefield as effectively as the dank mantle of night. Raising his head slowly, in the slightest of degrees, he dared to look down the hill where a gibbous moon cast a blue-white pallor on the tapestry of corpses. So many, he could barely discern the dark bosom of the earth that embraced them. A faceless terror iced through him—could such total carnage be possible? Had he truly escaped it, or did he now stare out upon the terra incognita of Hell itself?

Growing bolder, Fritz levered himself up on his elbows, allowing his senses to sharpen. The pungent air stung his nostrils and for the first time he heard the atonal chorus of agony drifting low over the dark hills like fog. The final sounds of the still-dying held him in their grip, and he held his hands over his ears in automatic response.

No use. The whistling breath from throat wounds, the gurgling bubbles of violated chests, the twisted moans of delerium. All grew more insistent.

Get out of here. Get as far away as possible.

The thought hammered at him, and he knew he should heed it. No way to tell what army had been victorious, and he didn't really care. He staggered down the rear slope of hill, away from the village of Solferino, towards the open road to the North. In that direction lay Austria. Somewhere. Far away. But definitely north.

But as Fritz wove amongst the bodies and body parts, he noticed that some of them lay naked or in their underwear.

Looters had already descended on the place, sharing time with the first wave of maggots and hungry dogs. Boots were prime targets, as well as wallets and jewelry, he'd heard, and he was surprised to see so much clothing missing as well. The wretched peasants of these hills could not afford to be selective.

And neither could he.

If Fritz planned to disappear back into Austria, he would need all the assistance he could get. It was a question of survival, and no need to consult one's moral compass. Besides, he'd never let any questions of ethics steer his life in the past. Had not his dealings with his customers always been as ruthlessly mercantile as possible. Chisel and connive your neighbor before he got the chance to do it to you. That was the commercial code of Darwinian economics; Fritz liked it that way. And there was always the simple truth that the corpses no longer had need of their valuables . . .

. . . and so he became a pillager of the dead.

For survival, he kept telling himself, as he rifled the jackets and trousers of bodies intact enough to allow one final violation. And Fritz held no favorites, stealing from countrymen as well as Frenchman or the occasional Sardinian mercenary.

But survival, as it often does, surrendered to avarice, and soon Fritz had hobbled himself with the weight of his plunder. His pockets bulging with marks, francs, and enough wedding rings to open a shop, he crested a hill splashed with moonlight and the angry stares of a squad of French dragoons. They wouldn't have cared had he looted only from his own scurrilous kind, but to desecrate the blessed remains of Napolean's army represented a crime of the most heinous stripe.

❖

Thus the military prison where he awaited trial and speedy execution by Lyonnaise fusilliers. Fritz had become resigned to his fate until a conversation with one of his guards gave him hope.

"They say you are in a haunted cell, *monsieur,*" said a young, dark-haired soldier who appeared during the night-watch.

Fritz pushed his blond hair back from his eyes, looked up from his cot at the Frenchie. "Oh really? Says who?"

"Some of the other prisoners. You know how men talk . . ."

Fritz shrugged, then: "Haunted by who?"

The guard leaned against the bar, grinned. "The locals say it was once the cell of an old man from Castiglione. It is said he was a gypsy, a kind of sorcerer. Nobody knew his real name . . . everybody called him *Il Mago*—The Wizard."

"And he died here?" said Fritz, smiling because he suspected the guard was trying to spook him. Better to undercut his feeble attempt.

"No, quite the contrary . . . he escaped from here—your cell."

"You are not making any sense," said Fritz. "If he escaped, how could he haunt the cell?"

The young guard hunkered down and leaned toward Fritz to speak *sotto voce*: "Perhaps 'haunt' is the wrong word, *monsieur.* Although it is said Il Mago occupied this cell more than 200 years ago—so he is surely dead by now, and it is therefore quite possible his spirit *does* visit this place."

Fritz rolled over, faced the wall. "You speak nonsense, boy. I'd rather sleep if it is all the same to you."

The Frenchman shrugged. "As you wish, but I was only going to tell you the rest of the story—that over the years, *other* men have escaped from Il Mago's cell."

Fritz did not turn back to him. "So what? Men escape from prisons every day, all over the world."

"Not from Cavriana Fortezza, monsieur. No one has *ever* escaped from this place . . . *except* the men who've occupied this very cell."

"What do you say?" Slowly, Fritz rolled over and regarded him cautisouly.

"And! . . . no one has ever figured out how they have done it. They have, in essence, simply *disappeared!*"

"Why do you tell me this?"

"*Monsieur,* any opportunity to relieve the *ennui* of this duty is appealing to me." He paused to smile, almost apologetically. "Besides, I have always had an interest in spiritualism. Have you heard of sessions of our esteemed Anton Mesmer?"

"Very well," said Fritz. "Is that the whole story?"

"Not completely," said the guard, warming to his subject. "But the rest is like a mystery . . . to be solved."

Fritz sighed audibly. "All right, I am listening . . ."

"Number one—the jailhouse legend claims that the spirit of Il Mago has visited certain prisoners in their dreams, telling them the secret of escaping this cell. Or two—he has actually spirited them away!"

"On the face of it, that sounds absurd," said Fritz.

"Perhaps," said the guard, checking his pocketwatch ostentatiously. "But, you have time on your hands—although not a luxurious amount—before your trial."

"That is true enough."

"So you have nothing to lose in trying, am I correct?"

The guard grinned, gave him a curt salute, and continued on his rounds.

The ever-diminishing glow of his lantern marked his passage down the long corridor of cells, and Fritz watched him until his light was as a firefly dancing in the night. He lay in his redolent cot, sunk into abject darkness—other than a small barred square of starry sky, through the window near the ceiling. Sleep would not drag him into its senseless depths, and he kept re-enacting his words with the guard.

Escape from Cavriana Fortezza?

Not likely. The prison fortress squatted high atop a craggy hillside, like a vulture on its rocky perch. Exiting any of the windows, even if one could squeeze through one of the impossibly narrow openings, would send a man plummeting to certain death. The building teemed with military guards—even if Fritz could somehow break the forged iron lock or bars of his door, he wouldn't get six paces along a corridor without being seen and shot.

But *someone* had done it.

Perhaps . . . thought Fritz, if one wished to believe in the tales of mad and desperate men.

But was not *he* now a desperate man?

Nodding to himself in the darkness, he felt suddenly foolish, but more than anything, desperate. And so he awaited the next sunrise, seizing on the tiniest fragment of hope . . .

❖

. . . and the days passed with unrelenting quickness, the hours punctuated only by the occasional fusillade from the execution squads. It seemed the more he considered the possibility of escape, the more urgently the minutes were ripped away from him. So many prisoners had been culled from the last battle, the docket had become crowded with cases, and there was no time to even notify a man of his appointment with the military court. Which meant Fritz could be summoned from his cell at any time, sentenced, and dragged to the courtyard with a blindfold.

He began a thorough investigation of the cell, making it as methodical and rational and comprehensive as possible. The only way to ensure not overlooking anything was to forget the ticking clock, and that is precisely what he did.

Every moldering stripe of mortar, every brick, every crack in the wall was examined with the eye of a jeweler. One by one, starting in the lower corner under his cot, on his belly, Fritz worked his way across the piss-stained floor, then back again. Over and over, until he found something that made his ragged breath catch in his throat like a clot of bile.

Etched into a brick was a faint, barely legible phrase:

In hoc signo, fugero.

Latin. Fritz became suddenly grateful for the classical education required by the aldermen of his village. The words, the thinnest of lines barely visible in the dim light, spoke to him:

In this sign, I escape.

And below the words—a symbol, a sign.

❖

For an instant, Fritz trembled without control. The words and the simple Maltese cross galvanized him—his life need not end in this squalid box. The soldier and the old stories had been true. *They had to be.*

Doubt abruptly gnawed through his gut. Could this be nothing more than a cruel joke? A message inscribed by the guard to amuse himself.

Fritz could not afford such thinking.

Every moment must now be spent under the belief that Il Mago, whoever he had been, had written that Latin message to anyone smart enough to read it, to find the Maltese cross, and in the process, find escape.

✥

Another day passed with hideous speed, each hour falling away from him like pieces of a leper's hand. He had forced himself to slow his search to an irritating pace, to ensure he missed nothing. Joint by joint, brick by brick, he examined the room with the gentle intimacy of an archeologist searching for a pharaoh's tomb.

Teasing splashes of moonlight struck his cell as clouds skated past the promontory, giving him barely enough light to continue his search. But his diligence was rewarded. And when he found the faintest of crosses scratched sewing-needle thin into the stone, he used his soup-spoon to worry the edges of the brick.

Slowly.

Carefully.

In silence.

It began to move, and Fritz was surprised to discover the face of the brick slide out to reveal an interlocking chamber, like a mortised jewelry box. Inside the cavity, a piece of parchment, inscribed in Latin:

> *You have been given a key to your freedom, but you are forewarned—do not use this knowledge unless you are willing to pay a great price, and to do exactly as demanded.*
>
> *Further, do not follow the path unless you wear the sentence of death. No man who will eventually live beyond his sentence would choose what awaits you.*
>
> *Therefore, choose . . . only because you have no choice.*
>
> *If you accept these terms, you will have freedom.*

Fritz held the parchment in hands palsied by excitement and fear. Although his thoughts tried to race ahead, spiked by the fear of running of out time, he forced himself to re-read the Latin words, to dredge up the rules of Roman syntax, and be sure his translation was accurate, unfailing.

Beneath the paragraphs lay a set of Roman numerals.

Nothing more.

Mathematics!

Fritz almost cried out in frustration. He was not good with ciphering, with calculation, or anything that required analysis by number. And yet this wretched bastard, this old magician, had pointed to the freedom's path with numbers!

Compose yourself. Think.

After a short time, he decided the numbers must represent locations on a grid—the configuration of the bricks in the wall comprising the southeast outer wall of the building. Allowing one number in the set to represent a row, the other a column, he counted bricks . . .

. . . and found another mortised chamber, containing a second Latin parchment, which he read by lunar light:

> *You have stepped upon the path. Beyond and below this wall lies a sluice for the vilest of waste, which is what you have become, and is thus an appropriate conveyance.*
> *Enter it. Allow it to take you to freedom.*
> *Lastly:*
> *Restore and replace these messages to their place in the cell.*
> *You will not be the last desperate man to lie within its dark embrace.*

Again, below the words, were sets of Roman numerals.

More this time, and Fritz believed they marked the location of the entrance to the sluice. So enthralled by his work, he had no idea how much time had passed or how much of the night he had left. Despite his rapier-edged awareness, he could feel his body tottering on the edge of exhaustion. It demanded sleep and he was powerless to stop it.

He knew he must clean up the cell before lapsing into unconsciousness—if the guards discovered his work, all would be lost. The briefest imagining of it sent a wave of pure dread crashing over his thoughts.

No. Unthinkable.

Stuffing the parchment into his blouse pocket, Fritz carefully nested the brick face into its cut-out place in the wall. Then crawling into his straw-stuffed cot, he surrendered to his body's need for sleep, until—

✥

—a guard's bayonet slashed across the bars, awakening him with such a start, his heart seized up in his chest.

"All right, *mon ami*," said a familiar voice.

Fritz rubbed his eyes, trying to focus on the man speaking to him. It was the young dark-haired Frenchman who'd told him about the legend.

"Oh, Christ, no!" said Fritz is a low, raw whisper.

The guard grinned. "Take heart, Corporal Essrig. I come only to give you a warning: your case is on the list to be heard tomorrow morning."

Fritz bolted upright, stared at the young sentry. "How do you know?"

Frenchie smiled. "After what I told you . . . how can you not trust me?"

Fritz swallowed hard, stood up and moved closer to the guard. "You know what I found?"

"I know."

"But how could you? I have not seen you since the day you told me about it?"

The guard smiled. It was a gesture which suggested great wisdom, maturity, and understanding far beyond his obvious youth. "Monsieur, when are you going to learn to trust me?"

When the man spoke, he exerted a subtle calming effect on Fritz, but the guard's demeanor and his smug clairvoyance was somewhat disturbing, and Fritz could not identify exactly why he felt that way.

"I . . . trust you." said Fritz with obvious effort.

"Then listen when I tell you . . . that you must be finished tonight. You do not wish to be here this time tomorrow morning." The guard touched the brim of his hat in a jaunty gesture of departure and turned to continue his rounds.

"Wait!" said Fritz softly. "I am not certain what I am doing . . . I am uncertain of the vocabulary. I think it speaks of a sluice . . . or a sewer . . . some kind of tunnel. Can you—?"

"Sadly, I cannot," said the guard as he stepped back from the cell. "Everything is in your hands. *Adieu . . .*"

Fritz blinked his eyes. "Wait!"

But the man was gone.

So quickly . . . it was impossible, thought Fritz as he found himself gripping the vertical bars tightly. In the blink of his eyes . . . ?

As he turned away from the corridor, he could not stop looking at the arrangement of bricks on the opposite wall. Fritz touched the breast pocket of his blouse and felt the parchment crackle there. He did not dare chance taking it out during the daylight, no matter how desperately he wished to go over its instructions, to calculate the location of the bricks that would grant him an escape.

Such irony.

Even though this could be the last day of his wretched life, he knew the hours would move at a glacial pace. Rather than dwell on such details, Fritz retreated to his fetid cot, closing his eyes and letting his thoughts drift where they might . . .

❖

. . . and, for the first time, allowed himself to think about returning to Berndorf, to his small butcher shop on Bekerstrasse. When Franz Joseph's conscription squads swept through his village, "enlisting" all the young men they could find, Fritz had been given 24 hours to put all his affairs in order.

Unlike many of his comrades, he had no children to kiss goodbye, no wife to lay with and lie to. Having grown up in the nearby Polen Orphanage, he had never seen the necessity of families or strong connections to others, and Fritz had spent his adolescent and early adult years proving it to himself. Women were only good for one thing, but they seldom let you have a grab at that stinking nest between their legs. Men were always out to get whatever you had for their own, and could not be trusted. It was no accident he had gravitated to the butchering trade (one of his village teachers had once told him) because there was a need to be dispassionate and detached from the work.

Fritz had been a very good butcher.

And now he could realistically plan on returning to his shop . . . albeit one small problem. When he left with his new artillery battery, Fritz had no choice but to leave the running of his shop in the hands of his assistant, a gnarled old man named Joachim Krauller.

"Odds are you won't be returning, Young Essrig," the old man had said as he tied Fritz's apron about his fat stomach and chuckled. *"And I will have a business of my own!"*

And Fritz had told him he would indeed be returning.

"Then it looks like we'll have to see who owns the business at that time, won't we?"

Old Krauller had winked, laughed aloud; Fritz had said nothing.

But he'd thought: *When that time comes it will be your heart in that chopping-block trough, you old bastard.*

And now, upon replaying the memory, Fritz smiled as he imagined the shock in Krauller's jaundiced eyes when Corporal Essrig returned. It would be a pleasure to gut and fillet that yellow-eyed thief. The village would have a surfeit of steaks and chops for weeks to come . . .

❖

Gradually, the bricks of the cell leached the heat from the enclosure, and the sun slipped behind the nearby hills. As a guard slipped a tin tray of jail food under his bars, Fritz jumped up and spoke.

"Excuse me, soldier . . . can I ask you something?"

The guard looked at him cautiously, stepped away from the bars, and lightly rested his hand on his holstered pistol. "What is it?"

"I was wondering if you knew the name of one of the guards who's been on the nightwatch . . ."

"And why is that, Prussian?"

Fritz ignored the attempted slur, and smiled obsequiously. "Well, he has been very humane to me, and I thought my family might wish to write him in gratitude—after I am . . . no longer here."

The Frenchman considered this for a moment, then nodded. "I see . . . all right, then, what guard is it?"

Fritz described the young, dark-haired sentry with the beguiling voice, and was not actually very much surprised by the guard's response: "You must be mistaken, Corporal—there is no one on the night-watch like that. Paul-Emile is bald and fat; Henri is blonde and bespectacled."

Thanking him apologetically, Fritz watched the guard smirk and shake his head, then turn down the adjoining corridor.

I have always had an interest in spiritualism.

The words of his guard-who-wasn't-there ghosted through his mind. Yes, Frenchie, I am sure you had *quite* an interest.

As Fritz turned towards the starry square of window, he had the sensation of something gauzy and cool settling over his shoulders. An unsettling effect, and he could not keep a shudder from wracking through him.

Soon it would be nightfall, possibly the last night of his life; and he was wondering what kind of forces he might be dealing with. Fritz sensed a lurking hysteria crouched just beyond the threshold of his rational thoughts. After drawing several deep breaths, he wiped involuntary tears of fear from his eyes, and resolved to press on with it. Unfolding the parchment from his pocket, he began to read over its Latinate instructions, to re-divine is numbers, and by the time the light of Luna spilled in his window, he was ready to begin the work that must be completed this night.

Fritz had been accurate in his reading of the numbers, and his locations of the proper bricks proved correct. By following the parchment's step-by-step direction, he slowly "unlocked" the wall as one might take apart an intricate Oriental puzzle box. Whoever had created the original construction had been some sort of genius or possessed preternatural abilities unknown to Fritz. As he unfitted each stone, carefully silent in the pale darkness, he could only marvel at the secret handed to him. Each brick had been fashioned in such a way as to be part of a larger, interlocking construction. There was only one way to take it apart; one way to put it back together.

Time powdered away from him like the grains of grout between the bricks from the wall. Finally, the space beneath his cot was filled with masonry—each stored in a special position according to the words of the wizard, and a cavity in the wall, just wide enough to admit the shoulders and torso of a man, awaited him.

There was also a final parchment.

> *Follow these words with great attention. Replace the stones in the wall in the proscribed order and manner. Do this and no one will follow—for no one will know the manner of your escape . . . until the need of the next desperate man.*

Fritz entered the cramped space within and beneath the wall, positioned himself so he could retrieve each brick, and inter-lock it back into its prior place. Instantly a hideous stench of decomposition assaulted him, permeated the air he gulped into his lungs. It was a fetor of such unrelenting power, Fritz knew he might vomit at any moment, and he fought to keep himself focused. As he labored to finish before dawn, he realized he had not replaced the second-to-last parchment from the previous evening.

The Prisoner's Tale

You will not be the last desperate man to lie within its dark embrace.

Well, perhaps not, he thought, but I am certain to be the last to follow this infernal path . . . Fritz grinned as he reached for the final brick, the last interlocking key that would reseal the wall and conceal his route to freedom.

When the final stone slipped into place, he was sealed into total darkness, and for an instant, a blade of sheer panic slipped coldly between the ribs of his reason. Paralyzed by the tomblike silence and lack of vision, and seized utterly by the thick scent of decay, Fritz forced himself to push onward in the tunnel-like enclosure. With each movement forward, the putrescence became more overpowering, and he noticed a lingering dampness on the walls of the sluice. It appeared to growing more wet, more slippery.

But he pressed on—there was no place else to go.

His breathing became labored as he began to think about how *closely* the passage contained him. Barely enough space for his shoulders to pass through, he progressed with arms tucked in, elbows at his waist, hands at his shoulders. Arching his back and lunging ahead like an inchworm humping along.

Total darkness.

The stench of the sewer.

It was enough to drive a man mad. But Fritz *knew* it was the path to freedom, he knew the parchments told the truth. No one would have bothered to construct such an elaborate plan, especially the interlocking bricks, as a jest or a ruse. To push ever forward, into pitch-dark uncertainty, he diverted himself with thoughts of returning to Berndorf and cutting out the heart of Herr Krauller.

The grim fantasy sustained him until he noticed the slope of the passageway had begun to change.

Downward.

Slightly at first, not more than several degrees, and he continued to inch along at his awkward pace.

Then he noticed the light, and he could feel all his muscles tense without volition for an instant. Was he really seeing it? Was it some illusion or trick of his eyes? Or could he really discern a white blur in the far distance?

As he edged forward, he could feel the incline of the tunnel increase more severely, and he recognized the white blur was an indirect reflection of light on the bottom curve of the tunnel far below him. Pausing to collect himself, he reasoned he'd been in the passage long enough for sunrise to have overtaken him. And the daylight could only mean one thing—an opening to the *outside*, to freedom.

The thought sparked him into motion and he surged forward in the tunnel towards the light, and suddenly the slope beneath tilted more radically. Now he was sliding *downward* on an ever-increasing angle until it felt as though he had fallen headfirst into a vertical shaft. Picking up speed, plummeting like a cliff-diver, the urge to scream being stifled by a surge of bile burning into his throat. Fritz looked down to see the source of the light expanding, filling the narrow aperture of his descent.

Any second now.

And he would be at the bottom . . .

Then suddenly he was being wrenched *upward*—his back arching so sharply it should be breaking.

But he could finally see the source of the light and he was rushing towards it with a final vertical surge. His first impression was a grate covering a drain pipe opening—the light was cross-hatched by thin bars.

In an eyeflash he was close enough to see what he was hurtling into—a rib cage.

Headfirst, Fritz impacted with the skeleton, and with such force the brittle bones literally *exploded* around him—all except the skull, which wedged itself into the space between his cheek and the wall of the tunnel.

So tightly was his body jammed into the space, he could move nothing but his fingertips.

No, this is not the way it was supposed to be . . . it was impossible! Cheek to cheek with the yellowed skull, Fritz stared straight ahead, to avoid its hollow gaze. The notion repulsed him, and he twisted his head the few inches the space allowed to roll his eye upward towards the opening above his head.

A deep, impossibly blue sky filled the space without distance or substance. It had no depth or density—it simply existed as the symbol for all that was fresh and clean and free.

And unattainable.

He stared at the sky for a long time before lowering his eyes, and it was only then that he noticed the inscription grooved into the stone interior of the passage that held him like a vise. Again, the familiar Latin:

> *To escape death required you be willing to pay a great price. That you are here affirms your acceptance of the terms. So be informed: the price is compassion. To put aside your desperation and leave hope for the next man.*
>
> *If you have done this, I will come for you, but I will not set you free—your own nature will have accomplished that.*
>
> *If you have not, you have already made the acquaintance of what awaits you.*

A sound startled him with its plaintive agony, and for an instant, Corporal Fritz Essrig did not recognize his own scream. His body sagged; and his gaze returned to ponder the emptiness of a socket that had once contained an eye no more caring than his own.

he first time Amelia saw her dead mother was on the stroke of midnight on the June night when she lost her virginity in the back seat of Jason Stringer's dad's Mondeo and fell pregnant with Lisa. It was very dark in the car—which was parked inside Jason Stringer's dad's garage—but not so dark that Amelia couldn't see her mother peering around the plastic headrest on top of the front passenger seat.

Her mother looked as if she were thirty again, with hardly a line in her face and her hair full, soft and luxurious. She was shaking her luxuriously-dressed head sorrowfully.

"You silly girl," she said. "You silly, *silly* Millie."

Amelia was slightly hurt. Given that she was over the age of consent—if only by a little bit—and had always exhibited exceptional precocity in non-sex-related matters, she felt that she was fully entitled to be criticised in a more mature manner. What her mother *should* have said was, "You stupid cow. You bloody stupid *cow*"—but being Amelia's mum she just had to say what she said in terms which implied that Amelia was still a cocksure little girl putting up a front of cleverness, which she wasn't. Hadn't she just proved it?

"I'll be all right, Mum," Amelia assured her mother, and honestly thought that perhaps she would, even though she knew perfectly well that what she'd just done was risky.

"That's what *I* thought," her mother replied, as if that were nailed-down proof that Amelia had got it wrong. "I was just as clever as you. I could have been a *contender.*"

Amelia knew that she should have made sure that she was protected, but she just hadn't known exactly how to go about it. She had grasped the fundamental concept of contraception, of course, but she didn't know how you actually got up the nerve to *do* it in a calculated manner, either by asking the doctor or asking the boy. If her mother had been alive, maybe she could have asked *her,* but somehow she doubted it. It wouldn't have been any easier to ask Mum than to go to the doctor or demanded that Jason go to the chemist's. Any of those strategies of preparation would have required far more courage than it took simply to open her legs and let Jason bring to a head, so to speak, all of the pressure that had been bearing down on her for months.

She didn't even fancy Jason, particularly, and she didn't imagine that he had any *particular* affection for her. He and she were both old enough to know that only twenty per cent of boys and twenty per cent of girls were really and truly *fanciable,* and that people who weren't in the relevant twenty per cents just had to make do. She had to do it some day, and so did he, just to get it out of the way and get on with life, and it had just been a matter of blundering around until an occasion presented itself at a time when one person's determination was running high and another person's resistance was running low and both of them happened to think "What the hell, go for it" at almost the same moment. Of course it was a risk, but every decision you took in life—not just the major ones but every petty day-by-day and hour-by-hour hesitation—was a risk. That was the human condition: risk piled on risk piled on risk. What good did it do to say "That's what *I* thought" as if one item of experience were enough to change the nature of life itself?

Anyway, Amelia thought, how many girls got pregnant the first time, fumbling around in the back of a car to no effect at all except to wonder what all the fuss was about and to conjure up the censorious phantom of your dead mother? Not many.

Unfortunately, Amelia Curtinshaw was one of the few.

❖

Amelia's mother—whose name was Faith, although she was not religious—had been a victim of medical negligence three times over. That was one more reason, if any more were needed, why Amelia didn't find it easy to go to the doctor.

There was no way of knowing whether or not Faith Curtinshaw would have survived any longer if she had not been the victim of medical negligence, but Amelia's father—whose name was Merlyn, although he was not Welsh—took the view that you had to accept that doctors working under pressure occasionally made mistakes, and that it was socially irresponsible to threaten them with the law every time they lost a patient, and that the chain of misfortunes that had happened to his wife was a million-to-one-shot. The insurance company who had to pay out on Faith's premature demise suggested very strongly to Merlyn that he ought to sue the local health authority for damages, but they had no power to compel him to do it and no right to withhold payment on the policy if he chose not to, so he chose not to.

"I have to think of Amelia," he said to anyone who questioned his decision. "What would it do to her to drag the death of her mother through the courts, prolonging her agony for years and years, in the hope of winning a little blood money? Isn't it better to get on with our lives? It'd be a lottery anyway, wouldn't it? Who really wins that kind of lottery? Only the lawyers. Not the people on either side of the court-room, and certainly not the art and science of medicine."

Merlyn Curtinshaw had a high opinion of the art and science of medicine. That was what the more ambitious boys in his class at his independent grammar school had gone on to study at university. Because he lacked their confidence, he'd settled for studying Biology and becoming a teacher, but he'd laid the foundations of a good career in an all-boys' grammar school similar in all essential respects to the one in which he'd been educated himself. In such a context, Faith once told Amelia in a moment of uncommon confidentiality, he had good reason to thank the whim of fate which had made his parents choose to spell his name with an l instead of a v. In all-boys' schools any teacher named Mervyn, even one who showed not the slightest trace of homosexual inclination, would inevitably be dubbed "Merv the Perv", whereas a teacher named Merlyn was a stone cold certainty to be nicknamed "the wizard"—as, in fact, he was.

Faith Curtinshaw had first fallen victim to medical negligence when a routine smear test had been cleared as a-okay by a laboratory in Barnsley whose staff subsequently turned out to have been overstressed, overstretched and not overly observant. When it transpired, after an interval of eighteen months, that several patients who had been given the all-clear had, in fact, been very far from a-okay, Faith was recalled, along with several thousand other women, to take another test. Because Faith's family, on Amelia's Grandma Booth's side, had something of a history of cervical cancer, she doubtless felt slightly more anxious than the thousands of other recall cases, but as she dutifully pointed out to

Merlyn and Amelia, there was unlikely to be one among them who was not anxious at all.

Unfortunately, the burden imposed on a laboratory in Lichfield by the thousands of extra slides resulted in its staff becoming just as over-stressed and overstretched as the staff at Barnsley. Mindful of their duty, they laboured long and hard to make sure that every slide had been double-checked and every slide which excited even the slightest hint of suspicion triple-checked, but this assiduousness threw their record-keeping system into such disarray that they lost the notes of several hundred cases, including Faith's. There was nothing for it but for her to report for yet another test, whose resultant slides were eventually adjudged by a laboratory in Darlington to be very suspicious indeed, probably indicative of a serious problem.

The result of the smear-test had, of course, to be confirmed by a biopsy. Unfortunately, a laboratory in Hull contrived to lose the results of the biopsy, not because its technicians were working under enormous stress—although they were—but because of a problem with its antique computer-system, which had never recovered from the effects of a diagnostic test intended to figure out how vulnerable it would be to the Millennium bug. Faith attempted to remain calm after turning up for a second biopsy, singing "Take Another Little Piece of My Womb, Why Don't You?" to the tune of Janis Joplin's "Take Another Little Piece of My Heart" all the way home in Merlyn Curtinshaw's second-hand Citroen, but by that time she was absolutely convinced that the roll of the dice was against her, and that metastasis was already making hay throughout her nether regions.

"Am I going to get it?" Amelia asked, when her mother was finally diagnosed as the victim of an exceptionally aggressive cancer and went back to the hospital to start a course of chemotherapy that had no better than a one-in-three chance of being effective.

"All you inherit is the risk," Faith told her daughter. "One day, maybe fairly soon, they'll be able to test your genes to see whether you've got the duff one. If you have, you'll just have to trust to luck to avoid the little accidents that might disable its healthy partner in one of the relevant cells. If you want all the jargon, ask your father—he's the biologist."

Given the way that luck had treated her mother, Amelia didn't think that it seemed very trustworthy. Getting pregnant in the back of Jason Stringer's dad's Mondeo while it was unromantically parked in Jason

Stringer's dad's garage didn't increase her faith in luck one little bit, nor even her faith in Faith's judgment.

❖

Merlyn Curtinshaw reacted to the news of Amelia's pregnancy with predictable stoicism. He didn't call her a bloody stupid cow, or even a silly, silly girl, although he did observe that it would play havoc with her A levels. Given that she was now scheduled to give birth a full fourteen months before she was scheduled to sit her A levels, Amelia had to concede that this was true.

"What do you want to do?" he asked, meaning did she want to have an abortion, or what?

"Jason asked me to marry him when I told him," she replied, "but I said no. He's only seventeen. I suppose he's bright enough—two short planks wouldn't stand a chance against him in an IQ race—but he's not what you'd call *together*, and his parents are monsters. He might make a father in ten years time, but if we married now we'd probably be divorced in three. Did Granddad Curtinshaw ever have a Mondeo, by any chance?"

"No," said Merlyn. "He was a Vauxhall man through and through, although he wasn't from South London. Why do you ask?"

"Just something Mum said. She was sitting in the front passenger seat of a Mondeo at the time." Amelia reflected that her father had probably been well and truly *together* even at seventeen, and was so together by now that he was practically set in stone.

"I can assure you that your mother would never be seen dead in the front seat of a Mondeo," her father assured her, showing how much he had still had to learn about his wife when the opportunity was rudely snatched away from him, "and you still haven't answered my question."

"I don't want an abortion," Amelia told him. "Not because I'm squeamish, or because I think it would be murder, and not because I have some bloody stupid idea about how cool it would be to be a teenage mother. I just don't want to take the risk of flushing something down the toilet that might turn out to be a-okay, if I don't actually have to. How do *you* feel?"

"I feel that you ought to be allowed to make your own decisions," he said, because he obviously knew that it was the sort of thing a good father would say. "You can count on me to do what I can. But there's one more thing I ought to tell you."

"What?"

"The reason you don't have any brothers or sisters is that your mother was afraid that having more children might increase her risk of carrying forward the family curse. That's what she called it: *carrying forward the family curse.*"

"Called what?"

"The fact that so many of her female relatives on her mother's side had died of cervical cancer. She felt—and after inspecting the data she'd gathered I had to concede the correlation—that the ones who had more children tended to die earlier. Stress to the relevant tissues, you see. Plausible argument, although I wouldn't call it scientific *proof.*"

"But she had me," Amelia pointed out.

"Yes," said Merlyn Curtinshaw, with a tear in the corner of his left eye. "She had you. At nineteen."

Amelia noticed that he did not add, although he certainly could have, that at nineteen Faith had not yet done the genealogical research which had stoked the fire of her anxieties and made her conscious of the risks involved in merely being alive. Nor did he mention that having a child at nineteen had forced Faith Booth to drop out of university and get married, incidentally making sure that she never would be a contender in any kind of fight for fame and fortune.

That must have ben a pity, Amelia thought, because Faith had probably been even brighter than her husband, who would himself have been able to give two short planks a ninety-nine yard start in a hundred-yard IQ race without having to hurry unduly.

❖

Amelia's pregnancy was routine—and so was life at home, which had become so very routine as to be positively formal. Even while his wife was alive, Merlyn Curtinshaw had never been a particularly demonstrative father, but after Faith's death he became very wary indeed of hugging and kissing his daughter. Perhaps he would have been wary in any case, simply because she was—to borrow a phrase from the late, lamented Grandma Booth—"filling out," but Amelia was bright enough to see that there were other factors involved. For one thing, a widower living with a teenage daughter had to be exceedingly careful to remain above suspicion. For another, something of Merlyn Curtinshaw that had withered when his wife died never had regained its turgor under time's supposedly healing influence.

Amelia observed that after her mother died, her father stopped complaining about the awful burden of expectation that modern society placed upon its secondary school teachers. He stopped groaning under the weight of the marking and other miscellaneous paperwork that he was forced to bring home. Indeed, his marking procedures grew increasingly conscientious. He was capable of sitting in front of the TV for hours on end, barely glancing at *EastEnders* or *Brookside* (although he always seemed *au fait* with the major plot-threads) ploughing through second- and third-year General Science.

"Hell, Dad, it's *science*," Amelia occasionally said to him. "Either the silly little buggers have got the answers right or they haven't. What's with all the deep thought?"

"It's not as easy as that, Millie," he always replied. "I have to determine the extent to which they've understood the fundamental concepts, and to what extent erroneous answers are merely the result of sloppy calculation."

Amelia knew, however, that her father had taken to hiding within his work, immersing himself in its toils so that he did not have to engage himself with any sort of life outside the home, or to engage himself fully with life within it. He even began to take a perverse pride in his cooking, abandoning Marks & Spencer Ready Meals forever.

Every Saturday Amelia would pore over the *Guardian* "Soulmates" column on her father's behalf, diligently pointing out likely prospects, but he always treated it as a joke. Amelia had always suspected that her father wasn't very highly sexed, but she knew perfectly well that despite her lack of siblings his marriage to her mother had been reasonably active, even moderately joyful. It seemed to her, once her mother had been dead for more than a year, that the metastasizing claws of the crab which had eaten her mother must have been unnaturally long, and that it was not merely her mother's nether regions that had been devastated by them. It seemed to Amelia, after the incident in Jason Stringer's dad's Mondeo, that her mother probably got out of her tomb more often than her father got out of his.

Not that her father was lonely, of course, in any non-sexual sense. He had her to keep him company most nights. She got out regularly, though, until the pregnancy reached its sixth month, at which point being out got to be a bit embarrassing. She resolved then that as soon as it became practicable after Lisa was born—she had named the child as soon as a sonic scan revealed its sex—she would get out again, at least once a week. When Mrs Lipton, the cleaning lady, quit during Amelia's eighth month, on the grounds that she hadn't time to clear up after babies and that an extra pound a week wouldn't come close to covering the hassle, it seemed as if it might not be practical for Amelia to get out even that often, but it turned out not to be that bad.

"We can cope," Merlyn said, as the day of Lisa's birth approached. "I'm sorry that you've had to give up school, and I certainly want you to have every opportunity to complete your A levels at the tech, so I shan't expect or allow you to be skivvying night and day, but we can cope. I've had practice, after all. We'll be all right, the three of us. We'll see it through."

⁂

The second time Amelia saw her dead mother was on the stroke of midnight on the night after she gave birth to Lisa. While the ward was temporarily quiet Faith walked right past the duty nurse, as bold as you please, and came to stand beside Amelia's bed, looking down at the six-hours-old Lisa asleep in her crib.

"Really rips the guts out of you, doesn't it?" her mother said, undiplomatically. "I was heaving for hours. The pethidine kept wearing off, but women don't go in for midwifery unless they're accomplished sadists. That's why there are so few female serial killers—our demonic sisters get more and better kicks from supervising births than Hannibal Lecter will ever get from butchery."

"If you've come to say *I told you so,*" Amelia began, "you can . . ."

"I haven't," Faith assured her. "I've come to warn you. That's what apparitions of the dead are supposed to be for, after all. The first time's just to let you know that we're around, to keep you on your toes. The second time's to tell you that you're going to need to be strong if you intend to see it through."

"And the third time?" Amelia asked, knowing that everything determined by legend and superstition happens in threes—especially misfortunes.

"We'll get to that," her mother said, darkly. "Let's not get ahead of ourselves. She lifted a hand to smooth her soft hair, and Amelia noticed that her nail varnish was slightly chipped.

"What's it like?" Amelia asked.

"What's what like?" Faith countered, although she must have known.

"Being dead."

"It's not *like* anything. It just *is*. It's not Heaven, it's not the Underworld and it's not the Other Side. Dead is dead. The atoms of your body are scattered on the wind and dissolved in the earth, breathed in and out or bound into weeds and grime; the reality of what you were is dispersed into the memories of everyone who knew you, neglected and forgotten by almost everyone."

"Not Dad," said Amelia, knowing that it would be superfluous to mention herself. "He remembers. He's still mourning."

"That man was born to mourn," said Faith, cruelly. "Your little family will suit him right down to the ground. Lisa will mop up what little time for thought and space for feeling he has left. He'll be far too good to you, in the saintliest way imaginable, and he'll be a real wizard with the housework. You mustn't let that kind of life consume you, and you mustn't think you owe him anything extra because of it. You inherited far too much from me as it is—you mustn't think of your father as part of the package. You can still be a contender, if you put your mind to it. It's just a matter of trying that little bit harder."

"That's the warning, is it?" Amelia asked, contemptuously. "Don't let Dad become too dependent? Put more effort into building a career?"

"Don't get smart with me, Millie," her mother retorted, still too dignified even in death to call her a bloody stupid cow. "I'm the one who knows what I'm talking about. Death has its privileges. I've been where you are, remember, and I know what comes after it. I know the risks. I'm warning you that it's a lot easier than you think to go to your grave without ever having lived at all, and all it takes is inertia. I'm warning you that people who sit around waiting for the future to arrive always miss the bus. I'm warning you that people who spend their lives in the back seats of other people's cars never learn to drive. I'm warning you that people who pay too much attention to understanding the fundamental concepts without ever bothering to tighten up their calculations always get the answers wrong."

"I think you mean *silly little buggers* rather than people, Mum," said Amelia, helpfully.

"I know what I mean," said Faith Curtinshaw, ominously.

"Sure," said Amelia. "You're the one who's dead, after all. Can you really see into the future?"

"Of course I can't, you silly, silly girl. That's exactly what I'm trying to tell you. Nobody can, because you have to *make* the future. If you just let it happen, it never arrives."

"And that's what you think of your life, is it? You hung around with Dad and me, waiting for a future that never arrived, and you resent it like hell?"

Amelia would have understood if her mother had just turned around and walked away at that point, but she didn't. Instead, Faith went to the crib to look down at the sleeping Lisa. "All you inherit," she whispered, not to her daughter but to her granddaughter, "is the risk. Play your cards cleverly enough, and you can still win, even against the odds."

"She can't hear you," Amelia whispered, "and even if she could, she wouldn't understand."

Faith left then, without a backward glance, not needing to add the observation that the kid wasn't alone in not being able hear the voices of the dead or to understand their warnings—and would never find herself lacking in *that* kind of company.

❖

As Amelia had anticipated, Merlyn Curtinshaw was a bloody good grandfather, hardly less than perfect. He looked after Lisa while Amelia went to evening classes at the tech to complete her A level courses in English, History and French. He looked after Lisa when Amelia went out with friends, of either sex. He needed no looking after himself, never giving the slightest hint that he was in any way dependent on his daughter. He continued to discharge his duties at the school without the slightest hint of negligence. His pupils continued to nickname him "the wizard."

"You ought to think about your own future, you know," Amelia told her father, the day her A level results came through and opened up the possibility of a university place. "You mustn't sacrifice yourself for me. You could get married again if you wanted to, start another family of your own."

"Most people," said Merlyn Curtinshaw, "spend their entire lives trying to be something they're not and arrive somewhere they aren't.

I'm one of the lucky ones. I always knew that if I aimed for the moon I'd never get off the ground. I calculated what I could actually achieve, and I went for that, and I got it. Yes, I was devastated when your mum died—but things don't have to last forever to be worthwhile. You and she were everything I ever needed, and I still have that. I'm not sacrificing anything."

Although he had no more ability to foresee the future than anyone else, it turned out that Amelia's father was right. He wasn't sacrificing his future on the altar of his daughter's needs and desires, because he had no future to sacrifice. Three days after Lisa's third birthday, he went to the doctor to obtain an opinion about a peculiar lump that had appeared on his left testicle and had finally become too big to ignore.

"You should have come to me sooner," said the doctor, before sending Merlyn Curtinshaw to hospital as a top priority emergency admission.

Three days later Merlyn emerged from the operating theatre one testicle short, and three days after that he started chemotherapy. The attention and treatment he received were wondrously rapid and efficient. It was, he gladly judged, enough to restore anyone's faith in the much-maligned National Health Service.

"It's called Hodgkin's disease," the unlucky man explained to his daughter. "It's uncommonly aggressive. There's no history of it in my immediate family—but my immediate family isn't large enough to constitute a representative statistical sample. We Curtinshaws have never been prolific breeders." Amelia did not remark that some few of his cells seemed to be doing their damnedest to make up for that lack of profligacy in no uncertain terms.

Amelia's mother had not reacted well to her chemotherapy, and had herself remarked that it was like having exceptionally bad PMS twenty-eight days a month. She had lost her smile and smooth complexion along with her hair, and had similarly remarked that if this was what death warmed up looked like it was no wonder that people tried to avoid the condition.

It was not until some time after the chemotherapy ended, and the death sentence had been confirmed, that Faith had begun to look slightly better again. As she had moved inexorably toward her end, buoyed up by morphine and the gradual if somewhat apologetic return of her hair, Amelia's mother had become more human again, more contented in her flesh, and more inclined to smile. Amelia had thought at the time that there was a certain irony in the fact that the defiant last stand of the art and science of medicine had only wrought havoc with the ghost in her mother's machine, while the acceptance of inevitability had allowed that ghost a brief resurrection of sorts.

Amelia didn't expect that things would be much different with her father, and to begin with they weren't. He lost his mask of composure along with his hair, and turned into a rottweiler in human form; had he had marking to do, any of the silly little buggers who got the answers wrong would have got zero marks—but he did not, of course, have any actual marking to do, so the only person who was marked, and left pointless, by the experience was Amelia. He spent a lot of time apologizing for his failures, and quite a lot weeping and grinding his teeth in wrath and frustration over the fact that however sorry he was, he simply could not avoid them.

After the chemotherapy ended, having failed to eliminate the rampaging crab, Amelia expected her father to recover a little of his old self, much as her mother had, but he never did. His hair did begin to grow again, after a fashion, and the morphine did ease his pain, but the process of becoming more human again did not gift to Merlyn Curtinshaw the least hint of contentment, nor any inclination to smile. He had always been a forgiving man, but forgiveness had somehow been cut out of him, and he was no longer able to forgive himself. The fact that he was entirely innocent of any sin made no difference to the relentlessness of his determination to bathe in blame.

"I'm *so* sorry," Merlyn said to Amelia, when she brought Lisa to the neatly-kept hospice where her father had elected to die. "I wanted *so* much to be with you, to see you through, to give you the support you needed. So bloody stupid of me not to have taken any notice of it sooner, so bloody stupid of me to wrap my feelings up inside, twist everything up into a knot, so bloody stupid."

"It's not your fault, Dad," she told him. "You don't get cancer because you're uptight—that's just an old wives' tale. It's a lottery. It can happen to anyone."

She was being generous, of course. For herself and Lisa she was frightened half to death. Both of the generative organs from which she had been conceived had now proven rotten. She was the inheritor of a double curse, and she just had to hope that Jason Stringer's genes would prove to be made of sterner stuff. His parents were stern enough—Jason's mum refused to speak to her if they happened to pass one another in the aisles at Sainsbury's and Jason's dad had told her father (unnecessarily, given Merlyn's dislike of fuss and bother) that his boy wouldn't pay a penny in child support, even if the CSA sent the debt collectors round.

"You need me," Amelia's father insisted. "You need me, and I'm letting you down. Your mother told me to look after you, told me she'd haunt me if I didn't, and I'm letting her down."

"Did she haunt you?" Amelia asked, letting a little of her own anger show through. "*Did* she? Of course she didn't. First of all, because you *did* look after me, and second of all because you're a bloody scientist and you don't believe in bloody ghosts."

"That's not the point, Millie," he told her, mustering the last vestiges of his best schoolmasterish manner. "She didn't have to mean it *literally*. All she meant was that I inherited her responsibility along with mine, that I had two people's jobs to do instead of just one, and that I had to do it right because there was no one else to do it if I let you down. And I have."

"No you haven't," said Amelia, firmly. "So shut up and smile. Shut up for Lisa, and smile for Lisa. Just because you're dying doesn't mean you have a right to frighten your granddaughter."

He tried, but he just couldn't do it. Even if he had contrived a smile, Lisa would probably have cried anyway, but he couldn't—and that, Amelia thought, was sad. What was the point of morphine if it couldn't set you free?

❖

The third and last time that Amelia saw her dead mother was the night of her father's funeral, when everyone had gone home. The funeral had been surprisingly well attended, given that nobody except for Amelia, Lisa and the absent Faith had ever *liked* Merlyn Curtinshaw. Even his parents had found it easier to respect him, and it was respect that had pulled in the crowds from his school. His colleagues were unanimous in declaring that they felt the highest respect for his abilities as a teacher and for the way he had coped with the tragedies in his life. Amelia would have preferred it if they hadn't pluralized the tragedy, thus implying that Lisa's birth and Faith's death were two of a kind, but they were teachers and had to be forgiven their narrowness of view.

Merlyn's headmaster gave the funeral oration, taking great care to give credit where it was due. Merlyn Curtinshaw had been a man who cared, he said: a man who was always careful to make sure that his pupils understood the fundamental concepts of science, never so petty as to penalize them for minor errors in calculation. Merlyn Curtinshaw had been a man who believed in serving the community, he said, a modest man who never sought fame or acclaim, a contented man who was satisfied to do what he could. Merlyn Curtinshaw's nickname was "the wizard," he said, and Merlyn Curtinshaw really had been a wizard in every meaningful sense of the term.

"Funerals are always farcical," Amelia's mother observed, when she presented herself at the foot of Amelia's bed, dead on the stroke of midnight. "Of all ceremonial occasions, they're the ones which best reveal the essential cruelty of humor. Take away the laughter, and what does comedy become? Death is Nature's best and worst joke, and it always leaves the audience rolling in the aisles, splitting their sides. Some people even howl. Not you, though. You have your father's dignity. I like that."

"Okay," said Amelia. "I misunderstood the warning. I admit it. It simply never occurred to me that Dad was going to keel over and die. I didn't take steps to free myself from dependency, and now I'm a little bit lost. Silly, silly Millie."

"He was insured," her mother pointed out. "You're the proud owner of a house with its mortgage paid off."

"And I'm a single mother only just out of her teens, whose chances of starting university in October now look a little bit thin. Have you any idea what professional childcare costs?"

"Of course I have. Just because I'm dead it doesn't mean I'm out of touch."

"So I've noticed," said Amelia, sarcastically. "I suppose Dad will be dropping in from time to time, to render his apologies if not to offer his excellent advice."

"Don't be silly. He's a scientist—he wouldn't be able to believe in himself. He had a hard enough job while he was alive; he's no chance now. And you can't rely on me to keep popping up every time you need something. Just because I'm dead it doesn't mean I'm at your beck and call for all eternity."

Amelia remembered then—without ever having quite forgotten it—that things connected with legend and superstition tended to happen in threes, especially misfortunes, and that there was every possibility that she would never see her mother again.

"Okay," Amelia said. "The first time was just to let me know that you were still around and that I wasn't the only bright girl ever to fall into the miscalculation trap. The second time was to offer me warnings that I wouldn't quite grasp, and taunt me with the possibility that I might lose out on everything life has to offer. The third time has to be a crunch of some kind—so what's the punch-line, Mum? Do I wake up now?"

"You woke up a long time ago," said Faith Curtinshaw, softly. "Some might think that you woke up far too soon, in the darkness before the dawn. But that isn't the deepest darkness—that's just an old wives' tale. The deepest darkness is still to come, and always is. Fortunately, the stars aren't scheduled to go out for another eighteen-billion years or so, so you have a little time in hand, and you're not alone."

She meant Lisa. She knew that *she* didn't count.

"That's it?" said Amelia. "That's all I get? Tomorrow is another day. I can get that from *Gone With the Wind* or *The Little Book of Calm*. For that, I don't need visits from my dead mother."

"So why *do* you need visits from your dead mother?" said Faith, wrong-footing Amelia yet again. "You tell me, Millie."

And that, Amelia realized, was the win-or-lose, do-or-die, put-up-or-shut-up question. She paused for a long time before she said: "Because I'm scared. Because I'm absolutely bloody terrified, and because even though I know damn well you can't see the future or make things right, I feel that I'm entitled. At the end of the bloody day, I'm entitled."

"There you are then," said her dear and dead but undeparted mother. "Count yourself lucky. Not many people get what they think they're entitled to. Even fewer get what they *are* entitled to."

"You just can't resist being glib, can you?" Amelia complained.

"Can you?" her mother countered.

Glib is good, Amelia thought, although she wasn't about to give her mother the satisfaction of hearing her concede the point. *Glib works. At least, it works a hell of a lot better than greed.* "It's not going to be easy, is it?" she said, aloud.

"No," her mother agreed. "That's the family curse. It never is easy, but you have to do it anyway. You have to try not to be silly, and you have to try to take charge. If you can make the best of what you have, you win the game. Even Merl understood that, although his idea of winning wasn't necessarily mine—or yours. You haven't lost, Millie. You haven't even given the rest of the field that much of a start. You've stopped being a silly girl and you've moved from the back seat to the front, but now you have to start moving up through the gears. You won't find *Per Ardua ad Astra* in *The Little Book of Calm*—or *Gone With the Wind*, for that matter."

"Dad told me that his father was a Vauxhall man," Amelia remarked, glibly.

"Through and through," Faith agreed. "Through and through."

And that, as it turned out, was all the punch-line Amelia got, at least from her dead mother.

✛

"Who was that woman you were talking to last night?" Lisa asked Amelia, when they sat down to breakfast the next day. "I thought everyone had gone home."

"Did I keep you awake?" Amelia asked, more concerned about that than the arguably startling fact that Lisa had been able to eavesdrop on her apparition.

"I was awake anyway," Lisa said, delicately dipping a soldier in a soft-boiled egg. "I couldn't sleep. But I didn't cry. I don't, any more." She didn't mean that she never cried at all, only that she didn't cry just because she couldn't sleep.

"No," said Amelia, "you don't. I'd noticed that."

"So who was she?"

"Someone who came to help."

"With the funeral?"

"Yes—with the funeral. Lots of people helped. Grandma Curtinshaw and Granddad Booth—and the headmaster, of course."

"I don't have any grandmas or granddads any more," Lisa observed. Being a wise child, she didn't count the elder Stringers.

"You can share mine," Amelia assured her. "I've only got two left, I'm afraid. Most people my age still have all four, nowadays, not to mention a few extras roped in by divorce and remarriage, but you don't really need a crowd." She didn't start adding up parents, lest her further reassurances should sound ever so slightly hollow.

"The headmaster said that Granddad was a wizard," Lisa observed, "but he wasn't, was he?"

Amelia did not feel competent to explain the meaning of the word *metaphor* to a not-quite-four year old, so she simply said "No, he was a scientist. That meant he knew a lot, like wizards were once supposed to, but what he knew was mostly true."

"Was Grandma Faith a scientist too?" Lisa asked, looking up from under her eyebrows with a speculative expression which suggested that she had somehow guessed—impossible as it might be—exactly who Amelia had been talking to the night before. Fortunately, she also had egg-yolk wandering down her tiny chin, so her accusative manner had a hint of the farcical about it.

"No," said Amelia. "*Everything* Grandma Faith knew was true, and she never let you bloody forget it, either."

Lisa did not react to the swear word; she already knew that hers was a family in which curses were not forbidden, provided only that they were used with discretion.

"The thing is," Amelia added, almost as if she'd been asked, "I'm almost exactly like her. Through and through. It might be the death of me, one day—but we'll just have to take the risk." Amelia tried for a second or two to forge a silent additional sentence which would glibly make use of the image of a spectre hanging over her, but the form of the words just wouldn't become clear so she gave it up. She hadn't the time to waste, she thought, and what did it matter anyway? "What you and I are going to be, my girl," she said, instead, as she wiped away the stray yolk, "is *contenders.*"

Ed Gorman
GHOSTS

Some nights were kinder to thieves than others.

Tonight, for instance. The October Saturday was prisoner to chill rain and rolling fog. All kinds of things could hide in such darkness.

The convenience store was an oasis in the gloom, windows bright with neon letters blue and green and red advertising various beers and wine, parking lot filled with the battered cars of the working poor, cracked windshields and primer-gray spots covering up damaged fenders and doors and leaking exhaust systems that shook the vehicles in orgasmic spasms, black radios booming rap, white radios booming heavy metal.

Byrnes was of the night and the fog itself, the damp slimy fog encircling him like glistening nightmare snakes, his own dark eyes glistening, too, anger, fear, need, loneliness, and a strange dreamy feeling, as if he were detatched from himself, just watching this dumb pathetic fuck named Byrnes do all this stuff.

The night smelled of coldness and traffic fumes and his own harsh cigarette breath. He was trembling.

He stood across the street from the store, black coat, black gloves, black jeans, black high-top running shoes, just the way he'd learned in prison up to Anamosa. Five-to-ten armed robbery. But because of his young age—and because of overcrowding—he'd served only four.

He'd been out six months. His young wife was gone, the baby she used to bring to the prison and claim was his, the baby gone, too. First month or so he'd been a Boy Scout. Did everything his parole officer told him. Showed up nice and regular at the job at a wholesale tire company where he put outsize rubber on truck fleets and big-ass farm equipment. Got himself a respectable little sleeping room. Stayed away from his old crowd. Even went to mass a few times.

Then Heather, this chick he met down to this Black Crows concert at the Five Seasons, she turned him on to meth and man, he hadn't been straight a moment since. Now, he was lucky if he dragged himself into work two, three days a week. Once a month, his parole officer checked with his employer, see how Byrnes was doing. Pretty soon it'd be his ass. The parole officer would demand a urine test and they'd find the meth in Byrnes and he'd be back in the joint for parole violation.

His only hope was to get enough money to lay by a few weeks' supply of meth and then head for the yards down by Quaker Oats. In the joint there'd been a lot of talk about bein' a hobo. The stories you heard in prison you had to cut in half—nobody loved to bullshit you as much as bored cons—but even cut in half the life of a 'bo sounded pretty cool. The idea of waking up in a gondola on a beautiful warm morning out in the west somewhere . . . and the life would be so healthy, he'd even be able to kick meth too. He'd be free again in all senses.

He had to stand there nearly forty-five minutes before the lull came. He'd hit eight stores in the past seven weeks and by now, he knew their patterns pretty good. Even the busiest convenience store had a lull. Even on a Saturday night. This store was having a lull now, parking lot empty, clerk working on a counter display.

Byrnes gripped the .45 in the pocket of his cheap black raincoat and walked across the rain-glistening street.

Clerk was a black woman in the orange polyester uniform jacket and silly hat Happy Campers made all their employees wear, the orange only emphasizing her already considerable size. She looked smart and friendly, smiling silently at him as he walked to the coolers in the back where the beer was kept. He was quickly checking to see if any customers were lurking unseen back there. None were.

He went right up front and pulled the gun and said, "Just make this easy for us, all right?"

She did something he wouldn't have expected. She smiled. Couple gold teeth, she had, and she smiled with them. She smelled good, a heady, spicy perfume. "You look more scared than I do."

"I just want the money, ma'am. Just please make it easy for both of us. All right?"

She glanced at the cash register. "Most I got in there is five, six hundred."

"Give me everything you've got in there. Now."

She sighed. "You're shakin', boy. You know that?" There was real pity in her eyes and voice. "I got a boy about your age. I sure hope he never do nothin' like you're doin'."

The car was in the parking lot, then, the beam of its headlights playing across the wall behind the clerk.

She'd been talking too much. Lulls never lasted long. She'd been talking too much and he hadn't stopped her. And now there was a car pulling in the lot.

"You better get your ass out of here," she said. "And hurry."

He couldn't believe it. She didn't seem intimidated at all by the gun. Or his black getup.

He said, "I just got out of prison, lady."

She grinned. "I did time myself. Now you git, you hear me?"

Thunk of heavy car door slamming. Then a second door shutting. Two people at least. Coming inside. Quickly.

"And lemme do you a favor and take that before you hurt somebody."

His mind was divided, part of it on the door and the two figures now outlined inside the fog. The other part watching as the woman reached out—slo-mo, just like in the movies—and started to take the .45 from him.

"Hey!" he said, wanting to cry out in frustration and bafflement.

The door opening. Two balding, middle-aged men coming in. And the clerk grasping the gun and twisting it to get it away from him.

And him so startled and angry and—

He fired twice.

He would never know if he'd actually meant to fire. Or if it had just been a terrible accident. He could never be sure.

He'd never seen anybody shot before. TV had conditioned him to expect an imposing and dramatic moment. But all she did, really, was put big hard-working black hands over the blood patches in the front of her silly Happy Camper orange uniform jacket.

There was this terrible silence—it couldn't have lasted more than a second or two—and inside it he could hear her start to sob. She was dying. He had no doubt about that and neither did she.

And then there was no room for silence in the store as the men crashed into aisles trying to find a safe place from his weapon. And him firing to keep them at bay. And then her screaming as she started to fall over backwards into the silver ice cream machine.

And then he was running, too. He didn't know where. Just running and running and running and the fog made it a bitch running you can believe that running into a tree once and stumbling over a sidewalk crack another time and then tripping over a tiny tricycle another time palms all cut to shit from the sidewalk and all the time cursing and sobbing and seeing her die there over and over and over seeing her die had he really shot her on purpose? Her dying over and over and over.

And him running through this midwestern night and sirens now and fog heavier now a halfworld really not the real world at all halfworld and faint halflighted windows and halfvoices in the houses and apartments lost in the gloom muted cries of infants and lusting lovers and angry lovers and droning TVs and him nothing more than slapping footsteps and whining searing breath in the windpipe in the night. Alone . . .

He made no conscious effort to reach this place. And when he saw it he had to smile. Maybe he wasn't as luckless as he'd thought.

Not easy to see the railroad yard in the fog. But he could make out the general shape of it. Smell the oil and heat and damp steel of it. See the vast brick roundhouse and the two-story barracks-like building where business was conducted during the day. The crosshatching of silver track. And the box cars, walls of them lined up into infinity into the fog and the night, unseen engines down the line, rumbling and shuddering and thrumming in this halfworld like great beasts of a prehistoric time, unseen but all-powerful as they stole a line of boxcars here and a line of boxcars there, and began moving them into the midwestern night borne for places as forlorn as Utah and as magnificent as California, and hoboes of every description (if prison talk was to be believed) riding fine and happy inside the dark empty wombs of them.

Riding fine and happy.

He'd be doing that himself in a few minutes.

✢

Three hours ago, Chicago Mike had enjoyed a gourmet meal at the local Salvation Army. Chicken and peas and mashed potatoes. This was a good town, far as free food went. He'd been planning on staying a few nights but the place was full up and they had to put the extras in this little building aways from the main action where all of Chicago Mike's friends were so he just decided to head back to the yard from whence he came and find a westbound train. He had to ask one of the yard clerks for help. Chicago Mike, a scruffy sixty-six years of age, could remember the days when rail workers had been the enemy. No more. They hated management so much for always trying to bust their unions that they were happy to help 'bos with information. A railroad dick tonight even walked Chicago Mike to a newish car and helped him up on it. Long long ago—back in the days when he still had teeth and had an erection at least once a day—Chicago Mike had busted his knee up hopping a freight and he'd moved real slow and ginger ever since.

He was ensconced now for the night. Tucked into a corner of the big car. He'd taken an apple and a Snickers from the Salvation Army. He figured these'd make a good breakfast. He had his .38 stuffed under his right thigh. Sometimes, you'd fall asleep and find yourself with unwanted company, a 'bo with bad manners or murderous intent. There were gangs on the rails these days, and they'd kill you just for pleasure. He threw his blanket over his legs and hunched down inside his heavily layered clothes. If it got real cold, he'd get inside his sleeping bag. Two things a 'bo needed to learn real good and they were patience and how to deal with loneliness. Long time ago somebody had taught him how to summon and while most 'boes didn't believe in it, nobody knew better than Chicago Mike just how real summoning was . . .

He wasn't sure just when the kid hopped on board, Chicago Mike. He'd been in a kind of half-sleep, a sweet soft summer dream of he and his wife Kitty on the pier in Chicago 1958, just after he'd put in his Navy years. Could there ever have been a woman as pretty and gentle and loving as Kitty? Fourteen years they'd been together until that night, dancing in his arms on a dance boat, she'd slumped forward and died. Aneurysm, the docs said later. And so, after burying her, Michael Thomas Callahan, respectable purveyor of appliances to the public in Oak Park, Illinois, became Chicago Mike, rider of the rails. For years, Chicago Mike believed that only in distance and the violent metal thrashing of speeding boxcars could he find solace . . . And then he'd learned about summoning . . .

The kid huddled in the far corner of the big, empty car with the wooden floor and the metal walls defaced in spots with some singularly uncreative graffiti. Trouble, Chicago Mike knew instantly. He'd been too long atraveling not to recognize it. Trouble. He wondered what the kid had done. Robbery, at least. You didn't hop a freight for anything less. Maybe even murder.

Chicago Mike took out his long black flashlight and beamed it on the kid. "You all right, son?"

"Just leave me alone, old man."

"Most of the people on the rails, they try to be friendly and help each other."

"Good for them."

Chicago Mike clipped off his flashlight. In a few minutes, the train started to move. And then they were in the prairie night and really rolling. Chicago Mike worried vaguely about the kid jumping him—scared people were dangerous people, and this kid was definitely scared. But he wasn't worried enough to stay awake. Chicago Mike dozed off.

The scream woke him. The kid's scream.

Chicago Mike pulled himself up straight, grabbed his light and shone it on the kid.

The way the kid looked, the way he was shaking, the way his face gleamed with sweat and his eyes were wide with frantic fear . . . Chicago Mike could pretty much guess what had happened.

He stood up and walked the length of the rocking car. He moved slowly, his busted-up knee and all. The kid opened his mouth a couple times, as if he was going to tell Chicago Mike to stay away, but he ended up not saying anything at all.

Chicago Mike sat down next to the kid and handed him the pint of cheap whiskey. The kid took it and gunned himself three quick drinks.

"What kind of trouble you in, son?"

The kid just glared at him. "I didn't ask you to come over here, old man."

"No, I reckon you didn't."

"And I don't want you hangin' around."

"All right, son, if that's the way you feel."

Chicago Mike started to push himself to his feet, arthritic bones cracking. The kid grabbed his arm.

"I shouldn't be in the trouble I am," he said. "I just meant to rob the place is all."

"But somethin' else happened, huh?"

The kid looked miserable, lost. "Yeah, somethin' else happened, all right."

Chicago Mike knew not to ask any more questions. The kid would tell him what he wanted to tell him. Nothing more.

"And then I had this—nightmare, I guess you'd call it," the kid said.

"Just now, when I was asleep. She—the black woman—she was in it and she was trying to get me to come with her. You know—to die."

The kid leaned his head back against the wall. Closed his eyes. The door was partly open so you could smell the cold autumn night and see the quarter moon above the cornfields. The kid said, "But that wasn't all. When I woke up—I could smell her perfume. I still can." The kid sat up and looked at Chicago Mike and said, "You know what that means? That I could smell her perfume?"

"What?"

"She was here. Right in this boxcar." He trembled. "Right in this boxcar, tryin' to get to me." He paused. "Her ghost."

"You think ghosts still have their perfume?"

"Hers did."

The pint of whiskey sat between them. Without asking, the kid picked up the pint and drained off a couple more good ones. "I appreciate it."

"My pleasure."

"You mind if I ask you to go back now?"

"No problem."

"Thanks again."

Somewhere in the night, somewhere near the Nebraska border, another scream woke Chicago Mike. But this time when he woke up, he saw the kid standing up and walking across the swaying boxcar.

"Leave me alone! Leave me alone!" the kid was shrieking.

And then he was firing the gun in his hand.

Chicago Mike had to put it together fast. Kid sees the ghost again. Grabs his gun. Starts firing. Two things wrong with that, one being that there's no way you can kill a ghost, the other being that the kid, not seeing what he's doing, is firing right at Chicago Mike.

"Kid! Kid!" Chicago Mike shouted, trying to free the kid from his nightmare. "Quit firing your gun!"

But the bullets kept coming. Chicago Mike rolled to his right, grabbing his .38 as he did so.

The kid couldn't have many rounds left but he continued to fire right at where Chicago Mike was. The kid was screaming at the ghost all the time. Telling her to leave him alone. Telling her it was an accident. Telling her he was sorry. All the time firing.

"Kid! Kid! Quit shooting at her!"

A bullet took a piece of fabric off Chicago Mike's jacket. And then he knew he had no choice—he had to fire back, injure the kid enough to disarm him.

But just as he fired, the train rolled around a long, steep bank and Chicago Mike's shooting was thrown off. He'd meant to hit the kid in the arm. Instead, the bullet moved over and took the kid in the heart.

The kid went over backwards, kind of a Three Stooges thing actually, bouncing off the wall only to pitch forward, arms windmilling, to run head first into the other wall as the train continued to curve around the steep bank. Then he did a little pirouette in the middle of the car, and fell forward. And died.

✢

There would be too many questions if Chicago Mike was found in a box car with a dead young man. Somewhere near Plattville, Chicago Mike pushed the kid out the door. He watched as the body hit the side of the tracks and sprawled on its back.

He'd seen it before, Chicago Mike, how a kid's first encounter with a ghost made him literally crazy. He didn't understand that the ghost didn't have any power to kill him. She was just angry that he'd killed her. Her soul hadn't passed over yet. That would happen in a day or so and then she'd forget all about him.

Chicago Mike remembered the first time he'd seen a ghost. What a wondrous experience that had been. It'd happened right after the old 'bo had taught him how to summon.

As Chicago Mike was doing right now.

He felt plain terrible about having to kill the kid. He needed a gentle and loving person to talk to.

And so he summoned. Closed his eyes as if in prayer and said the words the old 'bo had taught him.

And when he opened them again, there she was, pretty as she'd been back in 1958, the year he'd married her. His lovely wife Kitty.

She knelt next to him and kissed him and then just held him for a long time. He told her about what he'd been doing and how awful it had been accidentally killing that young kid, and then they just sat together holding hands and listening to the train spectral as the night itself, rushing into the solace of darkness.

Ramsey Campbell
RETURN JOURNEY

A
s the old train puffed out of the station, past the sandbags on the platform and the men dressed up as soldiers and a wartime poster with its finger to its lips, the three children who were managing to occupy the whole compartment apart from Hilda's seat began to demonstrate their knowledge of history. "I'm Hitteler," announced the girl with orange turf for hair, and shot up an arm.

"I'm Gobble," said the girl whose bright pink lipstick didn't quite fit her mouth.

Hilda didn't know if she was meant to be offended. When Hitler and Goebbels were alive they'd been just a couple of the many things her parents never discussed in front of her. It was left to the third girl to react, clicking all her ringed fingers at her friends and declaring "You'd get shot for that if we was in the war."

"We're not."

"They don't have wars any more."

"You'd get shot or you'd get hung," the ringed girl insisted. "Hung by your neck till you was dead."

They must have learned some history to use phrases such as that. Perhaps they remembered only the unpleasant parts, the opposite of Hilda. She was turning to the window in search of nostalgia when the ringed girl appealed to her. "They would, wouldn't they?"

"Did you know anyone that was?"

"Did you ever see any spies being hung?"

"I don't look that old, do I? I wasn't in the war, just in the wars."

They regarded her as though she'd started speaking in a dead language, and then they crowned themselves with headphones and switched on the black boxes attached to them. If they intended to shut up so much of their awareness, Hilda wondered why they were on the train at all—but she wasn't far from wondering that about herself.

She'd seen the poster on the outside wall of the car park of the telephone exchange where she worked. Since none of her colleagues had seen it, she'd felt it was aimed just at her. OLD TIME LINE, it had said, with a train timetable and the name of a town pretty well as distant as her hot and bothered Mini could reach for one of her Sunday jaunts. If she hadn't been aware of having settled into never driving anywhere that wasn't already part of her past, she mightn't have taken the chance.

The town had proved to be even more Lancashire than hers: steep hills climbed by red concertina terraces, factories flourishing pennants of grey smoke, streets so narrow and entangled they might have been designed to exclude any relative of the shopping mall that had taken over the view from her floor of the small house she shared with two pensioners whose rooms always smelled of strong tea. She would have liked to explore, but by the time she'd found a car park where the Mini could recover from its labors she'd thought it best to head for the next train. When she'd stumbled panting into the two-platformed station she'd had to sprint for the train the moment she'd bought her ticket, scarcely noticing until she'd boarded that the railway preservation company had gone wartime for the weekend, and at a loss to understand why that should make her wish she'd been less eager to catch the train.

She rather hoped she wouldn't need to understand while she was on it. The station and whatever it contained that she hadn't quite liked were gone now, and trees were accompanying the train, first strolling backwards and then trotting as a preamble to breaking into a run as the last houses stayed in town. The land sank beside the track, and a river streamed beneath to the horizon, where a glittering curve of water hooked the sun from behind frowning clouds to rediscover the colors of the grassy slopes. This was more like the journey she'd wanted: it even smelled of the past—sunlight on old upholstery, wafts of smoke that reminded her of her very first sight of a train, bursting out like a traveling bonfire from under a bridge. The tinny rhythmic whispers of the headphones were subsumed into the busy clicking of the wheels, and she was close to losing herself in reminiscences as large and gentle as the landscape when a guard in a peaked cap slid open the door to the corridor. "All tickets, please."

He frowned the children's feet off the seats and scrutinized their tickets thoroughly before warning "Just behave yourselves in the tunnel."

That took Hilda off guard, as did her unexpectedly high voice. "When is there a tunnel?"

"There has been ever since the line was built, madam."

"No, I mean when do we come to it? How long is it?"

"Just under a mile, madam. We'll be through it in less than a minute, and not much more than that when we come back uphill. We'll be there in a few puffs."

As he withdrew along the corridor the girls dropped their headphones round their necks so as to murmur together, and Hilda urged herself not to be nervous. She'd never been frightened of tunnels, and if the children misbehaved, she could deal with them. She heard the guard slide back a door at the far end of the carriage, and then darkness closed around the windows with a roar.

Not only the noise made her flinch. The girls had jumped up as though the darkness had released them. She was about to remonstrate with them when they dodged into the next compartment, presumably in order to get up to mischief unobserved. Excerpts of their voices strayed from their window into hers, making her feel more alone than she found she wanted to be. The tunnel itself wasn't the problem: the glow that spread itself dimmer than candlelight was, and the sense of going downwards into a place that threatened to grow darker, and something else—something possibly related to the shadow that loomed in the corridor as the girls fell abruptly silent. When the guard followed his shadow to Hilda's door she gasped, mostly for breath. "Nearly out," he said.

As he spoke they were. Black clouds had sagged over the sun, and the hills were steeped in gloom. In the fields cows had sunk beneath its weight, and sheep that should be white were lumps of dust. It wouldn't be night for hours yet; nobody was going to be able to stage a blackout, and so she was able to wonder if that was the root of her fear. "Thank you," she called, but the guard had gone.

She remembered little of the blackout. The war had been over before she started school. The few memories she could recall just now seemed close to flickering out—her parents leading her past the extinguished houses and deadened lamps of streets that had no longer been at all familiar, the bones of her father's fingers silhouetted by the flashlight he was muffling, the insect humming of a distant swarm of bombers, the steps leading down to the bomb shelter, to the neighbors' voices as muted as their lights. She'd been safe there—she had always been safe with her parents—so why did the idea of seeking refuge make her yearn to be in the open? It was no excuse for her to pull the communication cord, and so she did her best to sit still for ten minutes, only to be brought back to the war.

The temporarily nameless station was even smaller than the one she'd started from, and crowded on the closer of the pair of platforms with people in army uniform smoking cigarettes as though to celebrate an era when nobody had minded. The three girls were beating the few other passengers to a refreshment room that had labeled itself a NAAFI for the weekend, and Hilda might have considered staying on the train if the guard hadn't reappeared, shouting "End of the line. All change for nowhere. Next train back in half an hour."

The carriage shook as the engine was uncoupled, and Hilda grabbed the doorway as she stepped down onto the platform, which displayed all it had to offer at a glance. Most of the female passengers were queuing for the grey stone hut behind the ticket office, and the waiting room smelled of cigarette smoke harsh enough for Woodbines. The refreshment room had to be preferable, and she was bearing for it when a pig's face turned to watch her through the window. For as long as it took her to confront it she had the grotesque notion that the building had become not a NAAFI but a pigsty, and then she saw the snout was on a human head.

Of course it was a gas mask, modeled by one of the girls from the train. Three empty masks were rooting at the inside of the window. By the time Hilda grasped all this she was fleeing up the steps onto the bridge over the tracks, and the realization by no means slowed her down. She walked very fast until she was out of sight of anything reminiscent of the war—out of sight of the station. She saw the smoke of the engine duck under the bridge and rear up on the other side, where the rails used to lead to the next county—presumably the engine would turn so as to manuever to the far end of the train—and then she was around a bend of the narrow road bordered by sprawling grass, and the flank of the hill intervened between her and the railway. She didn't stop until she came to a hollow in the side of the hill, where she not so much sat as huddled while she tried to breathe calmly enough to believe she might grow calm.

Breezes and sunlight through a succession of shutters of cloud took turns to caress her face. The grass on the hills that crouched to the horizon hiding the town where she'd joined the train blazed green and dulled, shivered and subsided. She didn't know whether she closed her eyes to shut out the spectacle of the agitated landscape or in an attempt to share the stillness it briefly achieved. While she gave herself up to the sensations on her face she was able not to think—was aware only of them, and then not of them either.

She wouldn't have expected to be capable of sleeping, but some kind of exhaustion had left her capable of nothing else. She didn't dream, and she was grateful for it. Instead, as her mind began to struggle out of a black swamp of unconsciousness, she found herself remembering. Perhaps her stupor was helping her to do so, or perhaps, she thought as she strove to waken, it was leaving her unable not to remember.

Her parents had kept her safe from everything about the war, but there had been just one occasion when she'd had to shelter without them. She'd spent a Saturday at her aunt's and uncle's across town, which meant her teenage cousin Ellen had been required to play with her. Long before it was time for Ellen to see her home the older girl had tired of her. Perhaps she'd intended to be more quickly rid of her, or perhaps she'd planned to scare Hilda as a sly revenge for all the trouble she'd been, by using the short cut through a graveyard.

They hadn't progressed halfway across it when it had begun to seem to Hilda as vast as the world. Crosses had tottered towards her, handless arms as white as maggots had reached for her, trees like tall thin cowled heads without faces had whispered about her as she'd scampered after Ellen into the massing darkness, and she'd been unable to see the end of any path. Ellen had to look after her, she'd reassured herself; Ellen was too old to be frightened—except that as the sirens had started to howl, a sound so all-encompassing Hilda had imagined a chorus of ghosts surrounding the graveyard, it had become apparent that Ellen was terrified. She'd run so fast she'd almost lost Hilda at the crossing of two paths dark as trenches, and when she'd halted, her voice had betrayed she'd done so largely out of panic. "Down here," she'd cried. "Quick, and don't fall."

At first Hilda hadn't understood that the refuge itself was one source of her cousin's distress. She'd thought it was a shelter for whoever worked in the graveyard, and she'd groped her way down the steps after her into the stone room. Then Ellen had unwrapped her flashlight, and as its muffled glow brightened with each layer of the scarf she removed from it, her breaths had begun to sound more like whimpers. The walls had been full of boxes collapsing out of their long holes and losing their hold on any of their lids that hadn't caved in. For a moment Hilda had thought someone was looking at her out of the box with the loosest lid, and then she'd seen it was a gas mask resting on the gap between box and lid. Gas masks were supposed to protect you, and so she'd run to pick it up in the hope that would make her braver. "Don't touch it," Ellen had not much less than screamed, but Hilda had pulled the mask off—

She didn't know if she had screamed then; certainly she did now. The cry rose to the surface of her sleep and carried her with it, and her eyes jerked open. The view that met them could have been more reassuring. The sun was considerably lower than last time she'd looked, and its rays streamed up like searchlights from behind black clouds above the town past the horizon. One beam spotlighted a solitary oval cloud, so regular she had to convince herself it wasn't a barrage balloon. She hadn't quite succeeded when she became aware not just of the lateness but of the silence. Had the last train departed? Long before she could walk back to town it would be dark, if she managed to find the right road.

As she shoved herself to her feet her fingers dug into the soil, and she remembered thinking in the graveyard vault that when you went down so far you were beneath the earth. She did her best to gnaw her nails clean as she dashed to the bridge.

The platforms were deserted. The ticket office and all the doors were shut. A train stood alongside the platform, the engine pointing towards the distant town. The train looked abandoned for the night, and she was about to despair when the stack gave vent to a smoky gasp. "Wait," she cried, and clattered down the steps. She hadn't reached the platform when the train moved off.

"Please wait," she tried to call at the top of her voice. Her dash had left her scarcely enough breath for one word. Nevertheless the rearmost door of the last of the three carriages swung ajar. She flung herself after it, overtook it, seized the inner handle and with a final effort launched herself into the corridor. Three gas masks pressed their snouts against the window of the refreshment room, their blank eyepieces watching her as though the darkness was. She shut them out with a violent slam and retreated into the nearest compartment, sliding the door closed with both hands and falling across a seat to fetch up by the window. The station sailed backwards, and the humped countryside set about following. She was glad the masks were gone, but she wished the view would demonstrate the past had gone too. There wasn't a vehicle to be seen, and the animals strewn about the darkened fields were so still they might have been stuffed. She was trying to content herself with the rewinding of the panorama when she remembered that it would return her to the tunnel.

She didn't want to enter it by herself, especially since the lights of the carriage appeared to be dimmer than ever. She would put up with children so long as they didn't try to make anything of the dark. If there were any in her carriage she would have heard them by now, but perhaps there were quieter passengers. She stood up, though the movement of the train was against it, and hauled herself around the door into the corridor.

She was alone in the carriage. The empty compartments looked even less inviting than hers: the long narrow outlines of the seats reminded her too much of objects she was anxious to forget, the choked brown light seemed determined to resemble the wary glow of her memories. Surely there must be a guard on the train. She hurried to the end of the corridor and peered across the gap into the next one, down which she heard a door slide open. "Hello?" she called. "Who's here besides me?"

The carriage tossed, sending her off balance. She floundered towards the gap above the speeding tracks, and had to step across it into the middle carriage. It was swaying so vigorously that the lamps looked close to being shaken out, and she had to reassure herself that the sound like a nail scraping glass was the repeated impact of a blind against the window of the first compartment. If someone had drawn the blinds down for privacy, Hilda was loath to disturb them. Instead she ventured past in search of the door she'd heard opening.

Was the carriage out of service? The insides of the window of the next compartment were so grimy they might have been coated with soil. Through a patch that a hand must have cleared she saw movement—a stump jerking up and down—the movable arm of a seat, keeping time with the rhythm of the wheels. It must be a shadow, not a large black insect, that kept creeping out from beneath the arm and recoiling, though there were certainly insects in the adjacent compartment: fat blue flies, altogether too many of them crawling over those few sections of the windows that weren't opaque, more of them blundering against the rest of the glass, thumping it like soft limp fingers. She was trying to nerve herself to dodge past all that, because next to it was the door she'd heard, when she saw what was wedging the door open. She wanted to believe it had slid open with the lurching of the carriage, which had also thrown an item of lost property off one of the seats to be trapped by the bottom corner of the door—a glove with its fingers twisted into claws and as brown as shrivelled skin. Even if it was only a glove, it didn't look quite empty enough.

Perhaps she didn't see it stir, or perhaps the careening of the train made the fingers twitch. She only knew she was backing down the corridor, leaning against the outer wall for fear of being hurled against or into a compartment, her hands sliding almost as fast over the grimy windows as the twilit hills and fields were regressing outside them. She had to force herself to look behind her rather than retreat blindly over the gap. As she executed a faltering stride into the rear carriage, her lips formed words before she knew where she remembered them from, and then while she attempted not to remember. "It wasn't me," she mouthed as she fled along the carriage, and as she slid the door shut on the corridor that had turned too dim for her to see the end of it and clung to the handle, "I didn't do anything."

She hadn't broken into the vault or vandalized the contents, true enough. Days later she'd overheard her father telling her mother that some children had, and she'd realized they must have left the gas mask. "Pity they weren't old enough to be called up," her father had said for her mother to agree with, "and learn a bit of respect," and Hilda had felt his comments could have been aimed at her, particularly since Ellen had persuaded her never to mention they'd been in the graveyard. After that, every time she'd had to go to the shelter with her parents—down into the earth and the dimness full of shapes her vision took far too long to distinguish—she'd repeated her denial under her breath like a prayer.

"I didn't do anything"—but she had. She'd lifted the mask from the open end of the box—from the head poking through the gap. Whoever had pulled out the box must have used the mask to cover up the head. It seemed to Hilda that some of the face might have come away with the mask, because the vacant eyes had been so large and deep that shadows had crawled in them, and the clenched grin had exposed too much besides teeth. Then the light had fled with Ellen up the steps, and as Hilda scrambled after her, shying away from the mask and its contents, a steady siren had sounded the All Clear like a cruel joke. As though summoned by the memory of her having had the light snatched away, darkness erased the countryside outside the train with a stony shout of triumph.

She doubled her grip on the handle until the hot thick stale exhalations of the engine began to invade the compartment through the open window. Now that the journey was uphill the smoke was being channelled backwards, and she felt in danger of suffocating. She lunged across the seat to grab the handles of the transom and slide the halves together. They stuck in the grooves while her hands grew as hot and grubby as the smoke, then the halves stuttered together and met with a clunk. She fell on the seat and masked her face with her cupped hands, but when she saw her blurred reflection against the rushing darkness on both sides of her she uncovered her face. At least she'd shut out much of the uproar as well as the smoke, and the relative silence allowed her to hear something approaching down the tunnel.

No, not the tunnel: the corridor. She heard an object being dragged, followed by a silence, then a closer version of the sound. She was well nigh deaf from straining her ears when another repetition of the noise let her grasp what it was. Somebody was sliding open the compartment doors.

It could be the guard—perhaps he was responding to her call from before they had entered the tunnel—except that the staggery advance sounded rather as though somebody was hauling himself from door to door. She strove to focus her awareness on the knowledge that the train wasn't supposed to stay in the tunnel much more than a minute. Not much more, her mind was pleading, not much more—and then she heard the door of the neighboring compartment falter open. Her gaze flew to the communication cord above the entrance to her compartment just as two bunches of fingers that seemed able only to be claws hooked the edge of the window onto the corridor. The carriage jerked, and a figure pranced puppet-like to her door.

It might have been wearing a camouflage outfit, unless the dark irregularities on the greenish suit were stains. It was too gaunt for its clothes or for the little of its discolored skin she could see. Above the knobbed brownish stick of a neck its face was hidden by a gas mask that had fallen askew. With each sway of the carriage the mask looked in danger of slipping off.

For the duration of a breath she was incapable of taking, Hilda couldn't move. She had to squeeze her eyes shut in order to dive across the compartment and throw all her weight against the handle of the door while she jammed her heels under the seat opposite her. As long as the door and the glass were between her and the presence in the corridor it surely couldn't harm her. But her sense of its nearness forced her eyes open, and the figure that was dancing on the spot in time with the clacking of the wheels must have been waiting for her to watch, because it lifted both its distorted hands to fumble with the mask.

Hilda heaved herself up to seize the communication cord, and only just refrained from pulling it. If she used it too soon, the train would halt in the tunnel. Her mouth was yearning to cry out, but to whom? Her parents couldn't keep her safe now; they had never appeared when she'd called out to them in the night to prove they were still somewhere. Her fist shook on the rusty chain above the door and almost yanked it down as the fingers stiff as twigs dislodged the mask.

Whatever face she'd been terrified to see wasn't there. Lolling on the scrawny neck around which the mask had fallen was nothing but a lumpy blackened sack not unlike a depleted sandbag from which, far too irregularly, stuffing sprouted, or hair. All the same, the lumps began to shift as if the contents of the sack were eager to be recognized. Then light flared through the carriage, and Hilda tugged the cord with all her strength.

The brakes screeched, but the train had yet to halt when the lights, having flared, died. The train shuddered to a stop, leaving her carriage deep in the tunnel. She had to hold the door shut until help arrived, she told herself, whatever she heard beyond it, whatever she imagined her fellow traveller might be growing to resemble. But when the handle commenced jerking, feebly and then less so, she rushed across the invisible compartment and wrenched the halves of the transom apart and started to scream into the darkness thick as earth.

Charles de Lint
THE WORDS THAT REMAIN

Not yet," she said. Her voice was measured and calm, calmer than she'd ever thought she'd feel when this time arrived. "Give me a little longer. Just long enough to know who I am."

But Death had not come to bargain that night and took her away.

❖

"This place is haunted, you know," the night clerk told him.

Christy stifled a sigh. Normally he was ready to hear anybody's story, especially on this sort of subject, but he was on a book tour for his latest collection, and after today's long round of interviews, signings, drop-in visits to book stores and the like, all he wanted was some time to himself. A chance to put away the public face. To no longer worry if he'd inadvertently picked his nose and someone had seen and made note. ("While the author's premises are intriguing, his personal habits could certainly stand some improvement.") He needed to get back to his room and call home, to let Saskia's voice remind him of the real life he led the other fifty or so weeks of the year when he wasn't out promoting himself.

But he felt he owed it to Alan, not to mention his own career, to do what he could to promote his books. Ever since the surprising success Alan's East Side Press had had with Katharine Mully, particularly her posthumous collection *Touch and Go*, the media had taken a serious interest in what Alan liked to call their contemporary myth books, said interest translating into better coverage, more reviews, and increasingly more lucrative deals for paperback editions and other subsidiary rights. Alan considered Christy's and Mully's books to perfectly compliment each other, rounding out his catalogue, the urban myths and folktales

Christy collected telling the "real story" behind the contemporary fairy tales Mully had so effectively brought to life in her fiction.

He approached the various readings and signings with a genuine fondness for the readers who came to the events with their own stories and enthusiasms, and he made the rounds with as much good grace as he could muster towards those media types who sometimes seemed to be less interested in the actual work than they were in filling a few column inches of type, or minutes of airtime. Still, at the end of a long day, it was wearying and hard to maintain the public persona—not so much different from his own, simply more outgoing. Right now he seriously needed some downtime.

But, "Haunted?" he said.

She nodded. "Like in your books. There's a ghost in the hotel."

Christy could believe it. There'd been a mix-up with his reservations so that when he'd arrived from the airport to drop off his bags, he'd been shunted to this other, smaller hotel down the street. Truth was, he liked it better. It was an older building, its gilded décor no longer the height of fashion, furnishings worn and decidedly frayed in places, but no less charming for that. If there weren't ghosts in a place like this, then they'd certainly drop by for a visit. It was the kind of hotel where bohemians and punks and open-minded businessmen on a budget could all rub shoulders in the lobby. The staff ran the gamut from the elderly man in a burgundy smoking jacket who'd checked him in this morning to the young woman standing on the other side of the counter at the moment. Earlier he'd heard the big band music of Tommy Dorsey drifting from the small office behind the check-in desk; tonight it was the more contemporary sound of Catatonia.

Leaning against the counter, Christy made note of the woman's nametag. Mary, it read.

At first he thought the name didn't really suit her. Mary struck him as a calm name, a little on the conservative side, and the night clerk was anything but, though he had to give her points for trying. She could have been anywhere from nineteen to twenty-nine, her frame more wiry than skinny, her chopped blonde spikes twisted and poking up at random from her brown roots through an odd collection of clips, bobby pins and elastics. Her fashion sense was riot grrl attempting business chic; he could tell she was about as comfortable in the sleek black skirt, white blouse and heels as he was in a tie and jacket—it didn't feel like your own skin so much as some stranger's. Her multiple earrings and the tattoo peeking out from below the sleeve of her blouse, not to mention that mad hair, told another story from the one her clothing offered, revealing part of the subtext of who she really was.

"What sort of ghost, Mary?" he asked.

There was an old smell in this hotel, but he didn't mind. It reminded him of favorite haunts like used book stores and libraries, with an undercurrent that combined rose hip tea, incense, and late night jazz club smoke.

"A sad one," she said.

"Aren't they all?"

She gave him a surprised look.

"Think about it," he said. "What else can they be but unhappy? If they weren't unhappy, they wouldn't still be hanging around, would they? They'd continue on."

"Where to?"

"That's the big question."

"I suppose."

She fiddled with something on the desk below the counter, out of Christy's sight. Paper rustled. The monitor of the computer screen added a bluish cast to her features and hair.

"But what about vengeful ghosts?" she asked, gaze remaining on the paperwork.

Christy shrugged. "Vengeful, angry, filled with the need to terrorize others. They're all signs of unhappiness. Of discontent with one's lot in life, or should we say afterlife? Though really, it's the baggage they carry with them that keeps them haunting us."

"Baggage?"

"Emotional baggage. The kind we all have to deal with. Some of us are better at it than others. You've seen them, sprinting through life with nothing more than a carry-on. But then there are the rest of us, dragging around everything from fat suitcases to great big steamer trunks, loaded down with all the debris of our discontent. Those ones with the trunks, they're the ones who usually stick around when the curtain comes down, certain that if they can just have a little longer, they can straighten up all their affairs." He smiled. "Doesn't work that way, of course. Alive or dead, there's never enough time to get it all done."

She lifted her gaze. "You even talk like a writer."

"I'm just in that mode," Christy told her. "Too many days talking about myself, going on endlessly about how and why I write what I do, where I find the stories I collect, why they're relevant beyond their simple entertainment value. It gets so that even ordinary conversation comes out in soundbites. I've been at it so much today my brain hasn't shifted back to normal yet."

"I guess you can't wait to get home."

Christy nodded. "But I like meeting people. It's just hard with so many at once. You can't connect properly, especially not with those who're expecting some inflated image that they've pulled out of my books and all they get is me. And it gets pretty tiring."

"I'm sorry," she said. "I'm keeping you up, aren't I?"

Christy had long ago realized that, in one way, ghosts and the living were much the same: most of them only needed to have their story be heard to ease their discontent. It didn't necessarily heal them, but it was certainly a part of the healing process.

"I can never sleep after a day like this," he lied. "So tell me about your ghost."

She went shy again, looking away.

"Really," he said. "Share the story with me. I've done nothing but hear myself talk these past few days. Listening to somebody else would be a welcome change."

That wasn't a lie and perhaps she could tell, because she gave him a small, grateful smile when her gaze returned to him.

"Do you believe in what you write?" she asked after a moment.

That was a familiar question from this and other tours and he didn't have to think about an answer, the rote response immediately springing to mind. He left it unspoken and traded it for a more truthful answer.

"It depends on the source," he usually said. "I know for certain that the world's a strange and mysterious place with more in it than most of us will ever see or experience, so I can't immediately dismiss elements that are out of the ordinary simply because I haven't experienced them. But by the same token, I also don't immediately accept every odd and unusual occurrence when it's presented to me because the world's also filled with a lot of weird people with very active imaginations. The trouble is, unless you experience what they have, it's difficult to come to any definitive conclusion. I will say that, for all my predilection towards the whimsical and surreal, empirical evidence makes a strong argument."

What he said to Mary was, "Yes. It might not necessarily be true for me, or for you, but if it's in one of my books, it's there because it's true for someone."

The Words that Remain

"I don't understand," she said. "Things are either true or they're not."

"I think it's more a matter of perception. Just because ninety-nine-point-nine percent of the world has decided that something like a ghost or fairy spirit can't exist, doesn't mean they're right."

"Do you really believe that?"

He nodded.

"That's not what you said on the TV interview this morning."

Christy smiled. "You watch that show?"

"Only for the how-to segments."

"But a pumpkin carving contest aimed at speed rather than quality?"

She laughed. "Come on. Don't tell me you didn't think it was funny."

"This is true . . ."

Christy had had a hard time keeping a straight face while sitting in the green room and watching that segment on the monitor. Between the host and the three guest pumpkin carvers, they'd made such a mess that it was only through the director's clever manipulation of camera angles that his own interview hadn't appeared to be filmed in the disaster zone it had been. There'd been pulp and seeds everywhere, squishing underfoot wherever you stepped, and he was still surprised that no one had been hurt with all those flashing knives. He'd left the studio with the smell of pumpkin pulp lingering in his nose for hours afterwards.

"So why do you say what you do when you're being interviewed?" she asked. "I mean, if you really believe in this stuff . . ."

"I don't want to be dismissed as a crackpot," he told her, "because then they'll also dismiss the stories out of hand. This way, if I allow them to see that I have my own healthy skepticism, the stories get to stand on their own. We can talk about them, *ad nauseum*, but in the end, the words will remain. The stories will be there and taken more for their own merit, rather than being the product of some obviously deluded individual."

"Do you really think they get a fair shake because of that?"

"A fairer shake," Christy said.

She smiled. "You still talk like an author, you know."

"And you still haven't told me about your ghost."

She hesitated a moment longer, twisting her finger around one of the escaped locks of her short hair. The movement brought a stronger waft of rosehips to him and he realized it was her perfume, not tea he'd smelled earlier. From the office behind her, the CD player changed discs and Ednaswap began singing about a safety net.

"Well, the way I heard it," Mary said, "she was the daughter of the hotel's owner. Really talented and artistic, but unfocused. She could have been a painter or a poet. A singer, a dancer, a writer, a photographer. She was good at everything she tried and she tried a lot of different things."

"But?" Christy prompted when Mary fell silent.

"Her father wanted her to work in the hotel. She was all the family he had and he refused to let her go out into the world and ruin her life trying to make a living with anything so chancy. She could have just taken off, I suppose, but it was a different time. A teenage girl didn't do that in those days. Or maybe she simply wasn't brave enough. So she tried to be both. Dutiful daughter, working with her father in the family business, and the free spirit who wanted to create and experience and never settle down. But it didn't—couldn't—work."

"I knew it was going to be a sad story," Christy murmured.

"It gets sadder."

He nodded. "They usually do."

"One day," Mary went on, "she couldn't deal with it anymore, so she killed off the free spirit inside her. She called up an image of Death in her mind, you know, scythe, black hood and all—not too imaginative, but then she was trying to kill her imagination, wasn't she? So cowled Death came at her bidding and cut the free spirit out of her soul and together they buried the poor little dead thing—figuratively, of course."

"Of course."

"Over time she pretty much forgot about that spirit lying somewhere, buried deep in her memory, and the odd thing is, she did come to feel better. There was no resentment towards her father or the hotel. When she did think of that girl, she remembered her as someone she'd once known, rather than someone she'd once been. But the funny thing is— the *ghostly* thing—is that from time to time guests would see that free spirit roaming through the halls."

"But the woman never did?"

Mary shook her head.

"An unusual ghost," Christy said.

"Mmm."

"And what do you think is keeping her here?"

"Well, not vengeance," Mary said with a small laugh.

"Why not?"

"Well, if she was that sort of a person, she'd never have let herself be shut out of her life the way she was, would she? I think she's just, like you said, sad. In mourning for everything she lost. She can't go on because she never got to find out who she could be. Or maybe she just wants some recognition."

"But not from the guests."

"No. I think it'd have to be from the woman who killed her." She cocked her head to look at him. "Have you ever heard of a ghost like that?"

Christy shook his head. "But that doesn't mean she's not real."

"To me."

"And whoever else has seen her." Christy paused a moment, then asked, "I assume you have seen her?"

"I think everyone who's in this hotel for any length of time gets to see her. But most of them don't know she's a ghost."

"Now I'm really intrigued."

Mary smiled. "Use it in your next book. 'Course, I guess you need an ending to be able to do that."

"No, I just tell the stories the way I find them, anecdotal, fragmentary or complete." He regarded her for a moment. "You only know what I write from that TV show."

"I don't get into bookstores a lot. Pretty much all I read is what people leave behind in their rooms. I'm sorry."

"Don't be. I think there are far more people in the world who haven't read me than there are those who have. Or who even know who I am." He smiled. "And frankly, most of the time I'm happy to leave it that way."

"When aren't you?"

"Oh, when I'm looking at some rare first edition that I can't buy because I only have this month's rent in my bank account."

"I hear being rich isn't all it's cracked up to be."

"Did you ever hear a rich person say that?" Christy asked.

"Only when they're trying to pass as one of the proletariat."

"Now who sounds like a writer?"

Before she could respond, another of the hotel's guests approached the desk, asking if there were any messages for him.

"Thanks for the conversation, Mary," Christy said as she turned away to look.

"You, too," she told him over her shoulder. "Sleep well."

❖

The next morning, when Christy went to the front desk to check out, he had a copy of one of his books in hand. He doubted Mary would still be on shift this morning, but thought he could at least leave a copy for her with whoever was on duty.

The morning clerk could have been Mary's mother—she even had the same name on her nametag, but there the resemblance ended. She was middle-aged, forty-something—which made her roughly his own age, he thought ruefully. Funny how you forget that you grow older along with everyone else. Medium height, not quite overweight, attractive in a weary sort of a way, short brownish-blonde hair that had started to outgrow it's last cut, dressed in a skirt and blazer that appeared a little outdated.

Her taste in music, judging from the faint wisp of sound drifting out of the office behind her, ran more to the classics. Something by Paganini was playing. Solo violin. The smell of her coffee made him wish he'd ordered some from room service, instead of waiting till he got to the radio station where he was doing his first interview this morning.

"Does everyone working here have the same name?" Christy asked.

The woman regarded him with confusion.

"Your nametag," he said. "It has the same name as was on the one the clerk was wearing last night."

Now he wished he'd never brought it up. Maybe they only had the one nametag and shared it around.

"Jeremy was wearing my nametag?" she asked. She said it in the same tone she might have used if this Jeremy had been manning the desk while wearing one of her dresses.

"No," Christy said. "It was a young woman. Blonde hair, sort of punky looking—but in a nice way," he quickly added when the woman's frown deepened.

"We don't have anybody like that working here," she said. "The clerk on duty last night would have been Jeremy."

"And he'd have been at the desk here the whole time?"

"Unless it was particularly quiet. Then he might have been studying in the office in back."

Christy could see a portion of the office from where he stood. He returned his attention to the woman who was regarding him with some measure of suspicion now.

"Studying," he said.

"He's a student from the university," she explained.

Christy nodded. He knew now where this was going.

"Does your father own this hotel?" he asked. "Indulge me," he added as her look of suspicion deepened. "Please."

"My father passed away a few years ago. I'm the present owner."

"I'm sorry," Christy said. "Not that you're the owner, of course, but . . ."

"I understand," the woman said. "Can you tell me what this is all about?"

Christy shook his head. "Not really. It seems I had the most vivid dream last night."

The woman regarded him expectantly.

"I should just check out," he said.

He studied her, surreptitiously, while she completed the necessary paperwork. He could see the traces of the girl she'd been, now that he knew to look. Could almost smell the rosehips of the younger Mary's perfume.

"This is for you," he said, handing her the book when their business was done.

The suspicion returned, deepening once more when she opened it to the title page and read the inscription.

> *For Mary,*
> *May you finally be recognized for who you are.*
> *Christy Riddell*

"I don't understand," she said lifting her gaze from the book to meet his. "How could you know my name before you came down to check out? And what does this mean?"

She was pointing at the inscription.

Christy could only shrug.

"It's a long, sad story," he said. "But we met once, a long time ago. I doubt you remember—you must meet so many people in this business."

She nodded.

"The inscription refers to who you were then—when we met. You told me a ghost story."

She looked down at the book again, read the title. *Ordinary Ghosts, Hidden Hauntings.*

"Like these?" she asked.

He shook his head. "No, it was a rather extraordinary ghost story, pulled out of a rather sad situation that happens more often than any of us likes to admit."

"I don't understand."

"I know. But nothing I can say will change anything, or make it any clearer. I'm sorry if I've troubled you in any way."

He nodded and turned away, walking across the lobby. He paused at the exit.

"Goodbye, Mary," he said. "I hope you enjoy the book."

"Well, I'll certainly give it a try," the woman behind the desk told him.

Christy hadn't been talking to her, but he gave her a smile. He didn't get a response from the other Mary, but he hadn't been expecting one. Nodding again, he left the hotel and hailed a cab. There were only two interviews this morning, then a signing at a bookstore. Plenty of time to think about choices made and what could come of them. Too much time, really.

But then that was what life is all about, isn't it? The choices we make and how the people we are can be left behind when we make those choices because they're no longer a part of our story. For many, not even the words remain to remind us of them. There are only all those ghosts of who we were, wandering around for anyone to see. Except ourselves.

Because we rarely see our own ghosts, do we?

As he settled in the back seat of his cab he found himself wondering about his own ghosts, how many there were, haunting the places he'd once been, those products of choices he'd made that he would never meet, telling stories he would never hear.

Graham Joyce
CANDIA

That Candia, with its crumbling Venetian waterfront and its abandoned minarets, and its harbor sliding into the rose-colored sea further
by an inch every day. Just like Ben Wheeler when I first spotted him,
with his bottle of raki at his permanent station outside the Black Orchid
Café, a misted tumbler forever fixed at some point on the arc between
tabletop and bottom lip.

I had just climbed down from the rusting, antiquated bus, the sole
passenger to disembark in that dusty square, when I saw him, at a time
when I never expected to see again anyone I'd ever known.

His glass of raki arrested itself on its mechanical ascent, and he
peered across the rim of his tumbler directly into my eyes. He was sitting at a table on the concrete edge of the neglected wharf. Over his
shoulder the sun was punctured on a derelict minaret, spilling lavender
and molten gold across the motionless waters of the harbor. He took a
sip from his glass, and turned away.

"Wheeler," I called. "Hey, Wheeler!"

On hearing his name he spun around and looked at me again, this
time with an expression of incredulity and horror. Then he looked
around wildly, as if for egress. For a moment I thought he was actually
going to make a break for it and run away from me. I crossed the square
to the café and dragged a seat from under the table; but as he showed no
sign that he would allow me to join him, I was made to hover.

"Don't you remember me?" I asked.

Before I got an answer a singer struck up in the square. He had a
cardboard shoe-box for donations and was singing in that curious, deep-
throated and unaccompanied *resitica* of the dispossessed people from

the mountains. The sound was of almost unendurable melancholy and sweetness, and the guttural voice resonated along the baked brickwork.

Wheeler put down his glass and hooked his thumbs in his waistband, regarding me with an unblinking gaze. I wasn't fooled. He was clearly nervous. It was as if he had somewhere important to go, but in his astonishment at seeing me there, he couldn't tear himself away.

"So what are you doing here?" I asked.

He eyed me steadily. "I might ask you the same question."

He looked back at the square and stroked the white stubble of his beard. Again I got the impression I was detaining him from something important.

"I've come here to drink myself to death," I joked. At least, it was a truth hidden inside a joke, but he nodded seriously, as if this was perfectly reasonable.

The arrival of a waiter brought a moment's relief. Slow to spot him, Wheeler turned suddenly and fixed the waiter with his extraordinary gaze. The boy shuffled uncomfortably, tapping the steel disc of his tray against his thigh.

"Let me stand you a drink," I suggested.

Wheeler put his hand to his mouth, removing something very small from the tip of his tongue. "Sure." He let his eyes drop. "Sit down. I'll have a beer. Yes, I'll have a beer."

I sat, but I was already beginning to regret this. Ben Wheeler looked terrible. I could see a ring of filth on the collar of his short-sleeved shirt. The hems of his oil-spotted chinos were rolled and his bare feet were thrust inside a pair of rotting, rope-soled espadrilles. When the beer arrived, he slurped it greedily. We sat in a stiff silence for a while, the swelling vocalizations of the *resitica* man the only other sound in the square in the parched heat of the afternoon.

✣

Our paths had crossed briefly in the eighties, when we were both working for Aid-Direct, the notorious London based charity, three or four years before public scandal closed the outfit down. Wheeler, Director of Fundraising at the time, was a flamboyant character in a double-breasted suit. His sixties haircut that looked like it was woven out of brown twill. For some of the serious-minded charity workers he was too fond of champagne, parties and pretty girls, but he could bring in money the way a poacher can tickle trout from a stream. The eighties. New money wanted to log onto charitable causes, not out of any sense of philanthropy, but to clamber aboard the Queen's Honors List. Wheeler obliged by organizing fatcat charity parties, in which city stockbrokers and dealers would be photographed sipping champers from a Page Three girl's shoe, all before writing a check.

❖

After one of these all-night jamborees at the Savoy or the Dorchester, a sack of rice or two would end up on a truck bound for Ethiopia or Somalia. At the time I didn't care where the money came from, or how little of it found a way through so long as it assisted me in my plans to change the world. Or rather, I wasn't so naïve as to believe one could change the world, but I did believe it was possible to change one person's world, and that was good enough for me.

I'd only been working for Aid-Direct about six months before accountants were called in. No one was ever told why, but Wheeler was suddenly given an impressive golden handshake. After the farewell party, I got caught in the lift with him. He was smashed.

"Hey," he said that day, "Something I wanna do, 'fore I leave here."

"What," I said, my finger hovering over the lift button.

He swayed dangerously. "Young tart who works in your office. Wassname. Cat-like. Yum yum. Feline." I offered no help, and he supplied the name himself. "Sarah."

"What about her?" The lift started its descent.

"'Afore I go. Ten minutes wiv Sarah the feline. In the store cupboard. Hey. Ten minutes."

"Good luck."

"No no," he said, brushing imaginary lint from the front of my jacket. "I want you to ask her for me."

"Get out of here!" The lift door opened.

His huge manicured hand restrained me as I made to step out of the lift. Fumbling in his pocket, he produced a couple of banknotes and stuffed them in my breast pocket. "Ask her."

"Piss off."

More banknotes, stuffed in with the others. "Ask her for me."

"No."

Still more. Big denomination. "Just ask her for me." He patted my cheek with his beringed paw.

We got out of the lift and I went back to my office, where Sarah was audio-typing. With her lithe figure and her long, raven hair scraped back from her face and tied at the back, Sarah cut a figure like a ballerina. Who wouldn't want ten minutes with Sarah? I did. I'd taken her out a few times. Despite some lavish wining and dining, she'd resisted all my best efforts. Any man who has tried and failed to seduce a particular woman nurses a tiny malice, and I confess to giving way to a disgraceful and sadistic instinct to collude with Wheeler's drunken lust.

I gently lifted one of her earphones. "We need some more envelopes. Can you go get 'em?"

"Now?"

"Please."

"What's the rush?"

She looked at me quizzically as I turned my back. I heard her replacing her headset on the table. The door closed as she went out. Half an hour later she was back, flushed and looking like she'd learned some new wrestling holds.

I caught her eye, but I was the one to look away first. The expression of guilt, shame and humiliation on Sarah's face filled me with self-loathing and regret. She put her headset back on and resumed work, punching so hard on her keyboard I thought it might shatter. It disgusted me that Wheeler had found it so easy to make a whore out of a perfectly respectable young woman, and a pimp out of me. As for the money he stuffed into my breast pocket, I can't even bring myself to repeat how little it was. I only hope Sarah got a lot more.

I waited until Sarah left the office. I heard her heels clacking angrily on the linoleum of the corridor.

❖

That was the last time I'd seen Wheeler. Ten or more years had gone by. Now here he was, washed up in Candia, his face crumbling like a waterfront warehouse and with eyes like the oilslicked, scummy backwash of the sea. Did he remember that episode in the lift on his last day at Aid-Direct? I doubted it. But then people choose not to remember things. Or they pretend to forget. He put his fingers to his mouth again, plucking from his tongue what I thought was a loose strand of tobacco. Finessing it clear of his fingers, he drained his glass.

"Have another," I offered. My companionable behavior was more to do with my own intolerable loneliness than with any attraction in Wheeler's company. Besides, I was curious.

He shook his head, didn't move. I signaled to the waiter, who brought another beer, and a raki for me. "You heard about the company, after you left?"

A light went on. "You worked at A-D? That must be where I know you from." Recall the episode with Sarah? He barely remembered me.

I reintroduced myself. "William Blythe. I was in the Training department."

"Yes yes yes. I remember." Again his hand went to his mouth.

"What did you do after that? After Aid-Direct, I mean."

"Went here. Went there. Here. There."

It was dark by now. The *resitica* singer had gone, carrying away his shoe-box without a single donation. A breeze picked up off the swelling black tide and Wheeler shivered. The water sucked and slopped around the concrete breakers. Laughter carried across the bay from one of the bars, making him look over his shoulder. I guessed he was hungry. "I'm just going to eat," I said.

We went to a small restaurant converted from a spice warehouse in the narrow streets behind the waterfront. I ordered an array of small dishes and Wheeler fell on them like a man who hadn't eaten in days. After a few glasses of resinated wine, he began to drop his guard.

"How long have you lived here?" I asked.

"Some years. Four maybe. Not sure anymore."

"How do you survive?"

He drained his glass and looked at me quite sincerely. "I don't know. I don't do anything. One day runs into another. I'm always hungry, but I survive. And I don't know how." He became distracted, gazing at something across my shoulder.

Then his fingers went to his mouth again, unconsciously plucking something from the tip of his tongue before flicking it to the floor. He looked up at me with a sudden intensity. "Have you ever tried to leave this town?"

The question was absurd. I'd only just arrived. "It's not hard. Tourist buses come in and out every day in the summer months."

He laughed cynically. "Sure. But I'm no tourist. And neither are you. Tell me: where were you before you came here?"

I tried to think, but my mind went blank. He found this amusing. He laughed again and seemed to relax. He returned to his food, and then he did something I haven't seen anyone do in a long time. He picked up an almost empty plate and he licked the sauce clean with his tongue. "Terrific food here!" he said. "What was in that sauce?"

"Knowing this place," I joked, "it was probably a dead cat."

That was the wrong thing to say. Wheeler carefully set down his plate and pushed it away from him, staring at the dish as if it was on fire.

I broke his trance by asking him where he stayed.

He looked confused. "Anywhere. Anywhere they let me stay. Now I have to go."

"Don't," I said. "Have another drink. Look, it's my birthday." It was true, and though Wheeler wasn't first choice for company, I was feeling sorry for myself. The popping of a celebration cork is a lonely sound when you're on your own.

Wheeler looked astonished. "You're lying!"

"Why should I lie? September 21st. It's my birthday."

Wheeler stood up. "But that means it's the Autumnal Equinox to-day!" I shrugged. "And you arrived here today? You don't understand. This could be an opportunity."

"Opportunity?"

"If it really is your birthday, the Shades Club might be open!"

"Shades? Where's that?"

"You haven't been? I could take you there."

I wasn't sure I wanted to go to the Shades Club, wherever it was, whatever it was. But Wheeler insisted. He became more interested in me than at any other point in the evening. But what else had I to do? I had no one to go home to and nothing to detain me. I was ready to be picked up by any foul wind blowing in from the ocean. It was around midnight when I settled the bill at the restaurant.

❖

As we walked across the waterfront, sounds from one of the cafes drifted across the bay, another explosion of men's laughter and the eerie skirling music of the bow of a lira drawn across strings as taut as a devil's nerves. Wheeler led me behind the crumbling waterfront and into the derelict streets of what were once spice warehouses in the grand trading days of Candia. Damp odors of ancient plaster, brine, spice and exhausted trade breathed along the ratruns of those streets.

Then Wheeler was clambering over a pile of broken bricks. He spotted my hesitation and beckoned me to follow. "It was on my own birthday that I first discovered the Shades Club," he explained. He ducked under a fractured arch and I could see he was heading for the ruined mosque. The moon, obscured by clouds, barely offered enough light to illuminate the needle of the minaret.

In the glory of its trading days, Candia had prospered under four hundred years of Ottoman rule, but the infidel had returned, and the dome of the mosque lay sundered, like a cracked egg laid by some giant, mythical reptile. The minaret sailed defiantly above the mooncast ruins, but the exotic call of the adhan was no more than a ghost. A clump of jasmine growing amongst the rubble breathed a tiger perfume into the night.

I followed Wheeler through a fissure in the tumbled wall, and we emerged in a darkened street. A flight of stone steps descended behind the shadows of the mosque. The anapaest beat of music thudded from below. At the bottom of the steps a malfunctioning red neon light fizzed, spitting the words SHADES CLUB. The letter S flickered intermittently.

The place was almost empty. Two women sat at the shadowy end of the bar, both stirring tall cocktail glasses with a straw, both displaying a lot of leg.

"It's a clip-joint," I said to Wheeler, annoyed. The bar looked like any other place I'd been in where you pay for girls to sip coloured water, and at prices that would frighten a steeplejack.

"No. It's not like that. Sit down, it'll be all right."

I took a stool at the bar. An old-style juke box was grinding out early rock music. Someone behind me was cleaning tables with a dirty rag. I saw the girls give us the once-over, but the sight of Wheeler made them lose interest.

Wheeler surprised me by storming behind the bar and confidently mixing Vodka Martinis. "I'm known here," he assured me. Knowing he was broke, I took out my wallet but he waved it away. "Don't worry, it's free."

Overhearing, one of the girls snorted. "Free. He says it's free. Nothing is free."

The second of the two, the one who'd said nothing, was smiling at me, holding her cocktail glass to her mouth. The bar was lit by soft blue and ruby lights, and she struck me as extraordinarily pretty as she waited for me to come back at her friend's remark. Perhaps because Wheeler had reminded me of the incident, I was struck by how much she resembled Sarah from our days at Aid-Direct.

"You're a philosopher," I said.

Taking this as a rebuff, the outspoken one looked away, exhibiting the attributes of extreme boredom; but the other continued to gaze in my direction.

"You've made a hit," said Wheeler, coming from behind the bar.

"She's nice," I whispered.

Wheeler nearly dropped his glass. "You like her? You mean you really like her?"

I couldn't understand why he was so amazed. I checked her out again. Wheeler's response suggested he regarded her as some kind of reptile. "Doesn't she remind you of . . ." Wheeler was looking at me searchingly. I decided to let it go. "She's beautiful."

And she was, at least so she seemed in shadow: long, auburn hair and a china-doll complexion, just a hint of the oriental about her. Wheeler made some sort of gesture to her, because she got off her stool and came over. I got the chance to look at her in proper light.

She was even more striking than my first impression had suggested. It was not until she came over that I realized the two women were wearing some kind of fancy-dress outfits: leotards and sheer black nylon tights. Her eyes were heavily lined with mascara. Wheeler, in a state of some excitement, introduced us, and she slid onto the stool next to me.

"This is Lilly," Wheeler said, and almost from behind his hand he added, "and I think I've found my way out of this town."

I didn't know what he meant, and I didn't much like the way he said it. It reminded me of how little I trusted the man. I thought again of Aid-Direct, and how after he'd gone the depth of his corruption had been made plain. The organization, heavily in debt, collapsed like a house of cards. The executives, those caring-sharing liberal bleeding-heart charity workers began stripping the place before the liquidators came in. Office equipment was driven away by the van-load, the car pool drained itself overnight, and fabulously inflated expenses were cash-processed before the banks had wind of what was happening. My immediate superior stopped a consignment of rice before it left the docks and sold it on to a wholefood collective, pocketing the proceeds. I have to say that, demoralized, I joined in this feverish stampede.

But I was too busy getting along fine with Lilly to give much thought to Wheeler's odd remark. Lilly and I sensed immediate rapport. I can't remember anything I said to her, or she to me, but we had anchored and the next fifteen minutes melted in a miraculous and sympathetic exchange of thoughts. It was only when I offered to buy her a drink that I noticed Wheeler deep in conversation with the other woman. They eyed me intently. I sensed that they were striking some kind of deal, and that it involved me.

The jukebox went dead. Lilly jumped up to feed it with a coin, and it was only then that I noticed the tail protruding from the butt of her leotard, part of her fancy-dress. The other woman too, had a tail, sitting erect on the stool behind her. As Lilly bent over the juke box to make her selection, the tail swished slightly in the air.

"How d'you make it do that?" I asked, coming up behind her. I was feeling slightly drunk from the cocktail and all the raki I'd consumed earlier. The tail was actually flesh colored, with a furry collar half-way along its length, and another at the tip, as if the regions between the furred collars had been shaved. I grasped the brown, furry tail-end, which was still swishing gently as Lilly fingered Bakelite buttons on the juke-box, and I squeezed the tip hard.

It was the wrong thing to do. Lilly spun round, slamming into the jukebox. "Don't DO that!" she hissed at me. "Don't EVER do that!"

She was coiled like a spring, her eyes leaking venom. Astonished by this transformation I mumbled an apology.

"I hate it when men do that!"

"Sorry." I looked round for Wheeler and the other woman, but they were gone. So too had the shadowy figure clearing up the tables behind us. Lilly and I were left alone in the bar.

"Where did—"

There was a few seconds of vinyl hiss before honeyed saxophone music started oozing from the jukebox. Lilly's mood was restored, and she sidled up close, enfolding her arms around me. "Come here. Let's dance. I'm sorry I reacted like that. I'm sensitive. Here, dance a little closer."

The bar dissolve around us. I abandoned myself to Lilly's embrace. Her perfume, or maybe it was her natural cassolette, had me inflamed.

An hour later she was undressed in my apartment and I was carefully examining her tail. Her anatomy was normal in every other way. She had the physique of a centerfold, but she also had a tail. This time she let me touch it, but tenderly. She let me stroke it. She let me run my fingers gently along its sinuous curved length.

Three collars of brown tailfur had been left unshaved. These were at the tip, the location of my early offense, in the sensitive middle; and at the coccyx, where the tail joined the body at the base of her spine. The exposed, shaved skin was considerably lighter than the rest of her sallow flesh tone.

"Why do you shave it?" I asked as she stood over me, naked. I marveled at the way she could make it swish lightly from side to side.

She shrugged. "Fashion."

"Sure," I said. "Doesn't everyone shave their tails these days?"

She grew bored with my fascination for her tail, aggressively straddling me and pinning me back on the bed. For the next hour she rolled over me like a heatwave. Her tongue was rough, like a cat's tongue, and the odor of her body was an intoxicant, like the smell of a waterfront spice warehouse in the old trading days of Candia. I abandoned myself to her, and she to me, though all the time I couldn't help wondering how her tail was behaving behind her, or beneath her, or beside her. At the moment of her orgasm I instinctively reached around and grasped it above her coccyx. She gasped, sinking her nails deep into my back and tearing lightly at my skin with her sharp teeth.

❖

When I woke in the morning I somehow expected her not to be there. But she was already awake, her head resting on the pillow. She blinked at me sadly.

"What is it?" I said, wiping away a tear with my thumb.

She wouldn't answer me. She slipped out of bed, dressed hurriedly and then kissed me deeply and passionately.

"I've got to go."

"When can I see you again?" I didn't want to lose her. "Will you be at the Shades Club?"

"Sure," she said rather cynically. "When it next opens."

And she left. I made to shout after her, but there was something stuck to my tongue. I plucked it from my mouth. It was a dark hair. In distaste I flicked it away, but in that time Lilly had gone. My skin tingled in the places she'd bitten me. I had a high temperature.

In the evening I returned to the Shades Club, only to find it closed. The malfunctioning neon sign had been switched off. I couldn't find anyone around the place to ask when it was going to open again. I scoured the town for signs of Lilly, or of Wheeler, or even for the other girl in the bar. Exhausted I returned to my room, where I fell into a hot, feverish sleep lasting some days.

I don't know if this happened to me a year ago, or just the night before last. Time has a way of becoming a concertina of expanding and diminishing moments in this town. I spend the hours drifting in the streets, returning to the Shades Club of an evening, never to find it open. I ask the waiters at the other bars if they know anything about it. Someone was working there that night I met Lilly, but no one seems able to tell me anything. They regard me sadly, pour me a drink, sometimes they give me a meal.

I've made efforts to get out of this town, but every time I resolve to leave, then I'm distracted, by another hair on my tongue, or an involuntary twitch of my tail muscle. I don't know when the tail first appeared. I woke up one morning and it was there, as if it had always been there. I keep it self-consciously coiled inside my trousers as I go about the town, hoping its movements won't betray me.

But the discomfort of the tail is nothing compared to the hollow ache, the hunger, the yearning to make one moment snap together with another to form a chain of some consequence, some meaning. For I catch myself, washed up on this street or in that Club, with no sense of why I came there, or what it is I'm looking for.

I am haunted by the desire to know what I am doing in this place.

I haven't seen Ben Wheeler since that night. I know he struck some kind of a deal involving me, which helped him get out of town. Meanwhile I wait. I wait for the Shades Club to open its door again. I wait for an old acquaintance to turn up at one of the waterfront bars, so that maybe this time I can strike the deal. And every now and then, something appears on the tip of my tongue, a hair, a strand of fur, like something half remembered, or like the first words in a strange, impossible story I'm about to tell. A story about the town of Candia, with its sleepy waterfront, and its lost bars and missing streets, and its ruined temples dedicated to gods glimpsed only once in a lifetime. A story about Candia, the town that couldn't decide its allegiance between the Greeks and the Turks, and so invited its own downfall.

But then a kind of waking sleep washes over me. And I find myself back again in one of the bars on the waterfront, nursing a glass of raki while the *retisita* man decants from his bursting heart in this town of forgotten miracles.

T he little man was about two feet tall, as dark and shriveled as a Brazil nut, carved out of hardwood and studded everywhere with long iron nails. He was repulsive, Kat thought; and as he had been created to curse someone, he ought to be. But she could see the strange crucified beauty of him too, and that was one of the reasons she was good at her job.

She'd enjoyed haggling with his owner, a fat Jamaican woman in a purple turban who presided over her tin shed in the muddy market as if it were a palace and she a queen. But Kat wanted the little man, and she was ready to close the deal. "Fifty dollars American," she said. "Right now, cash."

The woman's broad face registered infinite disdain. "Fifty dollah, I maybe get you good stick of ganja fo' dat, but not my obeah man."

"What did you call him?"

"Obeah man. Obeah like Jamaican voodoo, you know, missy? You believe, den he got de power. But if you don' believe, he just a piece of wood." The woman saw that Kat was interested and took advantage of the moment. "Eighty dollah, las' chance."

"Okay," Kat said, and the woman's smile was worth it.

She nestled the fetish into her big straw tote and headed back into the steaming thick of the Kingston market, bracing herself for the on-slaught of humanity that instantly surrounded and accosted her.

"Hello, lady, you got to look in here—"

"What's up, blondie? You American? Speaken see Deutsch? Huh?"

"You buy two dese only hunnred dollah 'merican—"

"Lady! *Lady!*"

Kat plastered a vacant smile on her face—*sorry, no one in to take your calls just now*—and shouldered her way gently through the crowd, letting the reggae that played everywhere drown out the melee of voices, dodging the goats that roamed the market, scanning the stalls for anything that stood out from the mounds of tourist junk. She'd already bought some gorgeously dyed cloth and some decent beadwork, but she had a feeling that the little man was going to be her major find of the day, and he was starting to get heavy.

Back at her hotel, Kat stood the fetish inside the tiny closet and shut the door on him. She wasn't particularly superstitious, but the thing had been made with ill will, with the intent to hurt a man or woman. Wood and iron. Wood could bleed, and iron could remember . . .

Kat shook her head. She was tired, drained from the constant, vibrant, faintly hostile energy of this unfamiliar city. She needed a shower and sleep. Tomorrow she would find the Federal Express office and ship her purchases to Axel and Rob, the couple for whom she was shopping in Kingston. Kat was a traveling freelance buyer, a sort of exotic bargain hunter. Axel and Rob owned one of several Manhattan stores that bought her finds, priced them up considerably, and sold them to collectors of art, antiques, and curiosities. After nearly a decade of this, Kat couldn't imagine wanting to do anything else. She was just thirty and figured she had a good half-century left to pursue her career, which made for an interesting life and an eclectically decorated apartment.

She'd expected to fall into bed right away, but a long shower renewed her energy and made her hungry. She put on a full-skirted red cotton dress, pulled her damp hair into a knot, and hit the street again. She was staying in New Kingston, which was calmer than the market area, and she was able to have a peaceful dinner of jerk chicken and Red Stripe at a food stall near the hotel. Afterward, with the spices lingering on her tongue and the two beers buzzing pleasantly in her brain, she followed the lilt of reggae to a nearby street party.

It felt good to dance alone in the sweaty, noisy crowd, to sway with the music as the singer's voice rose and fell, to know that no one was going to grab her arm and claim her. This buying trip had come at just the right time. Finally she'd had a concrete reason to put an end to the all-night fights, the deceptions and reconciliations, to say with a delicious finality, "I'm leaving the country tomorrow, and I never want to see you again," then hang up on Tedd's answering whine. She'd felt cowardly telling him over the phone, but that way he couldn't transfix her with those puppydog eyes, couldn't play her the new song he'd written for her, couldn't make her listen yet again to the poor-misunder-stood-genius rap that every guitarist seemed to know from birth.

"Miss? 'Scuse me, Miss?"

Kat figured the deep male voice was talking to her, but she didn't want to deal with anyone, didn't want to flirt or resist flirting. She kept dancing alone, silently daring the man to grab her arm. Instead he tapped her very gently on the shoulder.

"Miss, it's really not safe for a white lady to be out here by herself tonight."

She turned and looked into the speaker's face. He was maybe her age, maybe a little younger. His hair was separated into little twists, as if he was trying to start dreadlocks. His eyes were tired and very intelligent. She wondered if he was feeding her a common pickup line, decided he probably was.

"I'm fine," she said. "I mean, thanks, but I've traveled all over the world. I can take care of myself."

"I bet you can. But this crowd is gonna turn ugly real soon, and there's some people would love to see a tourist get hurt in the mess."

"Ugly?" Kat stared at the man, then around at the crowd, which seemed peaceful enough if a bit rowdy. "What do you mean, ugly? And how do you know?"

"Look—" An expression of annoyance crossed the man's face, and he patted his pants pocket as if someone had just beeped him, which Kat supposed was entirely possible. "Aw, hell. I gotta go take care of something. I'll be back here in ten minutes—but if I were you, I'd just go on back to your room." He turned and within seconds was swallowed by the crowd.

Just go on back to your room. Kat put a hand to the back of her neck, brushed sweaty strands of hair off her skin. She was enjoying herself, dammit, enjoying being by herself for the first time in she couldn't remember how long. She didn't want to just go on back to her room. She looked around once more, half-nervous, half-angry, then shrugged and started dancing again.

It wasn't even ten minutes later that the drunk came out of nowhere and grabbed her breast.

Kat had lived in New York for most of her life; it wasn't as if she'd never been grabbed on the street. But it hadn't happened in a long time, and instead of scaring her as it had once done, it made her angry. She snatched the offending hand, which belonged to a wiry bare-chested man in his forties, and flung it away. "Fuck off!" she yelled.

But instead of fucking off, the drunk grabbed her again, and this time there was a knife in his other hand.

"Bitch," he spat in her face, his breath sour with rum. "Fuckin' white bitch t'ink you kin shake you titties in de street and nuttin' come of it— you see now—"

Kat froze, her eyes fixed on the blade, her breath trapped in her chest, unable to move or scream. The crowd had drawn away from the little scene in its midst, and she realized that no one was going to help her, that the drunk was going to cut her right here and all these people were going to watch him do it, and she was so *stupid*, why hadn't she listened to the young man—

Who was back now, shoving through the crowd, grabbing the drunk's wrist and twisting it so that the knife fell to the ground. He leaned down to whisper something in the older man's ear. The drunk's eyes widened in fear and he seemed to sober up several degrees at once. When the young man let go of his wrist, he disappeared into the crowd without retrieving his knife or speaking another word.

"Come on." The young man took Kat's arm, his touch very light. "I told you it was gonna turn ugly, and this isn't even the start of it. Now let's get out of here."

This time, Kat didn't argue.

✢

"Kingston's gonna blow sky-high one of these days," said Gideon.

They were sitting in a rum shop near Kat's hotel, and Gideon, as the young man had introduced himself, seemed to be baring his soul to her. Kat didn't know why; he wasn't drunk, and she'd never thought of herself as a particularly good listener, but somehow in the midst of the crowd and the chaos they had hit it off. He'd told her about his two years at the University of the West Indies, his attempts to work as a journalist. Now he was describing the street politics of the city, the rival parties JLP and PNP and their devolution in Kingston to a pack of rival gangs who controlled the slums, killing each other for the sake of party loyalty. Loyalty, it seemed, could be as important as a free election or as petty as drinking the wrong brand of beer. Gideon was drinking Red Stripe.

Kat thought he was very attractive, but was trying not to show it. With Tedd so recently in her past, a vacation fling was the last thing she needed.

"That guy who grabbed you? He used to be a big man in the Concrete Jungle, where I live. He'd throw street carnivals, have food and beer for everybody. He only started drinking so much after a JLP posse shot his son."

"That's terrible, but it doesn't give him the right to grab a woman and curse her on the street."

"No, 'course not." Gideon stared into his beer bottle. "That comes from the drinking. Different people grieve in different ways."

"What about you?" She willed him to meet her eyes, and he did. "Are you grieving for somebody?"

That got a rueful smile out of him. "You see a lot, Katherine."

"I already told you everybody calls me Kat."

"I don't like cats. Katherine is much more beautiful."

"And you're trying to change the subject. I'm sorry, I don't mean to be a nosy American."

"It's okay. It's just something I haven't talked about for years, 'cause everybody I know already knows about it. Ever heard of Orange Street?"

"I think I was on it today."

"Yeah, it's not so bad near the market. But down toward the harbor it gets pretty rough. Bunch of yards—tenements, and the people who live there are all PNP. So? So in 1976, a posse came and blew up one of those yards with Molotov cocktails, then shot the firemen who came to put it out. Five hundred people homeless, eleven dead.

"One of those dead was my twin brother Thomas. We were eight. We were identical twins, but he was always runty, and I took care of him. But not that night. I couldn't get to him, and he burned.

"Nobody ever proved it, and the newspapers wouldn't write about it. But everybody knew it was Seaga, Seaga the goddamn fascist and his JLP."

Gideon shrugged. "Everybody's lost somebody, everybody in Kingston, anyway. But I don't like to see innocent folk get hurt, and I especially don't like to see them get hurt by JLP. That's why I talked to you tonight. There's Shower Posse at that party, and it isn't their territory."

"Look." Kat held up her hands in a placating gesture. "That's horrible about your brother. I'm so sorry. But I think I'm in *way* over my head here."

"I understand. You come to Jamaica and buy up our treasures, but you don't want to see the dirty side."

"I—" Kat wasn't sure what to say; he had spoken in a pleasant enough tone, but his words were damningly true. "I live in New York, okay? I spend plenty of time worrying about getting shot. But yeah, basically I'm here to buy stuff from the nice lady in the market, and probably pay her a whole lot more than most people would. It's how I make my living."

"Living." Gideon looked faintly amused. "Americans always talk about their *living*. Jamaicans just spend their time trying not to die."

"So can I see you again?" he asked her in front of her hotel, in the flower-scented night, and Kat surprised herself by saying yes.

"I'm taking the bus to Spanish Town tomorrow. I want to check out the market there. Come with me?"

"I can't tomorrow." Gideon rubbed a hand over his short dreadlocks. "Something to do. How long will you be here?"

"Until next week, but I have to travel. I could be back in Kingston by Tuesday."

"Then I'll see you on Tuesday, Katherine."

❖

Her dreams ran hot and cold, smooth and sharp. A man was inside her, not Tedd, but a lithe black man who moved like heaven. A prick in her womb, a thousand pricks coming out of her skin. She woke with the taste of iron in her mouth.

She packed up the little man, swathing him in layers of bubble wrap so the nails would not poke through, and sent him to New York. She took the bus to Spanish Town, then up through the crystalline Blue Mountains to Port Antonio. She flew to Ocho Rios on a perfectly terrifying small plane. And all the time she could not stop thinking about Gideon.

In Ocho Rios, she called home; or called the gallery, rather, as her home was locked and empty. Rob answered the phone sounding uncharacteristically subdued.

"Yes, the packages got here fine. The nail fetish is particularly nice. It's not an antique—the lady you bought it from probably cranks 'em out at home; you ought to see if she has any more—but it's a beautiful piece. Worth several hundred dollars, I think."

"It's *worth* that much, or you think you can *get* that much for it?"

"In New York, what's the difference?" Rob laughed, and so did Kat. But he still didn't sound quite right.

"Anything wrong?" she asked. "Is Axel okay?"

"Well, he's having trouble sticking to his pill schedule. I made a big chart for the refrigerator, with gold stars like they used to have in nursery school. I think the drugs are really helping, though, Kat. I think he's going to beat this thing."

"I'm so glad," she told him, and meant it. She'd not been close to her parents; knowing Axel and Rob had been like getting a second chance. "But you still sound kind of down."

"Sweetheart, I didn't want to say. I wanted you to have a nice tropical vacation. But Axel made me promise that I'd tell you if you asked. The police came to the shop this morning. Apparently your ex-boyfriend was murdered."

"Tedd?" she said, absurdly; she'd been with no one else for three years. "What? What happened? Why did the police have to talk to you? What—"

"Ssh, ssh, let me tell you. Tedd came to the shop a few days ago wanting to know why you weren't answering your phone. I said I wanted to know why he was calling you, but he said he just wanted to make sure you were okay—"

Wanted to make sure I hadn't slit my wrists with grief over the loss of him, Kat thought, and then a wave of nausea washed over her as she realized just what she was thinking.

"So I told him you were away on a buying trip. He wanted to know when you'd be back, and when I told him it was none of his business, he started pulling out the testosterone stops. 'You fuckin' supercilious queens, I love that girl' and such. I always thought it was cute how he tried to use those big words."

"*Robbie.*"

"Sorry. Anyway, I'd just put the nail fetish out on the floor, and when I asked him to leave, he kicked it—just kicked it right over! That's when Axel came out from behind the counter, picked him up, and carried his skinny ass out to the sidewalk. I told you those drugs were working!

"That was the last we heard from him, and that's what we told the police."

"But what happened? Why—how was he murdered?"

"He was bludgeoned, sweetheart. One of the band found him in his apartment. Heavy object to the skull, not found at the scene. As coked up as he appeared to be at the shop, I'd imagine it was a debt gone bad."

"Probably," Kat murmured. She'd given Tedd money to cover cocaine debts more than a few times.

"There was one funny thing. Probably some kind of gang ritual, but I thought it was an odd coincidence seeing as you'd just sent the fetish. I didn't mention that to the police, of course—they'd probably seize the piece as quote-unquote evidence and it'd end up in some cop's rec room."

"Rob. What the hell are you talking about?"

"Tedd's guitar," Rob told her. "It was hammered full of nails."

It was strange arriving back in Kingston so numb; she had felt so lush when she left it. She'd meant it when she told Tedd she never wanted to see him again. But there was a world of difference between not seeing him again and imagining him alone in his nasty little apartment, face bloody and skull stove in, his thin body curled upon itself in final agony. His guitar. The lingering taste of iron.

She told Gideon all this when they met in the rum shop. "I was attracted to you when we met," she said, unable to make herself shut up no matter how much she wanted to. "But after this, I just don't think I can handle it. I hope you understand . . ."

Kat let her voice trail off. Gideon was nodding, a sympathetic look on his handsome face, but she suspected his mind was elsewhere.

"Where did you get the fetish?" he asked.

"At the Jubilee Market, like I said."

"Yes, yes. But from which vendor? A woman? What did she look like?"

Kat described the woman as well as she could, ending with the purple turban. "She said he was an obeah man. Do you know anything about that?"

"Oh yeah, I know about obeah." His eyes narrowed. "Comes from Africa. Ashanti. Nanny, one of our PNP heroines, she was an Ashanti slave. Obeah is black magic. Good for getting revenge on your enemies."

"You're PNP?"

"Katherine . . ." He sighed, gazed up at the twinkling Christmas tree lights strung from the tin ceiling. "I should have told you before. I'm the leader of a posse."

"A posse."

"Yes."

"Bombs and guns."

"Oh yes, lots of guns." He actually smiled.

"Gideon, 'posse' sounds like a word from an old cowboy movie."

"Yeah, some of the brothers love those old Westerns. They think that's how life would be if they were free—whatever free means to them."

"What does free mean to you, Gideon?"

"Paying them back for Thomas."

"Killing other people that somebody loves. That doesn't bother you?"

"Not if they're JLP," he said, and his eyes were as cold as iron.

She knew she would not see him again, but it was still awkward saying goodnight. There were ghosts of things between them, things that could have happened, though now Kat was very glad they hadn't.

As it turned out, she was wrong about not seeing him again. She saw him again the very next morning. It was her last full day in Kingston, and remembering that Rob had asked her to look for more nail fetishes, she returned to the Jubilee Market. The crowd pressed in as she searched for the stall of the woman who had sold her the little man. She smelled garbage and goat shit, and realized that she could hardly wait to leave this city.

As she approached the stall, she saw Gideon talking to the woman. She wondered whether to walk on by, but before she could decide, he finished his business, turned away, and saw her. His smile was broad and chilling.

"Remember, obeah is good for getting revenge on your enemies," he said, and disappeared into the crowd.

The nail fetish had been sold by the time Kat got back to New York. Rob was disappointed that she hadn't been able to find any others, but she told him to get over it, and he was so surprised by her fit of temper that he let the matter drop.

She called Tedd's parents, who told her he had been cremated and that there were no leads in the case. Though they intimated no such thing, Kat could not help but wonder if they blamed her.

She began noticing news stories that she had skimmed over before, stories about Jamaican gangs that controlled the sale of cocaine in the boroughs of New York. They had a reputation for being more dangerous than the mob, perhaps even more ruthless than the Chinese triads. There was one story in the *Post* that she cut out and stuck on her refrigerator with a magnet. Though it hurt her to look at it every day, she could not make herself take it down.

NEW FORM OF TORTURE?

A slaying in Queens has been linked to the John Wayne Posse, a Jamaican gang associated with the PNP, or People's National Party. The PNP was founded in Jamaica in 1938 as a democratic party for workers, but was later tarnished by relations with Castro's Cuba and more recently by associations with the crack cocaine trade.

Orlando Washington, 23, formerly of Kingston, was found dead in an abandoned warehouse in Queens. Washington, an alleged crack dealer for a rival posse, appeared to have been bludgeoned to death after being tortured with a nail gun.

Peter Crowther and Tracy Knight
CIRCLING THE DRAIN

Dawn arrived as a razor ripping Frank Percival's universe, cleaving away the callous of numbing sleep, splitting open the cocoon of unknowing. He opened his eyes and a taut grimace immediately stretched his 63-year-old cheeks.

"Maybe today," he whispered, his words sitting uncomfortably on the early morning stillness.

Frank's wife Mattie came into the room, delivering more silence to the silence that already had expanded into the farthest flung corners and the myriad nooks and crannies where, oblivious to the long drawn-out drama that was Frank Percival's departure from life, only an occasional spider held domain.

With a pained indifference, Frank watched his wife doing things: picking up magazines from the floor beside his bed, moving glasses—of which there were always many—out of the room and onto the bureau in the hallway, picking up Frank's robe from across the foot of the bed and straightening it out before throwing it back to pretty much the same place.

Actions performed on autopilot, Frank thought, when the brain was elsewhere: Wondering. Dreaming. Hoping. He labored to resurrect those long-lost brain functions, if for only a fleeting moment. But alas, the organism that was Frank Percival had no need for them, nor would it ever again.

It was as though Mattie were mentally attuned to him, sensing when he had just awoken, bustling into his room with the well-meant shuffle and orderliness that characterized all good attendants to the terminally sick. But that shuffle was markedly slower now, he had noticed over the days. Even though his vision was beclouded, it was clear enough to see the deadening strain his illness was having on her.

Mattie's hair, once carefully coiffured and colored, held thick streaks of dead gray and lay disheveled on her head. Deep wrinkles of worry fringed her mouth and eyes. She walked to his bedside. If Frank squinted hard enough, he could still see the pert beauty, the glowing, petite facial features that had first drawn him to Mattie those decades ago.

"Sit up, Frank," she said, her voice instructive but weary. "Let me straighten things out a little."

His sigh was informed as much by disappointment as by resignation.

"Maybe today," Frank repeated, leaning forward in his bed-prison, trembling against the shackles of pain and enfeeblement that had contained him so steadfastly these past three months.

He stifled a yawning moan as Mattie plumped up his pillows. It had become so that almost any movement around him, even of the air, caused Frank pain. Rapidly growing tumors have a way of leeching away life while geometrically multiplying pain, step by torturous step.

The tumor started every day rubbing itself in excitement, ignoring the steadily increasing ruin of Frank Percival's tainted insides, looking around at all the good stuff still to be consumed: liver, kidneys, lungs, stomach, colon, bowels, intestines . . . so much still to do and so little time left in which to do it!

It was a steady march—much too slow for Frank's tastes—toward beckoning darkness.

"Oh, tush!" Mattie smoothed the freshened linen around her husband, giving a tug here and yank there, and tucked the sides beneath the mattress, her every movement jerky and tense. "You start each day with 'Maybe today,' and end it with 'Maybe tomorrow.' I'm doing the best I can to care for you, Frank. Even if you don't care about yourself, it'd help my spirits if you didn't waste every moment wishing you were dead."

Anger roiled up within him, a blistering lump in his gut that sat snugly beside the three-pound tumor. "Listen, Mattie," he said, voice strained and trembling, "You're not the one going through this. *I* am. So if you can't underst—"

"Although you may have forgotten this," she said, looking him straight in the eyes, her own eyes shining with tears, "I didn't give you the tumor. You needn't make our days more painful than they already are."

"*Our* days?" Frank said. "You don't care," he added, more to hurt her than to express any real truth.

Mattie didn't say anything and Frank immediately felt guilty for having been so cruel. This wasn't him. This wasn't the relationship he'd enjoyed with Mattie. It was the tumor talking.

Frank looked deep inside himself and thought he glimpsed it, just for an instant, ducking behind a half-eaten, gray and glistening piece of bowel ducting that looked for all the world like a vacuum cleaner's concertinaed tubing. He thought he saw its malevolent Jack Nicholson stare'n'smile as it took another chomp at his guts, pulling the flesh free and throwing its head back to flip it into its mouth.

How he wished he could float away from Mattie and leave her before he'd hurt her any more.

Three months ago, Frank had been in his twenty-third year as Administrator of the local Office of Public Aid, the county welfare agency, when the cramps and pain—sometimes so severe as to blind him temporarily—had begun. Dr. Sachs, the oncologist, had studied the test results and the X-rays with a mixture of embarrassed regret at having to break the bad news and the understandable fascination of a medical man when confronted with an interesting specimen.

The prognosis was not good: Frank had three months to live.

Even with the chemotherapy that had rendered him frail and hairless, and the steroids that had swollen his body to the point it seemed ready to burst, the estimate was the same. The tumor sat on Frank Percival's gut like Humpty Dumpty. At times, the morphine took the spiny edge off his pain, but only that. Pain had become Frank's constant traveling companion; Death the inevitable destination. For Frank, the bus couldn't move fast enough.

Mattie walked to the window and pulled back the curtain.

"Oh," she said, suddenly lifting a hand to her throat, "what a beautiful morning. I think spring is finally here. Life is blooming all around. I wish you could see this, Frank."

To Frank's eyes the light seemed to enter the room in stages, illuminating small sections in isolation, as if ensuring that each individual task was satisfactorily completed before it moved on. He blinked three times and then narrowed his eyes. For a few moments it had seemed as though a shadow had coalesced in front of the old wardrobe, like a clotting of the air or a gathering storm cloud that had had second thoughts.

But after the third blink Frank saw that there was nothing.

"Now," Mattie announced, turning to Frank, her face darkened in silhouette. "What would you like for breakfast?" She tried to make the prospect sound enticing, or at least of vague interest.

"How about a pile of flapjacks and your telephone number, Babycakes?" a voice said off to Frank's right. Then there was a croaking chuckle that was quickly joined by several others.

"Wha. . . ?" Frank started to reply to the disembodied voice, then stopped himself. Another miniature thunderhead churned in his peripheral vision. He turned—even this simple movement producing turbulent pain—and searched for the origin of the voice but everywhere was as it always was . . . but, no . . . there seemed to be tiny spots in the room, presumably caused by the meeting up of swirling dust created by his wife's ministrations and the sudden intrusion of the sunlight, small places where the light didn't seem to penetrate.

"Are you okay, honey?" Mattie asked.

Frank closed his eyes for a moment and then opened them again. Just for a second there, he had thought he could see someone in the corner of the room, leaning against the side of the window, alongside the curtains, but that was nonsense. There was only Mattie and him in there and, given his present condition, that barely amounted to one-and-a-half people. He blinked against the sunlight. There was nothing there. Great: Now he was *seeing* things. Undoubtedly the tumor was now sending out metastasizing tendrils everywhere it could, even to burrow into and contaminate his visual cortex. As if the prospect of dying a hairless, distended caricature of himself wasn't enough torture, now the possibility that he would die a howling madman was cruelly taunting him.

"I don't care, Mattie," he said tiredly, attempting to thrust this new insight aside. "Breakfast doesn't matter."

"You should, you know, honey," Mattie said, tilting her head on one side, trying not to sound like she was ordering him. She smiled and for a fleeting moment looked twenty-three years old again. Sweet, open to the world, so full of promise. "The doctor said—"

"Mattie, I feel like I'm going to throw up, my guts are on fire, I have a headache and I need to use the bathroom . . . which means I have to sit on that goddam pan again and have you wipe my ass like I'm a baby." He let his head fall back onto the pillows and stared at the ceiling. "Now," he went on, lowering his voice, "just how hungry do you really think I feel?"

Frank didn't see or hear her leave but when he looked up she had gone.

"Way to go, Frankie," said a voice. This time there was no humor in it and the accompanying voices offered their assent only in short grunts. "Alienate the one person who cares about you before you hurtle out of the world. What a guy!"

When he turned to the window, the darkness at the side was back, and this time it was clearer. Slowly, it assumed a human form, the stormy darkness of its edges giving way to a patchwork of colors . . . then to the shape of a man. As the colorful outline filled in, Frank saw that it was an elderly man wearing a brown tuxedo, his teeth shining out of a broad smile in a coal-black face.

Death!

Jesus Christ, Death was a black man!

Frank felt a frisson of fear coupled with a strange excitement. He felt like he should smooth down his sheets, like he should have combed his hair at least—it must be all over the place. He reached up to tidy it and winced at the pain across his chest. This was it: heart attack.

"I'm going," Frank said, immediately wondering whether that should have been 'coming.' "I've been waiting for you," he added weakly.

The man's bulldog face held the most curious expression, his lips curled into a sneering smile even while his forehead and thick, single eyebrow were wrenched into something that could have been either ambivalent hatred or casual disinterest. The image reached up with its still-blurry hand and pressed the side of its fist against its lips, clearing its throat.

"You're waiting for *me*, Frank?" the figure asked, his voice husky and deep. "How'd you know I was coming, for Chrissakes?"

"Well . . ." Frank was taken aback. Did he need to point it out? Death certainly was an insensitive schmuck. "You know . . . I'm *dying.*"

"Mm hmm. And?"

Frank squinted, dropped his head to one side and stared. Death's face suddenly seemed familiar. "Wait a minute. Joe? Joe Marshall? Is that you?"

The man chuckled. "You didn't know? Who'd you think I was?"

"I thought . . . I thought you were Death."

Frank closed his eyes to the sound of gentle laughter.

In the darkness within his head, Frank's brain began inserting memories of Joe Marshall, the man who had been custodian at the office even before Frank took the Administrator's position. The memories tottered and tumbled out of the shadows, rearing up in front of him like papers blown by the wind against the windshield, with each time he recognized one the image being blown away to be replaced by another. And each remembrance brought with it a legion of sideroads that Frank's mind strolled up partway for a look-see.

Opening his eyes, he said, "Well, why *did* you come? Am I getting close?"

"Close to what, honey?" Mattie asked.

Frank looked around and saw that the room was empty over beside the window. He frowned and tried to sit up. "Where did he—"

Mattie placed a tray on the dresser across the room and turned around to face him. There was no mistaking the concern on her face. "Where's what, Frank? You lose something?"

He watched her follow his eyes and then turn back to him.

"You okay?"

Suddenly it was as if the last of his strength had been depleted. He fell back onto the pillow, closed his eyes, and let all his breath escape, every last bit of it, silently hoping that at long last this might be his final breath.

He waited.

Another breath came.

Maybe this one . . .

Another.

"I'm fine," he said, "really."

"Well, that's good," Mattie announced. She turned back to the tray and Frank heard crockery knocking and something being poured. He smelled fresh coffee. "I know you said you didn't want anything, honey, but I went ahead and brought it anyway. Coffee and fresh croissants." She held out her arms, her left hand holding a mug of steaming coffee and the right one a plate.

"Fresh?"

"Uh huh. I went down to the bakery."

Mattie walked across and rested the plate on the bedside table. "Saw Phyllis. You remember Phyllis Loganmire? Her husband Bob works at the hardware store over on Sycamore?"

Frank was trying to think, staring into the corner, waiting for Joe Marshall to grin across at him again out of that old black face.

"Anyway, she asked how you were getting along and I said you—"

Frank shook his head and stopped Mattie in mid-sentence. "When? When did you do all this?"

"Why, just now, honey. I went out right after . . . you know . . ." She waved a hand toward Frank's middle. "Right after I'd cleaned you up."

"Cleaned me up? Cleaned me up when?"

"After you'd used the bedpan, Frank."

"I used the bedpan this morning?"

Frank concentrated, eyes closed again. Doing a quick internal reconnoitre of his insides, he was surprised to discover that the feeling of needing to empty his bowels had disappeared.

He opened his eyes again, prepared to reach out and clutch his wife's hands, to ask her where time was going, where *he* was going . . . to ask her to forgive him for whatever forgotten sins might be lingering in his wake, to make everything okay again.

But she was gone, and it seemed to Frank that he heard the front door gently close.

Light twinkled at the foot of his bed and once again Joe Marshall stood there, arms crossed over his chest. His smile shimmered with the same sad rhythm as his body.

Shaking his head in pity, Joe said, "It's sad, ain't it, Frank? Now you can't even relish a good shit. When a fella can't enjoy voiding himself of gas and solids, and all the collateral satisfaction of the process, I'd say it's time to wave bye-bye, don't you, pardner? Time to switch off the lights and put up the old CLOSED sign."

Frank felt tears well up in his eyes and spill down his cheeks. "Joe," he said. "Help me, Joe."

" Help you what?"

"Help me to die."

Joe slapped his translucent cheeks in exaggerated disbelief. "Listen to you. You're asking the man who was the janitor in your office until he keeled over into a dumpster one icy winter night to help you die. Help you die? Listen, Frank, this is the first time I've been shoved down here to do anything like this. I'm not sure I know what to do. But I do know that you don't need any help to die. Jeez, you should've died at least two weeks ago, best as I can tell."

"Why didn't I then? Why can't I?"

The spectre of Joe Marshall shrugged and his eyes danced with diamond-like flickers of golden light. "That's the question, ain't it? Dying's no harder than letting loose of a rope. Letting go. And it's not like you're not experiencing enough pain to encourage you to shuffle off your mortal coil. What do you need, Frankie baby, an engraved invitation?"

"I *want* to die. I *do*," Frank said, feeling another tear trickling down his swollen right cheek.

"Those are your words, Frankie. But it looks to me like you're still lying right there in that plumped-up excuse of a body. Like I said, all you have to do is let go of the rope. C'mon!"

"Help me," Frank whispered. "Please."

"Sorry, Frank. As gifted a janitor as I was, dying is one mess you have to clean up yourself. That's just the way it is. That's the way it's always been."

Frank clenched his eyes shut and tightened his jaw muscles until they mushroomed with pain. Inwardly he instructed himself, "It's time. Go."

He felt his hot, swollen fingers clutching the cold sheets of his bed. And he waited.

"Frank?"

He opened his eyes.

The wavering figure of Joe Marshall had his fists pressed to his hips. "I'm waiting, Frankie. Look, it's not happening. C'mon, tell me what you need, what you need to know, what you need to happen. You're inches away, compadre.

"You got a tumor in your belly the size of Clinton's libido, your cells have split more times than they can count and just about the only part of your sorry body that ain't all curled up and looking to settle up and check out for parts unknown is your pecker and the only reason it's standing up that way is the artery that feeds it has collapsed and the blood has nowhere to retreat. It'll go black and gangrenous in a day or two . . . but that should be a day or two after you've gone. So, tell me, what can I do to help?"

Before Frank had the opportunity to respond, the morning silence was shattered by a sudden shrieking, a grating, grinding, piercing high-pitched note that seemed to come from outside, from everywhere.

"Oh, no," Joe Marshall whispered as he scudded to the bedroom window and peered outside.

"What is it?" Frank asked.

"Locusts. It's a damned sign."

"Of what?"

Joe floated to Frank's bedside. He almost had to shout to be heard above the buzzing roar of the cicadas. "It's an alarm, Frank, I don't know exactly how to explain it to you. But now I know why I was forced back to this plane. You're . . . not dying. That's what the alarm is about. It doesn't happen very often. But . . . here we are."

For a moment, Frank's curiosity almost overpowered his pain. "Because I haven't died, there's an alarm? That causes locusts to cry?"

"Yes. Now quick, Frank." Joe reached down as if he wanted to grab Frank's arm and shake him to his senses. But of course, being a spectre, he could do no such thing. "Tell me what you need so's you can die."

Frank sent an internal searchlight into the deepest caverns of his mind, looking for something, anything, that might answer his and Joe's question, that might release him, that might set the world right again.

Finally he said, "I always thought that I'd be called to heaven . . . by Jesus. That's what the people who almost die say when they come back, right?"

"Good enough," said Joe, taking his place at the foot of Frank's bed and raising his face toward the ceiling. "Say no more."

It was as though Joe Marshall were a forgotten candle. His features melted, and were replaced.

Frank looked up to see the visage of Jesus, the same Jesus he'd seen in the painting in his parents' bedroom growing up, or in the hallway of his childhood church. Flowing brown hair, nicely trimmed beard, and beatific blue eyes that shone with sadness and peace.

Jesus raised his arms. His white silken robe gently fell from his wrists to his elbows.

"There, Frank," Jesus said. "This good enough? Now please . . . come with me. Walk with me through the gates of Heaven."

Another lightning bolt of pain racked Frank's body. He arched his back and cried out.

Settling back into his bed, Frank sighed deeply and said, "That's you, Joe, not Jesus. I can tell."

Jesus scrunched up his face and spread his hands, bleeding palms facing upward. "C'mon, man. What do you want? What do you think those people who almost die see? It's us cosmic peons, the janitors of

the unseen universe, helping them decide to go back when they're trying to die out of order. Order is everything, Frank. It's the *only* thing.
Just pretend that I'm Jesus, okay? Pretend and let go."

"I can't. I can't die."

As he stomped soundlessly around the room, Jesus transfigured back
into Joe Marshall: The robes became faded blue bib-and-brace overalls,
the beard became a coal-black chin as wrinkled as a turkey's gizzard,
and the Son of God's healthily flat stomach turned back into a belly so
bloated by a lifetime's intake of Budweiser that Frank imagined he could
hear the material that encased it splitting at its fleshy seams.

"Well, this is as good as it's gonna get, Frankie baby," Joe said as
the final traces of Jesus vanished. "God Hisself is not going to come
down and take care of this. Hell, I haven't even seen Him. From the
scuttlebutt I've heard, he wandered away eons ago and lost his way
back. That leaves Earth, humans, death, all the mortal things, to us.

"Now c'mon, you have to tell me what you need. Is it guilt? Do you
feel guilt? And if'n you do, what about? Breaking the heart of your high
school sweetheart? Telling your co-worker's wife that he was cheating
on her and thus helping him decide to commit suicide? Speeding off the
road to hit that cat on purpose when you were in college?"

"How do you know all that?"

"Your life is an open book, Frank," Joe said, "though I wish that
weren't the case. It's a mite boring, to be truthful."

"I just. . . I just don't know. I can't understand. I've had a loving
marriage, a meaningful career. If I die now, I die with no dreams. That's
the secret of a fulfilled life, isn't it? Dying with no dreams?"

Nodding, Joe said, "Do you know how few people can say that
when they pass over? No more than a handful, my friend."

On either side of Joe's ghostly frame appeared small flickering orbs
of light, followed soon by identical displays in the uppermost corners
of the room, floating up and down alongside the antique dresser, bob-
bing left and right in front of the floor-length mirror.

If it were possible for a black ghost to turn pale, Joe did so.

"This. . . is serious," the old janitor said in a voice slightly trembling
with anticipation or fear, and increasing in pitch almost to the point
that it matched the single, ragged note the locusts sang.

"What is this?" Frank asked, trying to turn his swollen body to one
side to get a better look at the thickening swarm of lights.

"You've really done it now, Frank. You've stopped the death process on Earth. You've clogged the silently efficient machinery that underlies everything here . . ."

Slowly, very slowly, each of the points of light lengthened like warming dough, turned and squirmed in the air as they elaborated into human shapes of every imaginable size and shape.

"Oh my Lordy Lord," said Joe, wiping one hand back over the crown of his head, smoothing the tightly-curled black hair. "Frank, I think you're seeing something no soul has seen in years. I know I haven't. And I don't know what the hell to do about it!"

"What are they? More ghosts?"

Joe gulped. "No. These, Frank, are the spectres of the *almost* dead." Whatever expression of beatific peace that had lingered on Joe's face extinguished, and was supplanted with stark wide-eyed concern. "Congratulations! You've obstructed the death process! This is serious, Frank! No one on the earth can die until you do! Order is everything!"

"Wha—?"

"Quick, Frank, please!" Joe cried. "Tell me what you need to let go! Hell, I'd kill you myself if I could!"

The room filled with brilliantly incandescent figures who crowded Joe and shoved him left and right: a congested depot of suffering figures writhing to enter the last train leaving the station.

As Frank's weary eyes adjusted to the light, he could make out the spectres' bodies. Unlike Joe's, for the most part these bodies were not peaceful and healthy-looking. Instead, they displayed various types of injuries. There was the glowing visage of a horribly burned young woman, face liquefied into a crying skull; there was a wasted youngster with skeletal limbs, shrieking and crying firelight tears; there was an old man trying to hold his ruined skull together. The plaintive cries and screams of the assemblage threatened to drown out the piercing one-note song of the locusts.

By now Joe looked panicked. "Goddam it, Frank! You've got to help me!"

That moment, Frank realized that he felt no more pain. Perhaps his attention was so riveted by the roomful of dead and dying that he simply didn't notice, or perhaps his pain—as severe as it was—was a mere droplet in the ocean of pain represented in his crowded bedroom.

For the first time in recent memory, he smiled. "I don't hurt anymore," Frank said.

Joe leapt towards the foot of Frank's bed and began jumping up and down, thrashing his hands in some kind of holy tantrum. "Oh, great! Now there isn't even any pain to push you over the line! Somebody!" he continued. "Anybody! Help me!"

"If I may," a voice said from the back of the room. It was a quiet, measured voice, making it that much more surprising that it could even be heard amidst the violent din.

Joe wiped his brow and leapt back to the floor. "Whoever you are, come forward!"

The room continued to fill with the almost dead, shining bodies pressed against one another, most of them crying for release. Frank wondered if the room could burst from the burgeoning pressure of anxious souls.

Despite the congestion, the crowd of spectres spread out, making a narrow trail through which a small man swayed and rocked his ectoplasmic frame in a tortured attempt to reach Frank's bedside.

Frank leaned up so he could get a good view.

The man was a tangle of limbs so broken and mutilated that it was impossible to tell which belonged where. The left arm pointed backward, brushing the man's shoulder blades as it pointed to the right. The arm zigged and zagged with multiple breaks. Both of the man's legs aimed straight upward, toward the ceiling, toward heaven, so the man had to wriggle and manipulate his buttocks to move at all.

"Fell out of a window," the wobbly man said by way of explanation, a half-hearted shrug tugging at his shoulders like he was saying it might rain . . . but then again it might not.

"Hello," Frank said, unable to think of any other way to respond.

"My name's Artemus Grandling," the man said. "Call me Art. Forgive me if I don't shake hands."

"Hello, Art."

"Standing in this room . . ." Art said, "I couldn't help but absorb the facts of your life as they whirl around us all. And let me tell you, Frank Percival, you have enjoyed a good, productive existence . . ."

"I agree," Frank said, "but—"

"*But* is right. There is one large fissure in your life, a hole that you became so accustomed to you no longer noticed it's a hole at all. I think that's your—and our—answer."

The mystery of his own failure to die was now as intriguing to Frank as it was frustrating to Joe Marshall. "Tell me," Frank whispered.

Art turned his head upward and scratched his chin with his good right hand while his other hand spasmed up and down behind him. "Somewhere, deep inside you, Frank, you resist dying because you recognize that in doing so, you'll leave a mere space in the world that will soon be filled up by other lives. The parade will close around that space and march on just as it always has. Like all of us, you want to be more than just a statistic, an object lesson to others, an identity that fades like yesterday's clouds. Like all of us, you want your life to have meant something. You want to live on."

"I *do*?" Even as he said it, Frank realized it was true and he nodded. "I do."

"Everyone has their own way of living on, and most would say that you will live on in all the people you helped in your profession, all the people upon whose tables you helped set food, all the children who had clothing because you secretly handed their mothers some cash when they came to your office awaiting welfare. The planet is different, better, because you walked on it. But—"

"But what?"

"For whatever reason that isn't enough for you, now that you're here at the precipice where life meets death. Somewhere at the core of your being, you know that an opportunity existed that would have allowed for immortality but you let it slip away."

"Cut to the chase!" Joe interrupted, then cleared his throat. "Sorry."

For the first time since he became visible to Frank, Artemus Grandling looked perturbed. In fact, he tried to kick Joe in his butt, but his tangled legs only drifted left and right in the air behind him, like semaphore flags.

"Easily done," Art finally said in that same gentle voice. "Progeny."

Joe Marshall frowned. "Who's *he*?"

"You never had a child, Frank," Artemus Grandling continued.

"Now, hold on," Frank said. "Mattie and I decided—"

Art shook his head and smiled. "Not true, and you know that, Frank. *You* decided. Mattie, sweet companion that she is, merely acceded to your wishes. She wanted to be your best friend, your constant supporter, and she's still demonstrating that today, in every way possible. But she wanted a child, Frank. You know that, deep down. Furthermore, now that you're ready to move onward and outward, you realize—though perhaps you can't or don't articulate it—that you do, too."

Frank was speechless, trying to let it all sink in.

"Somewhere inside you, Frank, you realize that once you're gone, there will be no one on the earth to effect the little verbal mannerisms that have become the way you express yourself; no one who will posture himself or move the way you do—not exactly the way you do—when he sits; no one who will laugh in the unique way you laugh; no one who will dispense the same nuggets of wisdom and insight that you collected in your life and never had the opportunity to hand over to a littler human. In short, there is no one who will give quiet, unrecognized evidence that you were ever alive. No immortality. When you die, therefore . . . you just die. You disappear."

Frank was surprised to find tears streaming down his cheeks.

Art smiled sympathetically. "I'm right, aren't I?"

Frank shrugged. "I think . . . I think maybe you are."

Joe Marshall dramatically swept his arms wide apart. "Well, there we have it! Now come on, Frank. Insight equals change. Recognize that you flubbed up this one thing and let's go!"

"Not so fast," Art said. "Once a need is recognized, one must fill it in some way if at all possible."

"Why?" Joe demanded. "I certainly croaked with more than my share of unmet needs. What makes Frank so dad-blasted special?"

"Maybe because he doesn't feel fulfilled at all. Not at all. Not even the tiniest scintilla of fulfillment," Art said. "But he *is* fulfilled. We all are." He looked at Frank and Frank felt the man's eyes boring deep into him, so deep that he wanted to close those eye-windows and stop this strange, grotesquely twisted and deformed man staring into his soul.

"And now all we have to do is help him realize that," Artemus Grandling said. "Because, Frank, you're a special man."

"I'll second that!" The sharp voice came from the corner of the room and the countless entities turned their glowing heads at once to ascertain the source of the cry. Even Art, for whom head-turning was a formidable task.

The roomful of glowing entities once again fanned out, making a narrow path lit only by the midmorning daylight.

Mattie walked in, tears rushing down her face.

"Mattie!" Frank exclaimed. "You can see all this?"

"Yes, Frank," Mattie said.

Joe scowled. "We've got to be breaking all sorts of cosmic rules here."

Ignoring the old janitor, Mattie rushed over to her husband's bed and knelt beside him. "I saw it in you, Frank, all along, although you never spoke of it," she said, taking his clasped hands in hers. "You always wanted a little one. You knew how good a mother I'd be, how good a father you'd be, how much we both had to teach a child."

"I . . . I know," Frank said, stuttering with the tears. "I did. I knew that . . . knew it even then. I . . . I don't know why—" He leaned forward and cried into his hands. "I think maybe I was frightened."

Mattie wrapped her arms around Frank, hugging him tightly and kissing him repeatedly on the cheeks. "I love you so much, Frank!"

It felt wondrous to be hugged and kissed with no attendant pain. Frank reveled in the closeness with the woman he had adored for so many years. "I love you, too, sweet Mattie."

"I wish I had an answer for you," she said, the words pressing against Frank's cheek. "I wish that so much."

Art piped up, "I think *I* might have an answer for you."

Frank and Mattie looked toward the tangled man. Expectancy shone from their eyes.

In a disgusted tone, Joe Marshall said, "If you're wanting him to be carried out onto the street where he can impregnate a passerby, I think that's one too many steps over the line, pretzel-man."

From the look in Art's eyes, it was clear that he wanted to punch Joe in the nose . . . if only he had functional limbs.

"The idea is simple," Art said. "Back where I was standing in the corner, there was a young mother and her newborn. They both died during childbirth . . . or I should say, they're both *trying* to die."

"And . . . ?" the word was spoken simultaneously by Joe, Frank and Mattie.

"The child needs to know what life is like, since it's something he's not going to experience," Art said. "Of course, his mother could tell him—but I think I know someone here who would get more out of it, someone who would love nothing more than to teach a child what life is about, and what it means."

Joe bent down and gave Art a playful punch to his shoulder, almost knocking the tangled man to the floor. "You're a genius, Artemus," he said.

"I don't get it," Frank said.

Art turned his head toward the back of the room. "Madam?"

For the third time a path was created by the assembled dying and a small, young scared woman walked forward, a tiny baby in her arms.

"Please," Artemus said. "Hand the baby to Frank."

The young woman hesitated. "I was going to do it myself," she said.

Art nodded. "I think Frank's need is even greater than yours," he said.

But still the young woman held back.

"Don't worry," Art said. "You'll have him back. You'll journey together with your child when Frank sets us all free."

"It's a her," the woman said. "Her name's Hope. Hope Engleman." Then, slowly, she handed the baby to Frank.

Mattie plumped Frank's pillows so he could sit up and cradle the baby properly. Then, seeing that it still wouldn't be enough, Mattie crawled onto the bed, situating herself behind Frank, one leg on either side of him so he could lean back against her as he held the baby girl.

The child's body felt cool and malleable, as though Frank could take its tiny, blue-tinged fingers and mold them like clay into something else . . . something altogether different. Perhaps even into his own daughter. He looked up at Artemus Grandling.

"Tell her," Art said. "Tell her what life is like, Frank."

"Then we can all be on our way," Joe added.

Lying in bed, being cradled by Mattie, Frank gently held the baby girl, who looked up into his eyes. He could barely hold in his tears. "I don't know where to start," he said.

Mattie kissed the back of his head and whispered into his ear. "Start from the beginning, honey," she said.

And so Frank took a deep breath and began to speak. As the minutes spread out into hours, in a soft and almost singalong whisper, he told Hope Engleman what a summer breeze felt like on your cheeks and how wildflowers smelled when their scents danced in spring. He recalled for her the feeling of a scraped knee and of a mother blowing away Mercurochrome heat; the sensation of riding a bicycle on a damp autumn street; the sweet perfumes of mown grass and burning leaves. He explained the taste of good foods, the ache of first love and the dominating fullness that came with compassion.

The baby smiled and nodded with every word Frank uttered.

Soon the three of them—Mattie, Frank and even little Hope Engleman—were all crying and laughing as Frank painted, as well as any human can, a portrait of life.

The sussurant excited mutter from the almost-dead subsided even as it began, and the locusts fell silent, burrowing back into the earth until the next crisis.

"I think I'm done," Frank said, his voice sounding tired. "I have nothing more to tell her."

"I think you're right, Frank." Artemus Grandling nodded for the young woman to retrieve her child.

For just the faintest flicker of an eye, an additional shadowy figure seemingly attempted to materialize even as the others were growing indistinct. Then, Joe Marshall and Artemus Grandling and the young mother—who had never told anyone her name—and the child she had called Hope and even the new figure all grew hazy and faint and then, slowly and almost imperceptibly, they faded away completely, leaving only their smiles behind for the briefest of moments before they, too, disappeared.

"Frank?" Mattie said from behind her husband.

There was no response.

She cradled her husband's head and wept tears of joy and grief . . . but mostly, though she would have found it hard to explain, of contentment.

"You're a wonderful father, Frank Percival," she whispered, kissing him for one last time.

Outside the window, the world nodded in silent sunlit agreement.

Graham Masterton
SPIRITS OF THE AGE

ichael was sitting in Prince Albert's writing room when he thought that he could hear a woman sobbing. He sat up straight and listened. It was very faint, as if she had her face buried in a pillow, and after a few seconds it died away altogether, so that he couldn't be sure that he had heard it at all.

Outside, it was a blustery day, and for all its opulence Osborne House was notoriously drafty, especially when there were North Easterlies blowing across the Solent.

It could have been nothing but the wind, whining down one of the chimneys. It could have been water, quietly gurgling through the miles of elaborate nineteenth-century plumbing. But he stayed quite still, listening, and in the gilt-framed mirror over the fireplace his reflection listened, too—pale-faced, his glass tilted and his hair sticking up at the back.

After a long pause he went back to tapping at his laptop. It didn't take much to distract him. He was working as a research assistant for Buller & Haig, the art publishers, who were planning to bring out a lavish coffee-table book on all of Prince Albert's gardens. It wasn't the kind of job that Michael had ever wanted to do. He had left Middlesex university with a second-class English degree and ambitions of being a magazine journalist, the new Tom Wolfe, all coruscating adjectives and supercilious satire. But as one rejection followed another, it began to dawn on him that his entire university career had left him over-educated and out of touch. Magazines didn't want literary wasps any more. They wanted New Lads who told it like it was, with f*** in every other sentence.

The morning that his rejection letter from *Vanity Fair* arrived in the post, his girlfriend Sam called him to say that she was sorry, but she was leaving him for a Nigerian actor called Osibi with tribal scars on his face.

"He understands my *aura*," she said, as if that explained everything, and put the phone down. He hadn't been to the Isle of Wight since he was eight. All he could remember was catching tiny green crabs in a bucket and peeing in the sea. But when his university friend Richard Buller had offered him this small research job at Osborne House, he had realized that it was just what he needed. Although the island was only a twenty-minute ferry journey away from Portsmouth, and was actually in sight of the mainland, it was strangely dislocated from the rest of England. It didn't just belong in the sixties, it belonged in some other sixties that had never happened anywhere else, except within the imaginations of retired folk who wore beige cardigans and lived in pebble-dashed bungalows called "Meadhurst," as well as a few hippies with odd burring accents and mongrels on the end of a string. A community with a tenuous grip on reality.

But Michael badly needed to convalesce, and to concentrate on something other than his stalled ambitions and his lacerated emotions, and the Isle of Wight was the very best place to do it.

Queen Victoria had fallen in love with the island's detachment, too. She had built Osborne House here between 1845-51 as a country retreat where she and her family could be free from state ceremonial. It was a huge, sand-colored building with two Italian-style *campanile*. It was surrounded by woods and gardens, most of them planted and laid out by Prince Albert himself, and to the east, it looked along a broad stretch of open land directly to the sea.

Usually, Osborne was filled with shuffling lines of white-haired sightseers, but it was off-season now, and Michael almost felt that the house belonged to him alone. There was a home for retired servicemen in the Household Wing, and occasionally one of them would wheel past him and raise a walking-stick in salute, but sometimes he could go for days on end and see nobody at all except a distant gardener tending a fire.

Some days, bored with his work, he would wander from one room to another, each of them overwhelmingly decorated in high Victorian Gothic, with gilded and molded ceilings and gilt-encrusted furniture and chandeliers made to look like giant convolvuluses climbing out a basket. He found the Durbar Room especially overbearing. It was the state banqueting room, designed in the Indian style by Rudyard Kipling's father Lockwood and a craftsman from Lahore, Bal Ram Singh. It had a deeply coffered ceiling, like the inside of a temple, and for some rea-son Michael always felt uneasy there, as if he were intruding on a cul-ture that was not his own, as if he should take off his shoes.

It echoed, because it was empty of furniture, but it had strange dead places where it didn't echo at all.

Michael liked Albert's writing-room, though, where he was usually allowed to work. It was a modest size, with Adam green walls and early Renaissance paintings on the wall, as well as a portrait of Albert and his brother Ernest. Albert's presence was still remarkably strong. Ev-erything around had been invented by him or designed by him, from Queen Victoria's shower to the fastidious engraving of Osborne House on his notepaper, of which there was still a great deal left.

Sometimes Michael found himself talking to Albert as if he knew him.

"God, you made a bloody fuss over that *magnolia grandiflora*, didn't you, Bertie? And those myrtles. And all that special Kentish mulch."

It especially amused him when he found out that Albert's idea of hands-on garden "planting" involved him standing on top of one of the *campanile*, directing his gardeners by semaphore.

❖

It was mid-December, and by three o'clock in the afternoon it was starting to grow dark. Michael decided to call it a day and go into Cowes to do some shopping. He didn't need much: bread, milk, and a newspa-per. He packed up his laptop, but as he did so he was sure that he heard that sobbing sound again, and this time it was very much clearer.

He listened for a while, and then he called out, "Hallo? Is anybody there?"

There was no reply, but the sobbing persisted. He walked across the swirly-patterned carpet to the door which led to the Queen's sitting-room. This had a semi-circular bay with tall windows that led to a bal-cony. There were no lights on, and the only illumination came from the pearly-colored fog outside.

"Hallo?" Michael repeated, but now the sobbing seemed to have stopped.

He walked cautiously into the room and looked around. In the cen-ter were two desks where Victoria and Albert sat side by side. Both desks were cluttered with framed portraits and memorabilia. On the side of the Queen's desk were three electric bell-pulls: one to summon Miss Skerrett, her dresser; another to call for a page; and a third to bring in Prince Albert's personal attendant. Michael pulled each one of them in turn, but of course nobody came.

Except that he heard someone walking across the Queen's dressing-room, next door. There was no mistaking it. A quick, furtive rustling sound.

He opened the door and he was just in time to see a black figure disappearing through the door into the Queen's bedroom. At least he thought it was a figure. It could have been nothing more than a shadow.

He hesitated for a moment, and then he went into the bedroom. There was nobody there. But as he walked around the high-canopied bed, he saw that one side of the pale, embroidered bedspread had been rumpled, as if somebody had been sitting on it. On the bedhead hung a pocket for the Prince Consort's watch, and a posthumous portrait of him, which Victoria had kept in every residence, so that she could touch his dear dead face before she slept.

Michael straightened the bedcover. He didn't know why. He looked into the corridor outside the bedroom just to make sure that there was nobody there. He even went out into the stairwell, where two flights of marble stairs led down to the floor below. A distorted, echoing voice reached up to him, and footsteps, but when he looked over the cast-iron railings he saw that it was only one of the cleaners.

He walked to the main entrance to catch the bus. The fog was much thicker now, and all the myrtle and laurel bushes hunched in the gloom. The only sound was the crunch of his footsteps on the gravel path, and the mournful cry of foghorns from the Solent.

He was passing the red-brick wall around the kitchen garden when he thought he heard somebody else's footsteps. He stopped, and listened, but there was nothing but silence. It must have been the echo of his own footsteps against the wall.

He walked a little further, and he thought he heard the footsteps again, off to the right, toward the little octagonal summerhouse where Victoria's children sometimes used to have their supper. He glimpsed a triangular black shape disappearing behind the summerhouse, so quickly that he couldn't be sure what it was. A dog? A badger? Or somebody trailing a black sack behind them?

"Hallo?" he called, uncertainly. There was no reply, only the lost and distant moan of the Portsmouth ferry. "Hallo?" he called again.

He circled around to the front of the summerhouse. It was so dark that at first he couldn't see if there was anyone there. He approached it cautiously, and saw that the doors were five or six inches ajar. He had never seen them open before: the public wasn't allowed inside. Maybe it was a squatter, or a drunk, or somebody who needed some shelter for the night.

He climbed the first two steps and then he stopped, his skin prickling like nettle-rash.

There *was* someone there. A small figure dressed in black, with a black hood over her head, and a face as pale as a lamp. Michael couldn't see her very well. She seemed to be blurry, like a figure seen through greasy glass. She didn't appear to be frightened of him, though. She stood still and silent, and he couldn't even tell if she was aware of his presence or not. But there was something about her that seriously unsettled him. Some coldness. But it was more than coldness. It was an aura of complete self-possession, as if she were unafraid of anything, or anybody.

"Are you—do you need some help?" he asked her. She didn't reply. It was hard for him to say how old she was. Pretty old, he guessed, by her small, stooped figure. But she could have been a dwarf, or a little child, or something else altogether.

"Are you lost? I can help you find your way out of here."

"Not lost," she said, in a small, dry voice. "*Lost*."

"This is off-season. They don't have visitors here till Easter."

"*Who* has no visitors?"

"They. The English Heritage people."

There was a long pause—so long that Michael wondered if she were ever going to speak again.

"Lost," she repeated. "I expected to find him here."

"I'm sorry. You expected to find *who* here?"

"This *is* the year two thousand, isn't it?" she asked him.

"That's right. December 16, 2000."

"And the world has made many great advances, in the past hundred years? In science, in medicine, in saving human lives?"

"I'm sorry," said Michael. "I don't understand."

He could hear the little figure breathing, but no vapor came out of her nostrils, not like his. "We *have* found a cure for the typhoid fever?" she asked.

"Well, yes, as far as I know."

"And has the way been found to galvanize the dead?"

"I'm sorry?"

"Has the way been discovered to restore the human heartbeat through electrical shock?"

"Well, yes."

"Then where is he? I was assured that he would be here."

Michael said, "I think we'd better find somebody to help you."

"I don't require help," she said, in obvious distress. "I just want *him*."

"If I knew who you were talking about—" Michael began.

She stepped through the five-inch gap in the doors without opening them any wider. Even outside, her face was white and indistinct. "I . . . was assured," she said. "I was *assured* that by the end of the twentieth century, all diseases would have been cured, and that the deceased could be cured of those diseases from which they had expired, and brought back to life."

Michael tried to take hold of her elbow, but his hand seemed to pass through it like a velvet curtain. He was beginning to feel seriously alarmed now; and the fog didn't help; nor the utter silence. Even the foghorns seemed to have stopped.

"Listen, why don't you come back to the house? Perhaps we can call somebody for you? A daughter, maybe? Do you have any daughters?"

"I have to stay here. I can't go anywhere until I find him. He *must* be here. I was assured."

"Who assured you?"

"Abdul Karim, my *Munshi*. He said that he could foretell everything that would happen in the future. He said that people would be able to send their spirits flying around the world while their bodies remained in bed. He said that we would all be able to cure our loved ones, and bring them back to life, just the way they were. Living, breathing, laughing! The way that Albert used to laugh!"

"*Albert?*" said Michael. "You've come here, expecting to find *Albert?* Albert died 139 years ago."

She looked up at him, and he could feel the cold electricity of disapproval. "The Prince Consort built this house. His heart was here; and this is where Abdul Karim promised me that he and I would one day be reunited."

"Reunited?" said Michael, shaking his head. "You and Albert are going to be *reunited?*"

"Don't you understand who I am?" she demanded. "Has a hundred years erased my memory so completely?"

"I know who you are," said Michael, reassuringly. "You're Queen Victoria, that's who you are. Now, why don't you let me walk you back to the main gate and you and me can talk on the bus up to Cowes."

The small woman said nothing. But then she lowered her head and uttered a single sob of anguish, and turned around. She passed back through the doors of the summerhouse, and into the darkness of the summerhouse itself.

Michael followed her, flinging the doors open wider. The summerhouse was empty. He went all the way around it, feeling the walls, looking for any way in which the woman could have escaped. In the end he stood in the middle of it, his hand clamped over his mouth, wondering if he were starting to go mad.

❖

Abdul Karim had come to Osborne in 1887—first as a servant, and then as Queen Victoria's personal Indian Secretary. There was a fine painting of him in the Durbar Corridor. He was suave, handsome, with hooded eyes and a neatly-trimmed beard and moustache. Michael stared at him for a long time; but Abdul Karim had his eyes averted, and always would.

That evening, back in his room at the top of the Household Wing, Michael combed the Internet for all the information that he could find about Queen Victoria and her Indian servants. There was very little about Abdul Karim, even though he had been a minor celebrity famous in his time. But there was one book: *Queen Victoria's Mystic*, by Charles Lutterworth, brought out in a limited edition in 1987 by the Vectis Press—a small specialist publisher with an address in West Cowes.

Michael didn't sleep well that night. He kept seeing the summerhouse doors opening, and a pale lamp-like face watching from the darkness within. At 3:20 in the morning, his bedroom door opened, and he sat bolt upright in bed, his heart clamped with alarm. He went cautiously over to the door and opened it wider, and looked out, and he thought he saw a small dark shadow disappearing down the end of the corridor.

He closed his door and locked it. He lay back in his cold sweat-tangled bed but he couldn't sleep any more. Dawn found him sitting by the window, looking out across the woods and the first gray haze of light across the Solent.

❖

He took the floating bridge across the River Medina to West Cowes—him and a motley collection of cars and vans and cyclists and women with baby buggies. The morning was sharp as a needle but bitterly cold. His breath smoked and he regretted that he hadn't worn his woolly hat.

He found Vectis Press down a sharply-sloping side-turning next to a fish-and-chips shop. It had the name Vectis Press Publishers & Stationers written in gold on the door, and a dusty front window display filled with curled-up sheets of headed notepaper, faded calendars and dead flies. He opened the door and a bell jangled.

Inside, there was a cramped office with stacks of books and files and boxes of envelopes. Through the back door he could see an old-fashioned printing press, as well as a new Canon copier. He shuffled his feet and coughed for a while, and after a while a red-faced, white-haired man appeared, wearing a ski sweater with reindeers running across it and a baggy pair of jeans.

The man cocked his head on one side and looked at Michael and didn't say a word.

"I'm—ah—looking for a book you published. I don't know whether you have any copies left. Or perhaps you can tell me where I can find the author."

The man waited, still saying nothing.

"It's *Queen Victoria's Mystic*, by somebody called Charles Lutterworth. Published 1987."

The man nodded, and kept on nodding. "Yes," he said. "Yes. I think I can help you there. Yes."

Michael waited for him to say something else, but he didn't.

"I—ah—do you have a copy here? Could I—buy one?"

The man nodded. "I've got eighty-six copies left. You can have them all if you like. Didn't sell very well, see."

"Oh, well, I'm sorry to hear that."

"So am I, considering I wrote it."

"*You're* Charles Lutterworth?"

"Roger Frost, actually. Charles Lutterworth's my nom-da-ploom."
He went over to an old oak-veneered cabinet and opened it up. It
was crammed with books of all sizes. "Let me see now . . ." he said, and
at last managed to tug out a copy of a thin volume bound in blue.
"There you are. Six quid for cash. What's *your* interest in it?"

"I was doing some research. I came across some reference to Abdul
Karim's belief in the resurrection of the dead. I sort of got the idea that
Queen Victoria might have found it . . . well, you know, that Queen
Victoria might have been very interested in it, considering the loss she
felt for Albert."

Roger Frost tapped the cover of his book with an ink-stained finger.
"It's all in here. All meticulously documented. Chapter and verse. The
trouble was, most of the first-hand information came from other Indian
servants, and nobody believed what they said. Unthinkable, you know,
that our own dear Queen was dabbling in Hindu mysticism."

"Did she really think that she could bring Albert back to life?"

"That's what Abdul Karim led her to believe. He was more than her
Munshi, her teacher—he was a highly respected holy man and mystic. It
seems he told the Queen that by the end of the second millennium, all
disease would have been wiped out, and your dead loved ones could be
dug up, cured of what had killed them, and brought back to life."

"And she believed him."

"Well, why shouldn't she?" said Roger Frost. He hadn't realized
that it wasn't a question. "You've got to remember that Victoria's reign
saw unbelievable strides in science and technology, and enormous advances in medicine, so it must have seemed like quite a reasonabe pre-
diction. She knew the story of *Frankenstein*, too—that was republished
in 1831—and if it could happen in a story, why not for real? After all, a
lot of people still believe that resurrection is just around the corner—
otherwise they wouldn't have their bodies frozen, would they? Idiots.

"It was partly Albert's fault. He was so enthusiastic about science
that he convinced Victoria that, with science, absolutely anything was
possible. And if you combine that idea with the terrible grief she felt at
losing him—it wasn't surprising that she accepted what Abdul Karim
told her."

"And what *did* he tell her?"

"Some of it's hearsay but some of it's documented, too, at Windsor,
and in the library in Delhi. Personally, I think that Abdul Karim was
doing nothing more than trying to console the Queen . . . spinning her

a bit of a mystic yarn, like, to help her recover from Albert's death. But he performed a Hindu ritual which would ensure that the Queen's spirit would reappear at the turn of the next century.

"He actually left a letter attached to his will which required his executors and their assigns to resurrect Albert's body from the Royal Mausoleum at Frogmore as soon as it was scientifically possible, and to inform him that the Queen's spirit would be waiting for him on the anniversary of his death, at Osborne House, which is where they were happiest."

"Why didn't he leave instructions for *her* body to be resurrected, too?"

"She wanted Albert to supervise *her* revival personally. After all, she was the Queen, Empress of India, and Albert was the only man she trusted to ensure that all went well. She didn't know how she was going to die, you see . . . and she might have been taken by an illness that wasn't yet curable in the year 2000. In that case, she said, it would be enough to know that *he* had returned to life and vigor, and that she could remain as a shade at Osborne House to watch him fulfill his destiny."

Roger Frost handed the book over. "Unfortunately, as we all know, we still can't bring dead people back to life, no matter what they've died of, and no matter how much we used to love them. And I'm not saying that I don't believe in ghosts, but nobody's ever seen the ghost of Queen Victoria, have they?"

"I have," said Michael.

"I beg your pardon?"

"There *is* a ghost of Queen Victoria. I saw her last night. I *talked* to her, for God's sake. How do you think I knew about Abdul Karim?"

Roger Frost looked at Michael for a while with his lips pursed. Then he said, "It's all right. You can have the book for a fiver if you want to."

"I saw her. She was crying in her bedroom. Then I met her in the children's summerhouse."

There was a very long pause, and then Roger Frost said, "You're serious, aren't you?"

✣

It was eight o'clock, and dark. They stood together in Albert's writing-room, listening to the grief-stricken sobbing coming from the Queen's sitting-room next door.

"Do you want to see her?" asked Michael.

"I don't know," said Roger Frost. "I don't really think I do."

Michael went to the door and eased it open three or four inches. He could see the small black figure sitting at the writing-desk, her head bowed. He beckoned Roger Frost, and after some hesitation, Roger Frost came to join him.

"Jesus," he said.

❖

Michael said, "There's only one thing I can think of."

"What's that?" said Roger Frost, wiping his mouth and putting down his pint. They were sitting in the Old Anchor in West Cowes, a noisy, smoky bar full of yachtsmen.

"Well, we can't just let her wander around Osborne forever, can we? I mean, Albert's never going to come back, which means that she's going to spend the rest of eternity grieving for him. We've got to find a way to put her to rest."

"Loads of ghosts do that, what's different about her? Just because she's royalty."

"I can't let her do it, that's all. I can't let her suffer like that."

"So what do you propose? Get in a priest, and have an exorcism?"

Michael shook his head. "I read your book last night. In the appendix, you've set out the Hindu ritual that Abdul Karim used to bring her spirit back."

"That's right. That was in some of his papers. I had it translated. Thought it was cobblers, when I first read it."

"Well . . . supposing we use the same ritual to bring *Albert's* spirit back? Supposing we reunite them—not physically, we can't do that. But at least we can bring their spirits back together."

Roger Frost sniffed and helped himself to another handful of dry-roasted peanuts, which he churned around his mouth like a cement-mixer. "I thought you had a screw loose the moment you walked into the shop."

❖

In the Durbar Room, half an hour before midnight, Michael laid out a pattern of candles on the polished floor, and drew with chalk the *Shri-yantra*, a circular pattern filled with overlapping triangles. If you meditated on this *yantra* long enough, you could look back into the dizzying mouth of space and time, back and back, to the beginning of creation.

The room echoed, except for its dead spots, and the dripping candle-flames made it look as if shadowy spirits were dancing across the coffered ceiling.

Roger came quietly into the room and stood beside him. "I can't guarantee this is going to work, you know, just because I printed it in my book. For all I know, Abdul Karim was nothing but a shyster."

"Well, we can only try," said Michael. He picked up the book and turned to the ritual, the *Paravritti*, the "turning back up."

He began to recite the words. "We who are looking back into time and space, we call you to find the spirit of our lost son Prince Francis Charles Augustus Albert Emmanuel of Saxe-Coburg and carry him forward on the stream of creation. Let his spirit rise from where it lies asleep so that it can come to join us here."

Roger Frost, with a very serious face, began to recite the *"Om . . ."* There was a time when Michael would have found it ludicrous, but here in the Durbar Room, with midnight approaching, and the figures of Indian gods and goddesses leaping in the candlelight, it sounded sonorous and strange, as if it were a summons that could wake up spirits from days and years and centuries long forgotten.

"We call on our lost son Prince Albert to open his eyes and return to the house of his greatest happiness. We call him to rejoin the ones he loved so dearly."

It was then that Roger touched Michael's arm. From the far door, a small dark shadow had appeared, a small dark shadow with a pale, unfocused face. It made no sound at all, but glided toward them across the floor, until it was standing just outside the circle of candles.

Roger said, "I'm seeing things."

"No," said Michael. "She's there."

"What are you doing?" she said, in that tissue-papery voice.

"The ritual," said Michael. "Abdul Karim's ritual. We can't bring back the Prince Consort's body. We don't have the power to do that. But perhaps we can bring back his spirit."

"What? What are you talking about?"

"You can have his spirit back here, at Osborne. You can both be together again."

"What?" She sounded aghast. "Don't you understand? Once you've called up a spirit, it can never go back."

"What do you mean?"

"I mean that, once you've summoned him, he'll have to stay with me, whether he wants to or not, forever."

"But I thought that's what you—"

Michael was interrupted by a sound like nothing he had ever heard before—a low, agonized moan that made him feel as if centipedes were running up his back. He felt a sudden draft, too—a draft that was chilly and smelled of dust and long-enclosed spaces. The candle-flames were blown sideways, and some of them were blown out altogether, so that the Durbar Room became suddenly much gloomier.

Out of the darkness, a dusty-gray figure appeared, so faint that it was almost invisible. It seemed to be moving toward them, but Michael couldn't be sure. The small shadow-woman took two or three steps away from it, toward the door. Michael stood where he was, his fists clenched tight, his breathing quickening, his heart banging harder and harder.

The figure stood still for a moment. It was no more substantial than a gray net curtain hanging at a window. Michael thought that he could see a luminous white face, and the indistinct smudges of side-whiskers, but that was all. But gradually, as it came nearer, its substance began to thicken, and darken.

By the time it was standing by the pattern of candles, it was clearly Prince Albert, a small portly man in young middle-age, deathly-white, with a sharp nose and an oval face, and drooping moustaches. He was wearing a dark uniform decorated with medals and a large silver star.

His image wavered, in the same way that a television screen wavers when somebody moves the aerial. He turned this way and that, as if he couldn't understand where he was or what was happening.

"Albert," Roger whispered. "It's Albert, you've brought him back."

The figure opened and closed its mouth but didn't seem able to speak. Michael kept squeezing his eyes tight shut and opening them again, because he simply could not believe that this was real.

It was then that the shadow-woman walked around the *Shri-yantra* and glided slowly toward Albert with both arms outstretched.

"My love," was all she said. "Oh, my love."

Albert stared at her. At first it was obvious that he didn't recognize her. She came closer, and took hold of both of his hands, and said, "It is *I*, my love. They've brought you back to me."

"Back?" he whispered, his voice thick with horror. "*Back?*"

"This is Osborne," she said. "You never lived to see this room. But this is Osborne. We can be happy again, my darling. We can stay here forevermore."

Albert slowly pushed her away from him, still staring at her. "What's happened to you?" he asked her. "Can this really be you? What's happened to you? Your hair! Your skin! You've withered away! What kind of a devilish spell have they cast on you?"

Michael said, "No spell, sir. Only time."

Albert frowned at Michael like an actor peering into a darkened audience. "*Time?*"

"You died at the age of forty-two, sir," put in Roger. "Your Queen here was eighty-one when she went."

Victoria looked up at him in anguish. "I am still myself, my love. And I have kept my love for you intact, for so many years."

Albert's mouth opened and closed, but he still couldn't speak. Something glistened on his cheeks, and Michael realized that he was witnessing an extraordinary spiritual phenomenon—the sight of a spirit, crying.

"I am still your darling," begged the shadow-woman, reaching out again to touch him. "I am still your wife and the mother of your children."

"And they?" asked Albert, his mouth puckered with grief.

"Dead, sir," said Roger. "All long dead. I'm sorry."

Albert gradually sank to his knees, and his head dropped as if he were waiting for an execution that would never come. The shadow-woman put her hands on his shoulders, but he was inconsolable. She had lost her young husband, when he died, but now he had woken from the dead to discover that he had lost his sparkling young wife.

"Can you not find it in your heart to love me, now that I am old?" asked the shadow-woman.

Albert couldn't answer. All he could do was bury his face in his hands and remain where he was, too grief-stricken to move, while the candles in the Durbar Room guttered and died.

✧

Michael saw them only once more, on the afternoon that he was due to leave. He was carrying his suitcase out to a waiting taxi when he happened to turn and look along the broad avenue that led to the shore of the Solent. It was difficult to see them, in the foggy half-light, but it looked as if they were walking very slowly toward the house. She was leaning on his arm for support. He had his face turned away from her.

Michael watched them for a while, then climbed into the taxi.

"Are you all right?" asked the taxi driver.

"Yes, why?" said Michael, and it was only then that he realized that his eyes were filled with tears.

Ian McDonald
WHITE NOISE

L*iverpool lads, we are here; shag your women and drink your beer,* the hot air hand drier says.

Alone, he thought, in the bar toilets of the Manchester Britannia, Marsh turns. Alone, in fact. Smeary mirrors, sinisterly underlit; cracked basins facing the stained urinals across the excrement-coloured tiled floor; cigarette ends drowned miserably among the air-freshener cubes that cannot quite overcome the friendly, urinous hum. The warm jet of the drier—Lavisan, made in Salford, support your local sanitaryware industry—on his wringing hands, fluttering the turn-ups of his suit trousers. And a voice, reciting some bit of doggerel that had stood proud from the beery threats and testosterone territoriality of cubicle wit and made him smile.

Liverpool lads, we are here. No love lost between these hard northern towns. Shag your women.

And drink your beer.

Marsh jumps back from the drier as if it has shorted out and shocked him. Drops of water flick from his fingers. He bends his head to listen.

Just hope no one come in an catches me listening to the hot-air hand-drier, he thinks.

Down there, under the fan-rush and motor-drone, voices. No words, but sounds, like neighbours' telephone conversations, where you catch tone and inflection but no sense. A conversation in another room, that flows and eddies with the air currents that move through a house, sometimes close and clear, others distant and muttering.

Voices in the hand-drier.

Jesus. Way too much expense account single malt.

The machine clicks off. Marsh hits the button again. It is different this time, like a radio badly tuned in to an interview with a famous but uncharasmatic person. The pauses between the almost-voices are too exact, too human to be random motor noise.

. . .look, look; I can see your house, that's it there.

Sudden footsteps, the door bangs open. A fellow suit on a beeline for the porcelain maw. Marsh straightens, thrusts his hands under the warm wind. Caught on. Strange public toilet perversions, listening to the hand-drier. *Mutter mutter.* He tugs his jacket, adjusts cuffs and tie, leaves the man to his business.

He thinks he catches a tone of farewell from the still-whirring machine.

❖

"I once had that in my car." McLeod is a pudgy twentysomething looking well forty and Marsh has never liked going on business trips with him. He's too much the man with whom you end up in shebeens or strip joints or hookers' beds. A lads' lad. Shag your women and drink your beer. "It was in the winter, you see, had to have the heat on all the bloody time. Kept thinking there was someone in the back seat talking, or I'd left the radio on, or some idiot in the next car over had his stereo up too loud. You know, thud thud thud music? Turned out it was the fan. Straight. Some kind of resonance thing, the garage man said. Like it was making other parts of the car vibrate, and all the vibrations were producing all these weird sounds, like they were cancelling each other out and reinforcing each other. I don't know. But it was the fan motor."

The too-young waitress in the glossy black tights and clumpy black shoes brings the round. *She hates doing this,* Marsh thinks. *Business men. Traveling men. Suits give us power.*

"Keep the change," McLeod says. "And a receipt?" As she goes sullenly to the till, McLeod leans forward. Conspiracy of lads. "Jesus, would you look at her. Black tights . . . I don't know. Barely decent."

"Barely legal," says Peters, the ingratiating one, from the Stockport office. A taxi would take him home to Mrs Peters and Little Peters but it is company money and he does not want to miss out. The bar girl sets the receipt deliberately in a puddle of slopped Lagavullin. The black ink curdles. "If you ask me, the most likely bet is radio interference. The circuitry's picking up radio waves."

"Can it do that?" fat McLeod asks, following the wiggle of the short skirt back to its position by the bar. Feeling warm eyes on her ass, the bar girl tugs down her skirt.

"I had an uncle once could pick up the Light Programme through his fillings."

"Bollocks!" says Burnside, the difficult one.

"God's honest truth. The stuff—what do you call it?"

"Amalgam," Marsh says.

That. Amalgam. It was like a receiver, and his jawbone and eardrum were like the amplifiers. God's honest truth."

"But I heard it say "Liverpool lads, we are here . . .".""

"Liverpool what?"

Marsh explains the toilet doggerel. "How could the circuitry pick up something I'd just read?"

Disagreeable Burnside, with the North West's leading sales figures this quarter behind him and the authority that those bestow, is looking a Lagavullin challenge at Marsh.

"Okay then. Okay then. You come and see."

"Okay."

The men in suits march along the corridor hung with prints of old Manchester like a slo-mo from a John Woo movie. Austens from the sticks, at the business, reads a hint and zips quick.

"Listen." They bend their heads around the vent. Marsh hits the big chrome button. The motor whines. The hot wind blows.

"What am I listening for?" McLeod says.

"Like people talking in another room, or someone has a radio on but you can't make out the song," Marsh says. And as he says it, he hears them, exactly as he describes.

"Can't hear a thing," says Burnside, who wouldn't hear anyway because he's never liked Marsh, really.

"Listen!"

Fingers *shh, shh.*

. . .*a light snack and a drink from the bar* . . .

"There!"

"All I can hear is hand-drier," Peters says. Less generously, Burnside says, "Bollocks." But McLeod is frowning, holding up a hand for the others to shut the hell up.

"There's something."

"It said, "a light snack and a drink from the bar.""

"Could be anything." This from Burnside.

McLeod shakes his head.

"I can't make it out clearly."

"Can we go now?"

Marsh knows better than to argue against the North-West's leading loft conversion salesman. He follows meekly back down the flock-lined corridor to the bar where men's stuff is done. But again there is a parting prayer from the voices in the hand-drier.

. . . no love, I can't get Jonah the monkey, he's up in the locker . . .

In the bar, the heat oppresses him and the whiskey sickens him and voices have said too much of too little and he glances over at the harassed waitress who wants badly to go to bed and hopes that she will not misinterpret his look as a lumbering come-on. The lads are talking football. McLeod and Burnside are re-enacting golden goals with empties, cigarette packets and beer mats. *Bollocks*, Burnside is saying to McLeod. *Bollocks bollocks bollocks.*

That to everything, isn't it?

Suddenly Marsh wants badly to join the waitress in the black tights in bed. Glance: you know what I mean? Nothing salesman convention-ish. You in your wee bed and I in mine. A compact of sleep.

"See you, guys."

Grunts. The flicked beer-mat boomerangs through the Miller Genuine Draft uprights of McLeod's goal. Burnside rises, fists in the air.

In the room on the fifth floor Marsh thinks about washing face, cleaning teeth and then thinks, *hah*, because like all hotel bathrooms his has no window nor any direct ventilation and is clammy and smell of potential fungus and rots. He tumbles straight out of suit into skin into bed.

It's only when you're away from home that you sleep in the nip, he thinks. Thoughts of Josie and Emer and Niamh jolt him out of the long easy fall into the black. *Jesus, you were supposed to phone her, let her know when the flight is getting in.*

Sudden guilty insomnia. A little night music. Marsh fiddles with the headboard radio but his fingers are whiskey blurred and cannot settle on any night station. Fragments of Morse, of electromagnetic whale song, of manically repetitive bars from *The Lincolnshire Poacher*, basso rumblings in Slavic. Static. White noise. Half-heard voices from half-way around the planet, phasing in and out. It gives him odd comfort, the unheard words of others speaking urgently on the wakeful half of the planet. *Appleton and Heaviside layers*, he thinks. They reflect the radio voices. *Was there really someone called Heaviside?*

Then clear and unequivocal: . . . *an emergency hot-line number has been issued for friends and relatives* . . .

Gone. His fingers can catch only a German rock station and the outer edges of Classic FM. And suddenly the whiskey falls on him and drives him down into sleep.

❖

Good morning, this is your eight thirty alarm call.

Uhkh.

Reception girl repeats the message verbatim, down to the inflection of her reception-voice.

Oh Jesus.

Stumbling around the dark room, unwilling to switch on a light for reasons that are obvious and sensible at this moment and which Marsh knows, but the time he has his coffee and toast down him, will seem ludicrous and superstitious.

The toilet. He'd had them all in the toilet. No, you know what I mean. To hear the voices in the hot-air hand-drier. Jesus. He'd heard voices in the hot-air hand-drier.

Voices. Phone girl. Phone home. Before you forget, with everything else, before you have to think about flying and get worried. Do it first thing, before you even get up, and it'll seem like keenness and penance for your sins of omission and commission of the previous night.

Birr birr.

She'll be trying to tear Emer away from *Big Breakfast*, get Niamh to eat something proper, with fibre in it, get herself together for another kak morning in that kak dole office.

Birr birr.

Marsh hates that his wife has to do hateful work.

"Hello?"

"Hello, it's me."

"Oh, hi."

Two words, but after thirteen years married, it only takes two words to say I'm pissed off you didn't call when you said you would, double-pissed off you're hung-over and I'm not, and after thirteen years I can tell that from two of your words, *Simon Marsh.*

He gives her the information. She'll be there to pick him up from the airport. Yes, she's got the flight number. Love to Emer and Niamh. Yeah sure. Oh, and bring me a present. Sure. Love you.

Click.

Urr.

And inside the urr, mumbling in the cyberspace him of the broken connection, *them.*

. . . no sir, you can't come in here. You're drunk sir. Now if you'd just step aside, go over there . . .

With them, others.

. . . it's all right, I'll hold your hand, don't you worry about a thing . . .

. . . Hello? Listen, I'll have to call you back later, they're calling us now . . .

Urrr. With nothing inside it but urr.

Marsh sits on the edge of the hired bed. He feels mugged; a boot in his belly, a brick to his head, his inner wealth stolen. They've escaped from the night; they've broken into daylight and the sane, orderly things of the day, an infection of voices, a haunting of whispers.

He's losing it.

He plunges to the shower, eager for hot water and sachet shower gel scented with strawberry to wash away these things that should have stayed anchored to his Lagavullin dreams. The light switch activates the extractor fan. And in the fan noise, the mutterers.

. . . over an area of twenty five square miles . . .

Marsh jams the taps on full to drown out the voices in the extractor fan. Scalding water leaps at him from the shower head. With a yell, Marsh jumps back. He darts and weaves through the scalding spray, trying to knock the temperature control down by fractions of a degree. The water hisses. The hiss is blind noise, white noise. And through the white noise, the voices come into the shower cubicle with him.

. . . hail Mary, full of grace, the Lord is with thee . . .

. . . Oh Jesus! Oh Mother of Jesus! Oh God!

. . . Mummy, Mummy, Mummy!

The child's voice is so close and clear, so full of terror, it hits him like a physical blow. Marsh reels, loses his footing on the treacherous cubicle floor. The hard edge of the soap holder rushes at his forehead like a weapon. Seeing death, seeing his brain-blood spiralling down the plug-hole, Marsh grabs the shower curtain and swings himself clear. Curtain rings pop, his ribs catch the lip of the shower tray as he goes down. He cries out silently, winded, too stunned to drag his legs out of the still over-hot water.

Shower hisses. Fan sucks. The voices are gone. They are just machines again. Marsh rolls on to his front and crawls across the bathroom floor. Gasping, he gets to his knees. Shower. Got to turn the stupid shower off.

He braves the hot jets.

. . . reports are coming in . . . the voice of the shower says to him. He silences it with a savage jerk that snaps the plastic lever off the thermostat.

Bill the company, he thinks.

❖

"I'm getting worried about you, Marshie," says disagreeable Burnside. His disagreeableness includes smoking copiously over breakfast. Marsh spots flecks of ash floating in his coffee, tiny grey floes. "Really."

Marsh shrugs, there is no arguing with Burnside. The look on McLeod's face reads, *I want to ask you about what you think it is,* but Burnside sees the look and has a firm grip now and does not want to let Marsh go. The grip of Best in the North-West. Selling is just another kind of warfare.

"I mean, Jesus, voices in the bloody extractor fan. Get a grip man, I'm telling you, if Area hears about this . . . It's a bloody jungle, you know man? A jungle."

He sits back with a nod of rightness and authority. McLeod takes his moment.

"I mean, is there any sense to it? You say they're talking actual phrases, but is there any pattern in what they say. I mean, do they all add up to something?"

"Not really," Marsh begins to say, then pauses and corrects himself. "Well, actually, maybe."

"Like what?"

"Well, there seems to be a little girl in it, somewhere, and she's very afraid. Like something terrible is happening to her." Suddenly, Marsh has the attention of everyone at breakfast table twelve. "And there's something that sounds like it has to do with a drunk man trying to get somewhere and people won't let him."

"Sounds about right," says Burnside, knowing that he has lost terrain between the empty fry plates and the ashy coffee cups.

"Like maybe they're trying to tell you something?" McLeod says. "Warn you?"

"Ghosts," quiet Peters says and turns every head.

"In a hotel?"

"Best place for ghosts," Peters says. "I don't mean dead people come back to haunt you, all that ectoplasm crap. I mean emotions, events, things like that, that have sort of like become permanent, like a recording. In the walls."

"Scenes from the past, playing over and over again?" asks McLeod.

"Ghosts don't have to be from the past," Peters says.

Burnside has had enough, he surges up.

"Bloody bollocks is what it is and the DG's closing speech is in ten minutes and you'd better be looking pretty damn bright-eyed and bushy-tailed. And you're as nucking futz as he is." With an accuse of the forefinger at Peters.

⁜

After the DG's closing speech which is full of flat wit and vague aggression and High Business-ese, which Marsh has always found hilarious and has never understood how others take it seriously, McLeod joins him in the queue for the coffee urns.

"I've been thinking, about your voices."

"The ghosts of the Manchester Britannia?"

McLeod grimaces. Burnside, whose course towards the biscuits and the important people takes him past his two colleagues, overhears and grimaces. He is in poor humour. No longer Best of the North West. That orb, sash and sceptre have gone to a new boy, a twentysomething, thin and fit and with hair that sticks up at the front like a breaking wave for Brylcreem surfers. Darwin rules hard in the jungle of loft conversion sales. Shag your woman and drink your beer.

"Nah. That's bollocks. But I'm thinking, you're flying back over today, aren't you?"

"One thirty flight."

"You don't like flying, do you?"

"Not really." Understatement, Simon Marsh. You hate it. It's not that it scares you, being up the air, it is that is so monumentally unnatural. A gross violation of nature.

"Maybe it works like this. You don't like flying, you get all stressed up. Your head does weird stuff. Maybe these voices, they're like your subconscious working out all the stress, in these voices."

Men drink, birds fly. Men drink Lagavullin and their deep dark headspaces fly into voices in the white noise.

"But you heard it." Marsh sees how McLeod is frowning, not looking at him straight. "Last night." *You're trying to get out of it. You heard it too, and you're trying to get out of it.* "Did someone say something to you? Was it Burnside?"

McLeod glances a moment at the place he last saw disagreeable Burnside. But he says nothing, and shuffles a step closer to the coffee ewers and the bored looking girls in black and white.

"Think about it," he says, reaching for coffee and Nice biscuit and looking for a social pool in which he can wallow. "It's stress, that's all."

But I'm flying home, Marsh wants to say. *And it's only bloody loft conversions.*

One of the short-skirt girls is having a problem with the valve on the coffee biggin. She is keeping her head low and trying things with the levers and whispering to her colleagues. The urn hisses steam, like an espresso maker, which it is not.

Marsh hears other conversations in the convention room, conversations without words.

The voices have followed him into the public. They are hiding inside the urn, boiling in the black, hot coffee, muttering their maddening, muddy interviews.

. . . No, I'm sure the car park's this way, dear, says an invisible old lady in a voice so loud, so clear that the whole buzzing room must hear. But the loft men stand around in their groups and drink their coffee and dunk their Nice and laugh to each other.

Suddenly afraid, Marsh leaves to check out and settle his bill. His fingers can't find the right card. He fumbles, shuffles, deals, all but the right one. He can't look at reception girl; she'll be frowning, worrying about this mad man in a suit, crazy loft man. He signs the chits and the bill without looking at the numbers. Cheat, run up, scam, overcharge, I don't care. Out. I want out. They can't be out there in the street. They are what Peters said, creatures of the old hotel, embossed into the walls like the flock *fleur de lys.*

"Simon!" McLeod's voice, behind him. Don't look round. Don't get into conversation. "Marshie!"

The diesel smog on the street is like a blessing of incense. Traffic roar, city noise, peaceful as birdsong. A red Ford hurtles past, driven by a shaven-headed lad in sports fashion. Marsh is swept up in its sound wake: *thud thud thud thud thud thud.* Sonic territoriality. Big noise. Red noise. Black noise. Not faceless, toneless white noise, where the voices live.

A lifted hand calls in a taxi. The taxi takes him to the station. In the station there is noise and people and real voices. Caught up in the headlong rush of travel, Marsh has had the piss, zipped up, washed his hands and put his hand over the big chrome button of the hand-drier before he realises where he is, what he has done, what this is in front of him. A moment of fear. No. There are too many people here who would see a loft-conversion man in a suit paralysed by a hot-air hand-drier.

A *hot-air hand-drier.* Ridiculous. He hits the button. The motor whirrs. Hot air rushes and blasts. It dries his hands. Nothing more.

The train is fast and smooth and electric and takes him out through the southern suburbs in a quiet swish of power. Marsh listens to the hum of the engines, the hiss of the air-vents, the click of the rails for places where demon voices might lodge. They are not there. There are just obedient, efficient machine sounds.

Train to elevator. Elevator to travellator. The rolling way carries Marsh and his baggage trolley smoothly along, like a river, like time. Aircraft noises penetrate the clear plastic tunnel. Marsh can see little Boeings lifting sharply up over the terminal buildings into the clear air. Time to fly, soon. A thought to put a grip of tension in his bladder. Think about home, Josie, the kids. Josie's present. Think about the pressing urgency of that. He has an idea. He remembers there was a nice scarf in the tie concession, with ducks on it. Josie likes ducks, things that live on water.

He'll get her that scarf.

An elderly couple are approaching on the opposite travellator. They've got tartan luggage on their trolley, piles of yellow duty-free bags and the bright clothes and deep skin of people home from the Mediterranean. They seem to be engaged in gentle altercation. As they pass, Marsh hears the old woman say,

"No, I'm sure the car park's this way, dear."

Marsh feels his brain turn over inside his skull. He turns, numb-struck, but the relentless machine bears them away from each other. He wants to run after them, shout, *what do you mean, who told you that? Where did you get that from?*

He struggles with the cumbersome trolley, but even as he realizes that it would be a Red Queen's race against the flow of things, the moving walkway dumps him off it onto the airport concourse. Taken unawares, Marsh almost spills self and stuff over the polished mock marble.

Hissing in his ears. There's something like the sea, or the wind in trees, in his ears. In his head.

It's *in* there. White noise.

Panicked, Marsh obeys his preprogrammed routine of air travel. Roll up, check in. Window please. He likes to be able to see that everything out there is where it should be, doing what it's meant to do. Shopping. Get that present, buy yourself a magazine. Transacted through a haze of hissing white noise. Don't let them start, Marsh prays, fearful that the whole shop can hear the noise inside his head. The voices. Don't let the hiss break into mutterings and mumblings.

Coffee, though it makes you nervous. How can you be any more nervous that you are now?

Nerves. That's it. Pre-flight tension, that's the buzz inside his head. But you heard them say *no, I'm sure the car park's this way, dear.*

But they would. It's the way out. People are bound to be looking for the car park. Your mind just decorated the scaffolding.

He sips his high-octane coffee and watches the big birds taxiing on the field. A little feeder jet arrives around the end of the pier and turns sharply, nose into stand. *That'll be mine*, he thinks. Presently, the flight is called.

As he waits for the security check, he develops a new theory for the noise in his head. Lagavullin. Too much, too free; the guilt of a loft-conversion man who sleeps naked only when he is absent from his wife. Through the check and down the pier. Alone in a departure lounge, a middle aged woman fondles her rosary. Her lips mumble prayers, suddenly clear to Marsh as he passes.

"Hail Mary, full of grace, heaven and earth are full of thy glory."

Marsh freezes. The woman looks up. She has felt his eyes on her. She gives him a long, intimate look; part fear, part blessing, part damnation. *What do you mean? What do you understand?* Marsh wants to ask. Then the push of bodies carries him on, towards his departure.

At the gate security staff are arguing with a clearly drunk young man. His head is shaved, he wears track pants with popper panels up each leg. He is vehement, the flight attendant is adamant.

"No sir, you can't come in here. You're drunk sir. Now if you'd just step aside, go over there."

Like an automaton, Marsh hands his boarding pass to the flight attendant. He hardly hears her say, "Thank you sir, the flight is running about ten minutes late."

He finds a seat, sits with his flight bag clutched on his knees, like an emotional refugee from some existential atrocity. He looks at the people he is to fly with. The fellow suit with the mobile phone. The little girl with the toy floppy monkey. The obvious boyfriend and girlfriend, she leaning her heavy head on his shoulder while he absently strokes her hand. The nervous-looking elderly lady with the thick ankles, neatly crossed. Any of them at any time could turn traitor on him, speak the things inside his head. The white noise voices.

Marsh frets and festers. The ground staff are still arguing with the drunk young man in the sports fashion. There are two policemen with him now. The drunk man does not seem to notice the size of guns they are carrying. A flight attendant moves to the lectern by the gate and calls the flight. Boarding row numbers 20-40 first please.

The suit looks round. Marsh hears him say, "Hello? Listen, I'll have to call you back later, they're calling us now."

In a dream, Marsh is on his feet, carried towards the smiling hostess. As she swipes his boarding card, he feels impelled to glance backwards. The young drunk man has seen people getting on his plane and is angry. He's struggling and swearing, but the police have a firm grip of his baggy synthetic clothing. As they march him away, he turns. His eye catches Marsh's.

"Liverpool lads, we are here, shag your woman and drink your beer!" he shouts.

In his seat under the wing, where he likes to keep an eye on the engines, Marsh numbly buckles his belt and listens to the voices from the white noise.

"No love, I can't get Jonah the monkey, he's up in the locker."

"Thank you for flying with us today. Once we're airborne, we'll be offering you a light snack and a drink from the bar."

The stewardesses perform their safety ritual dance as the shuttle jet bumps over the concrete of the apron onto the runway. It halts.

"It's all right, I'll hold your hand, don't you worry about a thing,"

White Noise

Marsh hears the boyfriend say to the girlfriend, three rows in front of him.

Ghosts.

Now the feeder jet is powering up and Marsh is very very afraid. To shut out the cabin voices and the rising thunder of the jets, he turns on the overhead ventilator. Cold air rushes down on him. In the hiss, a new voice speaks, clear and unmistakable, and to him only, because it is his own voice.

Look out the right, his voice instructs him.

The plane leaps forward. Runway markings blur, then drop away with unexpected haste. The little jet climbs steeply, within moments the airport has dwindled to scattered toys. Flaps retract. Marsh watches them with paralytic fascination.

The engine, his voice says. *Watch now.*

He cannot look away. The cabin insulation muffles the bang, but Marsh has a front-row view of the pieces of metal that spray out of the inboard engine, then the tongue of flame that clings to the undersurface of the wing in defiance of the three-hundred mile-per-hour winds.

"Look, look; I can see your house, that's it there!" cries a man to his friend in Marsh's opposite number across the aisle. Oblivious.

Ghosts, Peters had said, do not need to be from the past. Ghosts of the future, speaking into the past. Warnings? Prophecies? Neither, Marsh understands. Ghosts are merely the blind replaying of some tremendous trauma, an outrage so far beyond normality that it has imprinted itself on the white noise that is the hiss of reality continuously recreating itself.

Watch, the reporting voice orders. Marsh watches. He does not have to do anything. There is nothing he can do. There is nothing that can be done. It is quite quick and very beautiful. The tongue of flame is sucked back inside the engine. Licks of fire leak from the seams of the engine panels. It explodes in a blossom of flame. The plane lurches, Marsh's attention flicks away for an instant. It returns to see the outer half of the wing tumble elegantly away through miles of clear, white air.

No message. No warning. No hope. Just pure reportage.

Then down is up and left is right as the little jet goes into its death dive. For a few seconds there is silence, broken only by the white noise of Marsh's air vent. Then the screaming starts.

Mark Morris

COMING HOME

Each time the baby kicked, Jane winced and recalled her mother gleefully telling her that she'd been a ten-pounder and that it ran in the family. It wasn't what she wanted to hear, but she knew Mum had just been trying to reassure her that her baby would be big and healthy.

Snow flurried outside, tapping slyly against the window, making the house seem cosy. Radiators breathed out heat; occasionally one burbled, and Jane hoped they wouldn't break down like last year, not when it was almost impossible to persuade plumbers to come all the way out here at Christmas. Sometimes she wished their nearest neighbor wasn't over a mile away, but mostly she didn't mind. If they still lived in London, they wouldn't be able to watch the sun setting spectacularly over the distant fields, wouldn't have had badgers ambling through their garden at night, wouldn't be spending their lives accompanied by the soothing rush of the river which paralleled the narrow road that twisted for two miles before reaching the village of Brackley where Gerry had his estate agent's.

The baby kicked again, so hard that Jane, crossing the lounge, had to grip the back of a chair to steady herself. She decided to lie down in her studio, and once the baby had stopped kicking made her way not to the kitchen where she'd been heading to find something to nibble, but to the staircase, which she ascended slowly, stopping every few steps to gasp for breath.

As she sank onto the camp bed in the cluttered room which also contained her easel, her boxes of chalk pastels, a dusty bookcase stuffed with reference material, and dozens of stacked frames and half-finished pictures, she wondered whether she would go the full term. Today was the 21st, the baby was due on the 29th, but already she felt fit to pop. If she had it within the next couple of days she might still be home for Christmas. However, ideally she would prefer to get Christmas out of the way before the endless round of feeding and nappies and sleepless nights began.

She was just drifting off when she heard a sound coming from the landing directly outside her door. It sounded like breathing, though it was heavy and liquid, somehow *sludgy*. Jane imagined the man (she was sure it was a man) pressing his nose against the wood. She lay rigid until the stealthy ticking of snow against the window became a sudden flurry, making her jump. When the flurry subsided, the breathing had gone. Jane lay and listened for five minutes longer, but all she could hear was the river rushing along outside.

When she told Gerry that evening he looked concerned, but tried to come up with reasons why she must have been mistaken.

"If the house was empty and the doors locked then you must have imagined it. Besides, why would a man break into the house and then leave without . . . doing anything?"

"Perhaps he thought the house was empty and fled when he realized it wasn't," she said, trying to convince herself. "Or perhaps we've got a ghost."

"Don't be silly. I won't have you scaring yourself witless over nothing, not in your condition."

"I'm not scaring *myself*, Gerry. I know what I heard."

Frowning, he said, "I could always drop you at Katy's before I go to work."

"No. I won't be forced out of my own house. Don't worry, I keep the mobile close by anyway in case of you know what." She pointed at her belly.

Despite her tiredness, she was too uncomfortable to sleep that night. She shifted with an effort from one position to another, rearranging the cushions she had been using to support her stomach and ease the ache in her back, but it was no use. In the end she gave up and gazed for a while into the wavering darkness, listening to Gerry's soft snoring, the river telling him to hush, the distant cry of an owl.

At length, inevitably, the pricking of her bladder prodded her from her cocoon. She shivered as she pushed the duvet aside, the night's chill coaxing goosebumps from her flesh. She pulled on her dressing gown and plodded to the toilet for the umpteenth time that day, then decided that she couldn't face returning to bed. With luck, if she made herself a hot drink downstairs and stretched out on the settee with her book, she might end up dozing off.

The lounge was still warm from the embers in the fire, whose glow lapped the walls. She picked up her book from the sideboard, then immediately dropped it with a cry of disgust. The cover was spongy and slimy, as if slugs had been crawling across it all night.

As if touching the bloated paperback prompted it, a smell suddenly touched Jane's nostrils. It was a damp, rotten, salty smell like decaying seaweed. She turned her head towards the kitchen door from behind which the smell seemed to be emanating, and heard a bumping, slithering sound, as if something large and soft and uncoordinated was moving about.

Though her instinct was to sink down into the shadows between the sideboard and the broken grandfather clock that Gerry was always tinkering with, she told herself firmly that she mustn't give in to her fear. She marched boldly across the hall, the tiles like ice beneath her bare feet, and pushing open the kitchen door to reveal a block of fetid and somehow bulging darkness, reached in and slapped the light switch.

Did something clammy, something disconcertingly like slug flesh, briefly caress the back of her hand before the room was filled with light? Apparently not, for the kitchen was empty.

No, not quite empty. The dank smell was still there, though fading now, and there were patches of wet leading across the lino to the back door. Jane licked her lips, then also paced across the lino, taking care not to step in the puddles. She inspected the door. It was locked and bolted from the inside. Suddenly she felt queasy and faint; she needed to sit down. She hurried out of the kitchen, leaving the light on, and back into the lounge.

She sank onto the settee, curled her hands protectively around her belly and stared into the crumbling embers of the fire. Next thing she knew it was morning, the fire was nothing but grey ash and her feet were numb with cold. She tried to massage some life into them, then padded back across the hallway to the kitchen. The wet patches on the lino had dried, leaving no indication that they had ever been there.

Katy, Jane's elder sister, picked her up at noon that day and took her to lunch at The Leaping Hare, a pub five miles and two villages away that was on Egon Ronay's recommended list. Jane had not told Gerry about her experiences in the early morning hours because he had woken up irritable as if *he* was the one who'd had a night of broken sleep. Neither, she decided, would she tell Katy, for daylight had diminished the power of the experience and she knew that relating it in the Christmas cheer of a country pub would only make her sound silly. Nevertheless the experience preyed on her mind enough for Katy to comment on how quiet she was.

"I'm not getting much sleep," Jane said, and placed a hand on her stomach.

"Soon be over," said Katy who had two school-age boys of her own.

The food in the pub was better than good. The leaping flames in the grate at the far end of the room reminded Jane of muscles that the bellowing fire kept flexing. Once she thought the tree guarding the cigarette machine had grown hot enough to burn, but the flames she saw dancing in its branches were only reflections in the baubles that the tree wore. Barmaids sported silver tinsel scarves and Noddy Holder yelled, "It's Christmaaaasss!" from the juke box, all of which helped Jane relax.

Nevertheless she was frowning as she wafted at a threat of cigarette smoke, thinking of the baby, when the landlord shouted, "Phone call for Mrs. Grainger."

As Jane reached the bar the landlord said cheerily, "Sounds like your man's got flu," and handed her the receiver.

"Hello," said Jane, pressing a hand to her exposed ear to block out Shakin' Stevens. She thought the connection had been broken until she realised it was not static she was listening to, but sludgy, tortured breathing.

"Who is this?" she demanded, sharply enough to earn several curious glances.

Did the breathing possess a voice that was attempting to form words? "Kaaaa," it seemed to be gurgling, "mirrrr."

Jane put the phone down. Though she was shaking, the pub suddenly seemed too stuffy. She stumbled back to her seat and plumped down, her breath coming in short gasps.

"Are you all right?" asked Katy, alarmed. "You look terrible."

Jane blurted out everything. She didn't care any more how silly Katy might think her. Her sister listened with pursed lips, then paid the bill and took her home.

Later, Jane was following a trail of dying fish up the stairs, their twitching silver bodies gleaming like Christmas decorations. Did the slow, squelching footsteps she could hear belong to her or to whoever had left the trail for her to follow? She inched open the bathroom door and caught a glimpse of the bloodless, slimy flesh of the figure in the bath as it turned its dripping ruin of a face towards her . . .

She woke with a cry, Katy sitting beside her. The late-afternoon darkness outside the window was hard and cold like black ice.

The next day was Saturday. As Gerry went to the supermarket and to pick up the tree they had ordered, Jane stayed in by the fire. She turned the radio up loud enough for the carol singers' voices to become distorted on the high notes. The sound she could hear in the pauses between hymns was not sludgy breathing but the gurgling of the river across the road from the house.

When the phone rang she almost left it, but eventually snatched it up and aggressively said, "Yes?" It was Katy, who seemed not to notice her tone, ringing to ask what time she should invade with her clan on Christmas Day. Soon afterwards Gerry arrived home, full of Christmas cheer and laden with goodies. They sipped wine as they dressed the tree, then settled down to watch *It's A Wonderful Life* as snow swirled around the house like a swarm of white flies looking for a way in. Gerry rested a hand on her stomach as the baby squirmed, and smiled soporifically.

"There'll be three of us next Christmas."

She kissed him on the nose. "There's still time for there to be three of us *this* Christmas."

Though she had only drunk two glasses, the wine helped her fall asleep quickly that night, but in the early hours she jolted awake as if someone had shaken her. Immediately she heard the sound of something rustling stealthily by the window. She looked in that direction and saw a figure with a pale, round head and rudimentary features. She sat up so suddenly that she wrenched her stomach, waking the baby, though even as the pain made her gasp she realised what she had really seen and heard: the glow of the moon through the curtains, the sound of snow settling on the window.

She was snuggling down again when she heard the screech of tires from outside, followed by a thunderous splash. Instinct made her want to leap out of bed, though her aching stomach forced her to perform the maneuver with care. She hurried to the window and yanked back the curtains. Could she see car headlights sinking beneath the river or was it merely an odd reflection of the moon? Certainly there appeared to be something large and black just beneath the river's surface.

"Gerry, Gerry." Try as she might, Jane could not wake him. He had always been a heavy sleeper and had drunk far more wine than she had. Dragging on her dressing gown and a pair of trainers she hurried downstairs and out of the house. It was bitterly cold, though the snow's kisses were gentle on her face. The river, its banks crusted with ice, flashed as if filled with churning chunks of metal. Taking care not to slip, Jane craned forward to peer into the water, but could see nothing.

Turning back towards the house she saw a figure standing by the front door that she had left ajar. It was only a momentary glimpse before a swirl of snow broke it up and carried it away, but she was left with the impression of bloated white flesh and dark clothes slick with water or slime. A pulse jumped in her throat as she stalked back to the house, her nervousness making her angry. Inside, she went straight to the phone and called the police, who arrived twenty minutes later and spent almost an hour searching the river, to no avail.

"Are you sure you'll be all right if I pop out for a couple of hours?" Gerry asked her the next day. It was Christmas Eve and his friend Graham, who he played five-a-side with, had invited him for a pint with the lads.

"I'll be fine," Jane said, secretly relishing the chance to be on her own for a while. Gerry had been bemused to find the police on his doorstep at three in the morning and had spent the day treating her with a kind of amused indulgence. When he said something about pregnant women's hormones doing funny things to their minds she had had to stop herself from thumping him.

She was angry when he wasn't back by nine, but didn't really start worrying until after eleven. By midnight her anxiety was a hard lump at the base of her throat. She phoned Katy, who was up late wrapping the boys' presents, and who came over immediately.

Jane had just decided to call the police when they arrived with a swish of tires on the snowy drive. Katy held her as the power of her dread seemed to make them say the words she had been expecting to hear. Coming back from the pub, Gerry had lost control of the car which had plunged into the river. The accident had happened several hours ago, but it had taken a while for police divers to recover his body from the submerged vehicle.

After the police had gone, Jane sat and stared into space as Katy wept and clung to her. Jane felt numb, unable to produce tears. The Christmas tree twinkled in the corner like a joke in appallingly bad taste.

Coming Home

The baby that Gerry had been so looking forward to but which he would now never see, moved inside her, but Jane felt distanced from it and its imminent birth. Later, in a flat voice, she said, "He tried to warn me."

Katy, bleary with tears and exhaustion, said, "What?"

"Everything that's happened. Don't you see, it was Gerry coming back. Why didn't I listen to what he was trying to say?"

Katy looked at her for a moment, then said softly, "Jane, you don't know what you're saying. How can someone come back to you before they're even . . ." She choked on the last word.

Jane's face was expressionless, her voice eerily calm. "He wanted this baby so much, so he found some way . . ." Then suddenly, shockingly, her face twisted and she was wailing, almost screaming, the grief pouring out of her.

It was five o'clock on Christmas morning when the knock came on the front door. Katy was asleep in an armchair, so exhausted that she didn't even stir. Jane was still awake, quiet again now, shattered though unable to sleep, staring into the fire. She padded into the hallway and pulled the door open.

When she saw what was standing outside she remembered the phone call in the pub and all at once realized what the caller had been trying to say. Gerry had wanted her to know that nothing in this world or beyond would prevent him coming home for Christmas.

Terry Lamsley
HIS VERY OWN SPATCHEN

Gerald decided he was too tired to tackle the long journey home along the motorway that evening. After breasting a high hill he found himself descending into a stretch of bleak, almost uninhabited landscape that occupied the space between the rolling country he had just driven through and a large town, the western edge of which peered at him out of the misty distance a couple of miles ahead. He had decided to throw himself at the mercy of the town's hoteliers when he saw a sign beside the road that offered accommodation at the High Trees Guest House situated two hundred yards ahead. Gerald drew up outside this establishment, the exterior of which was sorely in need of paint and repair, and briefly studied a notice board fixed to the stump of a dead birch at the entry to the carpark at the side of the building. In the failing light he was just able to make out that Mrs. Garstang, the proprietress, provided the usual facilities so he sauntered through the front door and tinkled a silvery bell that rested on the reception desk.

A woman behind the desk, speaking softly into a telephone, did not immediately turn to attend to him, so Gerald began inspecting a rack of leaflets advertising local stately homes and other attractions, from which he extracted a copy of a faded pamphlet that offered information about the Guest House. He glanced at its contents, then allowed his attention to wander to a framed photograph of the building itself, hanging nearby. Taken sixty or more years ago, if the design of the single car parked outside was anything to go by, it showed a section of the façade of the building packed tight in among mature trees, all of which had now been felled. With the exception of the lower section of the single, sad birch, that was, that probably owed its *post mortem* existence to its usefulness as a support for an advertisement board.

"You're too late for a hot meal," a voice behind him said.

Gerald turned and discovered a tall, narrow woman with deep-set eyes, staring at him critically. Mrs. Garstang, presumably. She still gripped the phone in her hand.

"A single room and breakfast would be fine," Gerald said, though he was extremely hungry.

"Number seven," she said, handing him a key and lifting the phone back to her ear simultaneously.

The room had a low ceiling and was over-full of bits and pieces of heavy furniture. The wash basin was cracked, one of the taps dripped, and the window would not quite close. Outside, the evening air was cold.

"It'll do," he told himself as he stretched out on the reasonably comfortable bed.

Exhausted as he was, however, hunger kept him from dozing. He found a map of the immediate district in a folder on the bedside table, and from it learned there was a village less than two miles away that boasted an inn and a restaurant. He brought in his luggage, put on a coat, and went downstairs again. As he passed the reception desk Mrs. Garstang put her hand over the telephone mouthpiece she had been whispering into and said, "If you're venturing out, be back by eleven."

"I'm going for something to eat in Sidbury. Would you recommend the restaurant there."

"I would not. There's cold ham here. I can do you a sandwich."

Gerald paused to contemplate what kind of job such a woman might make of a ham sandwich, and gave her the benefit of the doubt.

❖

He returned to his room. The sandwich, when it arrived, though thickly cut, seemed to contain little substance. After listening to the news on the crackly clock-radio at his bed-side Gerald realised he had eaten his supper too hurriedly and inflicted severe indigestion upon himself. He found himself fidgeting about the room in considerable discomfort and wandered out on to the corridor. A door at the head of the stairs bore, in faded letters just legible, the promise 'GUEST LOUNGE' and he made his way towards that.

He entered and, as he did so got the impression that, on all sides, people were edging back into the shadows. There were plenty of these dark places because the large room, that seemed well stocked with an assortment of chairs, was illuminated by a single, heavily shaded standard lamp. Directly beneath this light sat a person who Gerald at first took for the proprietress of the establishment, but he quickly realised he was mistaken. The woman bore a strong facial resemblance to the landlady but she was even more slender, with a straight-up-and-down figure.

She muttered something that he took to be a greeting. He nodded politely in reply and glanced about for a vacant chair, but they all seemed occupied. It was difficult, in the darkened room, to be sure. At last he went and stood in front of a large fireplace next to the woman, with his back to it, as though he were warming his backside, though no fire burned in the grate. The room, he noticed, was chilly: the air in it was not still. A draft was getting in somewhere. In a corner of the room somebody spoke a few words he did not catch and there followed a rustling sound, as though small pieces of very dry, thin paper were being slowly crumpled. This sound continued for some time.

There was no television in the room. He had been half hoping to watch something, anything, to pass the time until his stomach settled. It had been a surprise to him that a set of some kind had not been installed in his room but it seemed incredible that the so-called guest lounge did not contain one. What else did one do in such a place but watch the box? Read, perhaps, but there was no sign of newspapers or books: not even a pile of tatty, ancient *Reader's Digest*.

The woman beside him appeared contented to be doing nothing at all.

Gerald turned and peered at the small oil-painting hanging at a slight angle above the overmantle. It looked surprisingly old, and rather well done, he thought. He prided himself in his amateur's knowledge of English painting, and had attended a number of WEA courses on the subject. The solitary lamp lit the left side of the picture better than the right, but what he could see was enough to give him a feeling that he might have come across it before somewhere. In reproduction, perhaps? No; it was unlikely a painting worthy of commercial reproduction would be hanging in the lounge of a down-at-hell B&B establishment in the middle of nowhere, but the style was undoubtedly familiar.

Gerald pushed his nose up towards the canvas to get a better view. The scene was of a moonlit glade in a woods or forest. A path led into this space from the left forefront, along which walked three sorry looking figures, two of whom were rendered obscure by what Gerald decided must be quantities of leaves swirling around them. They were leading and following a sickly-looking woman, draped in what appeared to be a tattered, possibly bloodstained wedding dress. The couple fore and aft might have been whirling dervishes, or something of the kind, Gerald thought, creating their own uplifting breeze because, as far as he could make out, there was no indication in the rest of the painting that wind was blowing. The leaves depicted so carefully on the painted trees looked untroubled.

Closer attention to the figures gave Gerald no clue as to what kind of persons they might be, but it seemed from their postures they were looking over their right shoulders, toward him and out of the picture. In spite of the artist's naturalistic treatment, the painting had an air of artificiality. It crossed Gerald's mind that it might represent a scene from a ballet, perhaps, or an opera by Mozart, but he had a feeling the painting might well predate Amadeus by half a century or more. The thought made him quite excited, and he stepped back to get a better overall impression of the work. He then had second thoughts about the setting which may not, as he first imagined, have been the depths of a forest, because he could now see some kind of building in the unillumined right half of the picture, almost concealed among trees that extended back into the perspective from the far side of the rather disappointingly empty glade. It occurred to Gerald that the glade had a look of expectant vacancy, as though new characters were due to come on stage soon to change the mood of the drama, if that was what was represented.

The rustling sound, that had continued in the room for some minutes, stopped suddenly. Gerald stepped back from his contemplation of the painting into a silence that surrounded him rather awkwardly, and stumbled on the edge of a rucked rug.

The woman beside him said, "I see you are interested in our Spatchen. You know about such things, perhaps?"

"Enough to realize it might be by him, now you mention it," Gerald admitted. "A late work, I should say."

"His last: his swan song."

"It shows signs of the decline of his powers in his final years, and the subject matter is—uncharacteristic. An interesting work, though not a masterpiece. Worth a pound or two, nevertheless. I'm surprised to find it in such a place as this."

"It's safe enough here," the woman said.

Gerald doubted that. "I hope it's insured," he said.

"In a way, yes; you could say that."

"I'm glad to hear it."

Gerald was becoming increasingly aware of the presence of other people in the room, and got the impression they were taking an interest in his conversation. He wished he could get a good look at at least one of them, but they must all have been very retiring types, as they kept well back in the multitude of shadows outside the narrow circle of light provided by the solitary lamp. The draft, that seemed to rise from somewhere among them at one end of the room, had increased a little during the last moments. Gerald pulled his jacket together, buttoned it, and folded his arms.

The woman said, "Spatchen was born here and, after spending most of his short life in London, returned to die here."

"I was vaguely aware he came from this region."

"The area was wild then. His parents lived in the forest. When he returned at the end of his life he had their shanty pulled down, and built something more splendid on the site. If you look carefully you can see part of the house he built through the trees in that painting. He was our only great man. We have no one else to be proud of in these parts."

Gerald had nothing to say to this, reflecting that there were certain things in Spatchen's life that would, perhaps, have been glossed over by local people keen to make a hero of the man. He returned his attention to the painting, but could make nothing much of the representation of the master's last home beyond the outlines of a few dimly glowing windows and moonlit chimneys and rooftops.

"What about these figures, if that's what they are, in the foreground?" he said. "Who are they?"

"They are a little—*obscure*," the woman suggested, but offered no further information.

Gerald said, "Spatchen certainly had no problems representing the human form skillfully and accurately in his other paintings."

The woman nodded, as though she was aware of this.

"I suppose the two outer figures could be experiencing some unusual natural phenomena he observed, and captured in that painting," Gerald said tentatively.

The woman seemed impressed with this. "Captured! How clever you are," she said. "I'm sure you are almost exactly right."

Gerald wondered about the 'almost.' "Is his house still standing?"

"No. He had ordered it to be sealed up after his death, with him inside. It fell down at the end of the last century. The roots of the trees around it had undermined the foundations. This building we are in was built on the site soon after by my great grandfather, using much of the stone from Spatchen's house."

And probably he came upon the painting in the ruin at the same time, Gerald thought, but did not say. "And the trees?" he asked. "The ones in Spatchen's painting and in the photograph I noticed by the reception desk downstairs? They seem to have survived until recent years."

"My father had them all cut down when the road was improved after the second war. He thought it would make the place more inviting to passersby."

"That would make sense," Gerald mumbled, losing interest in the woman's increasingly tedious ramblings.

"It was a very bad mistake. The inhabitants of the forest had been forced closer and closer together down the years, as it had been cleared to provide agricultural land. When my father had the last stretch cut down, they were compelled to take refuge here. Where else could they have gone?"

"What do you mean?" Gerald inquired out of politeness more than curiosity. "Mice? rats? —things like that?"

"Not vermin, no. We never have been troubled by them."

Somebody shifted position in one of the chairs, and started, awkwardly, to rise. Gerald glimpsed what appeared to be a misshapen, ragged figure twist and turn a couple of times, as though in confusion, then sweep off into the farthest corner of the room, where it sank down into the shadows gathered there. Gerald wondered if the establishment had become, in its declining years, a home for the elderly and infirm.

It was time to make a move himself, he decided. The chilly atmosphere in the room had done nothing to encourage relaxation, and his peptic disorder had not abated, but the idea of stretching out under a quantity of blankets now had a strong appeal.

He wished the occupants of the lounge a good night, a civility that received no response, not even from the woman, who appeared to have fallen asleep, and returned to his room.

Once in bed, he found he still could not settle. The thought of the odd, unguarded and presumably, to the outside world, unknown painting, hanging a couple of rooms away from him, stimulated his mind in a number of ways and would not let him rest. Finally he decided he had reached that point of exhaustion, one step beyond ordinary tiredness of the body and brain, where it becomes actually impossible to sleep. He sat up, switched on the bedside lamp, and, desperate for diversion, began to inspect the only reading matter he had to hand, the promotional leaflet he had picked up when he had first arrived, that provided information about Tall Trees itself. It had been printed decades earlier, quaintly advertised the establishment's suitability as a halting point for charabancs and excursionists, and offered a bill of fare priced in pounds, shillings and pence. There was also a brief history of the building and a longer account of the site's association with the great man, Spatchen, which read more like myth than history.

Far from being a self-taught genius, as Gerald remembered he had been described by his WEA tutor, Spatchen, in his youth, had received instruction from a mysterious 'rustic polyhistor learned in arcane philosophy, the arts, black and otherwise, who knew the properties of herbs, metals and stones, and who was on exceedingly familiar terms with the spirits who lived around him in the forest.'

In spite of his insomniac irritability, Gerald smiled at this. The yarn had obviously been extracted from some earlier source probably composed, in a style already antiquated, in the latter part of the eighteenth century.

He read on to discover that the youthful Spatchen, who early on could demonstrate some artistic ability and possessed great ambition, had been taught to paint by this elder as part of a bargain. The old Magus somehow knew he was due to die soon, and wanted Spatchen to marry his daughter, who would otherwise have been left alone and unprotected. The girl must have been particularly plain or shrewish, because Spatchen was reluctant to comply at first but, when the 'rustic polyhistor' gave him a set of paint brushes that were deemed, in some way, to be 'special to the point of marvelousness' he gave in.

Almost at once, it was noted, he 'acquired the skills in draughtsmenship and colouring that were soon to gain him such high repute in London'. It was to the metropolis that Spatchen took his wife, almost immediately after her father's death. With them 'went two others, whom the old man, on his death bed, had insisted accompany his daughter, to wait upon and watch over her, wheresoever she should go, for perpetuity.'

There followed a hagiographic account of Spatchen's consequent fame, but not a word about his infamy. Gerald's WEA tutor had made much of the artist's debauchery, his various mistresses and his callous cruelty, widely commented upon at the time, but these aspects of the man's character were ignored. The mystery surrounding the never-explained disappearance of his wife, shortly before his abrupt, unaccountable desertion of the Capitol to return to the obscurity of his birthplace, and his hermit-like existence during the few years that were left to him, were likewise passed over.

"They're left out the best bits," Gerald said to himself, "and made him seem like a high-achieving dullard."

But while had been reading the leaflet, part of his mind had been running on a different, but parallel course, and this second line of conjecture had now taken precedence over his ruminations on the facts in the life of Wyckham Spatchen.

He got out of bed, stood for a few moments by the window, and stared down at the carpark. His vehicle was positioned at the base of the tree stump that was now illuminated by a dim light fastened above the Guest House's advertisement. He had taken the precaution of parking close to the exit, in case he became blocked in by other cars overnight but, as far as he could make out, no one at all had filled any of the other spaces. Perhaps he was the only non-resident staying that night?

He dressed quietly, emptied most of the almost worthless toiletry items from his overnight bag into a waste bin, and sidled out of his room onto the corridor.

❖

Anyone who knew Gerald would have been profoundly shocked by what he had done, but he had not taken himself by surprise. He had known for almost a lifetime what he was capable of, and had always made a conscious effort to control and suppress what he considered to be the potentially troublesome and possibly self-destructive side of his nature. But it had always been there, this urge to take from the world just whatsoever he wanted. Perhaps everyone contained the same potentialities, he didn't know or care: other people never had meant much to him, and he had little curiosity about them. But he kept an eye on the workings of his own inner self and tight guard on the activities of the exterior Gerald, and took pains to present a respectable front and always keep a distance between himself and the outside world. Always, that was, until tonight and, now he had broken his lifetime code of conduct for the first time, he felt sure he would get away with it.

In the small hours of the morning, driving through the deserted streets of the town he had observed from the top of the hill shortly before checking in to the Guest House, Gerald felt a tight, neat feeling of satisfaction in a job well done. He possessed *his own Spatchen*. He had always dreamed of owning something by one of the masters of English landscape painting—a scrap of drawing, perhaps, or some preliminary watercolour sketch. Previously, it had been nothing more than an idle dream but, as Gerald had always known, dreams can come true if you make them.

He was sure he had left no traces behind him; no clues to his identity. He had not been asked to register in a guest book or mentioned his name, had signed no check or even handed over any cash. His car had been parked sideways on to Tall Trees, so his number plates had not been visible from inside, and he was sure Mrs. Garstang had had no cause to venture out of the building, being too telephonically preoccupied inside. So nobody knew who he was, where he had come from, or where he might be going. He must have left fingerprints all over his room, but had never been in any kind of trouble with the law, so his dabs would not be on police records. The toiletry articles he had binned were all quite new, and could have been bought any Marks and Spencer's store. He glanced down contentedly at the overnight bag on the seat beside him. It had been, as he had calculated, just the right size to contain his booty and protect it from accidents he might have had, blundering out of the building in the dark.

The standard lamp had no longer been lit but some light from the corridor preceded Gerald as he had entered the guest room. The woman was no longer seated beside the painting though her toga-like grey cotton garment was draped across the back of the chair as though she had been squeezed out of it, like paste from a tube. A quick snoop about in the gloom convinced him all the other chairs had now been vacated. Everything was as quiet as he could have hoped, so he took the painting off its hook, stuffed it into his bag, and crept downstairs towards the front exit. When he came to the reception desk his heart nearly stopped because Mrs. Garstang was crouching there, mumbling into the telephone receiver. Luckily, her back was towards him. Gerald decided he would hit her with something if he had to—there was a choice of heavy objects that would serve as weapons to hand—but the woman must have been totally absorbed in her conversation because he was easily able to sneak past without disturbing her.

❖

So Gerald drove home that night after all.

Back in his austere and tidy flat he found somewhere to hide his overnight bag and its contents, toasted himself with a glass of celebratory port (here's to crime) and prepared for bed. As he did so, he noticed he had brought in a quantity of muck on his shoes—trails of damp, moldy leaves and black soil marked his recent passage over the previously spotless carpets. Peculiar, because it was early Spring, not Autumn, and the ground outside was frozen hard, imprisoning everything on and in it.

Never mind, Gerald thought, his carpet sweeper would soon sort that out in the morning.

It was four-thirty when he finally got to sleep.

And it was very late when he woke up, but it was the beginning of the weekend and he was used to spending most of Saturday morning between the sheets. He closed his eyes again, stretched out his legs, and felt some discomfort down there, around his knees and feet. Turning to adjust his position made him feel worse, because something itchy had somehow managed to get inside his pyjama jacket. Gerald reached in to scratch, and felt fragments of some substance scrape against his skin. He sat up suddenly, and peered down under the front of his jacket.

Leaves. There was no doubt about it. Half a dozen shrunken, splotched, sweat-dampened leaves were plastered against his stomach. They were hard to dislodge, as though they had some slightly adhesive quality. As he picked the leaves off his body one by one, he remembered how he had become the owner of his very own Spatchen.

It scared him, what he had done—he had *let himself go*. Broken the restrained habits of a lifetime. He had lost control, and perhaps his self respect, to gain, of all things, a Spatchen. He wondered if it had been worth it, and got out of bed to take a look at the painting.

In broad daylight, the picture was hardly recognizable as the one he had admired in the seedy Guest House. The overall composition was not good, with weak, under-painted spaces in the foreground, and the perspective was not quite resolved, giving the scene a slightly giddy look. Gerald wondered if Spatchen had been drunk or very ill when he had painted it. And if it was, as the woman at Tall Trees had told him, the artist's last work perhaps the man had died before finishing it. Gerald decided he didn't think much of it as a piece of art, and felt almost as cheated as he would have done if he'd paid for the thing, but it was still exciting to own what had to be in some way a significant work by the flawed genius.

He sat down, put the painting on his knee, and studied it more closely. Previously he had been under the impression that there were three figures in the lower left corner of the painting, but he had been mistaken. There were only two: an indistinguishable creature somehow caught in a whirlwind, surrounded by a spiralling column of leaves, leading a slender, ashen-faced youngish woman dressed in what Gerald now thought might have been a winding-sheet. These two strange creatures were obviously making their way from the building almost completely hidden by trees in the right upper portion of the painting. Gerald let his mind work upon the painting as though it was a problem to be solved until the sound of his front door bell snapped him to his feet with a guilty start. He almost ran to hide the painting, then opened his door to a postman with a parcel.

That broke the spell and brought Gerald to his senses. He was a fastidious man with settled habits. The rubbish he had brought in on his shoes the night before offended his sense of order and he set about tidying the flat. The leaves and others scraps of vegetation had dried, however, in the centrally-heated atmosphere, and become light as feathers. They flew into the air as he hoovered among them, and settled elsewhere. When he thought he had succeeded in clearing one half of his floor space he looked back and saw he had left trails of obdurate leaves where he had been, as though they were following him about, or hiding behind him. After a while the machine stopped picking them up and Gerald realized the bag inside was full, and that he didn't have a spare to replace it. He switched off the carpet sweeper angrily, feeling hot and bothered.

It occurred to him he had not washed for almost thirty-six hours: his skin itched and he had become grubby. He was in the mood for a long, soothing soak rather than a shower, so he ran a bath, anticipating a luxurious experience that would cure him of the gloom that had descended upon him. After lying back, with just his nose and chin above the steaming water, he shut his eyes and, for five minutes, attempted to detach himself from the rather anxious thoughts that jostled together in the back of his mind, but without success.

Activity, then, was perhaps the answer? Without opening his eyes Gerald reached out to the table beside the bath, found the shampoo in its familiar place, squeezed some onto his scalp, and began to rub vigorously at what remained of his hair. Normally this was a simple enough task, as his hair was cropped short, but today there seemed to be an unusual quantity of the stuff back there, clinging to his hands. He rubbed harder, but the more he did so, the more difficult it became to move his fingers—they were somehow becoming entangled. He jerked one hand free, grabbed a face-cloth, and wiped away shampoo that had fallen down his brow and opened his eyes. For a few moments his vision was blurred, and at first he thought his eyes might be playing some trick, but it was not so. As they cleared he saw that he was lying up to his neck in a blue-black pool of liquid mulch full of rotten leaf-mold, decomposing grass turfs, and other kinds of unidentifiable filth.

Gerald twisted like a tortured creature and floundered around in the pool of muck. His palms were slippery with filth and he found it hard to clamber out of the bath. When he was standing free he scraped at his skin with a towel but found it impossible to get clean.

The stuff was like half-set glue on him. And its quantity seemed to be increasing all the time.

In spite of his rising panic, he knew what had to be done. What was expected of him.

❖

Gerald parked his car at an angle outside the front of Tall Trees Guest House. As he ran to the building he noticed it was in far worse condition than it had seemed in the twilight of the previous evening, and now gave an impression of dereliction, even. Inside, the reception area was deserted for once. The phone was lying on its back on the desk and a faint voice could be heard endlessly repeating prerecorded instructions.

Gerald was in such a hurry to get up the stairs he lost his footing and almost dropped the painting, which he had been carrying under the winter overcoat he was wearing over his trousers and shirt to hide as much of himself as possible. He kicked against the door of the Guest Room and burst in.

The seat beside the fireplace was unoccupied. A length of old, none-too-clean grey cloth, wrapped in a spiral, was still draped over the back of the chair and trailed down onto the floor in front of it. The rest of the room looked as though a storm had blown through it. Most of the chairs at both ends were on their sides or backs. A window had smashed inwards and its heavy curtains had been torn down, providing more light than there had been on the occasion of his previous visit.

He felt about on the wall above the mantel until he found a protruding hook, then re-hung the painting with shaky fingers. He stepped back, saw it wasn't straight, and tried to adjust it. The plaster holding the hook must have perished because, as he fumbled around, the section it had been driven into fell away in a crumbling, dusty chunk. Gerald grabbed the frame as it fell, lost his balance, and fell himself. As the frame hit the floor there was a sound of breaking glass.

Gerald got to his feet and stared down at the ruined painting, which he could tell was beyond restoration. Whole areas of paint had flaked away from the canvas, which was ripped right across in a couple of places.

He stood for some time listening—expecting, because of the noise he had made during his entry and subsequently, that someone would come to investigate what he was up to. But the building was absolutely silent. Back in the corridor he scampered down the stairs, not caring too much about the sound he made now because he knew he was only seconds away from the reception area. At the foot of the stairs, however, he came up against a door which had certainly been open just minutes before but was now, he discovered, closed and locked. It was a remarkably heavy door, probably made of oak, and it didn't take very long for Gerald to come to the conclusion that he hadn't the strength to break its iron lock. An alternative exit had to be found.

He ran back up the stairs and must have made a wrong turning at the top, because he found himself in an unfamiliar part of the building in a section that had been disused for decades. The walls were bare in places and the floor's unvarnished boards were partially covered by lengths of ancient embossed wallpaper that had fallen down over the years. Someone had been that way before him though, and perhaps not too long ago, because he could just make out footprints in the white dust that had once been wallpaper paste and that now coated everything.

The footprints went one way only: whoever had made them had not come back, so the chances were that they would lead him out of the building. Or so Gerald reasoned. He followed them anyway, and shortly found they had been joined by a second set of prints, and then, moments later by a third. Memories of a favorite childhood story about a bear and a piglet hunting an elephant made him wonder if he was, in fact, merely going round in circles. He glanced back and was relieved to see his own prints were clearly distinguishable from the others, which he continued to follow.

The Guest House was much bigger than he had imagined. He had been walking briskly for at least fifteen minutes, it seemed, and must have covered the best part of a mile. By now there were dozens of lines of footprints leading him along, all merging into each other, as though a crowd had passed that way. Gerald was beginning to think the building must be of vast proportions when he turned a corner and found himself in a short, narrow passage that led into the ruin of what had once been some kind of conservatory. Rotten wood and broken glass crunched under his feet, and shreds of the structure's canvas roof or awning caught round his shoes and ankles and threatened to trip him. Cautiously he made his way out of this wreckage into a garden beyond.

Well, it had been a garden once: now it was a wasteland. The surrounding walls had collapsed in places and the almost jungle-like woods beyond had ventured forward through the gaps to within yards of the back of the Guest House. Vaguely, Gerald wondered about the presence of trees that he had certainly not noticed on his first visit to the building. But he had other things to worry about; his growing sense of becoming irretrievably lost and, more pressingly, the extreme discomfort he was now feeling under his clothing, against his skin, where the vegetable rubbish that still clung to him was beginning to move painfully about. The dead leaves were on the march around his carcass, it seemed, like so many soldier ants exploring the terrain of a vanquished enemy. Gerald felt again an irresistible urge to strip off and soak himself in deep water, but there was no deep water around.

He was, in fact, in a very dry place indeed.

He started to run again, still following the tracks of many feet, along a trail that led him away from High Trees, towards the other, looming trees. He stumbled over a pile of fallen masonry, part of the tumbled walls, and scampered forward into the woods that soon thickened into what he began to think of as a forest. He blundered on, driven increasingly distracted by his bodily discomforts. These were made worse by the sudden deterioration of his clothing, that was becoming unstitched, and was falling apart under the furious exertions of his limbs. Soon, he was almost naked, except for the leaves that no longer clustered round his body but broke free and swirled around him as he hurtled on and on.

❖

He had gone a long way through the forest, for what seemed to him an endless time, when he came to a clearing in the trees, and it was only then he began to realize where he was.

The two familiar figures, standing a short distance along a dirt path that led away into the trees on the far side of the clearing, appeared to be waiting for him. Meekly, he took his place beside them.

Then, very, very slowly, as though to do so was a terrible painful duty, Gerald turned his head 'round over his right shoulder, looked out, and saw just exactly what he feared and expected to see.

The room was, as ever, full of shadows but, as far as he could tell, was otherwise quite unoccupied.

Ray Garton
THE HOMELESS COUPLE

For Oscar:
we'll miss you.

oland Pearce walked to and from work every day, all year long, in rain, snow, or heat of summer. Ever since he'd lost his wife, the walk had been as much a part of his daily ritual as waking up in the morning and going to bed at night. Roland's job at the accounting firm of Schallert and Timmons allowed him no physical exercise, and he spent most of his time there—he nearly always arrived early and left late—so the brisk walk helped keep him healthy and trim. It was fourteen long city blocks from Roland's apartment to the building where he worked. That meant he had to leave earlier than he would if he took the bus or subway in order to get to work on time, but he didn't mind. By the time he'd spent the night alone in his apartment, he was ready to get out of there. He usually didn't sleep much, anyway, and was wide awake by five every morning, leaving him more than enough time to have some coffee and watch the morning news.

On this particular morning, it was raining hard. The charcoal sky seemed to hang just above the tops of the city's towering buildings. Roland held a large, deep, black umbrella in his right hand, and a matching briefcase in his left. The rain made such a loud roar as it fell on the umbrella that the sounds of the city seemed far away.

As he did every morning, Roland stopped at Mellenger's diner on the way for a breakfast of half a grapefruit and toast or a bagel with cream cheese and another cup of coffee. There was always a newspaper on the counter and he usually gave the headlines and the business section a cursory glance and exchanged empty pleasantries with the proprietor, an enormously fat man with a walrus mustache. Roland had been eating breakfast there for years, but he did not know the man's name, and it had never occurred to him to ask. The diner was just another part of his route, and he paid no more attention to it every day than he did the rest of his surroundings. The entire walk to and from work had become so routine, he hardly needed to look where he was going.

Occasionally, something extraordinary would occur during Roland's walk, and he would stop and take notice. The previous summer, he'd been on his way home when a woman had screamed across the street. He'd turned toward the scream, like everyone else around him, to see a woman clutching her purse as a small, filthy-looking man pulled on it repeatedly, trying to snatch it away from her. The man slammed a fist into her chest and she fell backward. He ran away with the purse, and the woman continued to scream for help as she struggled back to her feet. Roland had walked on then, along with the other pedestrians who had stopped on the sidewalk. He wasn't about to chase after a drug addict for a purse, and he'd thought that if she was smart, that woman wouldn't either. There was nothing she could keep in there that would be worth his life, hers, or anyone else's.

The year before that, a battered old pickup truck had jumped the curb half a block ahead of Roland and driven through the window of an American Cancer Society thrift store. The wreckage quickly drew a crowd, but as Roland approached, he stepped off the sidewalk and walked around it.

Such things seldom happened, of course, and that was fine with Roland. Since his life had changed so drastically seven years ago, he had come to appreciate routine, to crave it. He had no interest in change or surprises. So when he walked to and from work, he remained within himself, noticing as little as possible on his route, thus giving each walk a bland sameness.

Roland enjoyed letting his mind roam as he walked, letting it spiral up toward the sky like a helium balloon trailing a string that had been released by a child. He tried not to let anything get hold of that string and pull the balloon back down to earth.

There was one distraction that wouldn't go away: the Homeless Couple. He didn't know their names, so he thought of them only as the Homeless Couple. He'd first seen them midway on his route about eight months ago, beneath an aluminum awning that stretched about twenty feet from the entrance of a tiny convenience store to a phone booth. They wore what had once been clothes but were now little more than layers of filthy rags, and they never seemed to move from their spot, where the man asked passersby for change and always said, "God bless you," no matter what kind of response he received. He had done that the first time Roland had seen the two of them.

That first time, Roland had seen the woman first. She'd stood in the telephone booth against the wall of the building. Normally, Roland wouldn't have turned his head to look at her, but peripherally, there seemed to be something wrong with the way she was standing—slumped and leaning against the inside wall of the booth—as though she'd been injured. It was as an old-fashioned phone booth, the kind with a circular fluorescent light overhead that came on once you'd stepped inside and closed the accordion door. Roland hadn't seen one like it in years—the booths had been replaced by banks of open payphones that took up much less space—and he'd *never* noticed that particular phone booth before. It had been there for a long time, though. It was marred by graffiti and a couple of the Plexiglas windows were broken out. A strip of plastic over the doorway used to read TELEPHONE, but someone had used a marking pen to cross out TELEP and crudely change the N into an M, so it looked like this:

 H O N\E

The other reason he'd turned to look at her was that the door of the phone booth was open and, in spite of the sounds of traffic, Roland had heard the woman crying as she talked into the telephone receiver, sobbing between garbled words. He hadn't stopped, or even slowed his pace, just glanced to his left at the woman in the phone booth . . . and the man appeared in front of him, making it necessary for him to stop.

"Excuse me, sir," the man had said, running a hand over his hair, which was long and slicked back in an almost stylish way, except that instead of styling gel, it glistened with grease from not bathing. His voice was hoarse and his eyes were bleary and bloodshot, red around the edges and had pockets of puffy flesh beneath them. "Could you please spare some change? See, my wife and I—" He jerked his head toward the woman in the phone booth. "—we haven't eaten in a couple days, and we could sure use a little—"

"No, I'm sorry," Roland said as he stepped around the man and continued walking.

"You don't have to apologize," the man called after him. "God bless you."

As Roland walked away, the woman's deep, racking sobs had faded behind him.

He'd seen them every day since. A few months after they'd first appeared, the man approached him and started to ask for change again, then he'd recognized Roland and backed away with a weary smile.

Nearly every time he saw them, one or the other was in the phone booth, talking on the phone, and whether it was the man or the woman, they were always upset about something. Sometimes even the man was crying. Now and then, Roland would catch a few words as he passed.

"No, baby, it's gonna be all right. I promise, I promise. . ."

". . . listen to me, sweetie, don't cry . . ."

"I'm so glad we can talk . . . so glad . . ."

"I miss you so much."

It occurred to Roland that, for two people who couldn't afford to eat—and it was obvious from their appearance that they were seriously malnourished—they certainly had a lot of change to spend on emotional phonecalls in that booth.

Roland didn't understand the "homeless problem." He was forty-two years old and his grandparents had raised his parents through the depression. Back then, work had been almost nonexistent. The entire country, with the exception of the very rich, had been made poor overnight, and suddenly, everything from food to clothes was too expensive. They had to get by on wits and potato soup.

Apparently, it had been a different time that had produced a different breed. There was certainly no depression now. The economy was in great shape, Wall Street was singing . . . and yet there were homeless people begging on the streets. The only conclusion Roland could come to was that they had simply given up on the responsibilities that most people lived with every day. They had decided to go out and ask others for their money. Oh, sure, *they* didn't see it that way. *They* honestly believed they were at the end of their ropes. But that was only because they had decided not to reach out and grab all the other ropes dangling around them. A low-paying job was better than no job. Sometimes McDonald's was all that was available, whether for food or work. But they didn't want that. In being above such menial work, they had put themselves below everyone else . . . begging on the streets.

Roland refused to believe that he was not compassionate. He realized there were many people in the country who had the rug pulled out from under them and needed some help getting back on their feet. But in such a thriving economy, it was hard to believe so many people were "homeless" because of financial misfortune, and unable to recover from the situation. Most of them were simply people who had given up their lives in favor of drugs or alcohol, or both. They all reeked of booze as they staggered the sidewalks, asking for change. That was why Roland refused to give them handouts. They would only use it to buy more of whatever substance had them at the end of their ropes anyway, and he did not want to contribute.

Although Roland realized, as he turned the corner and headed into the business district, that the man who had stepped in front of him eight months ago had smelled of nothing but body odor.

But the most annoying thing of all about the Homeless Couple was that they never left their spot next to the phone booth, against the wall of the insurance building. The city was filled with shelters and programs to help the homeless get back into the mainstream . . . but they never took advantage of them. Just a few yards from where they stayed was a small convenience store. Every once in awhile, Roland saw them eating, but it was always food from that store: Twinkies, Hostess Fruit Pies, packaged sandwiches. He wondered if they had other people get the food for them when they could afford it, because they never seemed to get more than a few feet from the phone booth.

Something odd had happened twice in the eight months that they'd taken up residence there. Roland had been passing them when the telephone in the booth had rung. They'd been sitting on the sidewalk, their backs against the wall of the building, but the second they heard that ring, they'd shot to their feet and scrambled to the booth, nearly tripping over one another. He'd only been passing, so he'd heard none of the conversation . . . but he was sure it had been the same emotional wailing he'd heard and seen before. It didn't make sense. Who would be calling the likes of them? On a payphone?

⁂

Roland rounded a corner and passed through a storm of rap music coming from a group of teenage boys huddled beneath an awning outside a newsstand. On his right, a car horn honked repeatedly and someone shouted an obscenity into the rain. But Roland was remembering a vacation he and his wife had taken once, before they'd had the baby, to California's wine country. It had been a beautiful week, over much too soon. They'd sipped more wine that week than in both of their lives combined, before or since. It had been a honeymoon more than a vacation, actually, because when they *should* have taken their honeymoon, Roland had been roped into working because of a plague-like flu that had swept through Schallert and Timmons and had left a dangerous number of positions empty.

He was starting to feel a nibbling of guilt deep in his chest and immediately pulled his head out of the Napa Valley. He had to be careful with memories; even now, he sometimes found it very easy to upset himself.

He'd been lectured by well-meaning friends and his sister—*especially* his sister—about his failure to grieve. Not so much lately, but relentlessly in the year following her loss. They'd been worried because he'd remained so calm, even stoic, before, during, and after the funeral. It was unhealthy to hold back, they'd told him; it was natural, even necessary, to mourn, and if he didn't allow himself to do it, it would come out later, perhaps in some other way, some way that *wasn't* so natural. He'd listened to them all and thanked them for their concern, and he'd tried to tell them he was mourning, in his own way. When they didn't believe him, Roland had understood. None of them had ever really known him, not even his sister. The only person who would've understood *his* way of mourning—which, like everything about him, was very private and quiet and solitary—was his wife. Of course, by then, she'd passed the point of being understanding.

Roland took a deep breath, filling his lungs with the cold, damp air, then exhaled slowly, cheeks puffed, lips curled up in a small pucker. He would be at work soon. He needed a clear head, a place where numbers could dance.

"Mister! Hey, *Mister!*"

Roland barely heard the call, as if it were coming from the farthest end of the block.

"Mister! *Please!*"

The skin at the base of Roland's skull tingled and his brow wrinkled slightly.

"*Briefcase man!*" The voice was loud, but brittle and cracked.

Roland's step faltered and his shoes made scritching sounds on the wet sidewalk. He looked around quickly, his head moving in bird-like jerks, eyes squinting through rain-misted glasses. Roland spotted the homeless man behind him and to his left.

The Homeless Couple

Although the aluminum awning kept the rain from falling directly on him, the man was still soaked. His cheeks and temples had fallen away, making his face and head look too long and impossibly narrow. What there was of his dark beard stood out sharply against his pale skin; some of that skin glared through the wiry beard in spots were no whiskers had grown. He was sitting against the wall, legs stretched out, with what looked like a large bundle of rags in his lap.

"Help me," the man said, holding out a dirty hand. "Please, you gotta help me."

Looking around, Roland saw everyone else on the sidewalk moving around him from both directions, as if he were a tree growing in the middle of a stream. He looked at the man again.

"I-I-I . . . I told you once before," Roland began, shrugging, but the man didn't let him finish.

"No, not *that*, not . . . not *me*." He shook his head slowly, wearily. "My wife. Please, you gotta help my *wife*."

Roland frowned, took a couple short steps toward the man and leaned his head forward slightly, staring at the bundle of rags. After a few seconds, the image changed, clarified. It was the homeless woman, lying in a fetal position across her husband's lap, covered with something that might have served as a blanket at one time. With that realization, Roland's frown deepened.

"What, uh . . . what's wrong?" Roland asked as he took a few more slow steps, moving closer to the Homeless Couple.

"My wife," the man said. "She's sick. Duh-dying, I think." On the last three words, his voice broke, became throatier, as if her were about to sob. "I don't know what to do . . . what we *can* do. We . . . weeee . . . we have nothing." There was pain in his voice, not whininess, but a great, raw pain. He was either near tears or had been crying before Roland got there and was about to start again.

The surprisingly small bundle on his lap suddenly quaked with a series of deep, ripping coughs. She rolled away from her husband and her face became visible as she continued coughing. Bright red blood sprayed from her mouth with each cough and rained down on her skull-like face, spattering her ghostly-pale skin. There were already dried streaks of blood on her face where she'd tried to wipe it off with her fingers. When the coughing stopped, her hand appeared from beneath the rags and wiped the fresh blood, smearing it with the old.

Roland gasped at the sight. "My God," he said. "She's got to see a doctor."

"Well," the man said with a cold, hollow and unsmiling chuckle, "in case you haven't guessed it already, we don't have a doctor."

She coughed some more, sprayed more blood. Some of it speckled her husband's pale, sunken cheek.

"Well, she needs medical attention," Roland said. "Right away. If she stays out here in the rain like this, she'll—"

"Please help us," the man said, his quivering voice nearly a whisper.

"But I-I-I'm not a doctor. I don't even know why you . . . why *did* you call me over here, anyway?"

"I see you walk by every day. You're . . . familiar. I thought you'd . . . do something, I guess."

Roland looked at the woman's blood-stained face again and muttered, "Well, I-yuh, I could, uh . . ." He walked quickly to the phone booth, fishing some change out of his pocket. He closed his umbrella and stepped inside, hanging the umbrella on his forearm by its hooked handle. As he closed the accordion door, he heard the man calling to him again.

"Wait, wait, no, don't—"

Roland ignored him, lifted the receiver, dropped two quarters into the slot and put the receiver to his ear. His forefinger froze an inch from the 9 button when he heard a strange sound in his ear. He'd expected a dial-tone, but instead heard an open connection, echoing and whispery, crackling with static. Over the line came the nonsensical sing-song burbling of a small child, a toddler.

"Hello?" he snapped. The child continued. "Could you please hang up the phone? I have an emergen—oh, why bother." He pressed the lever down with two fingers, waited a couple seconds, then let it up again. The child was still there, distant and hollow-sounding. And then, from out of the nonsense words and baby sounds:

"Daa-*deeee!*"

Roland's jaw became slack and his eyes widened suddenly beneath his frowning brow. Gooseflesh crawled beneath his clothes as an image flashed in his mind, vivid as if he were walking in on it for the first time all over again. His wife Deborah on the kitchen floor, rocking their dead baby in her arms as she hummed a lullaby.

The receiver rattled when Roland slammed it back into its cradle.

The Homeless Couple

He fumbled with the door until it opened, then tripped out of the booth and opened his umbrella. He looked up and down the sidewalk, then across the street, for another phone.

"That telephone doesn't work," the homeless man said as Roland walked toward him. "Please, could you just—"

"If the phone doesn't work," Roland interrupted, shaken and suddenly angry for no reason he could readily identify, "why is it that every time I walk by here, one of you is *talking* on it?"

Before the man could reply, his wife heaved with more coughs. It sounded as if chunks of her lung were tearing away and were about to shoot from her mouth with the spray of blood.

"The county hospital is just a few blocks from here," Roland said. "They can't turn you away. I could call a cab and—"

"I won't take her there. She wouldn't want me to. They killed our little girl."

Roland slowly hunkered down beside the man and leaned forward slightly, his throat suddenly dry and scratchy. A wave of nausea passed through him and he swallowed hard a couple times. "They killed your . . . you . . . you lost a daughter?"

"She was just eighteen months old when she got sick. Just a year and a half old. She wasn't important enough, though. People like us . . . we're not important enough. They let her die. They killed her." He bowed his head and looked down at his wife's bloodied face, his upper body rocking slightly.

"Well, I-I . . . I don't have a car," Roland said. "I don't know what I can—"

"I don't know what I expected you to do," he muttered without looking up. "Sorry for bothering you."

Roland stood there for a long moment, just watching the Homeless Couple. The man never looked up again. The woman kept coughing. He walked on finally, still frowning, his pace a little slower than before, as unsettling thoughts flitted through his mind. But it wasn't the Homeless Couple he was thinking about. It was the voice on the phone, the child who had said, "Daddy?" And no matter how hard he tried, he could not shake the crystal clear image of his wife, in shock on the kitchen floor, rocking their dead baby in her arms. Nor could he shake the sickening certainty that the voice on the phone had been his daughter's.

"Years ago," he muttered to himself under his breath. "That was years ago."

✥

He was distracted all day. He made errors in his work, forgot about a meeting, and even forgot what he was doing at one point. It wasn't like him. Others noticed, and a couple people asked if he was feeling all right. He took advantage of the opening and said he thought he was coming down with the flu. Someone suggested he go home early and get plenty of liquids and rest. He paused to think about it, and it confused him a little. Go home early? Why? What would he do? If he really were coming down with the flu . . . well, that would be different. But to just go home early?

He told his coworkers he would make it to the end of the day, then went about his work, trying hard to focus, to ignore his dark, disturbing thoughts. That proved to be difficult, though. They would not go away.

Roland and Deborah had Melanie at the beginning of their fourth year of marriage. When they first married, they'd agreed they weren't ready—emotionally, and especially financially—to have a child and had decided to wait. As Roland got to know his new wife better, he was glad of that.

She was . . . fragile. During the year and a half they had known one another before marrying, he'd learned early on that she was very sensitive, that she was easily hurt, that she'd been abused as a child and again as an adult in two relationships before they'd met. But later, he realized that she was just fragile, a person with vulnerable feelings and a delicate personality. She wasn't just sensitive about certain things; she had a difficult time handling crises, drastic or unexpected changes in routine, or even the anticipation of those things.

That didn't bother Roland. If anything, it made him more protective of her. She had a job for awhile, working in an antiques store. But when she couldn't take that anymore, she just stayed home. He brought her something every evening: flowers, candy, a balloon, a sentimental card. They kept to themselves after she quit work, stayed home in the evening watching videos, or regular television, reading aloud to one another, or making love.

He came home one night to find Deborah crying. It wasn't the first time; he'd come home to find her crying quite a lot. But this time, it was about something. She was pregnant. "And we're not ready," she said. "We're just not ready yet." But Roland thought they were. He had already made advancements at work and was making more money than when they'd married, and there were more advancements to come. He told her they could afford it, and of course they were ready, because they loved one another so much and were so happy, and that was all anyone needed to have a baby, right?

Once baby Melanie was home, Roland saw a change in Deborah, a change he'd expected. She was happier than he'd ever seen her, ecstatic. Her entire life embraced the child, and Roland never came home to find her crying again.

Until fourteen months after Melanie's birth, when he found Deborah on the kitchen floor, back against the cupboard doors beneath the sink, legs splayed before her, holding Melanie in her arms. Deborah's eyes were wide, but in an empty way, and she seemed to stare at something a great distance away. She stroked Melanie's hair and half-sang, half-moaned some off-key lullaby as she rocked the baby in her arms.

Roland spoke to Deborah repeatedly, but she did not reply, or even acknowledge his presence. He took his daughter's right hand between his thumb and fingers; the ends of her tiny fingers were black and she felt unnaturally cold. Heart beating faster, he knelt beside them and pressed two fingers to Melanie's neck to find a pulse. There was none. He gasped and fell away from them onto his back, crawled backward a few feet, then grabbed one of the chairs by the kitchen table and climbed up, until he was standing again. "My God, my God," he muttered, staring at his dead daughter and absent wife.

An ambulance came, and with it, two police cars. A metal hairclip was found on the floor in the dining room beneath an electrical outlet. Apparently, Melanie had found one of her mother's hairclips and had stuck it into the outlet. And apparently, it was more than her mother could take.

Melanie was taken to the morgue, and Deborah was taken to the psychiatric ward of the Sisters of Mercy Hospital. Roland handled all the burial arrangements. Deborah's doctor told Roland that the funeral would only worsen Deborah's condition, so she did not attend. Roland visited her twice a day—once before work and once after—until she came home two months later.

Those two months were the longest and loneliest of Roland's life. Their small apartment seemed cavernous when he was there alone, and yet the walls always seemed about to close on him and smash him flat. He tried to keep himself occupied by eating dinners at a reasonably priced cafeteria and seeing a double feature a couple nights a week, no matter what was showing, at the Phoenix. His sister visited a few times, and he was always glad to see her because he thought it would kill time, fill some emptiness. But he always found himself wishing she would go a few minute after she arrived; her tears and condolences were needles driven into his skin, and when she said they could always have another baby, he wanted to scream, to break something. He didn't, of course. He held it all in.

When he was in the apartment, he kept the television or radio on to bury the silence, to cover up the absence of Melanie's crying or sweet babbling. He did everything he could to keep away the knowledge that he would never hear those sounds again, never change her diaper or make her laugh by playing tug-of-war with his tie. When he did let such thoughts in, they made him feel helpless, impossibly small, tiny as an insect, and they fell on him with breathless finality, blocking out all light, crushing him.

When Deborah finally came home, Roland was so happy to have her back that he didn't notice how drained she was. Drained of personality, of interest in anything, of life. She was to see her doctor twice a week and attend group therapy twice a week. Roland made arrangements at work so he could drive Deborah to her appointments. He'd expected her to be different, to need time to heal, and he was prepared to do whatever necessary to bring her back to the person she'd been before.

After a few months had passed and there had been no improvement, Roland became concerned. If anything, it seemed Deborah had gotten worse. She seldom spoke, and shook her head whenever Roland suggested they go out to eat or see a movie. He often found her crying, and sometimes awoke in the middle of the night to find her sitting up beside him, sniffling and muttering to herself. He finally decided to be very frank with her, sat down beside her and told her she was not to blame for Melanie's death, it was an accident, the kind of thing that could, and does, happen to millions of people, but it happened to *them* this time. Her only response was to shake her head and sob.

Shortly after three o'clock on an early, moonless spring morning, Roland was awakened by a sound. He assumed it was Deborah, crying again. But as he rolled over, he found she wasn't there. The room was cold and Roland was surprised to see the window open. When he heard someone shouting urgently down below, he gasped and threw the covers off, bounded to the window and leaned out. From fourteen stories up, it was impossible to identify the body on the sidewalk below with any certainty, but he knew it was Deborah.

More burial arrangements, another funeral. He'd gone home once again to an empty apartment, but with the knowledge that it would remain that way, empty except for him. He'd decided to move almost immediately.

At Deborah's funeral, her doctor had approached Roland. He'd said Roland appeared a little too calm, too composed, and suggested Roland make an appointment with him. When Roland did not, the doctor called him at home twice to make the suggestion again, with a little more urgency. "Grief is a natural and necessary process," he said. "Not grieving in the aftermath of a great loss is unhealthy and can lead to serious problems. It's entirely possible for one to experience a complete breakdown as a result of not properly grieving the loss of a loved one. I strongly suggest that you make an appointment with me, Mr. Pearce."

But he had not seen the doctor. Instead, Roland had moved to a new apartment. That was when he'd started walking to and from work, leaving the apartment early and coming back late.

✣

By the time he left work that evening, everyone else was gone and the sun—hidden behind charcoal clouds all day—had set. It was still raining, but harder now than it had been that morning. And Roland was still unable to clear his head of the upsetting thoughts that had been with him all day.

He considered taking a different route to avoid passing the phone booth, where he knew the Homeless Couple would be. He wondered how the woman was, and the thought made him wince, made him angry at himself. It was a useless, stupid thought, she was going to die without medical attention. The next thought came without warning:

And with his daughter and wife dead, he'll be all alone. Just like me.

Roland sucked in a sharp breath, as if he'd experienced a sudden pain.

Midway through his walk, he saw several red and blue lights spinning atop vehicles directly ahead, and he slowed his pace. An ambulance was parked at the curb along with two police cars, one beside it and one about a car-length behind it. As he got closer, Roland heard someone shouting desperately up ahead. There seemed to be a struggle going on, and Roland was about to cross the street and go around it when he recognized the voice.

"No, please don't, *please* don't take her. *PLEASE! DON'T TAKE HER!*"

Roland moved slowly closer to the group of people moving erratically on the sidewalk.

"God*dammit*, you son of a *bitch*, get your hands *off* her!"

Feet shuffled and scuffed on the pavement. There were grunts and muffled curses.

Traffic sped by, tires making *shush . . . shush* sounds on the wet road, as if to say the whole thing were a secret, to be kept under wraps.

Roland stopped in front of the convenience store and watched as two police officers fought with the Homeless Couple, tried to remove the woman from her husband's arms. Two paramedics stood nearby next to a waiting stretcher, talking to one another quietly. The police officers finally separated the Homeless Couple, knocking the man to the sidewalk, and the paramedics stepped forward.

As the paramedics lifted the woman onto the stretcher, Roland's mouth dropped open for a moment, then he snapped it shut. She was stiff. Her arms and legs did not move, her bent body did not straighten.

The telephone rang in the open booth. It wasn't the chirp of a cordless phone or cellphone. It was a genuine, old-fashioned ring, the sound of a rattled bell, and it cut through the night like a scream.

The paramedics loaded the corpse into the ambulance and the two police officers approached the homeless man again, one of them removing his handcuffs from his belt. The homeless man scrambled to his feet and shot around them, got into the phone booth and slammed the door behind him. The overhead light was dim and flickered erratically as the man grabbed the receiver and said, "Hello?" He said it so loudly—shouted it, really, in a raw, torn voice—Roland could hear it even through the pouring rain outside the closed phone booth. The man began to speak rapidly into the phone, clutching the receiver with both hands as he tossed nervous glances at the two police officers approaching the phone booth.

The doors on the back of the ambulance slammed and the paramedics headed for the front of the van.

The man in the phone booth pressed himself against the accordion door, still talking frantically, preventing the police officers from getting in.

Roland hurried over to the paramedic who was about to get into the passenger side of the ambulance.

"Excuse me," he said, "but . . . are they going to arrest that man?"

The paramedic turned and faced him. He was about twenty-five, already balding. A toothpick worked back and forth beneath his blond mustache.

"Sure," the paramedic said with a smirk. "He hit one of the cops. Punched him right in the face."

"Who called you?"

He shrugged. "Someone called and said there was a woman bleeding on the sidewalk here. She had blood on her, but she hadn't been bleeding in awhile. He wouldn't let go of her, so we had to call the cops." He climbed into the van.

Roland put his hand on the door before the paramedic could close it and asked, "What will happen now? To his wife, I mean?"

"His wife? You know this guy?"

"No, I just . . . I see them here when I walk back and forth to work, that's all."

"Well, if you know him, the cops might wanna talk to you. In case he doesn't have any ID, or something, y'know?"

There was an explosion of sound and Roland turned to see the two police officers reaching into the opened phone booth, trying to pull the man out. He was still clutching the receiver, in one hand now, its metal cord taut as he tried to hold it to his ear.

"I'm coming, honey!" he shouted. "Don't worry! I'm coming! I'll be right there, just—"

The receiver slipped from his hand and he and the two police officers tumbled backward out of the phone booth. All three of them fell onto the wet sidewalk.

The paramedic chuckled, shook his head, then said to Roland, "See ya." He slammed the door shut as the ambulance's engine came to life.

The two police officers got to their feet quickly and lifted the man up between them by his arms. The officer with the handcuffs began to speak to the man in a low voice with a sort of sing-song rhythm.

Even though he couldn't hear the words, Roland knew what the police officer was saying from a lifetime of television programs. He was telling the homeless man his rights.

The ambulance pulled away from the curb slowly, careful not to hit the patrol car parked beside it, and drove away, disappearing in the evening traffic.

Roland sighed as he stepped toward the curb, planning to get off the sidewalk long enough to walk around the two police officers and the homeless man. Before he took a full step, he heard two pained grunts and another quick scuffle of feet on wet concrete, then an outburst of voices all speaking at once.

"He's got my gun!"

"You just back off!"

"Drop the gun *now!*"

Roland turned to the three men and froze. One of the police officers was getting to his feet while the other stood beside him, fumbling his gun from his holster. The homeless man stood about eight feet away, facing them, holding a gun between both hands. The man's arms were stiff, elbows locked, but his hands shook severely.

"You wanna take me to jail, you're gonna have to *kill* me first!" The homeless man smiled as he shouted at them.

Before he even knew he was going to speak, Roland said, "No, don't do that! Please!"

The man looked at him for a moment, surprised, as if he'd just noticed him there. "Stay outta this," he said. "This is none of your business."

But it is, Roland thought. *I shouldn't have walked away.* He knew that once he found the payphone didn't work, he could have gone into the convenience store and used the phone to call an ambulance.

But the payphone had *worked*, he told himself.

Daa-deee?

Roland shuddered.

Both police officers were standing now, and the one who still had his gun was aiming it at the homeless man.

"Drop the gun, buddy! I'll shoot!"

"You duh-don't want to do this," Roland said, taking a step toward the man.

"Back away, Mister," the police officer with the gun said.

"Look, you tried to help today, and that was nice, but this is none of—"

The Homeless Couple

"No, I didn't do enough! And I'm sorry. Doing this . . . it won't help anything. I . . . I-I know how you feel right now, I know what you're—"

"You don't know *shit!*" the homeless man barked, keeping an eye on the police officers.

Another step toward him. "Yes, I do! I . . . I had . . ." His throat was suddenly very dry and seemed ready to close on his words as he spoke them. But even though it would make him feel as if her were standing naked there by the street, he wanted to say it, felt a *need* to say it. "I had a . . . a wife and daughter, too. And I . . . lost them. Both of them."

The man's eyes stayed on him for a long moment. "They're both . . . both dead?"

"Yes."

"God*dammit*, Mister, back *away!*" the police officer shouted.

The telephone in the booth rang. It startled the homeless man and he turned the back of his head to Roland to stare at the phone booth for several seconds. When he turned to the police officers, he was grinning. He raised the gun, as if aiming at something over their heads, and fired.

The police officer shot him twice.

The homeless man dropped to the sidewalk like a rag doll.

The telephone stopped abruptly, mid-ring.

Roland made a small, helpless sound in his throat.

The police officer who had fired grumbled into his radio as he approached the homeless man. The other officer hurried to Roland's side.

"You know this man?" he asked. He was winded from fighting with the homeless man; his lower lip was cut and his left eye swollen and bruised.

Roland shook his head slowly, never taking his eyes from the homeless man's limp form. "No, only . . . only in passing."

"You know his name?"

"No."

"What's your name?"

"Roland. Pearce."

"Well, stick around, Roland. We're gonna have to ask you some questions." He joined the other officer at the homeless man's side.

Roland took a couple steps toward them. "Is he . . . um, is he going to be okay?"

"No," one of them replied. "He's dead."

A headache began to form behind Roland's eyes. Everything was blurred and fractured by the water on the lenses of his glasses, and the rainfall on his umbrella had become an irritating drone that gnawed at his joints with a rat's needle-like teeth.

Another ambulance arrived, siren wailing. Another police car pulled up at almost exactly the same time.

The telephone rang again.

Roland started, as if someone had poked him in the back.

It rang again. And again.

No one else seemed to notice.

Stepping around the paramedics and their stretcher, Roland went to the phone booth and stopped just outside the door, staring at the phone as it continued to ring. He collapsed his umbrella, stepped into the booth and closed the door. He did not say hello when he put the receiver to his ear, just waited.

It was a crackly connection. Static hissed and popped, while another sound went on continuously beneath it, much quieter . . . a whispery sound, fluttering . . . like voices . . . many whispering voices blending into a low, echoey hum.

"Thank you," a familiar voice said.

"What? I-I . . . I'm sorry?"

"Thank you, Briefcase Man," the homeless man said. His voice faded in and out as he spoke. "I know you were trying to help, and I appreciate it. But I'm okay now."

Roland turned his head to the right and looked through the Plexiglas. The paramedics were putting the homeless man's body on the stretcher.

"You're dead," he said flatly.

The homeless man did not reply. Instead a small, smiling voice—a painfully familiar voice—said, "Dadd-*deeee!*" The word collapsed into a fit of giggles. The line fell silent. No dial tone, no sound at all, not even the resonance of an open line. It was dead.

"No," Roland breathed. "No-no-no, hello?" He put two fingers on the chrome tongue that protruded in the middle of the receiver's cradle and hit it several times, rapidly. "*Hello?*" The only thing he could hear was his own heart, throbbing rapidly in his ear.

He replaced the receiver, turned around slowly, and gasped when he saw someone standing just outside the phone booth, staring in at him.

"Mr. Pearce?" the female officer asked. "Could you step outside? I need to ask you some questions."

The Homeless Couple

Outside the booth in the rain, the officer took down Roland's name, address, telephone number at home and work, and asked him for a statement. Roland told her everything he'd seen, trying not to leave out any details . . . but it was difficult to focus on what he was saying. The officer told him he would have to come down to the station tomorrow to finish answering questions, thanked him for his time, then walked away.

By then, the homeless man's body was gone, along with the other two police officers. The ambulance's engine started up and its head-lights came on as if puled away from the curb.

Roland wiped a finger over each lens of his glasses, and started to walk away. After only a few steps, he stopped and turned back, looked at the phone booth with the crudely altered word written above the door: **HOME**. He walked over to the booth and leaned inside just enough to remove the receiver from its hook and put it to his ear.

There was only the flat, silent nothingness of a dead line. Just a grimy, cold piece of plastic against his ear.

But it hadn't been dead a little while ago . . . and Roland knew what he'd heard. The homeless man . . . and Melanie.

They're dead, he thought as he started walking. He picked up his pace, quickly putting as much distance between himself and the phone booth as possible. He heard Deborah's doctor warning him the last time they spoke on the phone:

It's entirely possible for one to experience a total breakdown as a result of not grieving the loss of a loved one. It's entirely possible for one to experience a total breakdown as a result of not grieving the loss of a loved one.

As he hurried home, Roland wondered if that was what was happening to him.

❖

He started to fix a quick dinner, but realized he wasn't hungry. He sat down to watch television, but he couldn't sit still.

Roland had two bottles of wine in a cupboard in the kitchen. He'd bought them when he first moved into the apartment. There had once been three bottles, but he'd used one for cooking. He seldom drank alcohol, but found himself craving some that evening, so he opened a bottle and, tossing manners aside, poured some wine into a tall water glass over ice.

Strong feelings were stirring in him, shooting through him like bullets going in one side and out the other. He finished one glass of wine and started on another. The wine was loosening his muscles, but not clouding his head. The sweet, giggling voice on the telephone kept sounding again and again in his mind: *Daa-deeee!*

A studio audience laughed inordinately on a television sitcom, but although he stared at the screen, Roland saw none of it. He was thinking about the Homeless Couple. Ever since they'd first appeared on his route, it seemed one or the other of them had been talking on that payphone every time he passed. Sometimes emotionally, loudly. He closed his eyes and thought back over all those walks to and from work, passing them there between the payphone and the convenience store in their filthy rags, eating junk food, doing nothing with their lives, just standing there, sitting there . . . or talking on that phone.

That telephone doesn't work, the homeless man had said.

To whom had they been talking on a phone that didn't work? And what had they said? What had he heard them say?

No, baby, it's gonna be all right, I promise . . .

. . .sweetie, don't cry . . .

I miss you so much.

He remembered walking by twice when the payphone rang, and seeing the Homeless Couple scramble to get to it, as if their lives depended on it.

They had lost a baby girl, too.

And what had the homeless man said on the phone earlier when the police officers were pulling him out of the booth?

I'm coming, honey! Don't worry! I'm coming! I'll be right there . . .

Honey? He was talking to his wife . . . telling her he'd be there soon. And when he'd fired the gun he'd taken from the police officer, he'd raised it first, raised it high so the bullet would go over their heads and they wouldn't be hurt. He'd done that knowing full well he would be shot immediately.

After resisting the urge for nearly an hour, Roland went to a rolltop desk next to the kitchen doorway and opened the top drawer. From the drawer, he took a framed eight-by-ten studio photograph of Deborah and Melanie. It had been a Christmas gift from them both. In front of a colorful wooded backdrop, Deborah was seated on a short stone wall with Melanie on her lap. They were both smiling, but Melanie looked as if she were laughing heartily. The picture had been on the living room wall for awhile, but Roland had never looked at it, couldn't *bear* to look at it, and had finally taken it down and put it away. He looked at it now, though, for a long time. His throat burned and the picture blurred as tears filled his eyes.

Daa-deeee!

His tears landed on the lenses of his glasses and he put the picture back in the drawer.

"I'm not having a breakdown," Roland whispered.

He knew what he'd heard. His baby girl had spoken to him over that payphone. That was why the Homeless Couple stayed by the phone booth and never seemed to get out of earshot of the phone's ring . . . because they'd heard *their* baby girl's voice over that payphone, too. And just before he was killed, the homeless man had been talking to his wife.

"I'm not having a breakdown," he said again as he closed the desk drawer.

He knew what he'd heard, and it had been Melanie's voice. And if Melanie could speak to him over that payphone, so could Deborah.

Roland moved quickly: slipped on his overcoat, took his wallet from the desktop and stuffed it in his coat pocket, grabbed his umbrella and left the apartment.

It was still raining, but it had gotten much colder. Traffic was thinner, there were fewer pedestrians and the loudest sound in the night was the rain on his umbrella. Roland walked fast, his breath puffing clouds from his mouth and nostrils, heels clicking on the shiny wet concrete.

The payphone was ringing before he even got there. He could hear it a good distance away, growing louder as he neared. He broke into a jog for the last several yards, bounded into the phone booth and nearly tore up his umbrella. He held it outside the booth as he grabbed the receiver.

"Hello?"

No one spoke at first, but he recognized the odd sound of the connection: crackling static and the hollow, echoing murmur of countless voices all whispering over one another.

"Hel . . . hello?" he said again.

"Daa-*deeee!*"

Tears came suddenly and tumbled down his cheeks. "Melanie? Mel, sweetie? Is that you?"

The beautiful sound of her giggles faded in and out. "Daa wook? Daa go wook?"

He started to laugh, but it became a sob. Melanie used to ask that over breakfast, before he left for work.

"Not now, baby. Daddy's going to stay right here and talk to you now, okay?"

"'Kay, Daa-deeee."

Holding the receiver with his shoulder, Roland turned, collapsed the umbrella, pulled it into the booth and closed the accordion door. "Is . . . is Mommy there, Melanie?"

"Mommy."

"Yes, Mommy . . . is she there?"

"Rollie?"

He fell against the wall of the booth, weakened by the sound of her voice.

"Duh-Deb-Deborah?"

"We miss you, Rollie. We miss you so much. Melanie's always asking for her daddy, and I . . . I'm so lonely without you."

"Deborah . . . oh, God, Deborah, I . . . sweetheart, I . . ." He could not find words. He was blinded by his tears and his heartbeat thundered in his ears as his lips worked, mouth opened and closed, trying to speak.

The static suddenly grew louder.

The connection was severed abruptly.

"*No!*" Roland shouted, rattling the chrome lever. He pressed his forearm to the phone and leaned his forehead on it, groaning. After a moment, he stood upright again and replaced the receiver. Stood there, running a hand through hair again and again, clenching his teeth.

He stepped out of the booth, opened his umbrella, and paced on the sidewalk.

She'd been there, on the phone with him, and he'd been unable to speak, tongue-tied like some nervous boy. There had to be some way to call back, to reach her . . . wherever she was. But if there was, he was unaware of it.

Melanie had called once. Maybe she would call again. Maybe Deborah would call because their conversation had been interrupted.

Roland stopped pacing and stood beneath the awning awhile, his eyes on the phone booth.

How often does it happen? He wondered. *Is there any regularity? Any pattern to the calls?*

The Homeless Couple

He paced some more. He would wait as long as he had to. All night, if necessary. If he got hungry, he could always grab a bite to eat at the convenience store. It was open twenty-four hours.

Roland went back into the phone booth, closed the door and leaned against the wall, staring at the phone.

He would wait as long as he had to. He would wait forever, if necessary. He wanted to talk to his family again. He'd lost them once and had been alone—all alone in the world for seven years—and he didn't want to lose them again.

Roland Pearce waited. He waited in the phone booth, beneath the marked-up word over the door, the word that had been crudely altered to spell **HOME**.

Gene Wolfe
THE WALKING STICKS

o saw something in the back yard day-before-yesterday, and that should have warned me right there. Got me started on this and everything. I should have gone to the big church over on Forest Drive and talked to somebody, yelled for the police and put this out on the net—done everything I am going to do now. Only I did not. It was a man with a funny kind of derby hat on and a big long black overcoat she said, and she went to the door and said, "What are you doing in our back yard?" And he sort of turned out to be smoke and the smoke blew away.

That is what her note said, only I did not believe her because it was practically dark, the sun only just up, and what does it mean when a woman says she saw a man in a black overcoat at night? So much has been happening, and I thought it was nerves.

All right, I am going to go back and tell all of it from the very beginning. Then I will put this on the net and maybe print it out, too, so I can give a copy to the cops and the priests or whatever they have over there.

Mavis and I got divorced six years ago. Guys always talk about what big friends they are with their ex. I never did believe any of that, and that sure was not how it was with us. As soon as it was final I went my way and she went hers. Mine was staying on the job and finding a new place to live, and hers was selling the house and taking off in our Buick for Nantucket or Belize or whatever it was she had read about in some magazine that month. Jo and I got married not too long after that and bought this place in Bear Hill Cove.

All right, here I better say something I do not want to have to say. A letter came to Mavis from England, and the people that had bought our old house from her carried it over and stuck it in our box. I ought to have opened it and read it and written to the man in Edinburgh. His name was Gordon Houston-Scudder. I should have said we did not know where Mavis was and not to send anything, but I did not even open it. I thought sooner or later Mavis would turn up and I would give it to her. Now I wonder if she was not behind the whole thing.

Around the end of September a pretty big crate came from England, and there was a good-sized cabinet in it. Jo and I got it out and cleaned up the mess. The key was in the lock, I remember that. And then inside the cabinet there was another mess of wood shavings that got all over the carpet.

Under that was the canes, twenty-two of them. Some were long and some were shorter. There were all kinds of handle shapes, and a dozen different kinds of wood. The handle of one was silver and shaped like a dog's head. It was tarnished pretty bad, but Jo polished it up and showed me hallmarks on it. She said she thought it might be pretty valuable.

About then I remembered the letter for Mavis and got it out of my desk in here and opened it. Mr. Houston-Scudder was a solicitor, he said, and his letter was from what looked like lawyers, Campbell, MacIlroy, and somebody else. He said the estate of some doctor from the 1800s had been settled and the canes were supposed to go to a woman named Martha Jenkins or something, but she was dead now and as far as they could see Mavis was her only relative so they were sending them to her.

I thought that was all right. We would just keep them for her and if she ever came back I would give them to her, and the cabinet, too. Those kids that got killed? I had nothing to do with that. *Nothing.* So help me God.

Anyway, that was that. We put the cabinet in a corner of the dining room, and I locked it and I think I put the key in my pocket. Only the cane with the German Shepherd head was not in there because Jo wanted to keep it out to look at. It was in the kitchen then, I think, leaning against the side of the refrigerator.

Here I do not know which way to go. If I just tell about the walking and the knocking, you probably will not get it. Maybe I should say that the key is lost before I get into all that. I think I must have left it in my pocket, and Jo put my jeans in the wash. For just a cabinet it was a pretty big key, iron. I have tried to pick the lock with a wire, but I could not get it open. I could break the doors, but what good would that do?

The thing is that I do not deserve to go to prison, and I am afraid that is what is bound to happen. But I did not do anything really wrong. In fact nothing I did was wrong at all, except that maybe I should have told somebody sooner. Well, I am telling it now.

It started that night, even though we did not know it. Jo woke me up and said she heard somebody in the house. I listened for a while and it was *tap-tap-tap, rattle-rattle.* I told her it sounded like a squirrel in the attic, which it did. But to shut her up I had to get up and get my gun and a flashlight and have a look around. Everything was just like we had left it when we went to bed. The front door and back door were both locked, and all the windows were closed. There was not any more noise either.

Then when I had turned around to go back to bed, there was a bang and a clatter, like something had fallen over. I looked all around with my light and could not see anything, but when I was going back to bed, passing the cabinet, I stepped on it. It was the one with the silver handle. That was the part I stepped on, and it hurt.

So I said some things (that part was probably a mistake) and leaned it back against the cabinet like Jo had probably had it, and went back to bed. Naturally she wanted to know, "What was that?"

And I said, "It was your goddamn cane. I must have knocked it over." Only I knew I had not. Then I asked why she had not told me there were little jewels like rubies or something for the eyes, and she said because there were not any, and we argued about that for a while because I had seen them, and went to sleep. Now I am going to have another beer and go to bed myself. I have locked the pieces in the trunk of my car, and it is not doing that stuff any more anyway.

❖

Here is what I should have written last week. The thing was that I had told it to go to hell, when I stepped on it, I mean. I think that was a mistake and I ought not ever to have done it, but a sharp piece had cut my foot a little bit and I was mad. Only I know it walked that first night before I said anything. That was what Jo and I heard, I am pretty sure.

A couple of nights after that Jo heard it again, and next morning it was leaned up against the front door, which was not where we had left it at all.

So that night I put it in bedroom with us and shut the door, which was a big mistake. About midnight it knocked to be let out, loud enough to wake up both of us. We got up and turned on the lights, and it was exactly where I had left it, and there were dents in the door. I said they had probably been there before and we had not noticed, but I knew it was not true. I took the cane out and leaned it up against the cabinet in the dining room again and went back to bed.

That was the first bad night I had, because it woke me up but it did not wake up Jo. I lay there for hours listening to it tapping on the bare floors and thumping on the carpets. It seemed like it was going through the whole house, room after room, and after a while it seemed like the house it was going through must have been a lot bigger than ours.

It was lying in front of the front door in the morning.

Jo said I had to throw it away, and we had a big fight about it because I wanted to take off the silver dog's head first and saw the wooden part in two, but Jo just wanted me to throw away the whole thing.

Finally I just put it in the garbage, because it was a Saturday and I did not have to go to work. Then when Jo went shopping I got it out and wiped it off and hid it down in the basement. When Jo got back the garbage had been picked up and she thought it was gone.

I know you must think I am a damned fool to do that, but I was wondering about it. In the first place, I was not really so sure any more that I had heard what I thought I had. There were the dents in the bedroom door, but I got to where I was not really sure they had not been there already. Besides, what if I had left it in the garbage and the garbage collectors had taken it away, and I heard the same thing again? Squirrels or something. I would have felt like the biggest damned fool in the world.

Anyway, that is what I did. And that night I did not even try to go to sleep. I just lay in bed listening for it, and when it knocked loud on the basement door to be let out, I got up and put on some clothes and went to the basement door. It was really pounding by then; it seemed like it shook the whole house, and I was surprised Jo did not wake up.

When I put my hand on the knob of the basement door it felt hot. I never have been able to explain that, but it did. I stood there for half a minute or so with my hand on the knob while it pounded louder and louder, wondering what was going to come out when I opened the door, and whether I really should. I was trying to get my nerve up, I guess, and maybe I thought pretty soon Jo would come and there would be two of us. Finally I turned the knob and opened the door.

And what came out was the cane. Just that cane, all by itself, with a sort of cold draft from the basement. As soon as it came out it went up and broke the light over the basement door, but I had gotten a pretty good look at it first.

After that I followed it through the house to the front door, and when it tapped on that to be let out, I opened the door and let it go. After that I closed the door and locked it, and went back to bed.

When I went out in the morning to get the paper, I was expecting to find that cane out there, probably lying in front of the door. I looked all around for it, in the bushes and everything, and it was gone, and the harder I looked for it and did not find it the better I felt. I was really happy. But now I am going to bed. I should be able to wrap this up tomorrow night.

❖

A cop came today asking questions. I told him I did not know anything about the dead girls except what I had seen on TV. He asked about Jo, and I had to tell him she had left me, which I think is the truth even if her car is still here, and all her stuff. After that he went next door. I saw him, and I think probably he was asking them about me.

Anyway, the next night I followed the cane again, only that time I followed it outside. I had heard it, I thought in the house. I had gotten up and gotten dressed very quietly so as not to wake up Jo and looked all around for it. Finally I heard it down in the basement again, walking and walking, tap-tap-tapping on the concrete floor down there, and I opened the door like before and let it out, and then I ran ahead of it and opened the front door.

And when it went outside, I followed it. I guess I kept about half a block back. Maybe a little bit less. There is no way that I can say how far it was. It did not seem to be doing very much walking, but pretty soon we were in a neighborhood I had not ever seen before, where all the houses were taller and a lot closer together, and the pavement was not even any more. I got scared then and went back, and when I got inside I locked the door like I had before.

Only something had made Jo wake up, and I told her about how the cane had come back and gotten into the basement somehow, and how I had been following it. She said, "Next time let me throw it out."

So I said, "Well, I hope there never will be any next time. But if you can find it, you can throw it out." After that we went back into bed, and

I did not hear anything else that night. In the morning I got up pretty early the way I always do on workdays and got dressed, and Jo fixed my breakfast. Then I went to work the way I always do, figuring Jo would take off for her own job in about an hour. That was the last time I saw her.

When I got home that night and she did not come, I thought she was probably just working late. So I made supper for myself, a can of stew I think it was, and rye bread, and drank a couple beers and watched TV. There was nothing on TV that night, or if there was I do not remember what. It got to be practically midnight and still no Jo, so I phoned the police. They said she had to be gone twenty-four hours and to call back if she did not come home, but I never did. That was the only time I called you.

While I was getting undressed somebody knocked on the door. I opened it and all the power went out. The light turned off, and the TV picture shrunk to nothing very fast, so I never did see the dog's-head cane come in and by that time I had cut it up anyhow, only I could hear it. I stood as still as I could until I could not hear it any more. Maybe it went down into the basement again, I do not know. I do not know whether the basement door was open or closed, either. It just sort of went away toward the back.

Well, I went in the bedroom and shut the door and moved the bureau to block it, and just about then the lights came back on and I saw there was a note on my pillow. I have still got it, and here it is.

Johnny,

There was someone in the back yard. I saw him as plainly as I have ever seen anything, a big man with a black mustache and a derby hat such as one sees in old photographs. He wore a thick wool overcoat, black or of some dark check, with a wide shawl collar, it seemed, and what may have been a scarf or muffler or another collar of black or dark brown fur.

I watched him for some time, wishing all the while that you were here with me, and asked him more than once what it was he wanted, threatening to call the police. He never replied; I know that you will laugh at me for this, Johnny, but his was the most threatening silence I have ever encountered. It *was*.

When the sun rose above the Jefferson's, he was gone. No. You would have *said* that he was gone, that with the first beams he was transformed into something like a mist, which the morning breeze swiftly swept aside. But, he was still there. He *is* still there. I feel his presence.

I am not going to work today, having already called in sick. But, I am writing this for you to cleanse my spirit of it, and in case I should decide to leave you.

I *will* leave, if you will not destroy every last trace of Mavis's stick. I know you did not discard it as you promised me you would last night, and *will not* discard it. I left my poor Georgie for you for much less. I hope you realize this.

I will go, and once I have I will be out of your life forever.

> Very, very seriously,
> JoAnne, with all my love

Now I think it is about over. I really do. Either over, or starting something different. Okay, here is the bad part, right up front. The bottom line.

Last night I thought I heard something moving around and I thought God, it's back. But then I thought it could not be back because of all the things I did. (I ought to tell about all that, and I will too before I turn in tonight.)

Anyway, I got up to see what it was, and it was all the other canes in the big oak cabinet in the dining room rattling around and knocking to be let out.

So it is not only the one with the silver top, it is all the rest too. But if that one is still doing it, why would the others want to step up? So I think what it really means is I have won. Here is what I plan to do. I am going to call up Union Van Lines and tell them I have got a certain item of furniture I want taken out and stored. I will get them to move the whole cabinet for me. (Naturally it will still be locked, because I have lost the key like I said.) They will put it in a warehouse someplace for me. I think New Jersey, and I can tell them I am planning to move there eventually but I do not know when yet. Every month or whatever they will send me a storage bill for fifty bucks or so, and I will pay that bill, you bet, for the rest of my life. It will be worth every nickel to know that the cabinet is still locked up in that warehouse. I will call them tomorrow.

All right, here is the rest.

There was a night (if you read the paper or even watch the news on TV you know what night it was) when I followed the cane with the silver top outside again. After about four blocks it went to the same place it had before, where the big high houses were up against each other so close you could see they could not have windows on the sides. Where the streets were dirty, like I said, and sometimes you saw people passed out on the cold dirty old pavement. That pavement was just round rocks, really, but the street lights were so dim (like those friendship lights the gas company used to push) that you could not hardly tell it except with your feet.

We went a long way there, a lot further than the first time.

When we started out, I was trying to keep about half a block behind like before, because I thought somebody would grab that cane sure, and maybe ask if it belonged to me if I was too close. But when we got in among those old houses that leaned over the street like I have told about, I had to move in a lot closer because of the fog and bad light. It was cold and I was scared. I do not mind saying that, because it is the truth. But I had told myself that I was going to follow the cane that night until it came back to the house, no matter what. I did, too.

I kept thinking somebody would notice a cane walking all by itself pretty soon, but it was real late, very few people out at all, and nobody did.

Then there was this girl. She had blond hair and a long skirt, and a coat too big for her; it looked like she was holding it tight around her, and hurrying along. I kept waiting for it to register with her that the cane was walking all by itself. Finally, when it got real close to her it registered with me that that was not how she saw it. Somebody was holding that cane and walking along with it, and even if I could not see him she could.

Just about then he grabbed her, and I saw that. I do not mean I saw him, I did not, but I saw that she had been grabbed and heard her yell. And then the cane was beating her, up and down and up and down, and her yelling and her blood flying like water when a car drives through it fast. It sounded horrible, the yelling, and the *thud-thud-thud* beating, too. I ran and the yelling stopped, but the beating kept right on until I grabbed it.

❖

It felt good. I never hated to write anything this much in my life but it did. That girl was lying down on the dirty pavement stones bleeding terribly, and it was horrible, but it felt good. I felt like I was stronger than I have ever been in my life.

People started yelling and I ran, but before I got very far the houses looked right again, and the streetlights were bright. I was getting out of breath, so I started walking, just walking fast instead of running. I tried to hold the cane so nobody would see it, and when I looked down at it, it was looking up at me. Sure, the handle was bent because of beating on the girl. Or something. But it was looking up at me, a German shepherd or something with pointed ears. The red things were back in its eyes even if Jo had not ever seen them, and it seemed like I could see more teeth.

Then in the morning it was all over the news. I had the clock radio set to wake me up at five to go to work, and that was all they were talking about, this girl that had been a babysitter over in the Haddington Hill subdivision (it is flatter even than here) and she was on her way back home when somebody beat her to death.

That night they showed the place on TV so you could see the bloodstains on the sidewalk, and it was not right at all, but when they showed her picture from the yearbook, it was her. She had been a sophomore at Consolidated High. I thought I would walk over there and have a look, and when I went out the door that cane with the silver dog on it was in my hand. It stopped me and made it hard for me not to go at the same time.

But I stopped, and that is when I did it. First thing I thought of was I would take off the silver head and put it my safety deposit at the bank where it could not do anything. But when I twisted it trying to get it off, it unscrewed. I had not even known it was screwed on. There was a silver band under the part that came off that said some name with a J only too worn to read, and M.D., all in fancy handwriting. It could have been Jones or Johnson or anything like that, but he had been a doctor.

Then inside that silver band the cane looked hollow. I turned it upside down and this little glass tube came sliding out. It was half full of something that was kind of like mercury only more like a white powder, some kind of heavy stuff that slid around very easy in the tube and was heavy. I took it way back to the back corner of the back yard where I had noticed a snake hole the last time I cut the grass and poured it in. Jo wanted to know what I was doing there. (She had seen me out the kitchen window while she was washing dishes.) I said nothing, just poking around.

But the funny thing was, when I got back inside the cane was just a cane. There was nothing special about it anymore. I sawed the wood part in two down in my shop like I had planned to, but it was nothing. It was exactly like sawing a broom handle. The next day I took the silver dog head down to the bank on my way home from work, but it did not matter any more and I knew it.

So I thought that everything was fixed until Jo saw that man and went away without taking her clothes or car or anything. Then just before I started writing this I saw him myself, and there was a woman with him, and I think it was Jo. That was what started me doing this. So this is all of it and maybe I will put it on the net like I said, and maybe I will not. I want to sleep on it.

❖

Another cop came a couple of hours ago, and after he went out back I found these papers, which I had stuck in a drawer. (It is December now.) He was friendly, but he did not fool me. He said the New Jersey cops got a court order and broke into the cabinet for them. I said, "What were you looking for?"

And he said, "Jo's body."

So I said, "Well, what did they find inside?"

And he said, "Nothing."

"Nothing?" I could not believe it.

"That's what they say, sir."

Then I told him there had been a collection of valuable canes in there, and they did not belong to me, they belonged to Mavis. He hemmed and hawed around, and finally he winked at me and said, "Well those Jersey cops have some real nice canes now, I guess."

I am not ever going to go near New Jersey, and I hope that those other canes do not decide to come back here, or anyway not many of them.

So then I told him about the trespassers and asked him to take a look around my back yard. He went to do it, and he has not come back yet. That makes me feel good and really strong, but probably I will have to call somebody tomorrow because his police car is still parked in front of the house.

Chaz Brenchley
THE INSOLENCE OF CANDLES
AGAINST THE LIGHT'S DYING

God, that's sad," Quin said, staring at the wall.

He didn't mean it nicely. Nice wasn't a thing that he did much any more; the thinner his voice became, the sharper it thrust. And it wasn't only his voice. The thinner he got all over, the edgier his relationship with the world. A razor-blade scratching down a mirror, was Quin in that last year we had together: doing no real damage—what could he hurt, after all? Not the image, certainly, and not the reality either, razors can't score glass—but trying hard none the less.

We were standing in the hallway of my uncle's house and both of us were staring at the wall, both feeling further even than we'd come, a very long way from anywhere that we understood.

My uncle Jarrold had been dead six months, so it shouldn't have been him who had marked the wall, the scratches looked too fresh; but what did I know? Maybe erosion worked more slowly up here than it did down south, or else the house had gone into mourning at his death. Maybe more than the clocks had been stopped.

Oh, it was sad, as Quin said, what some unseen hand had dug deep into the paintwork and the plaster; it was the work of some sad and sorry bastard, and it sure as hell sounded like my uncle.

He is gone, he is gone, I cannot find him. It was a cry from the heart, in letters two feet high; and I knew the sound of that bruised heart in all its grief, its stasis. I knew my uncle's voice as well as any, and sad though it was, though it always had been, I missed it still.

❖

Uncle Jarrold had lived and died in London, in a bijou little flat close to Parliament Square: a spinster of the Parish of Westminster, he used to call himself when he was in faux-jovial mood. He definitely wanted us to dispute that, to agree with his own unspoken view of himself, that he was a widow, the Widow of Westminster. We never did that even to his face, young and cruel as we were; behind his back we named him the biggest queen in Christendom.

He lived and died in London and was very much a Londoner, of that type that believes all civilization inheres in the capital; but he kept a house in the country also, like the Edwardian gentleman that he so earnestly aspired to be. It was the greatest sorrow of his life, that he had been born fifty years too late to wear a smoking-jacket and have his boots shined daily by the kitchen-boy.

No, it wasn't. That's a ridiculous thing to say. The greatest sorrow of his life was what defined his life, as so often it is; and though he made a good pretense of yearning for a bygone style and nothing more, he made it oh so clear that this was only a pretense, a diaphanous veil that he chose to lay across his heartache. He always took care to let us see the clear light of his pain, shining through that inadequate curtain.

I say us, but I don't mean Quin and me. Quin never met Uncle Jarrold. In those days, when I saw him often, I rarely had the same partner two visits running; he had the right perhaps to scorn me as he did. Even the first time, when he withered me: even then, with hindsight, he was dead on the money.

It wasn't the first time I'd met him, not by a distance. He'd been a constant Christmas presence throughout my life and an occasional visitor at other times, a fat and slightly foolish man who brought sweets more welcome than his kisses were. Smooth of voice and silky-smooth of cheek, smelling of bay rum and good tobacco, handing down boxes of chocolate and candied fruits: those were my childhood memories of Uncle Jarrold. Later, when I was adolescent, he was more interested in me; he'd take me off for the day and give me lunch in a country pub, making great play of seeking out a table in a discreet and shadowy corner where I could safely enjoy a couple of halves of ale. His words, repeated every time. He always used to claim that he'd taught me how to drink; I never bothered to disillusion him.

The first time I went to stay with him, though, the world had changed, or I had changed within it. I was a student then, and deeply snared in my first affair; I hadn't seen Jarrold for a couple of years, and it seemed such an obvious move. I wanted to show off my conquest, to glean approval. No hope of that from my parents, they'd have put us in separate rooms and scowled throughout. Not my uncle, though, or so I thought. I thought he'd rejoice in us, as we rejoiced in the wonder of ourselves.

How wrong can you get?

❖

We drove all the way from Cambridge, which was an adventure in itself: my first car, the classic student rattlemobile made of patchwork pieces and held together with string, kept going with prayer and over-confidence. Two hundred miles was a lot to ask, but we had that faith that flourishes in ignorance, and never thought twice about it.

Like his flat, like his life, my uncle's holiday cottage - his country house he called it, as we did not - was on an island, and largely cut off from the real world. Splendid isolation, he used to call it, though it was neither.

He'd told us about the tides, in the long letter of direction he'd sent me the week before, but we'd paid no attention to his warnings. We'd ignored the enclosed timetable, started later than we'd meant to and underestimated how long the journey would take; when we finally came to the causeway that should take us across, it was deep dark and our headlights showed us only surging water where the road was meant to be.

Never mind, not a problem. Not a problem in the least. We turned the car and drove a mile, back to the nearest pub. If the tide was high now, it had to be low by closing time, or low enough. Take enough beer on board, we could float across if need be; and there'd be no breathalyzers out here. One major advantage of the rural life, though almost the only one we could think of just then.

We scrounged a couple of bacon sandwiches from the landlady, ate her out of crisps and pork scratchings, played a lot of pool and drank without rest; closing-time came and went, and it was near midnight before I thought to check the clock.

Then, too late, I thought we ought to have phoned Jarrold earlier. No point in it now; we'd be on his doorstep in ten minutes. I thought.

In fact, it was closer to half an hour. The causeway was wet still, black and glistening as the sea was on either side, a scary drive to a lad unsober and barely three months past his test; and when we did come to the island, while I'm sure Jarrold's instructions were clear and precise, we were anything but. We got muddled, we got lost, we found the wrong cottage twice before we found the right one.

Brutally late and brutally drunk, I suppose we shouldn't have been surprised at the chill of our greeting, but we were. The young are selfish anyway, and drink can make that worse; I was looking for open arms and a beaming smile, a gesture of dismissal to any casual apology we might have offered, perhaps a 'pooh-pooh' and no more.

Which shows just exactly how wrong you can be. Uncle Jarrold was fatter than ever, but no jolly green giant, wrapped though he was in a jade silk dressing-gown with a purring ginger cat in his arms. It was sheer temper that made him throw the door open so wide, no welcome in the world; it was temper too that kept him silent as we staggered cheerfully in with our arms full of rucksacks and carrier-bags. We hadn't given a thought to a gift for our host, flowers or wine or whatever. Hell, we were kids; it showed.

When he did finally speak, after he'd closed the door behind us and thrown the bolts across, it was like a tubby kettle hissing steam.

"Don't begin to apologize," he said, which we hadn't thought of doing. We still hadn't even registered our offense: late, drunk, so what? Who wasn't? "If you don't have the decency to arrive when arranged"—his arrangement, not ours, though we were neither of us in a fit state to point that out— "or to phone through that you'll be delayed, there's no point pretending to have decent instincts of any sort. I hope you're not hungry," though his twitching nostrils told us what our breath was telling him, that we'd filled up on rather more than a couple of halves of ale, "your dinner will be inedible. Perhaps it would be best if you went straight to bed, and we all started again in the morning . . ."

Which we did: up steep twisting stairs to a small room off the half-landing, where a queen-sized bed was squeezed in with chest-of-drawers and bedside table, washstand: all good pieces, he told us, with a watchful frown. Measuring, I thought, to see if we were too drunk to be allowed his guest-room. I almost told him that we were; we had sleeping-bags in the car, and there was plenty enough floor for two downstairs. Far be it from us to trespass where we were unwelcome, among pieces that outranked us . . .

But he said nothing more, he passed us, if barely; and I was too young or too chicken to force a confrontation. So much easier just to let it go, to listen to his heavy feet climb higher and exchange a speaking glance with Frankie, all apology on my side and longsuffering on his.

Too pissed to suffer long, we slithered in between the sheets and whispered comforts to each other: how we wouldn't stay even as long as we'd meant to, how we'd stick it for a day or two for manners' sake then go on up to Scotland, just the twain, the two of us and let the world go hang, we needed none of it . . .

❖

Shagging on Uncle Jarrold's fine white sheets wasn't even an option; we'd come in hot but his icewater welcome had chilled us, and we were unconscious too soon to think about restoking what was quenched. We just snuggled up and drifted off on each other's beer breath and stubble, and I thought my life complete in spite of crosspatch uncles.

❖

But cometh the hour, cometh the man; every hero finds his moment. Uncle Jarrold's came next morning, and he seized it gleefully.

We woke, of course, to monumental grief, two of those hangovers that only the young endure, thank God, because only the young could survive them. Again no question of a good-morning shag: moving was too difficult, moving hurt. Lying still was better, huddled against the warmth of Frankie's weight. When I cracked my eyes open, a bar of hard light lay across the lacy counterpane; I winced. We were going to be as late to rise as we'd been to arrive. I could hear movement down below, and foresaw stormy weather.

Nothing to do but endure it when it came; I was in no condition to play the diplomat, too sore of head and sick of stomach to drag myself out of bed. I closed my eyes, and maybe groaned a little. Frankie's hand squeezed my thigh gently, as much as either one of us could manage and as good I thought as anything was going to get.

Until the stairs creaked, too loud, too soon; the door banged open much too loud and much too soon, and there stood Uncle Jarrold.

With a tray in his hands, two steaming beakers and a pot, real, fresh coffee: just the smell of it made my dry mouth ache with yearning.

"Up, you idle creatures, get you up!" He set the tray down carefully on the bedside table, with dire warnings against spilling a single drop on his precious linen; added that breakfast awaited us in the kitchen, which was far more than we deserved but that he was in the forgiving vein today, and swept majestically out.

As ever, coffee was sovereign. We sat up with exaggerated caution, cradled hot mugs possessively and sipped, gulped, poured and gulped again. No way would either one of us have let a drop spill, we needed it more than the bedclothes did.

Coffee does more than ale can, to justify man's ways to man. Inside twenty minutes we were up and washed, shaved (at my insistence: Frankie tried to claim holiday privilege, but Uncle Jarrold had earned so much, at least) and sweet of breath and groping our way unsteadily down the stairs.

To be met by another magnificent scent arising, the mingled odours of bacon and something herby, backed by more elixir, essence of coffee. My uncle was at the stove with an apron around his midriff and a wooden spatula in his hand; he waved it at us with an appalling bonhomie and cried, "Sit, sit! Breakfast is immediate!"

Breakfast was. He set plates before us and heaped them with crisp bacon and slices of black pudding, with sausage and fried egg, with tomatoes and mushrooms, too; he set a rack of toast between us, and said, "Eat, enjoy . . ."

So we did that. After a minute—or perhaps a couple of minutes—I managed to remember manners enough to mumble, "What about you, Uncle Jarrold, aren't you joining us?"

"Don't speak with your mouth full, Tom. And no, I had my breakfast hours ago. We don't all sleep the best part of the day away. It's nearly lunchtime. I thought I'd take you to the Queen's Head for lunch. Don't talk, eat. You'll need to line your stomachs. Unless your disgusting behaviour of last night has left you unable to face the sight of a few noggins of ale this splendid day?"

To be honest, I at least was still young enough that the thought of more beer could make me queasy; but I was young enough too to deny it fervently, "Hair of the dog, Uncle, it's the best thing," as I reached for another slice of toast. "After food, I mean. These sausages are amazing, I've never eaten anything like them. What's in 'em, do you know?"

"They are good, aren't they? They're pork, of course, with onion and leek. Sage and thyme are the herbs, I think, though there's another flavour that continues to elude me. Slow cooking is the secret, though.

You can't cook a sausage too slowly. These have been on for an hour or more . . ."

⁘

As he chivvied us out of the house, he raised a mute but expressive eyebrow at the car, and then said, "I must apologize, boys, for the unwelcome I gave you last night. Your behaviour was atrocious, but that doesn't excuse mine. You struck me in a tender spot, though; I am particularly sensitive to unpunctuality. Pray that you do not, but if ever you spend half the night waiting for someone who never comes home, then perhaps you will understand my reaction a little better."

"Oh, please, don't worry about it, Uncle," I said awkwardly. "It was our fault, we got cut off by the tide and never thought to phone . . ."

"I agree, your fault entirely; unfortunately, it played upon my most fragile sensibilities, and so I lost control. When you know me better, I think you will understand."

And his eyes turned to the wide sea, where it battered and sucked at a shelving shoreline.

⁘

The island was a rocky promontory, inhabited first by monks and monastery servants. Gradually a secular community had grown up around the religious; now the monastery was a ruin, and the locals lived by fishing and tourism. Pubs at both ends of the causeway pretty much depended on the tides for their trade; we had hardly been the first idiots to find the road awash, and ourselves suddenly with hours to kill before we could cross.

The causeway itself, Uncle Jarrold said, had been laid barely a century before, atop the safest of the several known pathways. Before that you took a boat to the island's fishing-harbor, or else you risked your life on foot across the sands.

"The tide comes in at a sprint, boys, so don't you go tempting fate," he said, with solemn tone and meaningful looks from me to Frankie and back to me again. "Nor is the tide the only danger. There is quicksand out there, quicksand that will draw you down and never give you up . . ."

And he stared out across the flat sands and the rock-pools, and I was astonished to see tears in his eyes.

✤

He took us to the pub—a ten-minute walk from the cottage, but that was universal: nothing on the island was more than ten minutes from anywhere else—and outmatched us pint for pint, and on what was for him an empty stomach too. It was impressive. We tried to pretend we were just slowed down by a heavy night and a heavy breakfast, but truth was he could have drunk us under the table, any night he chose.

That lunchtime, it seemed to me that drinking made him maudlin; later experience suggested that maudlin was his natural frame of mind, or else the state he chose to dwell in. He settled his eyes on us, two young lads sitting closer than we needed to, side by side on a settle, and he sighed mightily. Took a pull on his glass, and turned his eyes to the window, the inevitable view of glistening sand and mud and sea; and said, "You won't know this of me, Tom, your parents won't have told you, but I had a terrible thing happen to me here. A tragedy. A family tragedy, really, only your mother could never see it that way. I lost the one true love of my life, out there on the sands. That's why I keep the house here, why I can never truly leave. This place haunts me so . . ."

"Unh . . ." I didn't know what I was supposed to say to that, *do tell?* or what; but it didn't seem to matter. A grunt was enough.

"I wasn't a young man, even then," he went on, "and he was only a few years my junior, but it was a young love that we had; we'd been together barely a year. We both knew that this was the real thing, though, a lifetime commitment. Not like you two, we weren't playing at being men."

I felt Frankie shift in protest, and stilled him with a hand below the table. I wanted to hear this.

"We had arguments, of course, as lovers do. When you've been alone a long time, it's hard to make compromises, and we were both of us stubborn. I have a temper, too—well, that you've seen.

"We had a dreadful disagreement one night; it started from nothing, as these things do, and escalated into savagery on both sides. In the end he stormed out, as he often did. I was too upset to go to bed, so I just pottered around the house and waited for him to return. I knew where he'd be, walking on the sands, cooling off.

"It came on to rain, and I thought he'd come back then, he didn't have a coat. So I fetched a towel for his hair, and waited.

"He didn't come, though. I waited an hour, longer, and still he didn't come. He couldn't have been walking so long, in such weather; so I wondered if he'd taken shelter with a neighbor, though it was terribly late. I put on my waterproofs and went out to see. There were no lights burning anywhere, so I went on down to the shore. The tide was coming in strongly, the causeway was entirely underwater already—and there was simply no sign of him anywhere.

"I walked, I shouted his name, I woke all my neighbors and organized a search, but we never found him. Then, or later: his body never turned up. He must have gone out too far in his fury and been caught in the quicksand, or else simply outraced by the tide. It was dark, overcast, he might simply not have seen the water coming until it was too late. It was a terrible death, though, either way; and more terrible for me, I think, having to live on with the memories. Such a love only ever comes once in a lifetime, I can't look for so much luck again."

❖

"So what d'you reckon, then?" Frankie murmured later, as we lagged behind Uncle Jarrold on our way up to the island's height, where he was going to show us the monastery ruins.

"What? Sad story."

"If it's true."

"Frankie . . ."

"Oh, come on! It's the old 'I have suffered' routine, every faded drama queen has got one. Ask me, if this guy ever existed at all, he just lit out. Hitched a lift off before the tide came in."

"And then what? They were living together . . ."

"I dunno, do I? Changed his name, dropped out. Emigrated, maybe. Went straight, got married and he's raising kids in Arizona. Wouldn't you? With that to come home to?"

"Frankie, you're a bastard."

"Yeah, right. That's why you love me. But honestly, Tom, it's a fairytale. It's got to be. Christ, he didn't even tell us his true love's *name*, didn't you notice?"

I grinned, and slipped my hand into his back pocket. "We're not worthy."

❖

Later still, a lot later, long after the sun had sunk in glory behind the mainland, Frankie pleaded exhaustion and took himself off to bed, leaving me alone with my sad uncle and a bottle of malt. Looking for an excuse to follow, thinking that tonight we might just sully Jarrold's pure linen sheets, I slugged back my shallow share of the whisky and said, "Well, Uncle? Do you approve?"

"Approve? Of what?"

"Frankie. Frankie and me. God, I don't half love that boy . . ."

And that was when he ripped into me.

"Love? Love, do you call it? Don't insult me, Tom. Don't parade your adolescent conquest and call it by a holy name. You greedy, mocking apes—oh yes, I know you've been laughing at me behind my back, I'm neither blind nor deaf—you animals, what do you know of love? You sit there straining your jeans, your mind's already up there with him, you can't wait, you're almost drooling already with impatience to get your hands on his body—and you dare, you *dare* to call that love? Immature lust, physical obsession—it's nothing, do you hear me? Nothing! A tissue paper tango, and it'll burn out as fast as tissue paper burns and it won't even leave ashes on your tongue. Don't talk to me of love till you at least know what the word means, even if you haven't braved its touch . . ."

And so on and on, a tirade—fuelled by whisky, loss and loneliness perhaps, but a tirade none the less—that shrivelled me, that shredded all my certainties. When the brutal run of his words finally ebbed to silence, to a scornful gesture of dismissal, I slunk upstairs and found Frankie genuinely out for the count; and didn't wake him, only laid my cold body next to his and prayed for warmth.

In the morning we left, we went north and west to the wild Scottish coast, and found no comfort in it. So we went our separate ways instead, to our separate homes for what was left of the vac; and Uncle Jarrold proved to be absolutely right, rot him. Whether he'd sowed the seed of it or not, Frankie and I reaped a fiery harvest the following term, and wrote ourselves into college legend with the force of our mutual destruction.

And no, with hindsight, I no longer called it love, that frail, flickering thing we'd had, that pale light that had seemed to burn between us. St. Elmo's fire, perhaps, fool's gold but no true flame.

❖

In the years that followed I had other passions and many of them, other flames that seemed to me to burn hot and pure and true. Some of them I took to show to Uncle Jarrold after we'd made our peace, after family feeling and some need in me, in both of us had overcome my pride and his. But I never spoke of love, unless he asked me; and even then I was tentative, uncertain, and ultimately right to be so.

❖

But now he was dead, my uncle, and I was his inheritor: of this house, and all that it contained. Which was more and a great deal more than furniture and books and bric-à-brac. *He is gone, he is gone, I cannot find him*: but standing there in Jarrold's absence with Quin shakily at my side it seemed to me as though that *cri de coeur* had cruelly reversed itself. Jarrold was dead, and yet his spirit still pervaded this place and hence my life, I might never be free of him now; and Quin was altogether there, slender fingers clinging to my arm for support, and yet I thought that he was all but gone already, I could almost taste the loss of him and how that too would be a thing of which I could never be free.

"Come on, love," I said softly, "let's get you settled before I bring the stuff in from the car."

No question of the stairs, he didn't have the leg-power for a shallow flight of steps any longer, let alone the steep climb here. We'd brought a camp-bed with us just in case, but memory said there was a luxurious sofa in the living-room, and Quin was very used to nesting.

The sofa was there still, little more worn than when I'd last seen it. I turned it to face the windows and saw Quin comfortable upon it, packed him about with cushions and left him with the radio on and a kiss for company while I hauled in all the gear that we had to travel with, clothes and medicines, food and drink, towels and toiletries and chamber-pot. I could carry Quin up to the bathroom when he needed it, but not at night; no room for two on that sofa, and he wouldn't let me sleep on the floor. Not yet, not while he still had the will to resist. *Later* was a promise I'd made to myself, that I hadn't yet shared with him.

When the gear was all fetched in and distributed, upstairs and downstairs and in my lover's chamber, I asked him, "Are you hungry?"

"No," he said easily, almost cheerfully, recognizing the gambit of a familiar game.

"Well, but will you eat?"

"Some soup? Perhaps?"

"Perhaps so."

So I heated soup from our great supply, added plenty of pepper because he tried sometimes to use the blandness of his diet as an excuse not to eat, and added a wallop of yogurt also in hopes of getting protein inside him somehow. Served it up in one of Jarrold's pretty porcelain bowls—one of my bowls, I supposed, now—and stood over him while he ate.

"What about you?" he asked, dipping his spoon and tasting slowly, every mouthful only a taster and a very long way from a full mouth, using almost more energy to get the food there than he could possibly gain from swallowing it.

"Sick of soup," I said lightly, truthfully. "I'll fix myself a sandwich later."

"You've got to eat," he told me, frowning; and oh, that sounded so good coming from him, I could have cried. Instead I went back to the kitchen, sliced bread and beef and pickles, searched out the horseradish and assembled all into a massive bellyfiller. This was how we lived, largely; he could barely eat solids and I wouldn't cook properly for myself alone, so we got through a small reservoir of soup and I snacked on the side. I'd roasted and brought up a joint of beef big enough to last me a week; I had no plans to stay longer than that. We were really only here to sort through my late uncle's things, to decide what to keep, what to sell and what to burn or throw away. If Quin felt up to it, then I'd take advantage of the chance to show him the island and the coast: to try to show him a little of my uncle's life and what it had meant to me, why I really wanted to keep the house. *Expensive memento*, his first comment had been; and it was true, and I felt a great need to justify it to him.

I hadn't expected to find us both plunged immediately into the sad and sorry heart of Jarrold's obsessive grieving; but it fit, actually, it was apt. This was how Jarrold was in life, he left no margins, no neutral ground. In death, why should he be different?

I ate with Quin for witness, as he had with me, for me. We both needed that kind of watching. It should have been ironic somehow, but to me at least it only felt right. Of course I forgot my own body and my own needs, in caring for Quin's; of course he took care to remind me. How else should we live?

Reminded, I left him to doze while I went upstairs to get my own room sorted. On the way, inevitably, my eye was jagged by the graffito on the wall. I paused, and touched my finger lightly to one of the gouged letters; there was an immediate fall of plaster-dust onto the carpet. The floor should have been filthy with it already, and was not. There was a light film of regular dust everywhere in the house; I didn't believe that anyone had been in to clean since my uncle's death.

Well. It was another task for me before we left, and a little lighter than it might have been; no more than that. I trotted up to the old guest-room and made the bed quickly, unpacked a few clothes and necessities, hurried back down to Quin.

Found him lightly asleep, as I'd expected. He did little else but drift these days. I'd never told him so, but I hated to watch him sleeping, lying still and silent with his drawn face slack and empty. It was too potent a foretelling, a premature taste of that time to come when I'd find him emptied indeed, comatose or dead already, and what would I do then . . .?

The sun was setting vividly outside the window. To save myself sitting and watching him, anticipating a worse vigil, I moved quietly about the room setting candles to burn in all the corners; strong lights hurt his eyes, so we lived our long nights out among guttering shadows. It seemed appropriate.

I left the curtains open; moon and stars and distant glows delighted him as much as candle flames and firelight. There was an open fire here, coal and logs and kindling all set ready by my uncle's foresight the last time he left, never foreseeing that he would never return. Quin would enjoy a blaze; I turned to attend to that, and saw his eyes open.

I was caught, trapped, as so often at these moments: bereft of movement or intent, free only to be ensnared. We gazed at each other, and my breath was shallower and more tremulous even than his.

He smiled, before I could; and said, "Well. Here we are, then."

"Yes. At last." I'd had reasons in plenty, not to introduce him to my uncle while Jarrold was alive; chief among them—or perhaps the sum of all of them—was that simple snare that seized me, choked me time and again in Quin's company. Put it bluntly, say it straight, I was in love; and this love I had never been prepared to expose to my uncle's scathing. Jarrold had been important to me once, his approval had mattered; and for that memory's sake I could never bear to see him so belittle himself.

I sank down against the sofa, propped my elbow beside Quin's shoulder and rested my chin on it. "What shall we do? We could nip to the pub later, if you're up for it . . ."

"No. Not tonight, Tom. It's been a long day."

It had; too long for him, perhaps, though he'd slept through most of the drive up. "I'm sorry," I murmured, "but I couldn't leave you for a whole week . . ."

"Yes, you could. I've got friends enough, you know that. You just didn't want to leave me."

True, and not true. The whole truth was that practicalities aside, I couldn't bear to leave him for a week; individual days I found hard enough, not knowing what kind of Quin I'd come back to, sharp or dozy, asleep or sick or dead already.

"If you didn't want to come . . ."

"If I hadn't wanted to come, you'd have sulked and stormed and threatened to stay yourself, to sell the house by proxy, anything to make me change my mind. You know you would. Luckily I did want to come, and I'm glad I'm here. I just can't face company tonight, that's all. Other company than yours, I mean. And that's all the comfort you're getting, and more than you deserve. Get my pills and a glass of water, before you get too comfy; get a drink for yourself, and talk to me, okay?"

Better than okay, when such instructions were seasoned with a kiss, as they were. I did all of that and settled down again; and the first thing he said was, "Do you believe in ghosts, Tom?"

Ouch. I didn't want this conversation, not here and emphatically not now; but I never could say no to Quin. Specifically, this time, I couldn't say *no*. "I believe in being haunted," I said slowly. "By the living or the dead, or some dream that was never properly either one of those."

"What, you mean we make our own ghosts?" His voice was a whistle and a whisper, as reedy as any ghost's, a ghost itself of what it used to be. I closed my eyes, and was still haunted by it.

"Well, Uncle Jarrold did. All the time I knew him, he was haunted by his lost love." And now he was haunting me, and that wasn't fair, it wasn't right. I was haunted already, I'd brought my own ghost with me, still barely clothed in failing flesh and blood. My own lost love, and that

I hadn't lost him yet was only a confusion of the timeline, or else it was God's little joke . . .

❖

Quin was well used to nesting through the night on any convenient sofa, now that he was too weak to manage stairs but still too social to keep to his own bed at home like a good invalid should; what he wasn't so used to was sleeping through the night. Another of those little jokes, the ironies of illness: he could sleep at any time of day, all day often, but come the dark he was always wakeful. Sometimes I thought that he was frightened of the dark, scared to close his eyes against it, for fear of that greater dark to come when he would close his eyes and never open them again. I never taxed him with it, though, only stayed with him, kept him company as long as I could manage.

That night I fought off my own exhaustion for a while, for a long time, till we'd burned all the fuel on the hearth and watched the fire die to a sullen glow, barely any life left in it. At last he said, "Get yourself to bed, for God's sake. Christ, I can hear your jaw creak every time you swallow a yawn. You think it does me any good, watching your eyes sink to pits while you mumble like a moron? Christ . . ."

I smiled, kissed his cheek, put out all the candles for safety's sake except for one wee nightlight on a table, and took myself to bed.

And lay wide awake and fretful despite my weariness and the comfort of the bed; and so was still awake when something cracked in the quiet night. A sharp, destructive sound: I was up in a moment and running downstairs naked as I was, confused and anxious, frightened almost.

Stood in the living-room doorway staring in, and saw Quin's head turn to find me. Sobbed one breath in relief, the first I think since I'd heard that sound; and took another, far more calmly, as his acid voice said, "Sorry, sweets, you look nice as anything I've seen for months, but I'd be no use to you tonight."

Nor any night now, not that way; but never mind. "What was it? That noise?"

"I don't know. It was outside, in the street. I'd say someone had put a window out, except I didn't hear footsteps. It wasn't me, at any rate, I haven't broken yet. I haven't broken anything. Go to bed. And sleep this time, will you? Or you'll be no use to me in the morning . . ."

❖

Obedient as ever, I went to bed, I went to sleep. And woke in the late morning, and found Quin dozy but demanding, no change there. I fetched him pills and the coffee he was not allowed to drink, in exchange for his promise to essay a little porridge, which I made. It was an hour or more before I could go outside.

It only took a second to spot what had cracked in the night. The car's windscreen had starred in one corner, as though someone had flung a pebble at it; but out of the crazed glass ran lines of fracture, and those lines spelled out a run of words, *he is gone*.

I stood there looking for a time, for a short time that seemed longer than it should. Then I got into the car and with my elbow I knocked out all the glass in the windscreen, before I went back indoors to phone the RAC.

❖

That afternoon I took Quin for a drive around the island, stopping wherever I thought I might be able to beg some empty cardboard boxes: the few shops, the tourist information office, even the parish church. We finished the tour at the pub, which did us proud with crisp-boxes; it seemed only good manners to have a drink while we were there. Quin had a Bloody Mary, the evil of the alcohol—which he was absolutely not allowed to drink—offset, we decided, by the virtues of tomato-juice. I had a pint of my uncle's favorite ale, for old times' sake, and a quiet chat with the landlord. He'd known Jarrold since my uncle first arrived on the island, and offered a tradesman's conventional sympathy for my loss; said he was pleased that I was keeping the house on, and hoped to see plenty of me in the years to come. Plenty of me and my friend, he said; I didn't disillusion him. Instead, I asked the question that had been burning in the back of my head for years, ever since Frankie had set it to smoulder, the question I had never quite dared to ask while Jarrold was around; and yes, he remembered well the night that my uncle's lover had disappeared. Remembered the morning after, at least, the search: had joined in, indeed, as many locals had. Such a sad story, he said, and Mr. Farnon had never really got over it, had he?

No, I agreed quietly, he never really had.

✥

Back at the house, I piled up my booty of boxes wherever I could stow them and set about packing up Uncle Jarrold's things, under Quin's acerbic eye. The books he approved of, at least in theory, though some of the titles justified their existence by drawing a dry chuckle or a snort of amused contempt. The ornaments earned nothing but his scorn, even where they were porcelain figurines that carried the stamp of Meissen or Worcester. Quin had no patience with prettiness for its own sake, nor for the sake of market value. I was less precious; all this was money in the bank for me, and Quin was expensive.

I'd meant to leave my uncle's bedroom for the following day, but the work went faster than I'd expected, and having built up a head of steam it seemed a shame to waste it. Besides, that was the one room in the house into which I'd never ventured yet; curiosity drove me up the stairs, reluctance held me only a moment with my hand on the door before I pushed it open.

It was a dark room, even after I'd flicked the light on: heavy oak furnishings that must have been a trial to maneuver up the stairs, faded brown velvet curtains, bare boards with a scattering of rugs. A tester bed, a massive wardrobe—*his clothes, what to do about his clothes? Leave them for now, that's what. Sort them later, give them to Oxfam, whatever*—and another case of books, a dresser with more pretty things on doilies to arouse Quin's happy ire.

The dresser had a mirror; I saw myself reflected, and thought it likely that I was the first young man to be so framed since Uncle Jarrold's tragedy. I'd been feeling glad, in a strange and not very comfortable way, that the story had proved true, at least in so far as there had been a young man and he had disappeared. It had seemed to validate my uncle's obsessive sorrow, to justify the emptiness of his life. Ghosts need to be real, to take the bathos away from a haunting.

But now, as I stood there thinking those charitable thoughts—and thinking too, thinking inevitably of Quin and my own haunting to come, which could itself prove lifelong—I saw words forming slowly in the mirror, letter by letter, as if an invisible finger moved between the glass and the silvering.

He is gone, he is gone, I cannot find him . . .

And suddenly I had no sympathy and no pity in me, nor any trace of fear, only a blazing anger; I remembered how Jarrold had hacked at me in my own first gripping passion and I turned it all back on him, on whatever was left of him in this empty house.

"Oh, you shit," I whispered. "You sad, sorry little shit. You had your love and you lost him, yes, to the sea or to a pathetic argument, whatever; and you huddled around that little light and kept it feebly burning, you used that as your excuse against the world for all the rest of your life; and now you dare, you *dare* to shove it in my face, when all you had and all you lost can't hold a candle, not a bloody *candle* to what I've got waiting for me . . .?"

Tears stung my eyes, but I dashed them away in fury; and snatched up a shepherdess who might very well have been Dresden, only that I didn't stop to examine the base of her, I only flung her full force at the mirror.

More than the glass and the ornament was shattered, in that moment; more than shards of glass and porcelain fell crashing to the dresser, to the floor. I stood breathing heavily amid the silence until I'd stopped shaking, until I had some kind of weak control.

Then I turned and walked out of there, walked softly down the stairs, down all the stairs and into the living-room, that Uncle Jarrold had called his parlor and I would not.

Quin was sleeping, his face turned away from the light. Briefly—as so often at these moments, as ever—I thought he was gone already, I thought I'd never find him again.

Richard Matheson
AFTERWORD

O

h, there are ghosts for sure. Many different kinds of ghosts.

Some are manifested by mediums—and what more apt word could there be to describe these conjurors of the bodiless? *Medium: a substance or agent through which anything acts or an effect is produced.* (*World Book Dictionary*)

Some are apparitions unaware of their surroundings, performing certain actions over and over.

Some, as yet not conscious of their passing, appear as lifelike beings, leading—repetitively until the action is resolved—to some hidden object, or, in less common instances, to a lost and/or murdered body.

Some seek justice. Some seek revenge.

Some are seen in castles or in graveyards. On ships or airliners. In coffee shops or restaurants. In houses or apartments. In any location where the residual energy of their being substantiates itself in form and/or sound.

And yet, there are ghosts that no one is aware of as being ghosts. Legions of phantoms we experience every day and never realize it.

My personal definition of a ghost is "that which lingers." And what lingers everlastingly in and around us are the wraiths of mankind's eons of malevolent thinking. Century piled upon century of pernicious thoughts and actions which have exteriorized the innumerable specters which surround us—greed, intolerance, cruelty, violence, racism, fanaticism, et al—complete the list yourself, it's practically endless.

There are the truly harrowing ghosts that haunt our world.